I0452606

Silver & Smith

Belles & Boots ~ Book 3

By Louise Crouch

Copyright © 2020 Louise Crouch

ISBN: **978-0-6485484-7-8**

License Notes

This ebook is licensed for your personal enjoyment only. This ebook may not be re-sold or given away to other people. If you would like to share this book with another person, please purchase an additional copy for each recipient. If you're reading this book and did not purchase it, or it was not purchased for your use only, then please return to your favorite ebook retailer and purchase your own copy. Thank you for respecting the hard work of this author.

All rights reserved. This book or any portion thereof may not be reproduced or used in any manner whatsoever without the express written permission of the publisher except for the use of brief quotations in a book review.

Silver & Smith is a work of fiction. With the exception of public figures, the characters involved are purely fictitious. The opinions expressed in this story are those of the characters and should not be confused with the authors. The historical events that occurred throughout Colorado, Kansas and Texas during this time period have been used in a fictitious manner for the purpose of this story. Institutions, businesses, places, events, locales, and incidents are either the products of the author's imagination or have been used in a fictitious manner. Any resemblance to actual events or persons living or dead is entirely coincidental. If you are looking for factually correct historical information please consult the State Historical Society of your interest.

For more from Louise Crouch please visit

Louise Crouch Amazon

Dedication

To my family for their love and support

To my children for their patience

To my husband for saying yes

Table of Contents

Chapter 1

Cassidy Smith stood on the deck of the steamboat as the cool evening breeze speared through her caramel brown hair. Her brother, a street urchin she had befriended in Chicago, flipped stones from his pocket into the Brazos River. Jet's sandy brown hair was similar to hers yet his blue eyes, in stark contrast to her chestnut brown.

"Do you think it'll work Cass?"

Cass pressed her hands against her ribs for a brief second. "Yes, of course. He is supposed to be my husband, after all."

"Yeah that's fine for you, Cass what about me?" Jet flipped another pebble into the murky water, the sound enveloped by the unforgiving harpsichord music that shrilled through the late afternoon air.

The Texas sun slowly reclined behind puffs of white, the edges lined silver and slate, like tuffs of cotton across a tangerine field as the *Sally-Ann* approached the dock. Cass retrieved the locket that hung between her breasts, turning the golden orb twice, the worn filigree smooth under her thumb as she rubbed until her nerves abated, "Whoever my husband to be is, he cannot refuse to employ his new brides' brother, Jet."

Jethro Smith tossed his last pebble. "I hope you're right."

"I'm almost always right." Cassidy smiled as she bumped her elbow into his. The boy clutched the painted bannister.

"Almost," Jet snorted. "You sure?"

"Always." Cassidy winked. "Cheer up, we're almost…"

A door clanged, the harpsichord peaked as the fiddler screeched, and a couple stumbled onto the deck. Cassidy watched the man strut down the listing corridor. His shaggy blonde hair and unshaven cheeks matched his white shirt, unbuttoned at the collar and haphazardly tucked in around his narrow waist. Sand colored trousers ran down long legs into a pair of russet colored boots scuffed with trail dirt. The man's shoulders were broad and one of his long arms curled around the neck of a dancing girl. As her vibrant skirts sashayed down the narrow hallway, the flamboyant ruffles failed to conceal the scandalous whispers the man muttered into the girl's ear. The dancer eyed Cassidy with a smirk, as she played with the lace choker around her neck. The man's lips sunk to her skin, kissing her between propositions.

"Still sure Cass?" Jet sniggered into his elbow as he hunched over the railing. Cass looked for vacant air to rest her gaze, the varnished floorboards, the white bannister, even the bustling skyline of Waco, to no avail.

Cass's mind froze. What would she do if her husband-to-be turned out like this man, a licentious and salacious man pawing all over her without restraint? The man's eyes met Cassidy's for a moment, heat flushed her cheeks until she realized the difference between his gazes. Nodding his head in an innocent greeting to Cass, he continued on his way with his prize. Laughing and giggling the couple fell into a cabin at the end of the hallway. Would Cass count herself lucky?

"Well, I'm not so sure Mister Jackson isn't taking us for a ride." Jet said.

Cassidy almost reached for her locket again. "Who else are we going to find to take us to Colorado? We have enough coin and no sense. Oh here he is now." Cassidy neatened her appearance, tugging down her blush colored satin dress. She was twenty years of age and had taken a gamble that her father's fraudulent deal would land her a good man. A good man with a good heart, and nothing like Mister Jackson. "Good evening Mister Jackson."

"Aye, it is a good evening, Miss Smith," the way the man pronounced his 's' made Cassidy cringe. The man edged closer, his breath stank of whiskey and tobacco. Holding her breath, Cassidy twisted to the open railing. She couldn't afford to insult the man especially as they were about to disembark and Jackson was their guide. Jackson raked a thick finger along his clean-shaven chin, "I see the dress fits you just right."

Counting the steps to the dining room, Cassidy stopped fussing, "Yes, thank you although I don't see the sense in spending our money on such an expense."

"I knew your father, Miss Smith. He never wasted a cent for anyone, not even those he owed," Jackson grimaced. "But he'd want his daughter to have the finest of things. Besides," Jackson licked his lips, "First impressions count. Trust me."

Could she swim in all this pink satin? How many hoops did she have? Instead, she stepped around Jackson until he fell into step beside her. "It must be nearly supper time in the dining room, did you bring my father's funds?"

Jackson tapped his top pocket, "I surmise it's almost time for dessert," Jackson's fingers pinched Cassidy's elbow, turning until his fully belly trapped her against the boats wall. His wet lips met her cheek as his hand slithered around her neck, trying to twist her head.

Cassidy put both hands on his chest and shoved without effect, "Mister Jackson!"

Jet wrapped his arms around Jackson's shoulders. The malnourished fourteen-year-old boy was no match for the older mans' fist. Jet tumbled back clutching his nose.

Cassidy brought her knee up and then her heel down.

Jackson's backhand slammed into her cheek. Cassidy squealed. Her eyes closed, the sting sliced through the shock, plummeting into panic. Jackson's hands returned to tug at her pink ruffles. Cassidy pushed again and this time Jackson fell back. All the way back, in fact, tumbling over the rail and splashing into the Brazos River.

Cassidy ran to the rail just to see Jackson bob to the surface, stretching arm over arm to reach the bank of the river. A shout broke overhead just as the helpful citizens of Waco, Texas assisted the sodden Jackson to his feet. Cassidy watched the man disappear into the crowd of onlookers as the *Sally-*

Ann began to dock.

"Are you all right?" The man with the russet boots and the sandy hair stood in front of her. Sugar grey eyes, the edges ringed in flecks of gold met Cassidy's.

"Um...Yes, thank you."

Scents of rich plum and cedar wood cologne dissipated the scent of Jackson's whiskey and tobacco. An underlying flavor of bruised jasmine tickled Cassidy's nose.

The man stepped back and raked his fingers through his blonde fringe pulling it away from his crooked nose. He opened his palm to Jet, who willingly took it and pulled himself off the deck. "And how about you Champ?" the man slapped Jet on the back.

"I'll be fine." The scamp coughed.

"Good!"

Jet cupped his nose and wriggled it, trying to blink away the liquid that welled in his eyes. "Well, not really he had all our-"

"We'll be fine," Cassidy interrupted. She pressed her trembling fingers to her cheek, the skin hot to the touch. Something about the man's languid movements unnerved her. "Thank you, Mister-"

The man took Cassidy's outstretched hand, "Murphy, Shelton Murphy."

Cassidy's cheeks drained of color as her lungs raced to catch up with her thoughts. She ran her eyes up and down her savior. He was tall, too tall with straight blonde hair too long for his own good. The honey color of his skin suggested he'd spent his fair share in the sun and his calloused hands were rough against her palm. Barely dressed, debauched and with a painted lady waiting in his cabin, Cassidy's husband-to-be stood before her.

"Pleasure to meet you, Miss, if you need a hand with anything else don't hesitate to holler."

"Shelly!" The dancing girl's head peeped past the doorjamb as she twisted a blonde curl around her finger.

Awkwardly he smiled, dimples pinched his suntanned cheeks. A rush of something forced Cassidy into action.

"Mister Murphy, I'm afraid I will have to impose." Pulling a handkerchief from her ruffles, Cassidy dabbed at her invisible tears. "Mister Jackson had all our money." Cassidy emphasized the tremble in her words as she wandered down to his cabin. Jet bounced beside her until Cassidy clicked her fingers and the boy remembered to limp. "And now we're without a guide to take us into Colorado Territory."

Cassidy followed Shelton, taking stock of his room, the dancing girl reclined across the gaudy double bed, her skirt obscenely above her ankles. She sat upright as she realized more than Shelton entered the room. A tiny writing desk stood to one side with a stool, two glasses filled with a dark liquid waiting on the tabletop. A canvas bag tumbled at the end of the bed, the clothing half stuffed in or half dragged out, an arc of tanned leather rose from the center, the wood grain handle of a pistol just visible.

Shelton paused mid-step as both Cassidy and Jet entered the tiny room without hesitation, "Won't you please come in," He threw a smirk to the dancing girl who shrugged her shoulders and crossed one knee over the other.

"Thank you," Cassidy continued. "As my brother Jet mentioned, Mister Jackson was our guide into Colorado. I don't suppose you could assist us?"

"What business you got in Colorado Territory?" Shelton ran his eyes over Cassidy's gleaming pink layers and then Jet's stringy arms as he picked up one glass and took a sip, "You're not the usual Pikes Peak or bust crowd."

Pikes Peak she recognized, but what did the crowd have to do with her bust? Cassidy swallowed. "Ah, I'm due to meet my husband."

Sugar-grey turned to pewter, his brows deepened as Shelton cast new eyes over Cassidy, something dark behind his gaze. With a tremble in her knees, Cassidy took a seat on the closest stool.

"Oh, Honey!" The dancing girl cooed, "That's going to bruise if you don't get something cold on it now."

Instinctively, Cassidy put her hand to her cheek, only to have the girl pull it away again. "I hope not."

"I hope you socked him one back!"

"I tried," Cassidy sniffled; glad for the woman's sudden kindness.

The dancing girl rose. "I'll get ya something real quick."

"I threw him over the railing Mimi." Shelton called as her boot heels thundered down the deck.

"Not before– "Jet halted, his lips kinked revealing his incisor just as crooked as his spirit, "I'll be back Cass, give me one minute."

"Jet!" It was no use. The boy had dashed out the door, leaving Cass alone with Shelton.

She eyed his long legs, covered up to his calves with dark brown boots, the toes dusty and the heels worn. His shirt was clean if not pressed, his sandy trousers smudged where the fabric clumped around his thighs. He held a cheroot between his even lips and tapped his pockets for a match.

Well, that would have to change, Cassidy mused.

Shelton pushed his fringe back.

And a haircut.

Cassidy skimmed his features; deep-set eyes dark in this light, the crook to his nose clear from this distance. *Was he a fighter?* The match sparked, the flames highlighting the hard plains of his cheeks hidden under his unshaven cheeks.

Tall, too tall, but there was no changing that.

He took another sip of his liquor before pouring another and offed it to Cassidy. She cupped the glass with both hands and took a tentative sip. The flavors heated her tongue and stung her nose.

With the cheroot clung to one side, he grinned, "Cheer up..."

Cassidy sucked in a quick gasp at his words before the dancing girl spun through the doorway.

"Here you go, Honey." She handed a cloth towel to Shelton, and then took the cheroot, standing on the deck to take a long seductive drag, her red lipstick leaving a taint around the casing.

A spark of something dark and unexpected prickled in Cassidy's chest.

Shelton frowned as he crouched down to his haunches in front of Cassidy, the bundled cloth in one hand as the other slide upwards, his long fingers rested on the nape of her neck, his thumb caressed her ear. The resulting quiver found the spikes in Cassidy's chest and unraveled them point by point until she exhaled. The open collar of his shirt exposed glimpses of tanned muscle across his throat. Cassidy tore her eyes away, only to fall upon his roped forearms that cradled her face. His scent of plum and cedar wood faint under the reek of tobacco.

Yes, definitely no more cheroots.

With the slightest pressure Shelton applied the compress to Jackson's handiwork as he focused on rolling the coolness into position. His eyes fell on the edge of her jaw, then her mouth. Against her best intentions, Cassidy's lips parted as Shelton raked his gaze upwards, chocolate melted against steel grey.

"That better?" Shelton asked, the apple in his throat bobbed, his voice huskier than before.

"Almost," Cassidy squeaked, wishing she had enough ice for both her cheeks.

"Excellent." Jet grumbled from the doorjamb.

"Good." Shelton fell back and pulled out another cheroot, the dancing girl nowhere to be seen. In her place, Jet stepped in, his dark brown jacket now slung over his blue shirt, a pile of luggage at his feet and a rucksack sagged over his shoulder.

Cassidy winked in approval.

"So Mister Murphy, about our proposition...."

"Proposition?" Shelton dug around for his matches. "I'm

sure you meant, thank you."

"You're welcome, as I was saying," the girl continued. "Mister Jackson, who you so graciously sent for a swim, was our guide to Colorado and also in possession of all our money."

"Almost all." The boy added. Even with his back turned, Shelton could hear the tap of the boy's coat pocket against paper. Shelton kept his focus on the whiskey, his companion Mimi vanished like smoke on the wind, and now this girl, no woman, asked for his help. She was young at least three years younger than him, and no doubt her husband would appreciate her fresh face, and doe brown eyes, but Shelton had no time for delays. Mimi had been his last treat before he started his own trek to Colorado Territory.

Taylor Stone had meant to be his partner on this mining journey, only Old George at Windy Hill had declined in health to where the Ranch couldn't do without Taylor. Where Taylor's fortunes had risen, Shelton's father's hadn't. The Blue Cow Ranch suffered more losses this year than last. More than his father could support. Colorado waited for Shelton, his claim ready to pay dividends to bail the Blue Cow Ranch out from a mountain of debt. He didn't have time to escort a new bride and her bandy kid brother.

Matter of fact, he'd arranged with Cade Hamerton to help drive his latest herd up the Chisholm trail, in payment for one of Hamerton's worthy nags. No way was Shelton Murphy going up the Rocky's without a sure-footed mount underneath him. *But what to do about the girl?* Shelton had thrown her guide in the Brazos and he never left a man without a saddle. Shelton turned around.

Cassidy Smith wasn't any man. The lady sat quietly, her wide russet eyes flicking between her brother and Shelton. The pink dress clung too loose around her waist and too tight around her breasts, a gold chain dripped down her narrow neck and disappeared somewhere more delicate. Maybe if Shelton brought the bride to her husband, the man would pay Shelton for his efforts. She had tied her long caramel strands back, with odd loops tugged here and there, another sign of her struggle with the brute Jackson. Shelton wished he'd landed one blow before the man tumbled over the side.

"Well, Mister Murphy?"

Shelton stubbed his cheroot into the glass ashtray. "I can take you to the Sheriff."

"What?" The boy's eyes flew wide.

"No." Cassidy stood upright, "I don't think that's necessary."

Shelton smirked. He had no intention of tattling on the boy who just pinched whatever Jackson had left in his room. The Court would issue the man a fine for striking a lady, so in Shelton's books, Jackson had just paid. Yet something about Cassidy and her brother unsettled Shelton.

"Well, you say this Mister Jackson stole some of your money, I can take you to the Deputies in Waco, fill out a report and maybe if they catch him you'll get some back."

Cassidy tapped a single finger to her bow-shaped lips. "I suppose Mister Murphy," her slender brows puckered, her narrow chin resting gently in her delicate hands. The girl would no doubt freeze in mining country. She sat upright. "Should Jet and I make it safely to Colorado, you can have Mister Jackson's guide fee."

"Am I supposed to fish it out the Brazos, Miss –"

"Cassidy Smith," her cheeks colored to match her dress. This time the heat dashed down her slender neck ending at her exposed collar bones. Her oval face tilted to one side as if she waited for something. After a moment she continued, "You may ask my husband."

"Cass no," the boy rushed.

"What assurances do I have that your husband will pay up? I don't mean to offend you."

"You're not," Cassidy added.

"But is your husband going to follow through on a promise from his wife, is he a stand up kinda fellow?"

Cassidy's lips thinned, her slender fingers twisted in her

lap. "He will be. What do you say Mister Murphy? We still have the rail tickets."

Shelton turned his back, if nothing else than to control his gaze from returning to the beauty who pleaded for his help. She reminded him of sunset late in fall, fine alabaster skin, luscious rose colored lips and those eyes. Jasper polished with mahogany, long lashes that curled almost to her brows. Maybe Shelton should reconsider. He didn't fancy taking a precious woman like Cassidy Smith over the Chisolm, so he'd have to sort out Cade Hamerton. He hated to leave the man in a fix, but of all the men to understand it would be Cade.

Shelton had no brother of his own, only one older sister who'd taken off with the first man who could afford her dress-makers bill, so Cade Hamerton, Marcus Kearby and Taylor Stone had made up the rest of his family. Shelton threw another quick gaze over Miss Cassidy Smith, a wry smirk curled across his lips, and every one of his friends would envy his predicament.

"Fine, Miss Cassidy Smith I will take you to Colorado Territory."

Chapter 2

"I s'pose Mister Jackson will be back to get his belongings eventually," Jet said, tugging a wollen cap lower over his narrow nose. The *Sally-Ann's* whistle shrilled through the air, the click clack of heels on timber decks and the chatter of arriving passengers filtered through the tiny cabin.

"So we have an arrangement then Mister Murphy," Cassidy said. Shelton Murphy may not be ideal, but he was a damn sight better than Jackson and after all he was her husband. Well, almost. Cassidy had the journey to Colorado to meld the man into a suitable match. The whole man looked like he could do with a good clean and press. "Thank you, Mister Murphy." She took a step closer. Shelton shook her outstretched hand, his grip firm but gentle, the contact brief. "You can have Mister Jackson's rail ticket."

"Where to?" Shelton picked up his gun belt and slung it around his narrow waist.

"The Katy will take us across Indian Territory and then the Santa Fe through Wichita to Pueblo."

Shelton nodded. "I have instructions to buy supplies and a few mules before heading out from Pueblo myself. I take it you're headed to the California Gulch Placer fields?"

"Almost," Cassidy said. This man had signed the mining lease with her father and yet had not reacted to her name. Perhaps he hadn't read the fine print. Cassidy's father had taught her to always read the fine print. Always. But what was Shelton's fine print? His nose suggested he had a few fights under his belt, he smoked, he drank, likely he gambled, and spent his time with loose women. Cassidy had her work cut out for her. "We have rooms in town at the Regent."

"No dice, Precious," Shelton said. "I've got to see a man about a horse. I'll meet you at the station in the morning."

"Oh." Cassidy tugged her golden chain from side to side. The links grated against her skin, her mind brimming with images of saloon girls and soiled doves. She wasn't sold on Shelton Murphy as her husband yet, but she was certain she wanted his bed cold until she decided. Should she tell him? No, they still needed to get to Colorado to claim her father's parcel of land. Then Cassidy would tell Mister Murphy about the fine print on his contract and he could cut and run if he chose. She wanted a good husband with a good heart who would give her a family. He didn't have to be clever or pretty, and Shelton Murphy may be too much of both. "Well, would you mind escorting us to the Regent all the same?"

He shoved handfuls into his rucksack before pulling it up to his shoulder, "Fine."

Cassidy tried her most demure smile, hoping she would find something at the Regent to hold him from the Bordellos and Bawdy Houses.

Cassidy stood before the triple story timber monstrosity as the harpsichord music pumped wildly through the open windows. The reception area of the hotel bustled with arrivals, the manager in his emerald satin vest slapped keys in hands, as maids dashed up and down the wide carpeted staircase. The scent of tobacco washed over Cassidy, where she stood in the lobby with Jet beside her, so much so, that she had to pinch her nose. Behind them, the restaurant brimmed with cowboys enjoying steaming beef with biscuits and gravy, while deeper within, a bar spilled onto the adjacent street. Silk skirts swayed between the gamblers, hoping to catch the eye of a cashed up cowpoke. Mister Jackson had prepared well enough for himself, renting rooms at the closest hotel to the Two Street brothels as he could find. Heat climbed Cassidy's neck as Shelton's head turned, the hoots and hollers calling him forward.

Cassidy cleared her throat, "You said you had to see a man about a horse?"

Without ceasing his languid gaze of the parlor and its bevy of treasures, Shelton nodded.

Cassidy inhaled and smoothed her skirts. Why of all things did jealousy have to flourish? The man wasn't hers, not in any legal sense of the word and for what she had seen so far, he didn't seem worthy. Perhaps when she arrived at Colorado, she could find some exit clause to this contract and use the fine print to her advantage.

The couple in front accepted their room key and followed a porter up the first flight of stairs. A pressure settled in the small of her back and Cassidy flinched. Shelton's palm retracted, leaving an eddy of flames that pierced her composure. Shelton leant his elbow on the countertop, selecting a toothpick to chew as he reclined. Not one, but two maids flicked their gaze in his direction, while he twirled a dark Stetson between his fingers.

Cassidy heard only snippets of the manager's instructions as Shelton winked at someone, his long legs slanted; the pistol slack against his thigh.

A growl erupted from the street, "Silver tongue Murphy."

Shelton's shoulder flinched and Cassidy turned to appraise the speaker. A man covered head to toe in soiled black, with a Stetson raised high up his forehead to reveal a salt and pepper beard and dark furrowed brows.

"I didn't think you'd be brave enough to come back this way for a while."

Shelton sighed and stood upright. "Leave it, Frankie."

"Why don't you make me?" The man spat a wad of tobacco into the dirt.

Steel grey warped to molten lead.

Cassidy fumbled with Shelton's hat, only catching it before it hit the floor while Shelton strode outside. Cassidy clutched it to her chest, torn between following the man and running to the sheriff. She'd grown up in a small neighborhood in Chicago, relatively safe before the Great Fire in 1871. On instinct, Cassidy's chest seized, ash coated her tongue. She almost clasped her hands to her ears. Almost.

The sound of knuckles pounding flesh brought Cassidy to the present. In the street, encircled by a hoard of jeering cowboys, Frankie had Shelton by the collar as her soon-to-be-husband threw a left hook at the thicker man's jaw. Cassidy gasped, but Jet held her elbow.

"Uh uh, Cass, wait it out. Don't know why you promised him Jackson's fee. You don't even know who your husband is yet."

"He is my husband. It's his name on the lease." Cassidy rushed. "If he gets us to Colorado, he can pay himself!"

Jet snorted. "If Cass, if."

The man pulled Shelton's shirt over his head and pushed down. Shelton bent double. Cassidy winced as the man's fist collided, a solid *thunk* made the crowd erupt. Cassidy twirled her locket. Shelton slipped his blindfold. Standing bare chested, fist connected to cheek, nose then jaw. Frankie fell. Jet whooped and whistled. Shelton's punch landed again and again. The crowd fell silent. Shelton halted, his elbow raised, strands of taunt muscles frozen in place. His fingers released, Frankie slumped out of sight.

Cassidy's lungs filled, her palms sweaty against the firm fabric brim. Shelton retrieved his shirt from a bystander, rotating as he redressed. Too tall, yes, however the slabs of tanned muscles that rippled across his chest sent a rush of sensation down Cassidy's spine that ended in her toes.

"He's handy with his fists, makes an ordinary fight look like a prayer meetin'." Jet said, pulling a toothpick from the counter to bite down. Cassidy snatched it from his lips.

"It may be signed and sealed Jet, but I didn't say I would deliver." *The man was a savage!*

"I thought you wanted a husband, Cass?"

Cassidy shushed him as Shelton returned to the foyer, a red welt across one cheek, his nose still crooked.

"Checked in all right?" He retrieved his Stetson from her hands. "I'll see you at the station."

"Wait a minute, Mister Murphy,"

"Listen Precious, when I said leave it, I meant it."

Cassidy seethed, "You're supposed to be our guide, not some brute that launches into every street fight."

"I believe your husband would appreciate a brute by your side."

Cassidy's eyes flew wide. "And what if Frankie comes back?"

"Make up your mind Precious. Are you saying you want this brute by your side now?" Shelton laughed; a rich mocking timbre that slid under Cassidy's ribs and made her neck itch. "What's between me and Frankie and Frankie's wife is finished, and after that," He gestured with his chin, "I don't expect you'll have any trouble tonight."

Cassidy sucked in a shallow breath, her teeth ground down her jaw. "Is that so? And what about Mister Jackson if he shows up to claim his room?"

"I suspect Mister Jackson is skin deep in whiskey and..." Shelton replaced his Stetson. "I'll keep an eye out for him. See you at the station."

Shelton strolled onto the boardwalk, tangerine stripes crisscrossed the sky, splashes of lilac bled into violet, as the inky darkness of night settled over Waco. Scents of bruised perfume slithered through the stifling summer air, tobacco, manure, sweat all rolled into one. Shelton's veins pumped with energy after thumping Frankie, his boots eager to be away from Miss Precious.

Earlier in his steamboat cabin, with the ice applied to her cheek, Shelton could have sworn the woman would melt it faster than his heartbeat, yet just now, in the Hotel's lobby, Cassidy Smith had turned to ice. She may look all-woman in that low-cut dress, with bustles and hoops to add to her curves, but Shelton had seen through that. Her eyes had lashed wave after wave of frigid glacier blasts across his bare chest. He'd heard her accent slip too, Yankee. He thought the woman would freeze in mining country, how wrong could he be. Good luck to her husband thawing her rigid attitude. Shelton tapped his top pocket, searching for his cheroot tin only to find it gone. Damn he'd have to buy more.

He crossed the wide dusty street ignoring the catcalls of working girls and the deep jazz tones that hummed through his system. First he'd find Hamerton.

Nearing the stock yards, Shelton found him. The Double E ranch camp had set up with their stock penned in for the night, a handful of Hands wandered around the outside, keeping their sombreros low but their eyes sharp.

"*Te veo señor Shelton.*"

"Caught me, Tomas, where's the Boss man?"

"*Ci*, there."

Shelton thanked Tomas and slunk down to his haunches. He edged around the pen, keeping his eye on the tallest Stetson between the tents. Since Hamerton married Evie, he kept his camp and his men away from most of the trouble. Shelton would bet half his coin Hamerton let a few Hands sneak off to sample the delights of Two-Street. An image of luscious pink lips came to mind and Shelton almost clipped his own heel. Mimi, think of... wait, was it Miranda?

Shelton neared the big man, just as Hamerton started his evening prowl of the camp. Shelton slipped between the tents, hushing those Hands that recognized him. It wasn't until Hamerton reached the end that Shelton could take position behind him. Cade took one step, Shelton's boot toe jutted out, and the man cartwheeled forward, his brows furrowed, blue eyes alight.

"Well, look what the cat dragged in!" Cade chuckled, his fist releasing to an open palm that slapped Shelton hard on the shoulder.

"Howdy Cade where's all the fun with your camp this far out of town?"

"You look like you already stole the cream, Shelly, but I'm glad to see you." Cade shook Shelton's hand, who pointed to Shelton's bloodied knuckles. "By the looks, you've already had some fun tonight."

"A little, Frankie Delgado having a mouthful to say about the last time I hit him like he hits his missus."

"Ah." Cade pushed his Stetson higher on his head, his hair damp and a little longer than last time Shelton saw him in Dew Springs. "Well, come on and tell me about it. While we look at this brute of yours."

"About that, Cade..."

The older man turned to Shelton, his jaw cinched.

"I've taken an offer of guiding a couple up to Colorado Territory. They're paying a fee and since I'm going that way anyway."

"You can't make the drive?"

Shelton's gut clenched, he hated to let the man down. Cade Hamerton had come to his rescue more times than he could count. Dragging him drunk out of the saloon, sobering him up before he sent him home to his Ma and Pa, ending the fights that Shelly picked until he grew big enough to finish them on his own, "They've offered me their previous guide's rail ticket all the way to Pueblo."

"They? Previous?" Cade's wide lips twisted.

"Yeah, some girl and her kid brother, I kinda put them in the pickle by tossing their guide into the Brazos."

Cade snorted.

"Well, he was manhandling her all up the deck, back-handed her right on her cheek."

Cade's grin widened as they reached the horse's pen. "I see, and this girl..."

"It's not what you think Cade," Shelton leaned on the top bar and raised a boot heel to the bottom rung as a mix of mounts dashed inside the perimeter; geldings and mares, some with bridles, others tack-less. One horse stood a hand taller than the others, a narrow liver chestnut with a white stripe down his nose and four white socks, "She's a looker all right but she's meeting her husband in Colorado."

Again Cade laughed. "You know as well as I do, Shelton silver-tongue Murphy, a husband has never stopped you." Cade put two fingers past his lips, his shrill whistle cut off any rebuke Shelton may have had. Shelton hadn't even thought of a comeback to Cade's comments. The slender liver chestnut pranced over, his mane slightly darker than his coat.

"Cade, I told you –"

"Horseshit, man, take him. He's more of a dancer than a cutter, so I can't use him."

"Cade..."

"Shelly, by taking him you'll be doing me a favor and if you're worried about settling it up, pay me back when you hit a lode of gold." Cade ran his hand down the white stripe, the brutes wide brown eyes with long lashes made Shelton think about taming another animal entirely. "Come on, I'll show you what he can do." Cade jumped the fence and grabbed the main lead.

Together they spent the next few hours going over the horse and his traits, including his weaknesses. It was what made Hamerton such a master; his training enhanced the beast's natural abilities and instincts without breaking his spirit. They left the pen and returned to the main camp where Cade's Hand fixed Shelton a plate of salted pork, beans and sourdough.

"I can't thank you enough, Cade."

"You can with a trunk of gold."

"Pa first," Shelton mumbled. "Have you seen him?"

"Yeah, they're holding out. I brought a couple of his up with me. I've told him to pay my fee another day. I've offered him feed, and he's taken some."

Shelton's throat tightened. Not so long ago, it was Cade asking Shelton's father for a loan. How quickly fortunes change.

"And Kearby?"

"He's still chasing stagecoach robbers, and Taylor's got his hands full with Windy Hill."

"So I hear." Shelton reclined beside Hamerton's campfire, and took a sip from a flask of whiskey before passing it to the next vaqueros. The hours of the night dwindled away, the fire crackled and hissed, the embers flying higher as the night cooled, just as the stories grew taller.

"What was her name?"

"I can't remember but I'm glad her old man had a crooked eye. I never got those boots back." Shelton snorted into his whiskey.

"You could have made an honest woman out of her." Cade smirked.

"Ah, an honest woman will never suit Shelton Murphy. I ain't after a wife." He'd probably had enough whiskey for the night as an image of Cassidy's Smith flashed before his eyes. "Ice cold."

"Huh?"

"Never mind, I better turn in for the night anyway Cade, got an early train to catch tomorrow, and a blizzard to thaw." Shelton wished he could eat his words.

Hamerton didn't reply, only grinned from across the fire.

The straw peaked through the mattress to prickle Cassidy's back, the springs squeaking as she settled into place. Jet squirmed on his own cot against the other wall. Their room had been quaint and clean despite the crowd that gathered below. Before turning in, she'd asked the manager for another pitcher and basin and filled both to the brim. If she could, she would brace the door against intruders, with a chair to prevent it opening. But Cassidy knew better.

"Did you see the stairs?"

"Yes, Cass, front and back." Jet answered, sleep weighing down his answer.

"And if it starts upstairs?"

"I'm out the window, Cass but not without you."

Cassidy hated the necessity of her nightly routine. She rolled the pendant once more through her fingers before tucking it away for the night. "Night, Jet."

"Night Cass."

Tomorrow, the next stage of their journey demanded her courage. The Rail not so much, but sharing a cabin with Shelton Murphy would be trying to say the least. Colorado waited for her and in Colorado her new life. If her husband-to-be wanted to break the deal then he could. Like most miners, the man might suffer from gold fever already, caring for nothing except the illusive precious metal. Half her battle would already be won. Cassidy wanted a good husband, reliable, dependable, and not so pretty. She wanted a family. From what she'd been able to decipher, she would grin and bear her way through wifely duties if it meant she could have children. Cassidy pressed her cheek into the lumpy pillow to stop the slabs of muscles and ribbed abdomen that threatened to ruin her sleep.

Chapter 3

Billows of steam spilled from under the engine, departing passengers had already found their seats while Cassidy waved a fly away from her nose as she sat on the platform. Jet strolled around in aimless circles beside her, his hands in his pockets, now and then he'd break out to whistle a ditty. The sun beat down on her lime green bonnet, and she tucked a stray strand back into place. She'd taken Mister Jackson's idea of a respectable dress across the street and sold it. She hadn't a clue how much it was worth, but it lightened her heart and relaxed her shoulders, seeing it gone.

Cassidy glanced at the station clock one more time, the slow methodical movements of the hands in opposition to the rhythm she tapped their train tickets on her skirts. Shelton Murphy was obviously not a punctual man; reliable and dependable not in the man's repertoire. A tall figure stepped into sight at the far end of the platform just as a voice called behind her.

"Miss Cassidy, I hope you've reconsidered your behavior from yesterday."

Cassidy spun to face the pudgy Mister Jackson. The tickets slithered through her fingers and tucked into Jackson's pocket quicker than Cassidy could react. Jet jumped between them.

"I need not apologize. You were out of line, Mister Jackson." Cassidy retreated, pulling Jet with her.

"And where's my things, Boy?" Jackson launched at Jet as Cassidy tugged him so fast he tumbled on his feet.

Long fingers speared past Cassidy's shoulder to clutch Jackson's sweat stained collar, tightening the fabric until the man's cheeks puffed red.

"Mister Jackson, it's so nice to make your acquaintance again," Shelton grinned. "As you can see, Miss Smith has ended your services and engaged myself." Shelton's other hand patted Jackson's pockets and tugged the train tickets from inside. "Don't dig up more snakes than you can kill Jackson." Shelton's words heated as his grip released.

Jet had circled behind Jackson and caught his hefty frame. Cassidy flinched as she saw the youth's hand slip into Jackson's black piped waist coat.

"I'll call the Deputies!"

"Do it." Shelton pushed forward, his shoulder clipped Cassidy's bonnet, spinning it across her face. She heard Jackson huff before Shelton turned around. His pale blue covered chest filled her vision, the shirt neatly pressed, pulled across his broad shoulders, he wore a leather vest over the top and his denims were the cleanest she'd ever seen. His spiced plum odor even more alluring as the man had shaved, the strong lines of his jaw now revealed. His fringe still needed a trim; however, his sugar grey eyes darkened to slate molasses. "You all right?"

Cassidy nodded as her heel clipped her toe. Shelton missed her forearm and snatched her waist instead. The contact slammed Cassidy's breath into lungs as her ribs heated. Her elbow tugged backwards, and she twisted away only to stumble into the platform bench. Shelton snagged both her forearms this time and held her upright. "Sure?"

"Fine." Cassidy bit back, retreating to clear air.

Shelton exhaled, resettling his Stetson against the late morning sun, "If you say so."

Cassidy watched Jackson stroll down the platform, his eyes searching for something. A rail guard met him at the stairs. "I think it's time we boarded don't you."

"After you," Shelton gestured.

Cassidy snatched Jet's arm and fumbled with his pocket, her fingers closed over the smooth metal of Jackson's pocket watch. Cassidy let the trinket tumble down her skirts.

"Hey!"

"Go," Cassidy hissed. She pushed Jet forward and straightened her skirts to face the guard. Shelton remained beside her, his eyes on the guard and the engine. The whistle erupted.

Cassidy schooled her features. Her father had taught her well. She widened her eyes and pressed her fingers to her abdomen; biting the inside of her cheek, her eyes welled in response. She could feel Shelton's gaze upon her.

"Miss, this man is claiming you've stolen his belongings?"

"I would never," her chin quivered, her shoulders slumped. "His belongings are at the Regent Hotel. We stole nothing. It worried us..." Cassidy added a sniffle, "You must forgive me, Waco is such an impressive yet imposing town, I didn't know what to do, we waited but you never returned."

"And you Sir?"

Cassidy didn't let Shelton speak, "Mister Murphy here, came to our aid, I'm not sure you're aware Sir, but the hotel Mister Jackson booked, the Regent is right down–"

The guard held his palm up. "I know Two-Streets."

Cassidy tongue rolled around her sickly words, the taint climbing the back of her neck. Shelton's gaze hadn't moved. "We thought he had abandoned us, or otherwise occupied his time..."

"That must have been very confronting for a young lady like yourself." The rail guard raked his gaze over Cassidy's trembling form and back to Jackson.

"My watch!" Jackson howled as he patted his pockets. "They stole my watch."

"Have you seen this man's watch, Miss?"

Cassidy pulled a handkerchief from her pocket and dabbed at her nose. She swallowed hard and sucked in a breath. "Is that it over there?"

Shelton snorted quietly as Jackson hurried to retrieve his jewelry from the station platform. Cassidy settled her trembling fingers onto Shelton's forearm, her hip hard against his. "Is there anything else we can do? I have an appointment to meet my husband."

The rail guard took the tickets from Shelton's grip and stamped one end before handing them back to Cassidy. "No Miss, thank you, take care, Mister Murphy." The rail guard turned on his heel, shaking his head at Jackson, who tugged his crumpled suit over his portly frame.

Jackson pocketed his watch. His bottom lip puckered as he glanced between Shelton and Cassidy and back again. "She's more trouble than she's worth Murphy."

"I wasn't born yesterday Jackson, but you're as welcome as a rattlesnake at a square dance." Shelton said.

Cassidy climbed the five shorts stairs of the carriage, loitering at the top until Shelton finally climbed behind her. A Porter greeted her at the doorway and took her luggage, directing her to two rows of bench seats that faced each other. Shelton wandered down the aisle, his head narrowly missing the chandeliers that lined the ceiling.

Cassidy stepped into the cabin and found her seat. Flattening her skirts, the cool brown leather sunk through the fabric as the scent of charcoal and trail dust tickled her nose, so she pushed the double-hung window higher.

"Sorry," Jet said. He stood in the hallway on the other side of the sliding doors. Shelton appeared behind him, one arm holding loosely onto the railing overhead, the thickness of his arms accentuated.

"It's okay Jet, old habits die hard." Cassidy said.

The porter came to take Shelton's bags and instead Jet grabbed the handle, the older man held Jets gaze "There's no need, boy" The Porter rushed.

"Nonsense lead on Old Man. You'll be needing all the help you can get lifting Cassidy's unmentionables." Jet teased and plucked up the tiny but heavy rucksack.

"And it's George, not old man." The Porter sighed and moved onto the next passengers.

Shelton hesitated at the door a little longer before he sat, his long legs stretched to Cassidy's side, his boots cleaner than yesterday. His pale blue shirt had embroidery along the collar, the lines faint and all the edges sharp. *Why did the man have to look so neat?* Cassidy could feel his steel eyes on her and she refused to pull out her locket to twirl; instead, she looked out the window. Another rush of steam clouds puffed down the station, the carriages clinked, and Cassidy jolted in her seat. The silence in the cabin disturbed only by the train's sharp whistle.

The cabin walls seemed too narrow, the air just a little too hot, Cassidy exhaled slowly hoping her breath would create some distance between herself and the man who lounged only inches away, "Jet's known nothing different."

"And how about yourself there, Precious?" Shelton's voice came out more like a growl.

"Me?" Cassidy's voice raised a notch, and she tried to remain calm. "I'm trying to live a... an honest life." Cassidy could feel her lids welling. Her father's legacy was built on false promises and shifting sands. She'd never known whether he spoke the truth or another lie, she knew her father had made many shifty deals, the mining land only hers by fraudulent means, but she couldn't hand it back. Instead, it would give her a husband and she would build her life solid, consistent, and reliable.

"Well done, with your performance back there."

"Let those without sin cast the first stone, Mister Murphy," Cassidy replied.

"Is your husband a grafter like you?"

"I don't know what my husband is." This time, Cassidy met his gaze and regretted it.

Shelton's brow furrowed, the sun-kissed lines around his eyes intensifying his ridicule. "What?"

"We, we have an arrangement."

Shelton crossed his arms over his chest, and for a moment he watched Cassidy's face turn sour. The woman had some grit under all that doe-eyed, demure facade. It made sense, a mail-order bride, judging by her behavior so far, she was most likely swindling some poor fellow out of his mining claim, hoping to make it rich and leave the man at the bottom of the shaft without a rope. No wonder she had a guide. If her husband had laid eyes on her, perhaps he would have escorted her himself. Shelton would of. Admiring that delicate skin, her rose lips, those thick caramel strands of her hair. The man would get a pretty bargain, but at what cost?

"I see, Precious."

"If we are to be travelling together, Mister Murphy I'd appreciate you not calling me names."

Shelton nodded. She had a backbone. Just how strong? Mining country was tough, the winters harsh and the slopes icy. Judging by Cassidy's upturned nose and tight pout, her husband had a challenge ahead of him to thaw the glacier that was Cassidy. Shelton smirked at his own joke.

"Fine, you might as well call me Shelton or Shelly then, Mister Murphy is my Pa, and he's in Texas."

Swirls of pink flushed up the girl's neck as she nodded, "Fine. Shelton, I assume your saw the man about the horse?"

"I did, he's in the stock carriage now."

"Why the stock carriage? Surely he could have bought a ticket?"

Shelton laughed out loud and Cassidy flinched in her seat. She was a jumpy little thing, likely snap frozen under all those layers of emerald skirts. "No, Pre-, ah no Miss Smith, not the man, the horse is in the stock carriage. Cade is driving his cattle up the Chisholm and I should have lent a hand. The horse, a gelding would have been my payment, but Cade's heart is too good and he gave me the mount, anyway."

"Cade? Is he your brother?" Cassidy leaned forward in her seat, the scowl gone, the high society lady facade evaporated too.

Shelton watched the scenery of Waco slip by, the jostling of the train carriages gently increasing in speed. His stomach growled, and he hoped Jackson's ticket came with lunch. "No, not a brother." By embarking on this mining business, Shelton had to say goodbye to Dew Springs for now, and the feeling sunk in his boots. "But almost, you know." Shelton let it drop.

"Sort of like Jet," Cassidy mumbled.

For a moment their eyes met, soft chocolate brown seemed to peer through him, no not through him but at him, only deeper than the surface and only for a moment.

The door rattled as Jet slipped into the compartment, "Old George says the Red River Bridge is out thanks to the flood, so they'll put us on a stage and then take us across by barge. Then, wait it gets better." The boy beamed.

Another penny dropped for Shelton, Cassidy Smith might be all breeding and ribbons, but she'd adopted a street urchin, a pickpocket and taken him on this journey. Now Shelton ran a more thorough gaze over his latest employer. From her fluffy skirts to prim manners, her damsel in distress performances and yet her luggage mix-matched, her kid boots scuffed at the heels. What was she running from to accept a mail order arrangement? A beauty like her would have no trouble finding a suitor in many places.

Jet squished between Cassidy and the window, his eyes alight. "And then we're on a Pullman Sleeper, a real Pullman Sleeper all the way to Wichita."

Again, Cassidy met his gaze, no glacial stare, but a naïve hunger that ricocheted into Shelton's chest. His ribs compressed, and he fought the urge to lick his lips. The moment fleeting, as Cassidy turned to the window, a flush of color rose from her neck to the edge of her jaw threatening to overrun her high cheekbones with the softest pink. Shelton ran his hands down his thighs and exhaled slowly. For the second time that day, uncertainty rocked Shelton. Perhaps Jackson was right, travelling with Cassidy Smith might be Shelton's undoing.

Cassidy kept her eyes on the greenery that rushed passed, hoping the cool breeze that flittered in and out of the cabin would chill her cheeks. She didn't know why she confessed about Jet, something about Shelton's tone and his words. His association with the man named Cade sounded loyal, more than loyal and the notion sung to her. The words tumbled out before she could stop them. Although she couldn't take them back, it seemed fitting that honesty found its place between Shelton and herself, after all he might still be her husband. Might? How did he work himself back into a possibility so quickly? She needed to concentrate.

Jet and Shelton chatted about the gelding describing it as liver-colored which sounded unappealing until he described the splashes of white and called it a dancer not a cutter. Whatever that meant. Cassidy soon found out as Jet asked another barrage of questions. Shelton talked about his ranching life and the longhorn cattle. Cassidy's spine seemed to melt against the leather, and she twisted her skirts so she could watch Shelton as he spoke. The rich tone of his words carried Cassidy into his world. The fields of bluebells opening up as the train hit open country, while Shelton spoke about wieners and the cutting competition, a chili cook-off that sounded like it rivalled the World's Fair, long sunsets and early mornings roaming the stock. His friends, Cade Hamerton a rancher, Taylor Stone another rancher who had dreams of mining, and then another friend named Kearby who'd run off to the Rangers. Cassidy's mind wandered, visualizing Shelton's home town until an awful thought interrupted the daydream.

"So you have family still in Dew Springs?" She asked.

"Yes ma'am."

"Call me Cassidy or Cass please."

"Cass," Jet smirked.

Shelton nodded. "My Ma and Pa own the Blue Cow Ranch in Dew Springs, my sister married a Banker and moved to Houston."

Cassidy's breath caught in her throat. She found the gold chain around her neck, her fingers spinning the locket to cool her nerves. How forward could she be? The thought ran unchecked in her mind, her worry unclear whether she would break another girl's heart or whether her husband had already married.

"And what about yourself Mister Murphy? Any young lady awaiting your return from Colorado Territory?"

Shelton's lips split into a grin. "Several I hope." He even winked. "Right now I will wrangle us up some food."

The locket stopped spinning and Cassidy hadn't a reply ready before the sliding door whizzed closed, leaving just Jet and herself.

"Are you going to tell him?"

Cassidy tucked the locket inside her dress. "I'm not sure he's the right husband for me, at least not yet."

"He can fight, he's got a horse, and his family owns a ranch!" Jet pulled his cap back on his head and reclined with his shoes on the seat. "Did you see him set old Jackson in his place, I bet the man could wrangle a thousand beasts, shoot a can at a hundred paces...." Jet dug into his pocket and pulled out Shelton's cheroot case, he withdrew one slender roll and ran it under his nose. "I think he's a keeper." The boy put the cheroot to his lips and Cassidy snapped.

She tossed the cheroot out the window and pushed down on the clasp of the silver case, the metal tumbled, clanging on the windowsill. She clasped her fingers to her mouth when she saw the whole item spin wildly passed the spinifexes. Jet laughed as the door slid open. Cassidy spun to see Shelton standing with his Stetson in his hands.

"Yes." Cassidy jumped again.

"Settle down Precious, they're serving lunch in the dining cart, that's all." Shelton said.

"Right," Cassidy squeaked and gestured to Jet.

The youth rose to his feet, smirking. "Tell me about your friend the one that ran off to the Texas Rangers?"

"Marcus Kearby?"

"Yeah, what's he look like? How many stage coach robbers has he caught?"

"Well, Kearby stands six foot tall with his hat on."

Cassidy chuckled quietly behind as she followed both to the dining cart.

"He's caught a few, but he's chasing a different fugitive these days." Shelton's smile alluded to a fugitive of the female variety and Cassidy couldn't stop her next words.

"And what are you chasing in Colorado?" Cassidy asked.

"Gold." Shelton's lips thinned. He cleared his throat. "Ain't got time for anything else."

Cassidy's throat closed ever so slightly, she swallowed the flavors of ash until she could see the dining cart slowing filling with passengers. So her husband-to-be already had gold fever, the obsessive compulsion to pan everything in sight to the exclusion of all others, food, sleep and family. Cassidy was suddenly glad she tossed his silver case. The man might learn how to break an addiction. Cassidy didn't bother to explore why the hurt seemed to burn and why of all things, she would want Shelton all to herself.

Chapter 4

The waiters moved seamlessly passed each other carrying armfuls of plates slathered in delicious fare. Mouth-watering salted pork and steaming beef and beans, veal cutlets and dipped toast. While other Porters delivered carafes filled with red wine or served bottles of ale and returning to fill tumblers with whiskey and others with gin.

"Thank you Mister um…" Cassidy started.

"You're welcome, Ma'am, please call me Sam."

"Thank you Sam, please call me Cassidy."

Cassidy sat opposite Shelton with Jet beside her, the youth digging into his salted pork, the same as what Shelton ordered, while Cassidy pushed her roast beef and vegetables around the ceramic plate, the cutlery scraping in rhythm to the rattling of the dining cart, sending thorns to her insides. Shelton hadn't read the fine print of his mining lease, and not only that, he didn't have time or want of a wife. Cassidy should feel relief at the possibility of freeing herself from the wretched conditions her father has set upon her, except she wasn't. That alone sent another rush of frustration through her veins. It should relieve her. Shelton Murphy was absolutely not husband material.

When Jet had finished, he excused himself from the table exclaiming he would *wrangle* them up some dessert menus.

"So Mister Murphy,"

"Shelton, please."

"Shelton," Cassidy took a sip of red wine savoring the peppery sting barely concealed within the fruity flavors. "Where exactly is your claim?"

"Not so quick, Miss," Shelton replaced his cutlery in neat

lines across his plate and took a long sip of his ale, "Why do you want to know?"

Cassidy thought about batting her eyelashes realizing it would do no good. She would have to tell him somewhere along the line, unless she followed him right up the mountain to his front door. When? When would be the right time to tell Shelton Murphy that his signature had sealed her fate? When she felt certain of his decision; well, that's what she told herself. It had nothing to do about Cassidy's indecision, or the way his smile drove her curiosity.

"I'm curious how far we will travel, if we arrive at Pueblo and I have to make separate arrangements."

A waiter delivered another ale for Shelton and Cassidy looked at her empty wineglass. When had that happened? She didn't object when another good measure sloshed into the glass.

"I hope you're not forgetting the details of your arrangement. I'll deliver you right to his door so I can get my payment. That's another thing." Shelton waited until Sam had cleaned the plates, and thanked the man with a generous tip.

"I might see about bringing you back another whiskey, later." Sam said, tapping his nose.

"I like the way you think Sam." Shelton said. When Sam had left, he added, "When we get to Wichita, I think it's wise you send him a telegram. He's expecting Mister Jackson and I won't have him refuse payment when he realizes what's happened. I think it's sensible you tell your man the plan changed."

Cassidy rolled the wine around the edge of the glass. "Are you telling me how to talk to my husband Shelton Murphy?" The glass almost slipped through her fingers at the sound of those words together.

Steel grey crinkled at the corners, his lopsided grin almost endearing. "I didn't dare presume to tell Miss Precious how to talk to her fiancé."

Cassidy narrowed her gaze. "That man back in Waco,

called you Silver-tongue, but I have heard nothing other than derision. You're a bully in cowboy's clothing."

"Don't forget a brute and a rake." Shelton added with a wink. Cassidy expected anger instead of his cavalier attitude. Cassidy softened her tone, either Shelton or the wine, had made the long afternoon fuzzy in a manner where his hard lines and roguish attitude became more appealing. "I will consider your idea as I wouldn't want to affect any payment we owed you." Gold, he is only interested in gold, Cass!

"Thank you."

Now his civility worked tendrils of warmth under her corset. She needed air and leaned on the table to bring the wind rushing past her cheeks.

Shelton took a sip of his ale. "Is Jackson a friend of your husband's?"

"No, my father arranged Mister Jackson." Cassidy released the wine glass and instead drank from her tumbler of water. "My father was a businessman. He thought someone with Jackson's reputation would be a safe option."

"Your father? Tell me what does he think of his daughter running off to Colorado to marry a man she's never met?"

"My father?" Cassidy let the word roll off her tongue, "He encouraged it. He was a businessman and thought the arrangement prudent." She didn't dare talk anymore unless the wine had loosened her restraint too much. She could feel his gaze on her again, somewhere between pity and confusion, "So Mister Shelton, tell me where your fortunes lay."

Shelton waited until another porter, this time George, had passed and leaned forward, his voice low. "Its north of a place called Cache Creek."

Before leaving Chicago, Cassidy had memorized all her father's notes and maps, she knew exactly where the claim lay in relation to the Twin Lakes, Oro City and the California Gulch. She had read every scrap of information she could get her hands on about mining, ores, sediment, lodes and testing samples. She had prepared for every option. Nothing about her father had been honest and likely this parcel of land could be barren. But she would try anyway, a small part of her had daydreamed, learning all she could, so she could cement her loyalty to her husband-to-be. She would help him, this figment of her dreams, to secure their future together. Now she raked her gaze over Shelton unaware they had come so close. His crooked nose barely six inches from hers, his sugar grey eyes glistening with the reflection from the windows, the early afternoon sun sending flecks of gold through his blonde strands. Cassidy's next words came out as a whisper, "Cache Creek? That's near where I'm headed to Twin Lakes. There are a lot of claims there."

The noise of the train dwindled to a hum as Shelton's lips moved, his eyes hooded. "There are, but this land, is farther out, almost undiscovered."

Cassidy shivered, the distance between them less, and she didn't mind at all. "Is that so?"

"New, untouched."

The shivers erupted across Cassidy's skin, curling around her limbs and ending between her thighs. His eyes targeted her lips and her chest swelled, the corset too restrictive, her mind spinning from the wine and his intoxicating plum cologne. Shelton's words heated the air, slithering to her abdomen. Enticing her forward and promising her nothing. Curiosity peaked, what would Shelton's lips feel against hers. Her first kiss waiting to be plucked from the narrowing gap between them.

"There is lemon pie, coconut pie, apple pudding." Jet slid into the chair beside Cassidy and she jumped.

Shelton leaned back, slowly withdrawing to neutral space. It was the ale or the stuffy train cabin air that had Shelton's collar heating. Not the Precious piece across the table and her delicate pout or her lash filled lingering gazes. In an instant, the glacial demeanor returned, her back straight, her eyes focused on the other passengers, jaw set. Cassidy Smith had ice running through her veins for sure, and now Shelton's assumptions flipped on their head. Slowly, she had thawed before his eyes only increasing Shelton's hunger and her danger. The girl might not be trouble, but Shelton's enjoyment at making her melt threatened an easy payday. He had to be careful, yet careful wasn't his style.

"I think I'll pass on dessert and find myself the smoking lounge." He left another tip and strode down the carriage to the doors. He took a moment to stand on the platform between cars and patted his pockets. Damn! If he didn't know better, Jet's lightest fingers had just relieved him of his cheroots. But the boy didn't smoke, or at least Shelton would clip him over the ear if he dared. Maybe Jackson, no the boy had pilfered the podgy man's watch. Shelton resigned himself to a scam of some sorts, and pulled out a handful of coins to buy a pack from Sam or George if they had any. Cassidy Smith had him panicked. He liked a little panic; it kept a man alive. This panic seemed to increase the more time he spent in her company with only one resolution on Shelton's mind.

He could see through the rocking carriages when Cassidy rose from her chair and headed towards the main cabins, her ruffled travelling skirt causing her issues as she moved unsteadily passed the narrow tables. Damn, she was cute! Shelton moved into the lounge car and took his place at the bar, a cheroot much appreciated from the man to his left. He watched the gambling tables as he smoked, savoring the tobacco flavors as it rolled over his tongue and into his lungs. He had no interest in gambling himself. He had Hugo to think of, and it was Hugo's money Shelton would spend in Pueblo to buy supplies for the mining claim.

Shelton's business partner had enough money to start work on his own claim, except his reputation was as crooked as a dog's hind leg. Hugo James had been denied any further mining claims thanks to his overzealous claiming of mining land and not working it, bribing federal officers to get patents and above all else, the man had filed for bankruptcy only two years ago. Any creditor Hugo James had abandoned would sniff the mining claim as soon as he hit ore. Shelton had half a mind to refuse the offer, except his Pa's Blue Cow Ranch needed the funds. Shelton and Hugo would work the claim together, Shelton's name and Hugo's equipment. A fifty-fifty split so long as Shelton would be shoulder to shoulder with him in the tunnels and to Shelton, if that meant his Ma and Pa could keep the Blue Cow, he'd dig from sunup to sundown.

He stubbed out his cheroot and paid the man for another, listening as the Porter, George advised their vicinity to the Red River and for those passengers disembarking, the need to cross at Colbert's Ferry to reach Durant in Indian Territory. Shelton didn't mind at all, it would give him the chance to step out on *Tango* and see what the horse could do. Shelton wandered back to the cabin, his mind concentrating on the Blue Cow and Hugo's list of items he needed up the mountain. He closed the dining car door and glimpsed emerald green on the platform.

Cassidy stood facing the scenery in the direction of travel, her bonnet gone and her caramel strands torn away on the wind. Shelton regarded her frozen form, her eyes closed and her cheeks warmed with sunshine. Cute. No, definitely not cute. In this pose, with her lips at ease, her fingers delicately gripping the railing, she looked damn near perfect.

Ice coursed through Shelton's veins making him unable to move. Only the ice burned so hot in warning. His hands wanted to wrap around her waist, pull her against him and press his lips to hers to make her open her eyes. The train's brakes eased on and Cassidy's brown eyes peeled open, the pupils wide then narrowing.

"Yes, Mister Murphy?"

"Are you all right?" He managed. She looked a little wobbly on her feet earlier, a little too much wine maybe that made her skin paler than usual.

Her nose twitched. She twisted her head away and nodded. "Almost."

The sting of her upturned nose, the dismissive tone of her voice set Shelton's teeth on edge. He should be glad she could turn cold in a second.

"Right, we're nearing Denison so you'll be taking the stage to Durant and I'll take *Tango*."

Cassidy stared at him for a moment. "You're leaving to go dancing?"

Shelton laughed. "*Tango's* the horse. I'll ride *Tango* to Durant and meet you at the station."

"Oh," Cassidy said.

He spared her a moment more for a rebuttal that never came, and then turned on his heel, finding Jet with both elbows out the window and his knees on the seat.

"Hey, boy have you seen my –"

"Phew, don't shut the door, man." Jet waved his hand in front of his nose. "You reek! Cass will have a pink fit when she gets back?"

"Cassidy?" Shelton stepped over the threshold and left the cabin door open. "She doesn't like the smell of tobacco smoke."

The boy's features fell flat, he bit the inside of his cheek and nodded, "All types of smoke."

"Right." Shelton nodded. The case of his missing cheroot tin now solved. Cassidy Smith might be a pick-pocket after all. "Your sister Cassidy…"

The boy's blue eyes lit up again, and he turned from the window, "Yeah?"

"She gets a husband out of this deal. What about you Champ? Are you searching for gold too?" Shelton would find out one way or another, what type of charlatan he worked for. Then he could handle it, wait for the sting, and spring the final scam.

Jet regarded his boots and turned his cap between his hands. After a moment, he shrugged his shoulders. "I don't know, a home," The boy cleared his throat, "A new home, I mean, you know far away from the cities."

Shelton's gut clenched, he had just made Jet lay bare his misfortunes and his deepest dreams. He felt like an ass. The boy had nothing. Nothing except Cassidy. "A job too I bet."

"Yeah, mining sounds hard work though." His eyes bright again. Jet lay on the seat and put his boots against the open cabin door. He tossed his woolen cap down to the screeching of the train's brakes.

Shelton laughed. "Lifting a shovel is harder than lifting a wallet."

Jet snorted, "Or a watch, but still I reckon I'd give it a fair go, and the rewards wouldn't be all that bad." His eyes fell to his lanky arms and bony shoulders.

"Always," Shelton replied.

The kid twisted back up to a sitting position. He leaned out the cabin doors and regarded either end of the hallway before popping back in and sitting down. This time Jet leaned forward, his elbows on his knees, "Ah Mister Murphy? Do you mind if I ask you something? I mean before Cass gets back."

This sounded ominous to Shelton; however, he nodded.

"If her husband-to-be takes a disliking to me, do ya think you might find me work, I mean I could work for you on your claim if all things turn to horsesh-..."

Cassidy entered the cabin in a flurry of emerald ruffles and straight back disdain. "What's this?"

"Nothing, me and the boy were just talking, you know five-card stud, saloon girls and whatnot." Shelton winked.

Cassidy's lips thinned and she tapped Jet's shoulder until he shuffled over. When she finally sat, Jet looked back to Shelton. What could he tell the kid? He'd lived a hard life already, and he was only, what thirteen or fourteen? Shelton could imagine the situation; Cassidy mustn't have told her new beau about the boy. They had both taken a chance that her husband wouldn't mind a kid brother getting under foot. Shelton would need to discuss it with Hugo, yet good labor was hard to find on the mountain. Perhaps he could find work for Jet with him and Hugo or at the very worst, at another mining claim closer to town. Shelton slowly nodded and gave the boy a wink.

Cassidy ignored the exchange between Jet and Shelton, most likely just as unsavory as the man joked. She'd spent the last few minutes settling her stomach after all the wine only to have it turn upside down when Shelton arrived. That and the intoxicating plum overrun with tobacco. She mentally scolded herself for the thought. She'd thought about his last statement. Even though he agreed to accompany them, now he would take his horse for a ride instead. Cassidy inhaled and exhaled slowly trying to diffuse the tobacco scent from her nostrils. To think, she'd been daydreaming about kissing him. Served her right. Her mother had fallen for a fast talker, a smooth man who promised her the stars and delivered her a two-room squat in a back alley of Chicago. She didn't remember the early days only the later years when her mother's pining for her father had turned into fret.

His business deals turned south and the man would abscond, large men barging through the door taking what little they had. Her mother's jewelry, her father's good suits, suits he only wore to swindle the next naïve man who had too many dollars and not enough sense. Her mother had trusted Cassidy with her last trinket that now spun in Cassidy's fingers. Her father had given Cassidy nothing except a bad name and a bad business deal with a man not unlike himself. Cassidy wanted a loyal, reliable, dependable husband, not one that gallivanted off at will. To be fair, Shelton didn't know their arrangement. She hadn't informed him of her expectations and technically Cassidy hadn't paid him a dime. But still.

Cassidy turned her mother's necklace again and again until her thoughts cleared. The realization that her hurt came from somewhere unexpected didn't help either. She wanted Shelton to want to be by her side, and the disappointment stung. Business deals aside; Shelton Murphy was easy to look at and he almost made her laugh. Almost.

"I'll make sure you're on the stage before I head off."

Now he wanted to be gentlemanly? Cass, be nice. The man is being considerate, and you still haven't told him the truth. What would happen if she did? Cassidy felt her cheeks color and pushed the thought away.

"You're not staying with us?" Jet shoulders hunched.

"I'll take *Tango* across the river and meet you at Durant."

"Be careful." Cassidy didn't know why she said it, but as soon as the words fell from her lips, Shelton's gaze met hers. Well, she meant it. "We can't get to Colorado without you." She added, hoping to cool his accusatory stare.

"Always," Shelton said as the train squealed again and the whistle erupted. Cassidy very much doubted his answer. Shelton Murphy's always might mean never for all she knew.

Chapter 5

Cassidy stood at the Durant Station, her eyes bleary from the jolting ride in the stagecoach. The sun sat two fingers off the horizon, coloring the wide open fields, honey, tangerine and gold. Silver tufts sparkled amongst the farmers field, either wheat or sorghum, Cassidy wasn't sure. She should be thankful, the train hadn't been delayed, forcing her to stay in either of the two double story timber hotels that Durant offered. One even had an open fireplace and candle lit chandeliers, with only one set of stairs. Imagine all the pitchers and basins she'd need to be able to sleep at night. Jet pretended to understand but he didn't, not really anyway. He slept on the street for most of his life and Cassidy envied him. She would give anything to have that night over again; to sleep outdoors under the torched sky instead of listening to her mother's unheard prayers. *He'll be back.*

"No he won't." Cassidy said aloud.

Jet strolled passed the train carriages carrying her loaded rucksack and stood next to Cassidy, the biggest grin split his freckled features, "Guess who I found at the stock car?"

Cassidy held her tongue and Shelton materialized out of the billowing smoke. Four whole hours of bone jarring stage coach hadn't done anything for her nerves, as she watched the tall man saunter closer. His pale blue shirt replaced with navy checks covered in the same leather vest as earlier. Where had the man found time to wash up? Cassidy didn't want to speculate. A thin layer of trail dust covered his boots. Cassidy would have to find time to wash up on the train as her emerald green skirts had suffered a far worse fate than Shelton's boots.

"You weren't leaving without me were you?" He smiled.

Cassidy returned with a small smile of her own, "Almost." Handing over his ticket, they climbed onto the Pullman Sleeper car together. Rich fabrics coated the high backed chairs, the ornate wood paneling engraved with swirls and flourishes, chandeliers hung from the ceiling which Shelton again had to duck under as they walked down to their seats. A table stood between each bench seat to Cassidy's pleasure, another barrier between Shelton and herself. A porter took their luggage,

"Sir, where is the washroom?"

"The names Henry, Ma'am and it's at the end of the carriage."

"Thank you Henry."

She spent the next half an hour cleaning with pitcher and basin changing her dress into a simpler straight lined piece in plum with an overskirt lined with black lace. Only after she had retied her hair did she realize the color matched Shelton's tantalizing scent. Thankfully, her thoughts dissolved in the scent of beef and beans drifting through the carriage. Cassidy packed her things and followed the waiters down to her seat. The chandeliers had been lit and rocked softly in their casings. Cassidy eyed them with suspicion, however hunger won out. Supper had been laid out on the table between the bench seats, as the waiter offered a carafe of wine. Cassidy refused instead filling her glass with apple cider and Jet's with sarsaparilla. No sooner has she taken her seat then a plate of steaming filled beef and gravy with biscuits arrived.

This time Shelton asked the questions, "How was the stage?"

"Bumpy," Cassidy shifted in her seat her rump too sore to mention.

"Boring," Jet dug into his beans running his bread through the sauce. "No robbers, no Rangers, nothing."

Shelton snorted.

"I like boring remember Jet." Cassidy sliced through the slab of beef as best as she could manage, but truth be told, she hadn't a thing to eat since lunch. It melted on her tongue and she cut short her whimper of delight. "How did *Tango* go?"

"He did alright, still needs to get used to me I think."

Cassidy figured if she kept talking about the horse and not where or who pressed Shelton's shirt the knot in her stomach would release, "What do you mean?"

"He's a little shy. Not far off from green and I'll need to build some trust with him."

Cassidy wasn't sure she wanted to ask, but Jet did, "How will you do that?"

With a slow yawn, Shelton leaned back from his cleaned plate; the man certainly had an appetite. "Little steps at a time, firstly *Tango* needs to know that I'm leading."

"You're a bully." Cassidy said as she folded her napkin.

"No, Precious, it's gentle reminders of who's in charge. I am. I protect him. I make the decision and in those decisions he trusts me. I can't have him stopping halfway through a jump, or refusing to walk when I need him to."

"And how do you propose to protect a giant beast like a horse?" Cassidy wished to undo a few clips of her corset, hoping she had another inch or two for pudding. She'd never eaten so good. Luckily Jackson had found a buyer for her father's inks, stamps and engraving plates, the cash from the sale had bought their all-inclusive tickets and a small amount for expenses. The small amount had been swallowed by Jackson in the Brazos River. Maybe she should have let Jet keep the watch? No. Cassidy Smith would not live like her father. "Shouldn't the horse protect its rider?"

"Nah –uh, nobody, man or horse should touch him but me." Shelton's voice deepened. A giggle from another table erupted and the source caught Shelton's eye. She had a magnificent brunette bouffant with silver wisps at her temples, but it didn't stop Shelton's admiration of her cleavage.

"And then?" Cassidy almost clicked her fingers. Shelton's sugar grey gaze fell upon her and for moment he didn't answer.

"Gentle training with gentle reinforcements. Cade's taken

care of most of it, but *Tango* has to get to know me, know my personality and me of him."

Cassidy echoed that sentiment, what did she know of her husband-to-be? Not a lot, his parents owned a ranch and his sister married a banker. She decided to remedy that. A smile curled across her lips, thinking of Shelton preventing any horse or man touching *Tango* and how she'd done her darnedest to make sure no other filly gained Shelton's attention.

Henry arrived to clear their plates and Jet ordered apple pudding and apple dumplings while Shelton ordered himself a coffee.

"It sounds interesting and when he finally understands you, you'll have him in hand?"

"Then I can increase the training, gentle touches."

Cassidy's breath stalled in her throat. Why did his words heat the air between them?

"New things to sense uncertainty."

The hairs stood to attention on the back of Cassidy's neck, "And if you sense hesitation?"

"Patience." Shelton ran his forefinger across his bottom lip, his gaze unwavering. "And then when he's ready, I lead on."

The locket grew hot against Cassidy's skin, her fingers itched to twirl it to calm the whirlwind that stirred in her abdomen. Thankfully, their waiter, Henry arrived with dessert, two for Jet and a pudding each for Shelton and Cassidy. Shelton sat upright, his boot clipped Cassidy's under the table and she flinched only to wince as her buttocks tensed.

"Gees, Cass it's only pudding." Jet tapped Henry on his upper arm, "Good work Henry!"

The Porter winked before he placed a cup of coffee in front of Cassidy by mistake. She reached for the cup, her fingers colliding with Shelton's. She withdrew them as if burned.

Cassidy turned to the window, the darkness rushing past at breakneck speed. The reflection of the window trapped Shelton who hadn't turned away. There, Cassidy felt sure, beneath his derision something lurked. The glass panes rattled and Cassidy dug into her pudding, managing only four spoon-ful's before her corset refused to budge any further. Henry re-turned in time to clear the table. Shelton tipped the man as he rose to his feet and stretched, his shirt pulling free of his belt.

"In search of another smoking lounge?"

"Not tonight," He said, "I'm beat after today, so if you don't mind, could you get out of my bed?"

Cassidy snorted, "Your bed?"

She heard a clunk of chains behind her and swiveled to watch Henry open a panel above the empty seats and table be-hind them. The wood folded down to a platform, a mattress already in place. Another Porter wandered to the opposite end of the car, carrying long drapes he hung on hooks spaced along the ceiling. Cassidy stood upright, clutching the back of her chair. Henry opened their hatch and folded down the bunk. Under her fingertips she felt the rough edge of the fabric, flattened from many footsteps into the loft bed.

"Well I um," She stammered as Henry pulled the drapes loosely from each side and then lowered the table to match the seats.

"Would you like to retire to the bar while we finish your bedding, Ma'am?"

"No Henry, I'm fine, I'll just..."She eyed the chandelier. The glowing light so close to the linen.

Shelton sprawled across the lower bunk while Jet eyed the loft.

"You first, Cass." The boy said his voice clear until he neared her left cheek, then he whispered, "I'm sure they turn them off at night."

Cassidy watched the swing of the lanterns as they lined the ceiling. The train jostled on the tracks as outside, the blanket of darkness in Indian Territory mocked her nightmares. She returned to the dressing room. With each unclip of her corset she fortified her resolve. It was one single lantern. She would march out there and climb to the loft be damned with the chandelier. The tea gown tumbled over her calico shift and she buttoned it all the way to the neck, before pulling on her drab wrapper. Climb up and lie still and hope to God the track didn't bend. That's all she had to do.

Cassidy eyed the pitcher. She would look a fool if she carried wet towels to her bed and likely catch a chill. She pressed her palms to her abdomen and straightened her shoulders. With each step closer to the half drawn curtains Cassidy's strength dissolved. The light had dimmed but not extinguished. Drapes unfurled from several bunks, the thick fabric only inches away from the chandeliers. Or so it seemed to Cassidy. Golden orbs of death lilted from side to side as Cassidy made her way down the aisle. Inside the half drawn curtains she could see Shelton's long legs, his boots kicked off and his feet bare. Cassidy had switched her kid boots for slippers the only other pair of shoes she owned. Now as the heel hit the armrest of Shelton's bunk, Cassidy froze. Her fingers curled around the drapes as the train hit a bend, the chandelier nearest her raised bunk swung.

"Come on Cass." Jethro's whisper drifted down.

"What's the matter?" Shelton raised himself up on one elbow. His unbuttoned shirt fell apart, revealing a sculptured chest that Cassidy wished she could admire more if only she could ignore the flavors of ash in her throat. "Cassidy?"

She took her foot from the armrest and held onto the drapes, rolling them back from the edge. "I can't sleep up there."

"Well um," Shelton rubbed his hand through his fringe. Looking one way down the aisle and then the other, he said, "There ain't any spare beds."

"You sleep up there."

Now, Shelton got to his feet and Cassidy took a step back. He roughly tucked his shirt into his unbuckled denims, "Are you mad? I can't fit up there."

He was right, she knew it, but the ash taste wouldn't go away. Her fingers trembled fighting the urge to cover hear ears from the inevitable roar that tormented her dreams. "I can't sleep up there."

Henry came to stand beside her, his voice calm, "Is there a problem Ma'am?"

"No." Cassidy's whisper almost came out as a shriek. Shelton's eyes narrowed, his head tilted. Oh gosh, she couldn't tell him. He'd think her mad. What husband would want a madwoman for his wife? "I just need some more um... pillows."

"Pillows, of course, Ma'am." Henry dipped his head and returned moments later with four fluffy pillows, handing them to Shelton.

Her mind raced as she thanked him.

"Now what Miss Precious?"

Cassidy focused on the bottom bunk and the distance between herself and Shelton. She kicked off her slippers while Shelton handed a pillow to Jet. Cassidy dove on to the bottom bunk.

"Hey!" Shelton snapped.

"I can't sleep up there, I just can't." She pleaded.

"Shhh!" Shelton hushed. He leaned down so his head was level with hers, "No need to get in a twist." His shirt gaped and this time Cassidy could see all the way down to his taunt abdomen.

She tried her best kitten purr, the desperate damsel voice, except her panic made it real, "Please Shelly."

"Oh no, don't try that on me!"

Long legs clambered on the mattress, followed by an arm and then the rest of Shelton. Cassidy scrambled to the far end of the mattress, the layers of her nightgown tangling in her ankles until she ended up trapped. Shelton's knee brushed against hers and she flinched. Shelton leapt. A *thump* echoed through Jet's bunk as Shelton's curse hissed through his teeth.

With Cassidy's nerves already frayed, a giggle broke from her lips. Shelton cursed again and this time someone shushed them both. Shelton groaned into one of the extra pillows as Cassidy stifled another nervous giggle with her hands. Her heartbeat reverberated in her throat, the ash taste dissolving to a different type of panic. Shelton tugged closed the curtain.

"Top to tail, Miss." He ordered.

"Huh?"

Cassidy pressed herself backwards, the cool of the window brought rhythm to her breathing. The curtains had brought darkness and as her eyes adjusted, Shelton sounded closer.

"I said, top to tail Miss Precious, spin around so your feet are up here." He pushed a pillow over to her side and then another creating a false barrier between them.

Cassidy tugged, yet the layers of her tea gown and wrapper had her ankle good and proper jammed between the corner of the bunk and the window. "I can't, I'm stuck."

Shelton clicked his tongue. The sheets ruffled. Cassidy's breaths came jagged and heavy in her ears as the linen around her moved. His hand patted her leg twice and then settled around her calf. Slowly, he worked his grip down as the quivers across her skin rose upwards. Shelton reached the snare, his fingers dug under the fabric, lifting and pulling until she was free. In the rescue, his fingers grazed her bare ankle and Cassidy gasped.

Shelton's hand ghosted across her skin until it slid back to the linen, the contact searing through Cassidy's flesh. Maybe she should have risked the lantern of death; the prospect of being scorched alive safer than being scalded by Shelton's touch. His breaths deepened. His silhouette outlined against the heavy drapes, his face hidden in shadow. Cassidy carefully pulled her skirts and righted herself, her feet now at Shelton's head. Retrieving one pillow from the barrier, she shoved it under her loose strands. In all her worry about the chandelier she'd forgotten to braid her hair. Such a trivial thought yet it kept her mind from deciphering what Shelton's groan meant as he slumped against the mattress.

The window panes rattled and somewhere between the joins a breeze whistled through a gap and caressed her cheeks. Night's inky black sped past, the sky awash with glistening diamonds.

"You afraid of heights or something?" Shelton's voice enveloped her.

"Something."

With Shelton's frame between her and the lantern, the drapes drawn, it sealed off the world. Except the stars, Cassidy had the stars tonight.

Shelton listened as Cassidy's breathing evened out. He'd seen her *damsel*, he'd seen the blizzard but this was something different. Cassidy's body trembled without check, her eyes darting to the ceiling and back, doe-eyed chocolate wide and glistening in the half-lantern light. He knew his actions were improper and downright shameful. A small part of him thought better of himself. Only a small part, because then he touched her. Warm velvet pumped a raft of blood through his veins all headed to his loins.

Nobody on the train, except for Jet, knew they weren't man and wife, so he wasn't ruining her reputation. Where the hell was he supposed to sleep anyway? Cassidy should be thankful that it was him and not Jackson. Although, likely they shared the same desires, Shelton was more restrained. For now. The scent of honeysuckle and black current mingled with his breaths, he felt himself harden again. Damn, would he get any sleep tonight?

Shelton rolled onto his side with one foot touching the floor he shoved a pillow under his head. They had at least another two nights on the Santa Fe train to Pueblo. Cassidy better make other arrangements, for her sake. Shelton drifted off to sleep thinking about lodes and ores and tailings.

"Huh?" Shelton rubbed his palm into his eye, "What?" his toe kicked the chair rest and he bit down a curse. Somewhere a girl whimpered. The whimpers grew into whispers and the linen around Shelton's body trembled. He shook his head clearing the fog until he recognized where he was and with who. "Cass?"

She answered in whispers too faint for Shelton's ears. Carefully and without smacking his head a second time, he turned himself around. The new moon rose enough to splash tiny slivers of light over her slumbering frame. Except she wasn't asleep, not really. Cassidy trembled, no quaked as some night terror took hold. She faced the window and her shoulders rocked back and forth. Shelton had seen something similar before. Gently he lowered himself down behind her and placed his hand on her shoulder, "Cass, Cass?"

Cassidy flinched underneath his touch, spinning in the linen until she faced him, her fingers speared into his shirt collar, her voice high and hoarse, "It's here."

Spears of pity sliced in Shelton's chest, forcing his throat to close. Like a leaf adrift in a tornado, Cassidy's nightmare had her in its grip. Lowering his voice, he brought his lips to her ear, "Shhh, Cass it's alright."

Her grip tightened, her whisper curt, "Ma, it's here!"

Shelton's ribs compressed, he exhaled slowly as her pain reverberated through his chest. Running his hand down her shoulder, he trailed over her spine and down to the small of her back, he tugged, bringing her closer, until her forehead rested against his chin, "It's all right Cass, *I'm* here."

It took another full ten seconds before the tension from his collar released, her trembles eventually subsided. What had happened? It didn't matter, right now Cassidy needed comfort. Shelton brushed his fingers across her forehead. Even breaths caressed his exposed throat. He could do that. He could give her peace tonight.

Chapter 6

Cassidy stretched against the bed clothes, plum and cedar wood haunted her dreams. Dreams! Cassidy sat upright, the wood collided with her forehead and she let out a curse.

"Not a sweet mouth." Shelton's laugh cut through the drapes, "You decent?" The curtain tugged back before Cassidy had a chance to pull a pillow or blankets up to her neck, "You all right?"

She should be thankful that her modesty had been his first concern. However he still barged in to sit on the side of the bunk, today he wore a fresh brown shirt, the fold lines still visible. In the early morning light, his steel grey eyes were almost black as he raked his gaze over her condition. Cassidy blinked back tears as she pressed the heel of her palm into her forehead.

"Let me see."

"I'm all right."

"Ya sure? Show me."

Cassidy removed her hand and furrowed her brows as best she could manage. Shelton held up his hands in surrender. However, as she crawled closer to the exit, the carriage jostled on the tracks and she stumbled. Shelton trapped her arms and dragged Cassidy upright. She wriggled against his grip only to end up off balance, her hip trapped against his. Cassidy extended her arms, except when her hand came down on his chest it stayed there. To Cassidy's surprise her other hand clutched Shelton's upper arm. Snap frozen in place. His thick shoulder rippled under her right palm as with her left hand, she sensed his hardened chest. Cassidy almost cursed again. Shelton Murphy may be tall, but he was solid. The lingering touch drove wildfire into her abdomen.

"I said I'm fine." The words came out breathier than Cassidy intended.

Shelton's lips pulled up at one corner, as he gently tilted her towards the breaking dawn, "I don't want to hand you over to your new husband all broken and bruised."

Cassidy watched the new morning light alter his errant fringe from drab grey to honey as Shelton gently prodded her swollen forehead.

"You look just peachy to me Precious." He said.

"Is that your final diagnosis?" She didn't know why she said it. No, that was a lie. So much for living an honest life!

"Without conducting a proper examination...."

Cassidy gasped and dragged the sheets up to her neck faster than a scalded cat.

Shelton's laugh drove nails under her skin.

"I'd just as soon bite a bug!"

Shelton tugged shut the curtains and disappeared. Bite a bug? Another lie. Cassidy pushed her head through the drapes and watched the man wander down the carriage. She took her opportunity and sped to the dressing room at the other end. Closing the door, Cassidy sat down on the small stool and rested her head in her hands. Should she tell him? Although they had at least another two nights on the next train before they reached Pueblo. And then how many nights up the mountain to the mining claim? Cassidy shook her head. Silver-tongue Murphy. Cassidy hugged her arms around her middle. She wasn't ready. She knew it. She wasn't ready to tell him and all that would come of that disclosure. More importantly, Shelton wasn't ready. He may look at her with a man's hunger, but she would be an appetizer until he moved onto the next course. She straightened her shoulders. Cassidy Smith was so much more than an entrée.

The navy travelling dress Cassidy stepped from the dressing room in had been bought by her father. She wanted to hate it, but the cut with the narrow collar and lines of buttons down to her hips had made this dress her favorite. Her father no doubt had bought it with his earnings from counterfeiting. Honesty. Cassidy reminded herself.

She entered the carriage just as the station of Winfield approached. Seated at the now reformed table, Jet met her gaze. The boy had changed his clothes to brown pants with matching fawn shirt. His grey cap rested over his scruffy hair.

"So did you tell him?" Jet's tone caught Cassidy by surprise. Around them the Porters continued to reassemble tables and hand out breakfast menus.

"About Chicago?"

"No about the contract?"

Cassidy shook her head, "I don't think that's wise, Jet. Not until we reach Pueblo."

The boy leaned forward, "He's going to find out."

Cassidy lowered her voice, "He could leave and then where would we be."

Jet smirked at Cassidy as he leaned back, "I don't think he'd leave Cass. I asked him you know."

Cassidy's cheeks infused with heat, "You asked him what?"

Henry returned to take their order and once again Jet ordered the largest meal he could find. The boy would be a foot taller by the time they reached Colorado.

"I asked him if, things go bad between you and your *husband,* well I suppose I really mean, if things go well between you and your *husband* and I'm not welcome, would he take me on. Give me work or find me some. See Cass, he's stuck with us either way."

Cassidy laughed at Jet's ingenuity, "You'll never, not be welcome Jet." With a quick wit and youthful charm, Jet had a bright future. Hopefully none of Shelton's silver-tongue nature would rub off on the kid. "But that's very clever of you." Something about the way Shelton spoke about his friends, made Cassidy certain he wouldn't renege on that deal. Then why did Jet demand Cassidy tell Shelton the truth? She asked her *brother* this and his answer surprised her.

"I feel bad. I know, we've done some shifty deals Cass, but this one's permanent. Or at least it feels that way. I don't want to keep lying to him, he's..."

Cassidy's greatest ally had begun to waiver. She smiled at the youth. His father had run off before Jet turned four, his mother died of pneumonia before he turned ten. When he tried to pick Cassidy's pocket only to have her retrieve her purse and the latest watch he'd stolen, they instantly became friends. Cassidy should be happy Jet liked Shelton. And if an honest life was their future, it was a good sign the boy felt guilty about being dishonest.

"I'll tell him Jet, just when it's the right time, otherwise you'll end up running the mining works and I'll be on a train back to Chicago."

"Not on your own, Cass. I'm with you all the way. Just not Chicago." Jet placed his other hand on top of Cassidy's.

"Fine, Texas." Cassidy wished her words back in her mouth.

"Just tell him before Pueblo. Then we arrive in Colorado with a fresh start."

"Okay." Cassidy's hands retreated. Jet pulled out a notebook and began scribbling away.

"What you doing there?"

"Writing it all down. Well, as best as I can."

Cassidy gently pulled the book across the table so she could read Jet's messy handwriting. "That one is spelt with an e." She corrected. The boy fixed his spelling and put the book down again for Cassidy to recheck his words. "Perfect." She said. "Next you'll be writing one of those dime novels."

"Ha! Nothing interesting about sitting on a train, Cass."

Cassidy laughed, "I'm sure the Turners Gang disagrees with you."

"Ah yeah. Well if it's going to be a dime novel, something interesting better happen soon."

The carriage door squeaked and Cassidy lost her concentration. Henry brought a serving of French toast and two plates of bacon and eggs, followed closely by Shelton. His fresh burgundy shirt accentuated his sun-kissed skin and the light grizzle across his cheeks. He tipped Henry and Jet scooted across the bench seat and Shelton slid in beside.

"Mornin'. Why do you two look like flies in the glue pot?"

"Good morning, Shelton." Cassidy replied.

Jet grabbed a plate of bacon as Henry poured two cups of coffee. "How'd you sleep Ma'am? I trust the pillows were sufficient?"

"Fine." The color drained from Cassidy's cheeks. A tendril of a memory lurked in her mind, coated in cedar wood and plum. She had dreamed. Fire slithered across the floor, igniting everything it touched, climbing the walls as the air disappeared. Her lungs seared behind her ribs. The heat licked her cheeks until the scent of plum peppered the flames. Stars, she remembered the stars, and a different kind of warmth. Soothing, solid, steadfast. "Yes the pillows were more than sufficient."

Cassidy sliced her French toast thinly as Shelton dug into his breakfast without another word.

"Wichita soon," Jet said, "Is it true what they say about Delano?"

"Why you asking me kid?" Shelton smirked. After last night he considered visiting the wild streets of Delano to slake his thirst, only he knew it wouldn't. He wanted to taste Cassidy's rosy lips, press against them until she thawed. Anything in Delano would be a disappointment. Even the stately woman who sat at the table across from them, dicing her eggs had caught Shelton's eye. In the lounge car, a young woman travelling West with her family, had a fine shape in pink ruffles, yet it reminded him of a different dress and a different girl. Everything he looked at seemed a carbon copy of his desire. He sensed his downfall. "There's plenty of things in Delano to keep a man entertained but I'll be looking to stretch *Tango*."

Cassidy's eyes stayed on her toast, even when she took a sip of coffee.

"Can I lend a hand anywhere?"

"Shouldn't you be looking after your sister here?"

"Why can't she come too?" Jet looked at Cassidy's wide-eyed stare. "The train doesn't leave until two."

Shelton scooped up two pieces of bacon and crammed it between two pieces of bread, "If all goes well, then maybe I can take you for a run." He bit down and egg ran down his little finger. Without thinking he sucked it clean with a squeak. Cassidy's gaze darted from his lips to his plate and then back to her own.

"I will have to send a telegram first."

That's right, he'd told her to warn her husband. The knots in Shelton's stomach caught him by surprise. His thoughts drifted to claiming Cassidy's lips amongst others things and yet she thought about her husband. Perhaps it was for the best. He didn't want to get between a miner and his woman. Well she had said fiancé. Betrothed is different to married, and they hadn't even met yet.

"You might need to find a new pair of boots too, Miss."

Her pout turned into a scowl.

"It's cold up the mountain. Your dainty boots aren't going to last one week up there. You too scamp. They'll be a lot cheaper in Wichita than at Pueblo."

Shelton hated sounding responsible. Hated it down to his toes. The woman's husband should have warned her. He bit into his bacon and egg roll thinking about the old scruffy miners he'd seen. Beards halfway down their chest, not a clean pair of socks between them. Cassidy had saddled herself up with one of them, although he could be a mine owner or supervisor. Shelton finished his sandwich and coffee by the time the train's brakes winced.

"I'll meet you down the end of Douglas Avenue."

It took another hour and a half before they arrived and

finally disembarked in Wichita. The station filled with greeting families and departing passengers that Cassidy and Jet scrambled through the crowds only drawing breath when they hit the street. They carried their cases as they made their way down Main Street, their luggage getting heavier with each step.

"God, Cass you got rocks in here or what?"

"No, just books, keep any eye out for a shoemaker."

Cassidy took the largest satchel from Jet and threw it over her shoulder. They should have paid a courier except now she needed boots. Jet had managed to find some of her father's money in Jackson's room aboard the steam boat; but they would still need supplies at the mining claim. She had no illusions as to what the cabin would look like. At most she hoped for a stove. She prayed for a stove. Not an open fire.

Cassidy stored their luggage at the Santa Fe lines, picking a book to read for when they eventually made it to the train. They wandered down the wide streets of Wichita, the boardwalk timbers dusty, the summer heat sending beads of sweat between Cassidy's breasts. Citizens dashed from under hooves and steel wheels. A fair portion of the crowd consisted of cowboys, making their way north on the long drive. Perhaps Cassidy and Jet wouldn't have made it this far after Jackson's licentious behavior. Cassidy should be thankful. Instead she thought of Shelton's morals, or lack thereof. His comment about an examination still echoed in her mind. The tempting plum scent that lingered on her skin irked her even more.

Cassidy stopped outside the closest resemblance to a reputable hotel and paid for a hot bath for herself and Jet. Cassidy scrubbed as fast as she could before the sand slipped through the hourglass, glad for the reprieve. Before too long the door rattled, the maid barked through the keyhole and Cassidy extracted herself from the tub. Hopefully Jet had spent his time wisely and washed his unruly hair. As Cassidy looped the final button of her navy travelling suit, the door rattled again.

When Cassidy reentered the street, Jet was already waiting; his shirt damp around his narrow shoulders and his hair bone dry under his grey cap. Cassidy held her tongue.

Together they found the outfitters. Two old gentlemen leaned against the rail, pipes in the mouths, bowler hats on their heads. Inside Cassidy wandered down the aisles, the tanning oil thick between the rows of boots. She ran her fingers over the leathers, some embroidered, and others had short nails along the toe and heel. Jet picked up a pair of brown boots that went half way up his calf with a pointed toe and engravings around both sides. Cassidy picked up a pair with blue threading swirled into dragon flies. She turned them over and put them down to pick a hobnailed pair.

"I think we'll need both." Cassidy said.

"Got enough after our dip?" Jet whispered his eyes darting to the storekeeper and the front door.

Cassidy clicked her tongue and pulled out her purse, "Yes plenty." Even after the bath, she'd leave at least fifty dollars for supplies in Pueblo. Flour, canned goods, blankets. How cold would it be up the mountains? The scent of plum and cedar haunted her taste buds. Maybe she should have soaked longer in the tub.

At the counter, Jet eyed the leather belts and selection of knife pouches before Cassidy sent him outside. Stepping onto the boardwalk, the late morning Kansas sun stung her cheeks. Boots fell into step beside her.

"Done alright then?"

Cassidy almost cursed again, "I thought you were looking after Tango?"

Shelton tipped his Stetson hat higher on his forehead. His gun belt slung low around his narrow waist yet the holster was empty. "I took him for a quick sprint to steady the nerves." Shelton scooped up the dragon fly embroidered boots in Cassidy's arms, "Good choice. Did you send your telegram?"

"Not yet," She reached, her fingers collided with Shelton's and she snatched the boots out of his hand. "We... I will."

"Good, we'll head to the post master now then."

"I..." Cassidy started

"Did you change your hair?"

Cassidy's elbow bent but she resisted, "We found a hot bath."

Shelton smiled.

"You don't need to escort us, we passed the Post Masters office on the way here."

Shelton stalked down the boardwalk and unhitched *Tango*, the giant chestnut horse twitched and then settled as Shelton ran his hand slowly down its shoulder. Jet came up behind Cassidy and whistled. The horse's ears twitched again and Shelton whispered something to the animal. Jet stepped down cautiously to the street while Cassidy kept on the boardwalk.

"It's fine, there's a nice little patch where the Big Arkansas River meets the Little, so we'll head to the Post Master, send your telegram and get a bite to eat."

Cassidy regarded the timber boardwalk as it ended outside the butchers, "I told you Shelton there is no need." Cassidy stepped down the street, with Shelton only a stride behind.

"Ah," Shelton used his finger to tap aside his nose, "If I hadn't watched your brother snitch a watch from Jackson and if I hadn't seen you batter your eyelids to make a grown man dizzy, I wouldn't be concerned. Besides, if he is as amenable as you believe then there ain't no issue telling him Jackson is done and it's me he has to pay."

Cassidy slowly nodded her head. She had no intention of sending a telegram to her fiancé considering the man walked beside her to the Post Master yet his words clung to her skin leaving an oily taint to her thoughts. Dishonesty ran in her bones! She should just tell him. And what if he left her high and dry in Wichita? Cassidy sighed and headed to the Post Master. Shelton handed Jet a handful of coins and directed him to the nearest café.

Within moments, Cassidy could smell the plum scent impinging on her thoughts as he followed her into the Post Office. Shelton worded two telegrams of his own while Cassidy fumbled with the paper. When the Post Master finished with Shelton's message he stood before Cassidy. Quickly she scrambled a short message, smirking as she re-read her words. She handed it over with her coins and pressed a single finger to her lips. The Post Master looked from the paper to the man behind and nodded.

"All done. I'll await his reply in Pueblo." Cassidy said just as Jet returned to stand beside *Tango*. In his hands he carried three thick parcels that leaked gravy through the parchment paper. Shelton tucked three bottles of sarsaparilla into one saddle bag. The scent of roast beef made Cassidy swallow hard. "We will pay you back."

"Of course, Precious. I'm keeping a tally of all my expenses."

Cassidy exhaled, her jaw cinching tight. "Of course." She said flatly. She would find a way to pay him back. An honest day's pay. She could wash, mend and cook. There would be work in Oro City for certain.

Chapter 7

"Are they real Rangers?" Jet pointed to two men who stood outside the sheriff's office, their holsters empty as they received a wooden tag in return. Shelton led *Tango* behind them as they wandered down Central Avenue.

"Sure as a shower of sh...."

"Shelton!" Cassidy hushed him in a hurry.

Shelton had to smirk. Outraging Cassidy Smith had become his new favorite hobby. With her brows dipped and her pout tight, he wanted to scowl at her and now, after her bath, it wasn't just his lunch that made his mouth water.

"Will you teach me to shoot?" Jet asked.

Shelton looked to Cassidy. After all, the woman had taken responsibility of him.

"I've read about grizzlies." The boy continued.

Cassidy's teeth worried her bottom lip, "I think it would be prudent for us all to learn our way around a firearm, don't you think Shelton?"

"Sure. Grizzlies, not to mention coyotes, and the odd mountain lion up there to worry about. Lots of predators in the mountains." Shelton risked a glance at the woman whose neck bent, her hands went to her throat twisting her necklace. "But not in Wichita with those deputies breathing down everyone's neck. When we get to Pueblo."

"I guess a few things will have to wait till Pueblo." Jet said. His tone unusually thick.

"Oh," Cassidy said. Shelton looked up.

The street opened up to wide lawns decorated with groves of sycamores and burr oaks, hackberries and dogwood trees. The land descended towards the wide curve of the Arkansas River. *Tango's* nostrils flared, his front hooves toeing the ground and Shelton tightened his grip on the reins. He ran his palm down *Tango's* white nose whispering as they neared a large sycamore.

"It's so beautiful." Cassidy mumbled. "Is your home town like this?"

"Dew Springs?" Shelton held his laugh. "The town is only one street of what Wichita has to offer. But Blue Cow...." Shelton thought about the sun setting over the rear pastures as he stood on the rear porch. The colors of amber and honey blending into fingers of gold that seemed to touch every corner of his parent's ranch. If Shelton didn't find gold in Colorado the sun would set for the final time.

"I'm going to take *Tango* for another sprint." He handed Jet the rolls of beef and gravy and the sarsaparilla before climbing into the saddle. *Tango* sensed his eagerness and galloped across the open lawns. The emerald hills flew under hoof, ducking under low branches, Shelton picked the track nearest the river, his lungs expanding as the fresh air worked into his body. A rush of heat trickled down his spine and into his limbs. Up here, the world made sense. No jokes, no mockery, no batting eyelashes or honeysuckle to concern him. He spied a thicker grove on his left, a large log had fallen between two oaks and Shelton crouched low over the pommel. He urged *Tango* forward, ready if the horse baulked. Hamerton had given him instructions, one sharp whistle to halt, one long loud whistle to return and two quick chirps to jump. *Tango's* ears twitched, his neck raised. Shelton patted the horse's neck and chirped. Shelton shifted his weight and clutched the pommel, the ground tilted, *Tango's* muscles bunched, and Shelton leaned forward. Too far forward, the descent rocked through his forearms and knees, his boot scrapped the nearest tree, twisting the stirrup wide. *Tango* recovered better and returned to a gallop before Shelton had righted himself back in the saddle. He let out a sharp whistle and the horse halted so fast his chest collided with the animal's neck.

"Whoa boy!" Shelton patted the gelding's neck. "You didn't baulk. You'll get a cube for that." Shelton dismounted and gave *Tango* some sugar from his pocket, he dropped the reins and the horse's muzzle pressed against his pocket. At least he held his seat and the animal hadn't thrown him. Wandering back to the fallen log, Shelton stepped out the hoof prints. He lifted his Stetson to slide back his fringe. He searched the tree, his fingers finding the groove his stirrup left behind. Four, if not five feet in height.

"You're a dancer all right, that was a damn pirouette." He gave *Tango* another treat, his muzzle nudging Shelton's shoulder, ears twitching like crazy. "Come on, let's try that again." Shelton climbed into the saddle and brought *Tango* out to the far-bend of the river. He pushed the horse into a trot. The fallen tree neared and Shelton chirped again. *Tango* leaned back on his rear legs, the ground tilted and Shelton matched his weight to the horse's movements. They came down smoothly on the other side.

"Now let's go find that filly." Shelton cringed; glad no-one but *Tango* heard him.

He found Cassidy in the shade of a sycamore, her back against the bark, her knees up and a book against her thighs. She flicked pages back and forth making notes in the margin as Jet lay on his back, his hand behind his head. Cassidy had removed her bonnet, her caramel strands like silken threads dangling down to her creamy neck. Maybe Shelton should take *Tango* for another sprint. Jet suddenly sat upright and raised his hand. "Too late now." Shelton mumbled and *Tango* snorted as he pulled him up to a trot.

"How did he go? Is he fast?"

"Fast, yeah, but he's a jumper."

"Really?"

"Yeah. No wonder Cade couldn't use him. A horse has to stand his ground, cut the wieners, no point having one leaping over them instead."

Cassidy had risen to her feet and took a step closer, "He's

still a good horse though. You're not going to get rid of him. I mean even if he's not what you want, you'll keep him?"

Was the city girl a horse girl? Unlikely judging by the size of her eyes as she started at *Tango*. "I'm keeping him. He's brand and training is worth more than any other horse in any other stockyard."

"Is it about his value?" Cassidy asked.

Shelton tied *Tango's* reins to a low hanging branch and stepped into the shade. One beef and gravy roll and bottle of sarsaparilla remained and Cassidy handed it to Shelton. "No. He's personality's growing on me."

"Good." Cassidy stepped back and resumed her seat against the tree trunk.

"Can I pat him?" Jet asked.

"Just hold your hand out, and let him sniff you. If he pulls away, stay still and wait." Shelton instructed around mouthfuls of bread and beef. He kept a close eye on Jet as the boy neared *Tango*. The horse shifted his muzzle away for a moment. Ears alert. Shelton moved closer between the boy and the animal as the horse's front hooves danced away. "Give him some time." Shelton swallowed his last mouthful.

Jet's shoulders slumped and he nodded. He picked up his beef and gravy remnants and headed down to the river. A raft of ducks swam into shore as Jet approached and he flicked his crumbs to his new adoring crowd. Shelton reclined against the sycamore trunk and took a swig of his Sars.

"He's eager to learn." Shelton broke the silence.

Cassidy watched Jet by the riverside, his head down, shoulders hunched. Should she console him? She thought of his admiration for Shelton. Unlikely the boy would appreciate the extra attention right now. "He is," she replied. "He wants to learn new things. Be useful."

"He will be. I said if ah, well if your new husband isn't keen on taking him on. I'll find work for him."

Cassidy rolled her lips inwards. Should she tell him now?

"Thank you, Shelton. I hope that will not be necessary."

Shelton rested his hand on one knee and rolled the bottle between his long fingers, "Why didn't you tell him about Jet before you agreed to come out?"

How did she explain this? Cassidy put a marker in her book. Because her husband didn't know she existed? Her husband didn't read the fine print let alone an extra mouth to feed?

"I couldn't leave Jet behind. Not where..., where he was. I didn't want to jeopardize my arrangement. I have faith that my fiancé will see the benefit in having myself and Jet, rather than a deficit."

Shelton smiled, "There's a shortage of women up the mountain, I'm sure ah," he cleared his throat, "Someone like yourself would find a suitable match as soon as you arrived. Probably seven or eight."

The heat climbed Cassidy's neck her throat suddenly dry, "Thank you Shelton, but I had specific requirements in mind."

He leaned back, his head resting on the tree trunk, "Right."

The tone caught Cassidy by surprise, "Not that I have to explain myself, but there are certain qualities in a husband that are more desirable. I'm sure when you marry you will no doubt have some demands of your own."

Shelton smirked, "Yeah, and what are these qualities Precious?"

"Manners for one."

His laugh seemed to rattle the leaves and Cassidy reopened her book, "For some people that's more important than appearances."

"Oh yeah," Shelton said, his blonde fringe hung across his nose, yet she sensed he still watched her, "Watcha reading there Precious?"

She lifted up the edge to reveal the cover.

"*A Practical Treatise on Mine...*" Shelton leaned over and plucked the book from her hands, "*Mine Engineering* by G.C Greenwell."

"Hey!" Cassidy reached out but Shelton had already risen. His long strides took him under the sycamore and out of reach. Cassidy ducked under the branches. With a flick of her ankle she stuck out her toe and clipped his heel.

"Hey!"

Cassidy dove forward as Shelton stumbled. Only he stayed upright. Cassidy stopped before she collided with his chest.

"Did you just trip me?"

Her book only inches away. What had Shelton said about training *Tango*? Cassidy tilted her neck and threw him her darkest glare. "Manners, Shelton." She opened her palm.

Shelton placed the book in her palm but didn't let go, "Making yourself useful to your new husband?"

The air vanished from Cassidy's lungs at the thickness of his voice, "I think it's prudent to be prepared."

"Prepared?"

As his gaze altered, Cassidy swallowed hard. Heat climbed her neck. She shifted her weight from one foot to the other. Tiny vibrations fluttered in the hollow of her throat and the locket around her neck seemed to hum. Shelton's eyes traced down to her lips and then back to eyes.

"Just give him that look, Precious." Shelton cupped her cheek.

Trouble. Shelton knew it as soon as his fingers touched her velvet skin. Trouble. There she stood so close, the dappled sun through the leaves highlighting her delicate features. He thought she'd slap his hand away. Except she didn't. His fate had been sealed as his lips pressed to Cassidy's. A shield of ice seemed to settle over her soft lips now unrelenting. Shelton ran his other hand behind her neck and twirled through her hair. He brought her closer, slanting his lips to revel in her silky kiss.

"So soft," He mumbled. He heard Cassidy gasp, and Shelton dipped his lips again. Withdrawing only a hairs breath away to kiss her again and again, her scent wound through his veins awakening a darker thirst. Lingering over their final kiss, until her breath tickled his cheek, Shelton rolled the lobe of her ear between his thumb and forefinger. The warmth of Cassidy's skin seeped through his palms, lightening pulsating through his blood. Slowly he brought his kiss across Cassidy's lips, his whisper lost, "Open for me, Precious."

Cassidy's knees wobbled, the shade of the tree had been replaced with Shelton's heat, searing through her lips down to her abdomen. His kisses tender, yet firm. Shelton's whisper repeated, "Open for me." Not a demand, a promise.

Cassidy complied, startled as Shelton's tongue, hot and wet darted across her lips. As if sunlight coursed through Cassidy's veins, she was lost. The press of his lips, the mingling of their breath drove thorns of pleasure under her corset. She could feel her body responding to the slow slake of his tongue across hers. Glorious plum teased, as curls of desire stretched like tendrils of silk. Her swollen breasts now ached, the weakness of her knees now tremors as her heartbeat reached fever pitch. Tentatively Cassidy reached out, her hands finding solid muscle. Another lick of heat curled through her abdomen as she explored.

Her thoughts of more, echoed in Shelton's movements as his palm descended down her shoulder, until it settled in the small of her back. A noise strangled from his throat, the sound reverberating through Cassidy as he pulled her hard against him.

Shelton's fingers trembled as Cassidy melted in his arms, her tension gone, and in its place the supple delight of a woman ablaze. Her warmth seared through his shirt, his body aching for more. Shelton dragged Cassidy onto his arousal, the soft press of her body torture as he craved every last touch before she inevitably broke away. Except she hadn't. The girl was supposed to flinch, pull away, save herself from his shameless behavior. Cassidy's tongue darted forward to meet him and Shelton unraveled. If he didn't stop, if she didn't stop, they risked more than discovery. The blizzard of Cassidy had thawed leaving an inferno that threatened to consume him. Shelton withdrew, peppering light kisses to her swollen lips.

Cassidy stood breathless; her senses on edge, demanding something, only Cassidy didn't know what. A soft breeze drifted between them, Shelton held her waist as Cassidy fought the urge to run her fingers across her lips. Her first kiss from her husband and she'd relished the pleasure.

Steel grey turned to flint. Cassidy spun on her heels and pressed her hands to her stomach. She took measured steps to the other side of the sycamore. Shelton said something but her feet wouldn't stop until she reached the river bank. There, when she was certain, she brought her hand to her mouth. Tall, he was too tall, too pretty and his kiss scared her. *How did she ever think she could marry a man like Shelton? No, the kiss didn't scare her. Not Shelton either.* She walked along the bank of the river, the breeze cooling her cheeks.

"You all right Cass?"

Cassidy jumped as Jet strolled over, his lunch crumbs gone, the ducks well adrift on eddies of the river.

"Yes, I'm fine."

"Ok, well I suppose we should be heading back to the station soon."

"Yes." *The Train!* Cassidy would have to brave the top bunk. She couldn't in all good conscious sleep next to the man again. Not with the tornado of flames he had induced. "Yes you're right. Just give me a minute. I'll follow you up soon."

"All right."

Shelton watched the exchange between Cassidy and the youth. Damn! Thawing Cassidy Smith had been easier than he thought only the wildfire that burned under the surface had all but destroyed him. Worse, he wanted more. He wanted to follow that spark all the way to detonation and to hell with the casualties. Except Cassidy would be a casualty. Shelton exhaled slowly as he watched Jet wander up the hill, moments later Cassidy turned and followed. When she reached the shade of the sycamore, Shelton sighed. He should be happy the icy glare had returned, the blizzard in full swing behind her chocolate irises. And that meant even more trouble for Shelton. Since he knew what lurked beneath the ice, he wouldn't be able to resist.

"Time for the train?"

"I believe it is Mister Murphy."

"Mister Murphy?" Shelton smirked. *Yeah, trouble alright.* Shelton shut down his train of thought immediately. A husband of sorts, waited for Cassidy and Shelton would have to stand before the man and ask for his payment. All that Shelton earnt would go back to his parents at the Blue Cow. Colorado gold, not girls, should be his focus. He'd hoped there'd be girls along the way, but Cassidy Smith wasn't the kind of girl Shelton had in mind. She had a husband and new life ahead of her, and all Shelton had to do was play it safe until he brought her to Twin Lakes. Safe. Except Shelton never played it safe.

Chapter 8

Cassidy sat at the table facing the direction of travel, she held G.C. Greenwell's book in her hands while the locket grew hot against her skin. She heard the whistle and still no sign of Shelton. Perhaps that was a good thing. If she was going to marry him, he would need to be reliable and restrained. She wanted three children, not a hundred. Cassidy wished her thoughts back into the corner of her mind, as the man himself sauntered down the aisle.

"Are you ever punctual?"

"Punctual goes with manners, Precious." Shelton replied. He tossed himself down on the spare seat next to Jet and took his Stetson from his head. "I was settling *Tango* in the stock carriages and sorting out my ticket."

"Your ticket?" Cassidy asked.

"Yeah, I figured since there are three of us, I could either find myself a berth to warm every night or I sort my ticket before we leave Wichita."

A sliver of something dark curled through Cassidy and she turned to the window as the train whistle finally blew. After a moment she turned back, the words thick on her tongue as he picked up her book, "Well that's prudent."

"I thought so." Shelton bit back.

Was he annoyed that Cassidy had cost him money? Perhaps the kiss had been not to his liking? What would Shelton do if Cassidy told him about the marriage arrangement? Lightening sizzled through her chest down to her abdomen. Cassidy cleared her throat.

"So I'm at booth six." He pointed to the bunk a row back and on the opposite side of the aisle. "In case you're looking for more pillows."

Maybe she was wrong about the kiss? She re-read the same paragraph about strata faults, "Unlikely Mister Murphy."

"It's Shelton remember. You still reading Greenhill's engineering papers? Shouldn't you be undertaking more lady-like hobbies?"

"Like?"

"Painting."

"I don't paint." Cassidy said. She wouldn't pick up another paint brush if her life depended on it.

The book tumbled from her hands and slid across the polished pine table.

"How much mining experience do you have Shelton?"

"I know Longhorns, Bobcats and Coyotes." He answered.

"Then how are you going to get the most out of that claim?"

Shelton flicked a page with one hand and the other he used to tap his shoulder, "These."

"You can work a shovel? Well strong arms will only get you so far. What if you're digging in the wrong spot? What other rock formations or geological signs will point you in the right direction?"

"Cassidy's real smart, you know." Jet piped up from jotting in his notebook. "She knows a fair amount about rocks and stuff."

Shelton skimmed the pages, "I don't need to know all types, just one or two."

Cassidy leaned forward, her lips twisting into a grin, "Like the ones that form gold?"

Shelton returned to the front of the book, "Maybe." His eyes narrowed, "Why does it have Chicago Public Library stamped in the front?"

"Never mind that," Cassidy snapped the book shut and handed him another one from beside her.

"*Elementary Geology* by Edward Hitchcock." Shelton opened the cover, "Well would you look at that, New York Society Library."

Cassidy's cheeks heated as she peeled back the pages to find the right chapter.

Shelton skimmed reading aloud specific words "...porous quartz... silver, copper, lead....total value to the mint..." He let out a whistle. "I see your point." Shelton turned a few more pages, his eyes scanning the tiny black print. "You still didn't explain how you have two library books in your possession?"

"Four." Jet smiled.

Cassidy didn't answer. So much for living an honest life! The thought of Shelton changing his ticket had dissolved with the grin he threw her across the table.

"Four books on rocks and mining and that's not counting the..."

"All right Jet." Cassidy whispered.

"Relax, Cassidy I'm not going to bring Pinkerton's Agents on you. Tell me, how is gold formed?"

Cassidy smiled and pressed her back into the chair, "When the hot fluids from deep inside the earth cool or come in contact with other rocks, they can leave behind gold. If you're looking for lodes of gold, metamorphic rocks can be good indication, sometimes the color of the soil, other times two different types of rocks colliding at sharp angles can indicate possible gold-rich locations."

Shelton gestured to the books, "I hope he appreciates your efforts." The man threw a quick look to Jet, the boy's future hung in the balance of Cassidy's ability to win over her new husband.

Jet sat upright, "I told you she was clever Shelton. She taught me to read and write, she can cook, and mend and..."

"Thank you Jet, but I'm certain Shelton doesn't need –"

"She's a real catch," Jet finished as he dragged Cassidy's book across to his side of the table and began sketching Sluice boxes.

"I don't doubt it, Champ."

The Porter arrived and handed them the Bill of Fare. Shelton eyes met hers over the top of the card. Cassidy pulled the menu up higher as the heat climbed her neck.

"Apple Pudding and dumplings and coconut pie, I'm set." Jet said.

"Mister um...?"

"Everyone just calls me George, but my names Sunny."

"Sunny it is then." Cassidy smiled.

"Thank you Ma'am."

After they placed their orders for dinner and breakfast, Shelton stretched both arms outwards along the top edge of the seat, "So you intend on working this claim with your husband?"

"Of course." Cassidy straightened her shoulders. "I want my husband to have success. I'll help him anyway I can."

Shelton's eyes paused at her hands that rested on the table top. His lips twisted to one side, "If he lets you?"

Now Cassidy smiled, tilting her head just slightly downwards, looking up through her lashes, "As if my husband could refuse me?"

Lightening rushed through her limbs thanks to Shelton's gaze. Deliberate, lingering, wanton, his steel grey eyes paused at her lips and then her neck, downwards until she swore, he counted every button across her blouse. "That I don't doubt Precious." He tapped Jet gently on the shoulder and slid out of the bench, replacing his Stetson as he strode down the hallway. Without so much of a backwards glance, he entered the next carriage.

"Tell him Cassidy."

"Hey, you said I had until Pueblo and Pueblo is when I'll tell him."

"Fine, and when he's got his tail up, I'll be here."

"Am I supposed to find that comforting?" Cassidy dragged the book back from Shelton's side, leaving Jet to sketch designs for contraptions with lines and pulley's.

"I'll tell you I told you so first, but I'll always be there for you Cass, like you've been for me."

Cassidy wanted to throw her arms around his neck, only he sat consumed by his images across the table. He had been her constant for so long, the street scamp with a soft heart. Softer than hers had been when they met. Cassidy owed him a proper life, if only for the way he made her care about others again. They were family. He knew all of her secrets, and she, his. Which is why the next words out of her mouth seemed to clog her throat, "I don't think he's a bad man."

"I don't think he is either, Cass." Jet said. "Plus he's going to teach us to shoot, and take us up the mountain and I don't think he's going to run out on you once you tell him."

Cassidy sighed. Her stomach twisted in knots at the idea of Shelton's reaction. He felt duped already after witnessing her simpering damsel in distress performance with the rail guard; the same performance that landed Shelton as their guide. Then Jet stole Jackson's watch and here she was with two stolen library books, well seven to be exact. He didn't trust her and he shouldn't. The moment she exposed her father's 'fine-print' the game was up; feelings of betrayal would come crashing down, with Cassidy as the target. It wouldn't matter what Cassidy's reasons were.

The image of Shelton storming away, calling her a fraudster, a grafter, liar, cheat, swindler seared into Cassidy's lungs, the ash flavor coating her tongue. She scooped up her necklace and twirled it at least ten times for good measure. Her father had trapped the man, any man that would sign the lease, with the burden of his worthless daughter. Cassidy ran her fingertips along the edge of her lids, wicking away the moisture. Yet, if Shelton felt something for her... could it be permanent?

"Pueblo Jet, you said I had to Pueblo."

Jet nodded and twisted his page to Cassidy's eye line.

"Oh I see it, yes! If the land runs to the creek, then the slope of the land will take away the tailings."

A wide grin split Jet's narrow cheeks.

Shelton stood at the bar, a bottle of ale in his hand, inhaling the second hand smoke of a dozen cigars from the 'lounge' car. He considered buying another packet of cheroots, only unable to justify spending the money if Jet or Cassidy would filch them anyway. That's what he told himself anyway. A table of five card stud had been dealt and Shelton watched each player in turn before he would take his seat. He could at least win back the cost of his ticket upgrade.

Booth six! The distance between his sleeping berth and Cassidy's, seemed not enough and too much all in one. He'd have a whiskey at supper and read George-whoever's mining paper that would send him off to sleep. Shelton should admire her courage and spirit, traversing the country-side to meet a stranger. Her words sounded loyal, yet with Cassidy, Shelton guessed, a man never could tell. One moment she was all Precious Lady, the next a thief! The next moment he faced a blizzard, only to have it change into a wildfire that would ruin him if left unchecked. The memory of Cassidy melting in his arms thundered into his chest and wound down to his loins. What of her night terrors? She hadn't mentioned them, and he wouldn't. Curiosity clouded his mind and he missed the next hand. He cursed and ordered another ale.

By the time Shelton wandered back to the main car, dinner had been served. Cassidy sat straight backed fidgeting with the locket around her neck. Slender fingers. Delicate. Shelton imagined her hands blistered by the pick or the shovel, her soft skin cracked by the harsh Colorado winters. He shouldn't have had the last whiskey because for a moment he imagined her standing in an open field. No, not just any field, specifically the Blue Cow's rear paddock. An ocean of emerald under her bare feet and the Texas sunlight cascading over her creamy complexion, her eyes closed like he'd witnessed before they disembarked at Wichita. Damn, no more whiskey.

Shelton dragged his fingers through his fringe, tugging it back into something respectable before he took his seat.

"Did you win?" Jet slid in beside him.

"Yeah, enough."

"Enough to pay for your ticket change?" Cassidy asked.

Shelton nodded. Now why did her lips thin? After all he was doing it for her benefit. If Shelton had his way…No he stopped that thought before it grew legs. Soft, velvet, slender legs.

"Can you teach me?"

Cassidy twirled the locket again before tucking it into her navy neckline. The rows of buttons framed her ample bust and down to her narrow waist. Cassidy's husband would be well pleased when they finally met face to face.

"If your sister say's it's all right."

The waiter arrived with carafes of wine and he took a bottle of ale and sipped it slowly.

"Maybe in between teaching us how to shoot? Can we try the pistol?"

"The .44 is a bit much for either of you, and at close range you'd want your accuracy to be dead on. The Winchester on the other hand and then there's the shotgun."

"How many guns do you have?" Cassidy's head snapped from the window to his bleary eyes.

"How many library books did you steal?"

"Seven." Cassidy answered.

"Four." Shelton replied.

"What did you use them for?" Her chocolate eyes widened, her hand tracked to her throat, but the necklace remained hidden.

"A few mountain cats, some coyotes, cattle, rattlers."

"Ever shoot anyone?" Jet asked.

The penny dropped in Shelton's mind as Cassidy's cheeks paled.

He sipped his beer, "Thankfully not yet."

"Not yet!" Jet hooted and took out his notebook.

Out of the corner of his eye, he caught her hands slowly returning to her lap. The air between thickened and Shelton's tongue loosened, "Although I came close once with Marcus, not intentionally mind you."

The boy's face lit up, Cassidy's lips curled.

"We were chasing some deer down a gully and well Marcus got ahead of us on the trail."

"Marcus Kearby, the Texas Ranger?"

"Well he wasn't at the time." Shelton laughed. To his surprise Cassidy chuckled softly. He leaned forward, "We come around the bend and see this outline. The sun was in our eyes,"

"Any moonshine in your canteens?" Cassidy chimed in.

"Of course, Windy Hill makes a clean brew. Up ahead we hear this God awful sound, like a male…" Shelton cleared his throat, "…anyway we thought it was the Buck. So Taylor and I start crawling along the bluff, on our bellies, mind you. Cade's stone cold sober laughing at how ridiculous we look. Marcus hears us, jumps up to tell us to shut up and loses his hat for his efforts."

Jet laughed and so did Cassidy. The lilting sound of her giggle, worked under Shelton's ribs and he smiled, "Marcus dives for cover so fast we think we hit him. We scramble down the scree tumbling head first into a patch of thistles. Until we hear him laughing in the bush. We reckon that's the day that Marcus officially stopped growing."

They laughed again and Shelton couldn't help but join in.

"How old were you?"

Shelton tugged his fringe as Cassidy's eyes widened, "Ah older than you, Champ. Much older."

Cassidy covered her lips with her slender fingers and she turned to the window until her grin had disappeared.

"What's your ranch like?" Cassidy asked just as Sunny brought dinner. "Thank you Sunny,"

"Always a delight Ma'am." The man said.

Shelton dug in, his stomach thanking him for the solid food. He should be smarter, knowing how tight Cassidy had him wound and how little he cared for her husband or their arrangement.

"Ah, in summer the fields are like an ocean of emerald." If only his tongue would ignore his reckless thoughts. "If you stand on our back porch it's a sea of green. The Cherry bark oak in the front lawn is twice as tall as the house, and in the Fall, drops leaves the color of ruby's to blanket the front porch. We share a border with the river that cuts through Cade's Double E and Kearby's Crooked K ranch, except it trickles slower past the Blue Cow. The banks are wider, lined with live oaks. At dawn it looks like their heavy branches are climbing out of the river, at dusk, when the sunsets all lilacs and tangerines, the trees appear as if their taking a drink after a long day with the cattle."

"Wow." Jet said.

Cassidy sat still, her knife and fork beside her hands, her dinner untouched. Damn. Shelton cleared his throat. The image of the rear river bank held tight in his mind; his favorite place to pull up for a rest after long days in the saddle.

"Does your Ma cook good? I might wanna come and visit someday." Jet joked.

A knife clattered onto Cassidy's plate and she scooped it up.

"Yeah my Ma makes the best apple pies, she's not so good at Chili, which is a shame."

"Do you like Chili?" The woman asked.

"Ah no, but she keeps trying so I have to keep tasting."

Thankfully they laughed again and Shelton felt his shoulders release.

"What about you two? One library book says New York, the other Chicago. Which is it?"

"Both." Cassidy said. "We both lived in Chicago for most our lives. My father took me to New York once." The fork scratched along the plate, "And Indianapolis and Philadelphia, Washington, even Louisville."

"That must have been quite a trip." Shelton hesitated. He watched Cassidy tug on her necklace, the locket not visible.

"It was business, so ...." Cassidy shoveled a forkful of potatoes into her mouth.

"Right, and you Champ, Chicago born?"

"I guess so. I used to think it was interesting, I mean anything can happen in one day. But there's buildings as far as the eye can see and not a soul to say hello." The boys tone flat and he shrugged his shoulders.

"Except for Cassidy?" Shelton said.

A smile wormed across the youth's cheeks, "Yeah except for Cass. Will you be heading back to Texas during the winter?"

"Hopefully." This time an image of Cassidy perched along one of the low live oak branches near the river popped into his mind. He took another sip of his beer to wash down the beef. "I suppose in the winter you'll be retreating to wherever your new man lives. Where does he hail from?"

"Ah," Cassidy wiped at the corners of her mouth, "He's from all over, he mentioned Texas and Kansas." She mumbled, "Did you order dessert, Jet?"

"Sure did. Well I hope if Cass's husband goes to Texas we could swing passed and get an apple pie from your Ma, Shelton."

Shelton snorted. He couldn't imagine Cassidy meeting his mother and just passing through. Temperance Lovena Murphy would wrap her arms around Cassidy and hold on until she smothered her or Cassidy's husband told her off. His mother had hoped to have him settled by now, with at least one grandchild. Twenty-four felt like the prime of Shelton's life, no way he was settling down. Marriage and children were serious responsibilities. Responsibility didn't suit Shelton and he was never serious about anything. Ever.

"Sure, if Cass's husband don't mind." Shelton managed around his gravy and biscuits.

"I guess we'll see then." Jet rubbed his hands together as Sunny returned with his pudding. "Thank you my good Man!" Jet tapped Sunny on the shoulder. The Porter rolled his eyes but smiled all the same.

Shelton wiped his napkin across his mouth and left it in his plate he added a tip for Sunny. Cassidy resumed staring out the window, the sun had set, the darkness highlighting her reflection in the glass. Her teeth worried her bottom lip until she caught Shelton's gaze.

"Well I might take this time to freshen up before bed." Cassidy slid out along the bench chair and wandered down the aisle to the dressing room.

Shelton's mind worked overtime not to imagine what occurred behind closed doors.

"What were you drawing earlier today?" He asked.

Between spoonful of dessert, Jet pulled out his notebook. They lost themselves in discussion of sluice boxes and panning placer gold, ignoring the other patrons as the porters set tables into beds and pulled down bunks. By the time Shelton's bunk was made, Cassidy still hadn't appeared from the dressing room. He kicked off his boots and unbuckled his belt. Pulling off his shirt, Shelton crawled into Booth six with Greenwell's papers and decided to read hoping to catch sight of Cassidy one more time before sleep. Within moments, the pages blurred, the heavy meal with beer and whiskey had done its trick and Shelton let sleep claim him.

Chapter 9

Dreams of gold trickled through Shelton's fingers as somewhere, someone whimpered. He turned on his side, the gentle rattling and rocking reminded him of the train. The journey to Colorado. Gold fever raced through his veins. He beat the pillow until it softened and yet the whimper teased his ears.

Shelton rolled out of his bunk, his bare feet cold along the slats. He rubbed his palm into one eye, squinting as the dimmed ceiling lamps blinded his sleep haze. Like a whisper from within a deep well, the whimper chilled Shelton's chest, goosebumps raised across his bare skin. Cassidy?

Tiptoeing across the aisle, Shelton leaned against the rear of the seat, the heavy curtains brushed against his lips.

"Cass?"

A sob strangled from behind the drapes and Shelton moved. Darkness enveloped Shelton as he crawled across the mattress. Sinking down, he sensed Cassidy's back to him, her hair unbraided spilled onto the pillow. With slow movements, Shelton curled himself around her tucked frame, his knees behind hers, her buttocks against his thighs.

Shelton touched her shoulder, "Cass?"

Cassidy's upper arm tensed. He ran his palm down her shoulder, the light fabric of her tea-gown bunching as he skimmed further, her soft skin exposed below her elbow. His fingers found her fist clenched around the linen.

"Cass, I'm here." Shelton whispered. He worked his fingers over her knuckles as slowly they unwound.

In the darkness he listened. Short sharp breathes evolved into gentle exhales; her shoulders slumped and Cassidy leaned back. Long strands of caramel tickled his bare chest and Shelton knew he should return to his bunk before the sunrise, only her blackcurrant and honeysuckle scent had infiltrated his senses. Mixed with Cassidy's warmth against his flesh, the pleasure an intoxicating elixir he couldn't resist. Sleep found Shelton before sunrise.

Cassidy stretched her arms over her head, her limbs relaxed and warm. She turned on her side, listening as the porters tiptoed down the aisles quietly placating awake patrons while the others slept on. The hint of a dream teased through Cassidy's mind. She ran her palm through the empty sheets, cold yet her movement stirred faint traces of plum. The linen scratched against her nose as she rubbed. Last night as she wandered down the aisle, a stab of disappointment struck her when she spied Shelton asleep. His fringe askew, Greenhill's mining book propped open across his nose. Cassidy hesitated for a moment before pulling it free, trying as she might to keep her eyes off his sculptured bare chest. Sleep claimed Cassidy in a whirlwind of dreams.

The scent of bacon and eggs drifted through the drapes and Cassidy sighed. In her dream Cassidy couldn't see her feet for the wheat, a white washed homestead on the horizon and the afternoon sun seared her skin. Shelton's words had been better, painting a portrait of Dew Springs that lingered in Cassidy's mind. Shelton. Her sheets smelt of Shelton so much so that Cassidy bolted out of bed, only to stand in the aisle in her tea gown. Shelton's booth was empty, all more to the point, it had been remade into a table and an elderly couple shared a pot of coffee over dipped toast.

"Mornin'" The lady raised her cup. The gentleman nodded.

"Morning" Cassidy replied.

"Oh you're up."

Cassidy thought she climbed the ceiling as Shelton appeared behind her.

"I am, I'll just be a minute." Cassidy's heels didn't touch the ground until she closed the dressing room door. She pulled her tea-gown up to her nose and inhaled. Her fruity perfume filled her nose, she shook her head. A mad woman would not do for a wife. Cassidy had refilled the pitcher and basin twice until she felt clean and dressed slowly, the tremors in her hands subsiding by the time she wound her hair at the back. She ran her hands down her emerald travelling dress. When they stopped at Pueblo the first thing she would do would be to find another hot bath. Well the second, first thing, she needed to tell Shelton his signature had sealed their fate.

By the time Cassidy sat down to breakfast, Jet had his book open to a rough sketch of loops and numbers, while Shelton had a length of rope between his hands.

"When you nail the Bowline, I'll show you the Spanish Bowline, now you try." Shelton handed the rope over and the boy revisited his notes. Shelton closed the book, "Without looking this time. Morning Precious."

"Morning. Again." Cassidy sat down. "Knots?"

"He wanted to learn."

Cassidy hoped the slice of toast she slipped into her mouth hid her grin.

"I think I've read all I can of mine engineering and the like, and instead figured you could just fill me in on the details."

"Oh really." Cassidy took a sip of her coffee, the bitter brew warming her tongue.

"Think of it as a trade-off for my ticket upgrade."

Cassidy sipped her coffee again. Shelton couldn't pay himself. She'd have to find some way to pay him back. "I thought you won enough at poker?"

"I won enough."

"I don't understand." She sliced her toast thin.

"People chase their losses. I like to let my losses go and move on. I won enough yesterday but if I gamble today, who knows I might end up losing what I had yesterday."

"That almost sounds prudent. Almost."

Shelton frowned, "No need to insult me."

Cassidy couldn't help but laugh. Jet dropped his work in

front of Shelton.

"Done?"

"Yep, looks good. Ready?" Shelton asked.

"Yep." Jet picked up his notebook and began jotting down Shelton's instructions. Cassidy let the conversation wash over her until Shelton leaned forward.

"Now, you can teach me about rock formations."

Where did she start? "Okay the basic rock types are igneous, sedimentary and metamorphic..." Cassidy began as the train put more miles under their belts. Each passing hour brought Pueblo closer. They had another night aboard the Sante Fe and then half the morning before Jet's deadline would force the truth from Cassidy. Shelton listened to her list of rock types and how they related to the elusive precious metals. With one eye on Jet's handiwork, he asked questions here and there.

"And you learnt all this from your textbooks?" Shelton asked.

"I did, I can't wait to experiment with the processes, see how the ore is separated."

Shelton nodded, "You are quite clever aren't you?"

Cassidy blushed, "I read a lot. Not everything is in books, you know, I have no idea if the chemicals will work, the temperatures needed, not until I try."

"Try your luck I suppose and your husband will be one lucky man." Shelton said.

Jet's gaze seared through to Cassidy she almost checked she hadn't turned to ash.

"Speaking of luck, I might take a look at this poker, excuse me," Cassidy slid out of the bench, glad for the breeze that assaulted her cheeks when she stepped between carriages. Pueblo, she had until Pueblo.

Cassidy wandered to the lounge car. A cloud of tobacco slammed her as she opened the carriage door. Round tables sat to one side, a dealer handing out the cards to each player as a group of onlookers clustered around the bar. An organist trilled the keys, his merry tune adding to the fast paced atmosphere. A bevy of ladies reclined in wing-backed chairs, a gentleman behind each of them. One of them laughed, her shrill giggle cut through Cassidy's ears and she was suddenly transported back to Chicago and the first time her father asked her to swindle. She straightened her back. Since Cassidy made off with half the estates silverware under her hoops before the night was out, she could make it through this. Cassidy moved into the lounge car and took a spot at the bar.

The next few rounds passed, easing the tightness in her chest, as Cassidy watched the punters bet and ante against each other. She needed distance from Shelton, if only to organize her thoughts. As much as she loved Jet, she couldn't tell Shelton with Jet watching. She didn't want him to see how Shelton's rejection would crush her. The lunch call went out and Cassidy resolved to tell Shelton the morning they would arrive in Pueblo, then at the base of the mountain she could find their way up to the claim. When Cassidy finally returned to the booth, both Shelton and Jet leapt as if the hound had found a fox.

"Still working on knots?"

"Shelton was just telling me about cattle."

"Cattle?" Cassidy flicked her napkin across her lap.

"Did you learn anything up in the lounge car?"

"I did, so tell me what you know about cattle Jet?"

"Um," Jet ran his finger across his bottom lip, his blue eyes sparkling against the reflection from the window. "I know they're scared of fireworks."

Shelton tugged his fringe running his hand all the way down to cover his mouth.

"Is that so?" Cassidy rolled her lips inwards.

"You know explosives are frequently used in mining." Shelton said.

Before Cassidy could retort, a squeal rattled the windows. The other passengers murmured to each other, Shelton watched the long prairie grasses pass by as the train slowed.

The elderly couple across the aisle clicked their fingers

loudly, "Excuse me!"

"Yes Ma'am."

"George, what's happening?"

Sunny strolled towards the couple, and Cassidy leaned towards the aisle, "There's a landslide over the track down a ways, nothin' too much of a delay and figured since the day's so nice, a picnic will do."

"A picnic!" The woman waved a fan in front of her sinking jowls.

"Sounds delightful Sunny," Cassidy replied. "Don't you think Shelton?"

"Gives me another chance to stretch *Tango's* legs and my own."

The older man nodded, "You'll survive a picnic Gertie."

The woman sighed, "Oh I know I'll survive. You should be more concerned about yourself William."

William grimaced and rolled his eyes at Shelton and Cassidy, "Marriage sometimes it's just about who can outlive the other."

"William!" Gertrude slapped her fan across Williams knuckles.

"Well best wishes to the both of you." Shelton chuckled before he leaned forward, "See your future, Cassidy."

"I assume you're never going to get married then?"

"Not if I can help it." Shelton returned to Jet's notebook to review the boy's notes on dynamite. Dangerous but effective. Doubt that Hugo would have a supply of dynamite on hand or would trust Shelton to use it. He tapped his pocket lightly, Hugo's list of supplies ready and waiting for purchase in Pueblo. If only he could outlast his own thirst on this damn train. Cassidy didn't remember or didn't acknowledge his presence last night. Which was likely a good thing. With her head so full of marriage and mines, Shelton stood on perilous ground. He had no intentions of marrying. He couldn't support his Ma and Pa, he sure as hell couldn't support a wife.

"Can I...?"

"Sure Jet, try again, see if *Tango* likes you this time. If he does, I'll show you how to saddle him."

Shelton shook his head. Marriage. Responsibility didn't suit Shelton.

By the time the train came to a full stop and the Porters had set the passengers in a farmers' field between two huge cottonwoods overlooking a wide branch of the Arkansas River, Shelton finally made it to the stock car. The stout thick trunks and long low branches shaded the plush field from the midday sun while the river trailed past, the scent of the water filled *Tango's* nostrils and he snuffed. Shelton eyed the cluster of passengers who wandered between tables, the rigid back of one with long caramel hair.

"Time to dance." Shelton patted *Tango's* ruddy neck, the horse's hooves eating the distance. Too much time cooped up not a mare in sight, Shelton shared the horse's sentiments, before he remembered *Tango* had been gelded and didn't care a lick about mares. Lucky bastard. Shelton clapped a hand on his Stetson as the wind cooled his cheeks. *Tango* galloped down the length of the train before Shelton directed him across the farmer's field. Within minutes he'd found a fence line. Shelton chirped twice and the horse glided over the obstacle.

"Fancy boy." Shelton praised him with a rub down his neck. He enjoyed the feel of the power underneath him and the cool air down his collar. He took *Tango* on a wide arc back across the fields towards the train, finding a dried gully, that when it rained, likely ran to the Arkansas River. Shelton chirped again and the horse cleared the distance with ease. Shelton pressed inwards with his heels and *Tango* galloped along the train until the sight of the landslide came into view. A bevy of porters and train engineers had shovels and picks digging at the rubble that clogged the tracks. Sleeves rolled up, some shirtless, others with rings of sweat down their back.

Shelton brought *Tango* alongside the gang of workers and

dismounted, "Need a hand?"

"Nah Sir, you head on back for lunch?" Sunny called.

Shelton eyed the pile of rocks and quickly counted heads and shovels. He turned back to the shade of the cottonwoods, as Jet dashed across the field. Shelton brought *Tango's* reins over his muzzle and stretched them to Jet. The boy picked up the pace, his running hampered by an apple in his hand.

The boy's nerves seemed to multiply as he closed the distance.

"He's all right now." Shelton soothed *Tango* and gestured to Jet.

The boy placed his hand open to the giant horse the plump red treat ready for sampling, "Cassidy figured I could win him over with food."

"Smart." Shelton dismounted as *Tango* chopped it whole. "Take him back to the shade with you. Trust me, he'll be fine. If anything he'll want the river. If he wanders off I can bring him back."

"What about you?"

"I'll help out here." Swinging a shovel might ease the tension from the blackcurrant dessert he wanted to sample. "He'll be fine. Just if he gets up on you, push him gently away, but don't move your feet. Okay?"

Jet nodded and carefully led *Tango* towards the passenger's picnic. Shelton turned back to the shallow valley that the track drove through. The embankment stretched to shoulder height falling slowly away to towards the farmer's field and the Arkansas River. The debris that congested the steel tracks had a mixture of heavy boulders, loose gravel and sand. On the opposite side to the field, a tributary crisscrossed the sand hills. No doubt Cassidy could tell him the names of each type of rock and possibly why the tributary had washed this area out. Shelton unbuttoned his shirt setting it aside with the others and set to work.

"What did he say?"

"He's helping the others." Jet said.

Cassidy placed a hand over her brow, catching sight of Shelton's broad back as he removed his shirt. She couldn't stop the sigh that dashed across her lips. She stood at the fringes of the largest Cottonwood, while a row of tables had been placed at intervals in the shade, as two porters dashed between passengers serving lunch. Cassidy decided to set out place settings and napkins to control her thoughts.

Another passenger, a young woman with enough frills around her waist to clothe the entire Senate, also raised her hand to her forehead and surveyed the group of diggers, humming in approval as she fanned away the heat with a large oriental number. The gentleman who stood beside, tugged at his collar. He turned to the excavation activity and back to his lady's unwavering gaze. He offered her his half-filled glass, "Excuse me Elizabeth. Come on Samson, let's set to it."

Samson, in pressed slacks and waist coat, stood from his reclined position in the grass. The young lady beside him failing to take his bottle of pop as she silently watched the crowd of bare backs glistening in the sun. "Saffy?"

"Oh," Saffy took Samson's bottle and discarded it on Cassidy's table, returning her attention to the rippling scenery in the distance.

"Right, Fredrick." Samson said.

Both Fredrick and Samson unbuttoned their cuffs and removed ties as they crossed the field.

"You know Saffy, I don't think Fredrick's..." Elizabeth's voice trailed away as Fredrick's pale skin shone under the midday heat. Elizabeth bent her head to her friend and they giggled into the oriental fans. Saffy threw a heated look to Cassidy, "They might even work up an appetite."

"Certainly," The cutlery clattered onto ceramic as Cassidy kept her eyes downcast from the horizon and the broadest pair of shoulders amongst the rabble.

Elizabeth even winked as both women moved deeper into the shade.

A snorted blasted in Cassidy's ear and she jumped, "Jet!"

"Shhh, Cass, Shelton said to push him away, gentle but without moving your feet."

"Huh?" Cassidy threw her arm behind her as *Tango's* velvet lips brushed her neck. The whiskers tickled, the horse's breath hot against her cheek. "Why can I not move my feet?"

"I don't know, probably showing him whose boss, hang on."

Heels and hooves scuffed in the dirt.

Cassidy twisted to the side, and with both hands against his bristly jaw, gave *Tango* a shove. The horse snorted and stepped back. Cassidy turned on her heels, her fingers catching the leather reins and tugged it to the side. Jet pulled the horses muzzle towards himself and *Tango* obediently followed. "I'll take him down to the river."

"Be careful Jet."

"Always."

Cassidy wiped her hands down her thighs, considering whether to sit down amongst the other passengers. On the other side of the tree trunk William and Gertie sat at a low table. Gertie clicked her fingers in the air as William pointed to something untoward on his plate. Cassidy returned to the table and decided to hand the settings out instead.

As the sun reached its peak, the railroad crew didn't cease for lunch and even Elizabeth and Saffy reappeared at Cassidy's table, their fans unable to beat the heat.

"Working up an appetite indeed," Elizabeth said. Her dark curls sagged down her neck, her high cheekbones flushed with color.

"They could use some refreshments I suppose." Cassidy said as she grabbed a slab of bread and started carving.

Saffy stopped twirling a finger around her blonde strands, "They'd be thirsty too." She disappeared and reappeared within minutes, two pitchers filled with lemonade in her hands.

They chatted while Cassidy, with the help of Elizabeth

made pork sandwiches. When they made enough for all the workers, they roped a few of the children to help them carry the plates across the fields.

Cassidy watched Shelton as she crossed the distance, his tanned shoulders blushed, his Stetson damp around the hairline. He turned to the approaching company and stood upright, wiping his brow and removing his hat. Shelton grabbed a canteen of water and splashed it over his face, flicking his hair backwards as he stood. Closing the distance, Cassidy wished he wouldn't have bothered, as the beads of water trickled down his ribbed abdomen. How had Shelton managed to look even more handsome covered in muck?

Cassidy half wished he'd put his shirt back on if only to calm her thoughts. She watched Elizabeth and Saffy make their way to Frederick and Samson despite all the men looking less than satisfactory. Cassidy took a jug of lemonade and some mugs, making sure every man received a good measure of the cooling liquid before she came to stop in front of Shelton.

Chapter 10

Shelton rolled his shoulders. His muscles ached, yet the sensation only brought him satisfaction. He'd sleep well tonight. A breeze coasted down the gully as the last of the track glinted in the afternoon sun. The scent of salted pork reached his taste buds as he watched Cassidy stroll through the Porters and engineers, smiling as she handed out lemonade. She stopped in front of him, her grin vanishing as his swollen fingers held the mug as she poured.

"Are you hurt?"

"It's nothing, just warming them up for when I dig the claim." Shelton smirked, "Excepts it's hotter than Hades out here." He sculled the cup in one and Cassidy poured another.

"Find some shade and rest you've definitely earnt it." Cassidy turned to the train engineer closest and refilled his cup, "I'll bring you a plate in a moment." Cassidy moved over to Sunny who clung to his empty cup.

Shelton took her advice and wandered to the far side of the line and sought shelter in a scraggly grove of Salt Cedar, the deep pink blossoms dusted the top of the shrub while Shelton rested under its thin woody branches. He sat on his haunches and watched Cassidy move between passenger and porter, waiter and engineer handing out sandwiches to the men. Her two helpers, young women in frills and pearls, rouged lips and fancy bonnets attended to their beaus. Shelton had never seen the shade of red, the man named Frederick, now sported across his back. He'd be asleep by dinner and sore tomorrow.

Cassidy's caramel strands lilted in the gentle breeze, her bonnet absent, her attention on the task at hand. Sunny and the other porters thanked her as she passed. Maybe Cassidy

Smith wouldn't freeze in Colorado? Her smile seemed to rival the afternoon sun and Shelton couldn't help but listen as she chatted, congratulating the men on their hard work. When she'd finished the first round, Cassidy returned to Shelton, plate in hand, a serving of pork sandwiches and even a side of jam biscuits.

"Had enough of Gertie and William?" Shelton teased. The tight lines of her travelling dress accentuated her hips and narrow waist while the emerald green offset the chocolate brown of her eyes. Her cheeks were flushed with heat and for a minute he wanted to run his finger along her bottom lip. The memory of her buttocks against his thighs stirred his groin.

"They found companionship."

Cassidy's gaze wandered to the other two women who strolled, arm in arm with their men back to the shade of the Cottonwood Trees.

"Marriage at it's best?" He had no right, yet with her standing so close, her nose upturned, her scent of blackcurrant upon the prairie wind, Cassidy was downright delightful. He took a huge bite of his sandwich to forestall any more comments.

"William is pretending to nap while Gertie recounts all manner of his medical ailments."

Shelton almost choked so much so he had to take a swig of his lemonade.

"Delightful," He managed between gulps. "Is Jet managing with Tango?"

"He is now."

"I didn't mean to scare the poor boy but I figured helping here was more important." He gestured to the rails, from this angle, the air an inch above the steel warped.

A small grin slid onto Cassidy's lips, "Yes, I think you did well. Jet is managing just fine."

Shelton chuckled. That almost sounded like a compliment. "Your idea of feeding Tango the apple was a smart idea." He bit into his sandwich again pausing only to take a breath before he finished the gravy soaked morsel. "You know, to win him over with food."

Cassidy raised her chin as Shelton regarded his empty plate.

The woman cleared her throat, "Yes well now the tracks clear, I suspect we'll be on our way." Cassidy stood with her hands on her hips, her weight shifted from one heel to the other. Shelton watched the shade from the Salt Cedar dance across her flushed cheeks, the cerise flowers matching her cherry lips. Cassidy leaned forward and Shelton waited. Slowly Cassidy picked up Shelton's cup and plate from the ground. Chocolate gemstones wandered across his bare chest as her golden chain spilled loose.

Shelton's thumb trapped the locket, like a pendulum of doom, his tendons hummed ready to pull her closer. Ebony lashes battered over velvet brown, "Beautiful."

The girl's fingers slid over his to retrieve her trinket, "Thank you," Cassidy whispered. "It was my mothers."

The image of tight linen clenched within her delicate fist slammed into Shelton's gut and he released his grip.

"Then I guess it's time for me to clean up. Don't let that train leave without me." As Shelton rose Cassidy shuffled backwards. She swallowed hard and retreated, her emerald skirts swishing across the field. Shelton turned to his dusty comrades, "Last one to the Arkansas buys the first drink!" He undid his belt buckle as he crossed the track, the sloping sandy banks to the river beckoning his throbbing muscles. He spared a final glimpse to the girl across the field, only to see her halt. Her head turned slightly until she discovered Shelton watching. He kicked off his boots, smirking as he watched her hips roll with haste to reach the Cottonwoods.

"Second last, buys the next round!" Shelton added as he dashed to the river. The splash of the racing men drenched the latecomers and Shelton relished the fresh water cooling more than just his temperature.

Cassidy couldn't sit still. The passengers had ambled back to the train, glad for the shade and the promise of cool winds. William attempted to read a week old newspaper while Gertie nattered on about his table manners. The two women Elizabeth and Saffy had invited Cassidy to join them in the lounge car for an afternoon drink while they awaited their Beaus cleaned and pressed. Cassidy declined politely and decided to hide in the rear of the kitchen area. Since the picnic ended, the porters, those that remained fresh after the excavation, had the job of resetting for the dinner service. Instead of practicing what she needed to say to Shelton, Cassidy had perched herself on a stool to dry the glasses and cutlery. The porters didn't mind, every now and then the cook, a large dark-skinned man named Jack would narrow his eyes, double checking Cassidy's efforts with a sly grin.

Jet strolled back and forth down the train, running water to wash basins and towels to the passengers and workers who'd taken a dip in the Arkansas. Cassidy gripped the stool as the carriages clunked together, a slow chug of the engine thundered down the floor boards.

When the Kansas sun slipped beyond the horizon and the gas lamps blossomed with light, Cassidy took her leave.

"Thanks Miss."

"You're welcome Jack, many hands make light work after all." Light fingers make an easy payday, her father would have said. Her father would have found a way to exploit any situation. Cassidy counted the silverware, on instinct her elbows went to her hips, her palms to her pockets.

"I reckon them girls will thank you too."

"When they get the time, Jack. No need for me to distract you any further, you can concentrate on them puddings, or Jet will blame me."

Jack's double chins wobbled, "He likes the dumplings or the pies best?"

"All of them Jack, all of them."

Jack chuckled again and winked.

Cassidy smiled back, her stomach slightly unsettled at the thought she'd managed to swindle an extra dessert for Jet. The last Kansas sunset trickled through the curtained windows, oranges bled into lilacs as a sliver of pink carved through the horizon in a riot of color. Tufts of white dotted the sky as if an artist had dabbed their brush, each cloud a feathery master-piece. Cassidy halted between carriages to admire the vibrant hues contrasted by the delicate fleece. The door to the next carriage opened.

"You hiding from William and Gertie?"

Cassidy didn't turn at Shelton's voice, instead she asked, "Does it remind you of home?"

Shelton leaned his forearms against the railing, his fresh cream shirt had been rolled up to the elbows, his collar damp from his hair, the scent of plum coated her tongue. Pleasantly surprised at the lack of cheroot, Cassidy inhaled deeper.

"It does, except Dew seems greener, most of the time any-way." His voice took on a dark note before he lifted his gaze, "The fields are oceans of emerald, the trees olive and sage against the sunset. In winter, in the morning, the frost looks like the fields have been dusted with sugar from the night be-fore."

"It sounds beautiful."

"It is, I hope it stays that way." Shelton's brow creased, his thumb trailed along callouses on his other palm.

"Are there reasons why it wouldn't?"

Shelton's lips thinned, "Nothing just Ranch life."

The sound of his half-hearted laugh caught Cassidy by sur-prise, "You sound serious."

Now Shelton laughed genuinely, "Serious doesn't suit me."

Something tiny compressed inside Cassidy's ribs and sud-denly she wasn't so sure. "Nothing your big shoulders can't fix, right?" She added, smiling when a real smile returned to Shel-ton's lips.

"That's right, anyway, why are you sulking out here?"

"I'm not sulking,"

"Then cheer up, Precious, because tomorrow's a Colorado sunrise."

Cassidy's throat clenched, her fingers reached inside her collar and twirled the locket back and forth until she felt her lungs expand. "It is, isn't it?"

"Yep, you can send your man another telegram when we get to Pueblo. Did he give you a list of supplies he needs?"

"We need." Cassidy added. As the night slipped away so did her chance at clearing the air before Colorado.

The carriage door swung back and this time, Frederick wandered through, Samson under one arm, a glass of whiskey in the other hand. He saluted Shelton as he passed, his heavy lids over glassed eyes.

"A hot meal will sort him out." Cassidy said.

Shelton stepped back and opened the door for Cassidy to wander through, "A hot meal will send him to bed, and a fair few others."

Cassidy slid into the booth seat, Jet already had the menu out and had poured them all a glass of water. As Shelton sat down, Jet straightened his back, "I checked on him in the stock cart, they put him in right. He didn't get out of hand, only gave Cass that one nudge."

Shelton's eyes met Cassidy's "A nudge?"

"Well it was more like a kiss, I told her what you said, keep her feet planted and push him away. She did it too, worked a treat."

"Did she now?"

Cassidy took a sip of her water. Well she wasn't about to tell him, his horse made her jump out of her skin only to nuzzle her neck. He would have laughed. Carefully she replaced her glass, "Tango was just being friendly. Jet pulled him back in line."

"I see."

Sunny strolled down the aisle with a carafe of wine and decanter of whiskey, "Here's to first place." Sunny filled Shelton's glass, "And here's to the best and fairest." He added as he filled Cassidy's wine glass.

"Thank you Sunny," Cassidy took a shallow sip if only to stop her hands from clasping her necklace.

"The best and fairest," Shelton took a sip his sugar grey eyes didn't leave her face.

"Well tonight I think I'll try the soup, and then the roast, what's for dessert tonight?" Jet continued to quiz Sunny before he finally settled on apple dumplings.

"You didn't want to play cards with Saffy and Elizabeth?"

The wine sizzled on her tongue, leaving little hiccups in her mind. The window panes rattled, the breeze reaching Cassidy's neck. She shivered. Pueblo approached and soon she would have no choice. Shelton unfolded his napkin and rested his blistered hands on the table, his knuckles only an inch from hers. Perhaps she had too much sun as well, as she lost herself in thoughts of soothing his hands, and Shelton had to ask his question again.

"Um, no I thought to save my pennies for supplies, once we reach Pueblo."

Jet looked up and thought better of it, scratching away in his notebook, all the details he had learnt from today with *Tango*.

"Fredrick's an interesting character. His uncle owns the smelter at Pueblo. Seems he got into some trouble in Philadelphia and his father sent him out here. With Elizabeth in tow. Samson's a land surveyor, seems Fredrick's uncles got his eye on patches across the river, and the railyards. He's hoping to change his fortune."

"You three have so much in common." Cassidy joked.

Shelton's jaw clenched and he took a sip of his whiskey, "Didn't you say you'd been to Philly?"

Rich flavors of roast beef and vegetables flooded the carriage and Cassidy leaned back, "Yes my father took me there."

"Tell me about it."

She straightened her place setting before looking up,

"Well, it was for business." Illegitimate business, but she held her tongue.

"You must have seen something of the city?"

Cassidy wondered how Shelton would describe the bustling metropolis of Philadelphia. He had such a way with words; she knew why he'd earned the 'silver-tongue' nickname.

"The wide streets were filled with all manner of people and transport, horses, carriages and rail, so much you had to watch where you stepped for fear of being trampled. The banks of the Delaware overflowed with industry, the plants and warehouses echoing the sounds of the workers along the docks, a dozen languages competing with the hawkers and the whistles for the Doves." Cassidy let her gaze wander to the window, "East of 7th street, the boarding houses were filled with families from across the Atlantic, the scent of their unfamiliar recipes trickling through the alleyways, coating the washing strung across between tenements. Italian insults shouted to the German washer woman, the Irish family with a dozen children in tow, in trouble from the young Polish men who slept five to a room. At night it seemed that small part of the world never slept."

Cassidy took a moment to slice her beef. Shelton's whiskey now refilled, he reclined in the bench seat, "Go on."

"During the day we wandered up to Independence Hall and Congress Hall, the trace of significant decisions heavy in the air. I watched the workers building City Hall wondering the weight of every brick, and the strength of the mortar. I wanted to visit the Zoological Gardens at Fairmount Park, but father disagreed." Cassidy's father had asked where the money was in a zoo. Instead he'd made them pace around the financial districts searching for opportunities. Her father knew all too well the Treasurers and Brokers were as crooked as a barrel of fish hooks.

She could feel Shelton's eyes on her. "At night we headed to the estates up Main Line and attended a Ball."

"That would have been swanky." Jet managed around a mouthful of potato.

Cassidy decided to begin her dinner hoping eating would settle down the butterflies jittering in her stomach. Shelton's plate was clean. As Sunny returned to clear his plate, he yawned.

"I am I boring you, Mister Murphy?"

"On the contrary, you worked hard today, I'm merely waiting for you to finish your dinner before I hear about this Ball."

Not just a ball, a grand ball, held for a Grand Duke. Cassidy swallowed the rest of her dinner and chose her words carefully, "It was swanky, the room filled with frills and sashes, rich paisley drapes and fleur-de-lis upholstery, the silverware polished to a high shine, every table had an ornate flower arrangement, even a chamber orchestra to while away the hours."

"Lots of silverware?" Jet smiled.

"Lots, diamonds and rubies sparkled under the chandeliers, the crystal glasses glistened between lace gloved fingers." Her father had peddled his counterfeit skills while Cassidy had lifted as much jewelry as she could hide under her hoop.

Shelton twirled his whiskey glass between his fingers, the amber liquid rolling from side to side, "And you gave all that up at a chance to mine in the snow?"

Cassidy sighed. It hadn't been any realer then, than it sounded now. "When you looked closer, the frilled hems had been soiled as they trucked through the same streets the immigrants slept in, the silverware reflected the shallowness of their schemes for wealth. Wealth accumulated from the hard work of others." Cassidy took a sip of her wine, "Those expensive drapes had been long closed on the true nature of Philadelphia's streets. We stayed for three days," They left that night after the Ball, rushing away before anyone could work out their swindle. "In those three days, a boiler exploded, a sugar refinery and a paper press burned down, workers died, fireman rioted."

The fires had billowed black smoke into the skies, the tenements of the immigrant housing pressed inwards and Cassidy had spent a sleepless night, praying the chaos wouldn't reach them. Cassidy pushed aside the memory of those that should be helping, landing blow after blow on each other, while the screams of the helpless were consumed by the inferno. Her father whined at the disturbance to his sleep, his harsh words had silenced Cassidy that night.

"It must have been difficult."

Cassidy searched Shelton's words for any derision and found none. She should have held her tongue. Jet started on his desserts while the other porters rearranged some of the booths for passengers to retire. "Are you going to play a hand tonight?" Cassidy gestured to the lounge car.

"I think I'll give it a miss, I'm looking for my bed more than a dime right now." Shelton yawned again and Jet slid out of the booth to let the man out.

Cassidy returned to watch the ebony night rush by the rattling window. Some time tonight they would slip into Colorado Territory and time would slip from Cassidy's grip. She had to tell Shelton about the fine print and tell him before lunch time tomorrow.

Chapter 11

Shelton stretched in his sheets, the need to relieve himself won over his need for sleep. Rocking on each foot, he wandered down the aisle, the low lamps guiding his way. Cassidy's drapes overlapped one another, and Shelton wondered about her view of Philadelphia. Although her recount sounded honest, she'd left Shelton with more questions than answers. As he passed her booth, his steps slowed, ear straining. On the way back Shelton dawdled again. A sigh slipped through the heavy curtains. Shelton ducked his head into the booth. Pointless, as the interior lay thick in shadow. Instead Shelton listened, Cassidy's breathing shallow and out of rhythm. Another yawn cracked his jaw and he lowered himself to her bunk, his shoulders ached with the slow pace.

His fingers speared through hers as Cassidy released the linen. Shuddering, a sighed escaped her lips. Directed by the whiskey-haze, Shelton curled up behind her.

Cassidy stirred. Flames licked along the window sill, the skyline changed from the clogged Chicago horizon to lines of linen engulfed. Cassidy's eyes snapped open. A chill crept through the glass panes and Cassidy tugged the linen up to her shoulder only to find it snag. She spun to the obstruction. Heated plum sizzled under her skin, the faint flavor of whiskey on Shelton's warm breath caressed her cheek.

"Shelton?" Cassidy whispered.

"Mmm," Came his groggy reply.

Tentatively she brought her hands up, her fingers ghosted across his bare chest.

"Shhh, Cass. It's all right. I'm here."

Like opening a floodgate, liquid welled in Cassidy's eyes, her throat constricted. The taste of ash replaced with spiced plum. Carefully she rested her palm against his bulk as she snuggled her nose into his neck.

"I'm here." He mumbled again and Cassidy choked back a laugh.

The light beamed onto Cassidy's cheeks sending warmth though her skin and intensifying the plum and cedar wood scent that lingered. Her palm smoothed over the heated linen, empty. Cassidy sighed. She rolled to the window, the scenery rushed passed, the wide open plains remained only slightly greener. As if the train echoed her thoughts, racing along a collision course she couldn't alter. Cassidy pulled the linen up to cover her face. Chicago and then Philly had left its mark, unable to shift the memories, the night terrors had returned. If she lay in bed all day could she avoid Shelton and the truth, how could she meet his eye if he'd heard her whimpering? Jet had told her she talked in her sleep sometimes. *How much had she said?* Regardless of Shelton's kindness last night, she had to tell him.

Breakfast had been delivered by the time Shelton wandered into the carriage. Jet had already started on his eggs. Cassidy met Shelton's eyes once and regarded her latest text book. The thought of his reaction to her secrecy seemed to leech through her corset icing her ribs.

"I guess I should say welcome to Colorado." Shelton sat down and Sunny poured him a coffee. "I was seeing to *Tango* since we only have a few hours until we reach Pueblo, you got that list for your husband. I don't know if you have rooms booked, but I recommend we stay at least one night to get organized. I've got a few errands."

"Um," Cassidy started.

Shelton's businesslike tone added more ice to her ribs. Jet seemed to sense the change as well.

"I'm going to see if the chef has some leftovers, that bacon was tasty." Jet rolled out of the bench seat, "And after that I'm going to pack." Jet raised a single eyebrow.

Cassidy cleared her throat. Where did she start? She had a copy of the lease agreement in her luggage. No, paperwork didn't seem the right direction.

"You all right?" Shelton asked.

His manners bolstered her confidence.

"Did you sleep all right?"

The cutlery clattered onto Cassidy's plate. "I did," Cassidy took a sip of her coffee, the bitter liquid scalding her tongue. "Thank you," She turned to the window hoping it would stop the heat from rising past her neck.

"Good." Shelton said.

"Listen Shelton...." As Cassidy turned back, the man had already taken three steps down the aisle, his coffee untouched.

Shelton exhaled slowly as he stepped onto the platform between carriages. Colorado air whooshed passed, tugging at his shirt, and clearing his mind. Cassidy's heated cheeks had told him enough. He'd been having fun, enjoying thawing Cassidy's glacial composure, until last night. The scent of her bedclothes seemed to haunt his thoughts, the echo of her hand in his, a little too snug. She was sweet, innocent, and if he kept on this track, eventually he would win and she would lose. The woman had a husband; one Shelton hoped would pay him fairly. Shelton for once, decided Cassidy Smith was not worth the trouble. Except... no, no exceptions. Cassidy had a life ahead of her and Shelton had the Blue Cow ranch waiting for his lucky strike. Maybe an educated strike?

If he dug for too long, the bank would have the ranch. Maybe he could ask Cassidy to run her eye over the terrain, and save him some time. Shelton tugged his fringe out of his eyes. Nope, it sounded like a business deal even if he knew otherwise. He could only hope that her husband had decided to meet her at Pueblo. Until Cassidy's husband laid eyes on his new bride, Shelton could manage his own willpower. Training *Tango* would surely distract him. The paper rustled in his top pocket, he had supplies to buy, a good canvas tent would see him get a good night sleep for once. Thoughts of Cassidy's nightmares echoed through his chest, would she? Perhaps she hadn't even thought of their sleeping arrangements? Damn, Shelton would have to be responsible again.

As the train pulled into the station, Cassidy scrunched her gloves between her fingers, wringing the velvet until it almost squeaked. Pueblo has arrived and with it her confession. Only Shelton was nowhere to be seen; a quick word to Jet about his horse and gone.

Morning had passed and taken with it Cassidy's courage, now as she disembarked into the bustling Colorado settlement, a seed of regret worked under the corset.

"You have to tell him before noon Cass."

"As soon as I find him Jet!" She threw the boy a soft look, annoyed that in her frustration she'd raised her voice. "I'm sorry Jet." Stumbling through the crowded Pueblo platforms, Cassidy adjusted her rucksack, the book spines jabbing into her ribs.

"Need me to take that?" The bag lifted from Cassidy's shoulders and into Shelton's hand, "I'll get you settled in the Victoria and then check out the stock."

"Stock?"

"Yeah I'll need to find us some good mules." Shelton tapped his pockets and Cassidy winced.

Was he looking for his cheroots?

"We'll save some time, if when you're sorting out your husband's supplies you can sort out mine, while I arrange the mules. Don't forget the canvasser for some good sturdy tents. Check for rips and tears. I'll meet you back in time for supper."

Shelton stormed ahead so that Cassidy had to hitch her skirts and lengthen her strides to catch up. Jet dashed after them both, his head swiveling from left to right catching all the sights offered by Pueblo, Colorado. The railyards ran adjacent to the main thoroughfare; all manner of businesses ran either side of the wide street, that Shelton identified as Union Avenue. They stepped between horses with carriages and wagons, some loaded with supplies and some empty ready to collect from the rail. As they passed one wagon, a load of flour tumble into the street, a carriage lead by two horses couldn't stop and the bag split with the collision of horse's hooves. A puff of white dusted through the air as a woman shouted, the babe in her arms wailed and her husband, weary from whatever travels, simply wiped a hand down his face. Cassidy's steps faulted but Shelton had already crossed the next block. Jet snatched Cassidy's wrist and pulled her along, doubling their efforts to reach Shelton before the crowd swallowed him whole.

With one hand on her bonnet, Cassidy peered upwards at the three story timber monstrosity that stood before them. Shelton took the steps two at a time and Cassidy had no choice but to follow him inside the high ceiling lobby. A reception desk stretched down one side of the hotel. Billiards clinking and men cheering could be heard past the wide double doors that separated the main dining room from what Cassidy only assumed would be the bar. The chandeliers remained un-lit, the narrow but tall windows affording the Colorado sunshine to trickle through the panes, highlighting the dust that drifted in from the street. Scents of cigar smoke mingled with salted bacon, making Cassidy's nose twitch.

As soon as the concierge had their rooms organized, Shelton handed over his list of supplies and banknotes, his fingers touching Cassidy's for the briefest moment. Awkwardly, Cassidy accepted her task, tucking the money away. She sucked in a quick breath and pressed her hands to her abdomen, "Fine, but Shelton before you go..."

"The canvasser is on D Street, the Mercantile too."

It was now or never. Cassidy swallowed hard, "Shelton?"

"Look the quicker I get the stock sorted the quicker I can

get you to your husband."

"Yes but," Cassidy started but Shelton had already replaced his Stetson.

With one hand on the door jamb and another on the brim of his hat, he gave Cassidy a quick smile, his crooked nose all the more alluring with his lopsided grin, "I'll be back by Supper."

Deflected, Cassidy simply nodded as the man entered the street. Could she wait until Supper?

After settling into their rooms, Cassidy resolved herself to her task, first finding pots and pans, then food; sugar, flour and other canned pantry items, sending them over by delivery to the Victoria.

"Ma'am, I'm hoping you have more flour." The woman from the street rushed through the mercantile, her head turning every now and then to the street. Cassidy looked out the dusty window to see the woman's husband holding a tiny bundle in his arms, while their elder son sat leaned against a railing, arms crossed. "The last one had a bay ride through it, then a grey and then another bay."

"Oh dear Alice, I'll get Peter to check out the back, we'll be getting another delivery tomorrow, can ya wait that long?"

"I suppose we can if we have to Meredith," Alice rushed, "It gives me a bit more time to talk sense into Leroy." Alice's gaze once again returned to the street, where, who Cassidy presumed was Leroy, rocked their child slowly in his arms.

"You'll be alright, follow the stage line as far north, they'll be a few others heading your way, Twin Lakes is getting busy this time of year."

Cassidy rechecked her list as Peter returned to give Alice the bad news, "That was the last of it, until tomorrow. Would you like me to send it over to the Royal when it arrives?"

"If you don't mind. I s'pose it'll give me more time, before we set off."

Cassidy watched as the woman returned to Leroy who carefully handed over their baby into his mother's arms. The older boy looked about 17 or 18 years old, his eyes seemed to dart back and forth through the crowd, only falling into line when his father raised his hand as if to clip his ear. Cassidy concentrated on her own task. Not until she paid for her own goods that Cassidy remembered Shelton's list.

Oddly, his requests had been organized into two columns, with separate items in each, some doubled up, and at the bottom of the list, in bold writing, had been written 'H. James'. Clearly Shelton had taken responsibility for another's supplies as well. Cassidy took a pencil from the mercantile assistant and crossed off the items as she found them.

By noon, the money had slipped quick enough through her fingers, Cassidy wasn't sure she'd have enough to buy a meal at the Victoria, let alone two. Perhaps, she could wash dishes or a sell something?

Scorched by the sun, Cassidy returned to the Victoria, her heart sinking as she counted her bank notes. She tossed the meagre funds aside and flicked through her library books. Each one of them was worth their weight in gold in knowledge. She eyed Greenhill's Mine Engineering tome, and decided to pick the priciest, yet least important of her stash. Unfortunately, the next hour Cassidy spent traipsing around Pueblo finding the best price for Erichsen's "*The Science and Art of Surgery*" instead of practicing her confession to Shelton. Jet hadn't let Cassidy out of his sight and dogged her every footstep. Cassidy didn't have the energy to watch the boy's every move as he slipped through the Pueblo Crowd, the sun getting lower as the bars swelled. Hoping Jet's fingers didn't slide into too many pockets was the best Cassidy could do right now. After finding a handsome price in a less then reputable surgery, who didn't mind in the least the book had Penn Medicine stamped in the front, Cassidy bought herself and Jet a sandwich from a café.

Pity no-one was interested in her other text books.

"So, shall we find the stock yards?"

Cassidy tried to ignore the worms that wriggled in her gut.

Jet was right, she knew it. But she didn't have to tell him.

"I was thinking the same thing myself."

"Really?"

"Almost." Cassidy stifled a laugh, "Come on, hopefully Shelton has fared better and someone can buy you dessert tonight."

Jet crossed his arms, and gave her a wink, "You never know, dessert might be on me tonight?"

Cassidy winced. Her feet hurt, the sun had scorched her cheeks and now her mood deflated, "I thought you said you wanted an honest life?"

"Yeah Cass and so do you, so when you tell Shelton the truth, I'll start keeping my hands to myself."

A weight sunk in Cassidy's already leaden legs, the boy could end up in jail or worse, in some misplaced game of chicken. Bolstered by Jet's declaration, that she too, had to do the right thing, Cassidy stood up and shouldered the rest of her books. "Then there really is no time to waste is there, come on."

Jet winked again and bowed low directing Cassidy towards the street, "After you, me lady." He mocked. Cassidy bought a sandwich for Shelton and a bottle of sarsaparilla, hoping it would sweeten her sour message.

Another mile later, after crossing the 8th street bridge, Cassidy found herself squeezing between pens and barriers, weaving her way to the tallest Stetson in the stockyards at East Pueblo. Adjacent to the Fountain River, the stockyards had been penned, their paddocks now filled with mules that milled about. Cassidy spied Shelton with his arms crossed, clearly still haggling with the merchant.

Slowly, Cassidy wandered past the outer fencing admiring the soft slate colored coats, the animals' round white muzzles adding an endearing almost comical expression. The dark fur around their eyes coupled with their long lashes made it look as if someone had outlined their glistening black baubles with kohl. One mule pushed his muzzle against Cassidy's chest, she flinched and opened her empty palms. The animal tilted his head, his ears pricked and rubbed his jaw down Cassidy's upper arm.

"Friendly fellow," Cassidy giggled. Tentatively she raised her other arm and stroked between the mules peaked ears. If only she could sooth the anger she anticipated from Shelton when she told him the truth. Even more annoying was the lurking thoughts that Cassidy held, the disappointment in the face of his possible rejection, or the alternative, taking seed in her chest, that Shelton accepted the arrangement. She concentrated on the first, rejection, anger, disappointment and the fact that Jet was right. If she intended to live an honest life, it needed to start in Colorado.

"Cass?" Shelton's voice made Cassidy step back. As he neared, she worried her bottom lip with her teeth. It was now or never. Plus telling Shelton the truth would stop Jet from lifting every watch in Pueblo.

"Is something wrong?"

"No, I um..."

"Did you need more banknotes?"

"No."

Shelton tugged back his fringe and reset his Stetson. *Be brave Cass!* She straightened her shoulders, "Jet and I finished the supplies, and thought we'd explore the city." *Liar!* She cleared her throat. "And we brought you lunch."

Jet stepped forward and handed Shelton the wrapped sandwiches and bottle of sarsaparilla. He threw Cassidy a dark look, "I might look around a bit, find something to entertain myself."

"Jet..." Cassidy started, but the boy had already stalked off.

"Ah here," He pushed the sandwich into Cassidy's hand, "I'm halfway between fifty and a hundred for three, I'll come find you when I get to sixty for five of his best." Shelton popped the top off his sars and retraced his steps to the burros' merchant.

Standing by herself, Cassidy had no other alternative but to retreat to the nearest shade. Two Douglas firs sprouted side by side beside a slight hill covered in big bluestem grass. Cassidy picked up her hem and climbed the rise, finding a spot where the tall grasses would hide Shelton from view. She tossed down her rucksack and pulled out her Chemistry textbook. The pages offered no suggestions on how Cassidy was to break the news to Shelton. Perhaps she should have brought the mining lease. What if Shelton decided to acknowledge the conditions?

Cassidy concentrated on acid washes when she heard footsteps. She stood bolt upright. The big bluestem grasses concealed Shelton's long legs.

"Deal's done." He said as he lifted his Stetson back from his forehead.

Now that Shelton stood only inches away, Cassidy's courage fled. The afternoon sun dwindled through the sky as the Fountain River snaked around the low banks. Time was running out.

"You picked a nice spot," Shelton lowered himself to the ground where Cassidy had sat. Reclining with one leg in front of him, Shelton un-wrapped his sandwich and consumed it with four large bites.

The silence between them rattled Cassidy's nerves and she took a seat beside him if only to stop her legs from trembling. "We had all the supplies sent to the Victoria."

"Good," Shelton skulled the remainder of his sarsaparilla, "We'll load the mules at first light and head out."

"Good." Cassidy rolled her lips between her teeth. "How long will it take?" She straightened her back, sitting just in front of Shelton so he sat on the peripheral of her shoulder. Cassidy retrieved her locket and gave it three spins for courage.

"Ten days as best. What are you reading now?" Shelton tilted the book upright, "Another library book no doubt."

"Ah Yes, from New York...."

She needed a textbook on how to tell the truth. *Chapter One, I'm your wife, an introduction. Followed by Chapter two; My father tricked you.* Cassidy let out a nervous giggle, *Chapter 3, Reading the fine print and other common lease mistakes.*

"Is this another attempt at being useful to your husband?"

The locket tumbled from her grip, the gold cool against her skin, "Yes, now that you mention it."

Cassidy turned on her hips to face Shelton, only to find the man had moved into a sitting position, his clean shaven cheeks only inches from her lips. His forehead dipped to read her cover. Suddenly he looked up and sugar grey eyes melted like molten steel. A cheeky lopsided grin split his cheeks making Cassidy's own smile blossom, except his hands rested calmly on his knees, unlike Cassidy's fidgeting.

"Chemistry?" He read aloud.

"Yes," her voice breathless.

The distance between them narrowed. Shelton's eyes targeted her lips. A surge of heat slithered through Cassidy's veins as she fought the urge to lick her lips, "Some things you can't learn in a textbook."

"I know." The words whispered against Shelton's cheek.

Like a magnet, Cassidy leaned closer, Shelton's plum cologne enticing her further. Shelton paused and then withdrew, his brows furrowed, "I need to apologize for my behavior earlier, in Wichita."

Cassidy swallowed hard, the air between them now cooled. Stunned, "No need to apologize," she ran her palms down her skirts. Her abdomen churned. Apologize? From what she had seen of Shelton so far, he didn't abide by morals, it only meant one thing. Clearly Cassidy had fallen short. Doubt clawed at her insides. Mimi the dancing girl, Frankie Delgardo's wife, even the stately matron on the train, had drawn Shelton's gaze. How could Cassidy, compare? She was twenty and Shelton had been her first kiss. "I understand, you would, um, have to excuse me, I mean if it was unsatisfactory..." Heat colored both her cheeks and she turned back to the river.

Clearly Shelton's tastes weren't satiated, her inexperience showing through.

"On the contrary,"

Cassidy froze with her hands clutched the textbook in her lap, not wishing to turn.

"I meant for stealing your husbands first kiss."

Now she couldn't resist. Twisting, she met Shelton's gaze, the molten steel still there. Heat infused so rapidly through Cassidy's spine rushing up to her neck, she thought she might melt. Shelton leaned closer, the brim of his Stetson shading her from the afternoon sun. The words were out of her mouth before she registered the impact, "And the second."

Shelton smiled. The weight of the textbook slid from her lap as Shelton's lips slanted across Cassidy's.

Chapter 12

Cassidy relented to the gentle pressure of Shelton's kiss, his tongue slowly slaking across hers, as she sensed her skirts move. His palm, warm and firm encircled her ankle, bringing both her legs across his lap, trailing his fingers up her calf. Cassidy gripped Shelton's collar, pulling his bulk closer until he wrapped his other arm around her back, his forearm aligning with her straight backed spine, his long fingers stroking her neck. For safety, she leaned into his bulk, curling around his neck, the soft nettles of the grass bristling against her back. Plum and cedar wood competed with the tang of sarsaparilla and the scents of fresh earth, as Shelton's weight settled over her. Licks of flame followed Shelton's grip as he worked higher under her frills.

"So soft, Cass. Like the softest velvet a man's dared to touch."

His words fueled the flames and Cassidy removed his Stetson, running her fingers through his hair.

"And your lips," Shelton whispered as he trailed his kisses down her jaw to her throat, "The lushest a man could hope for. " He suckled and nipped his way to the hollow at her throat, "You drive a man wild with your whiskey brown gaze, all glacial wildfire, I expect to be burnt when I touch you, except I can't resist and I want that spark, I want your fire Cass."

Waves of warmth curled through Cassidy's body, spiraling downwards to slick between her thighs. Shelton's palm cupped her upper thigh, his fingers caressing her tender skin.

"I feel scorched, deep inside," His tongue returned to delve the soft corners of her mouth. Cassidy felt as if her feet had left the ground, floating upwards to the clouds with only Shelton as her anchor.

His pressure increased, as more of his body eclipsed hers. First his chest met her chest, her breasts swollen, the centers aching. Then his hip, the hardness of his arousal pressed against her hip and Cassidy's abdomen flipped.

"I want you Cass, despite your husband."

Cassidy smiled against his lips, "You are my husband, Shelton."

Shelton's moan consumed by Cassidy's mouth, when he finally resisted the pleasure of her lips, he leaned back, "Huh?"

"You are him, Shelton."

Cassidy's words twisted in his mind. He must be mad, the passion gone to his head. Her skin supple, soft, velvety in his grip as his fingertips touched the lace of her drawers, "What?"

"You are him, Shelton James Murphy is on the mining lease...." Cassidy's arm curled around his neck, her knee hooked near his thigh.

Slowly he propped himself upright, "No," and offered his hand to Cassidy. She took it and he pulled her upright from the grass. "You're not making sense Cass."

"Yes. You signed a mining lease with Julius Smith, to work the plot of land under his patent, known as Pip's Pit, for a period of five years paying 10% to Smith or his agent, and on the condition that you marry his daughter. Me, Cassidy Smith."

Shelton's mind spun. Shelton James? Hugo James. Hugo had set him up! He drafted the mining lease, Shelton just signed it. Shelton's middle name was August. Shelton could feel trembles work into his knuckles, his legs suddenly itching to be away. He had signed the lease for The Blue Cow, his parent's ranch. He didn't have time or money for a wife. "I ain't got time for a wife."

Cassidy's hand fell from his palm, as if burned.

Rising to his feet, the heat ratcheted Shelton's ribs. The pennies fell into place, Cassidy's scheming, her battering eyelashes, the unnerving sense Shelton had the entire time he'd met her that something was up. Jackson would be Smith's agent no doubt, pushing Cassidy out front to take his cut from the profits. Shelton was a fool. Hugo James, Jackson, Cassidy even Jet had played him.

"I guess you mean you haven't got time for your wife, just everybody elses!" Cassidy replied.

He'd ghosted Cade to bring this hustler up the mountain in the hopes of an easy pay day. Shelton scoffed, "Well I guess other people's wives pay me. Am I supposed to bill myself my services for this journey?" Shelton scooped up his Stetson and replaced it on his head. He turned to find navy blue skirts dashing through the grass. Only a fool would chase after a woman with this much heat still boiling in his veins. Shelton dusted off his denims and watched as Cassidy tore off across the field.

Who'd want such a scoundrel as a wife? Clearly Hugo knew the terms of the lease and sent Shelton in his place. He wouldn't want a wife dividing half his payday when they hit a lode. Seething, Shelton stumbled down towards the stock yards and shoved his hands into his pocket if only to loosen his fists. Likely Hugo's debts wasn't as bad as he made out, Shelton had believed him. Kicking another shrub with his boot, Shelton paused. What of Cassidy then? She'd known he was supposed to be her husband but held her tongue until now. Why?

His thoughts rolled over one another as the Pueblo sun sunk lower, adding an itch between his shoulder blades; the honking of the mules taunting Shelton's mind for an answer. Likely, Cassidy had been weighing Shelton up for husband material, hence the disappearing cheroots, the questions about his family and if he had a girl back home. He swallowed hard, his throat tight, as realisation dawned. Even worse, Cassidy had finished assessment, misguided as it was that Shelton was somehow worthy of the title husband!

Well, Shelton would just have to show her how wrong she was.

Cassidy threw herself down on the coverlet, the late afternoon sun seemed to blister her tears and sting her resolve. All the words had been left unsaid, trickster, fraudster, charlatan, only Shelton had simply said he didn't have time. Cassidy wanted to believe his kisses told another story, only they didn't. Shelton wanted a woman, not a wife. A wife cost money, and Cassidy had already cost the man his guide fee and his expenses. Something tangled in the back of her mind, only unravelling when the door slammed back.

"Damn Cass, sorry," Jet rushed into the tiny room and sat on the wire cot on the other side, "How'd it go? Bad?"

"Almost."

"Worse?"

Sitting upright, Cassidy scrubbed her cheeks, "It's better now the air is clear, you can stop thieving and we can make our way to the claim without...." As if the dawn had just peaked behind storm clouds, she smiled.

"He's not going to take us up to the claim now?"

"Almost." Cassidy winked and rose to her feet, quickly she smoothed out her dress and pushed back her hair, pinning it into place as fast as she could. "I'm heading to the Royal."

"The Royal, what for?" Jet slipped something from his pocket under his mattress and Cassidy didn't bother to discuss it. She'd find a way to hand it in as lost to the concierge.

"To repay Shelton, are you coming?"

Jet jumped up and tightened his vest across his gut, "Sure, but um, how are we going to do that?"

"Honestly, Jet. Honestly. Now what did we do with our flour?"

As the stairs flew under foot, Cassidy's plan solidified. Only getting Shelton to agree to it would be the next hurdle. Although the way the man focused on money, it shouldn't be too difficult. Would he trust her? She didn't have time to worry. Pueblo's sun had sunk below the false fronts, the street crowds thinning of respectable citizens as the night-time patrons thickened. It took another four blocks before they made it to the Royal and found Alice's husband, Leroy packing their wagon in the stables.

"Sidney, tie down the canvas." Leroy ordered.

The older boy, Cassidy had seen earlier at the mercantile threw his father a sullen look as he slowly obeyed. Strapping one rope over another, he ran his gaze over Cassidy. Jet's elbow collided with Cassidy's "Cass..."

She helped drag the flour from Jet's shoulders and dumped it onto the half covered wagon.

"Hey what you doing?"

Cassidy cleared her throat, "Excuse me, I was in the mercantile earlier today and I couldn't help but overhear your wife Alice had some trouble ordering flour."

Leroy stepped closer, "Ah that's right we did," The scent of straw dust, manure, and animals became muted as Leroy's meaty scent intensified.

"What's it to you?" Sidney snapped.

Suddenly Jet stepped forward, his wiry body between Sidney and Cassidy. Although flattered by Jet's gesture, it was a quick word from Leroy who sent the tall, dark haired youth into the long shadows of the barn. Cords recoiled from the canvas as Sidney worked silently at the rear of the wagon.

"I've thought I'd share some of ours since no doubt we'll see each other on the trail."

Leroy pulled his bowler hat off his head and wiped back the few dark strands that remained there, the dark circles seemed to eclipse his brown eyes, "Will we?"

"Oh yes," Cassidy lifted her voice an octave higher to match her chin and nose. Clipping her words she twisted her accent to one of High Society. "Your dear wife mentioned Twin Lakes, my party is heading out tomorrow as well."

"That's mighty charitable of you Miss um..."

"Cassidy Smith." She answered.

"Miss Smith, but I ain't got anything to pay you in return." Leroy wiped his hand on his trouser thigh and began to lift the flour bag.

"Use your head Pa, she wants an escort." Sidney's shout echoed from within the darkness.

A horse whickered and Cassidy counted to three as Leroy's hand hovered over the flour.

"Thank you for the offer, however that's not necessary."

Leroy's expression crinkled in confusion.

"We already have a guide, a Trail Boss from Texas who's been up the mountain, oh…" Cassidy exhaled slowly and Jet picked up the rest.

"Too many times to count," Jet said, he shoved his hands into his pockets, raising one eyebrow to look over the half-packed cart, "Trained with a Texas Ranger sometime back and put Frankie Delgardo in his place quick smart only last week in Wichita."

There was no chance either Leroy or his son knew who the devil Frankie Delgardo was or even if he was someone important, yet Jet's tone carried such an air of authority that even Cassidy let her mind wander to that night and Shelton's flying fists.

"You're guide trained with a Texas Ranger?"

"Isn't that what I said, Sidney." Jet smirked. Cassidy knew all the twists and turns this conversation could take and decided to call it early.

"My father was frugal and smart," Now her tongue coated in ash, Cassidy inhaled sharply and pressed her stomach with her trembling fingers, "He thought it prudent to arrange the guide with the best skill, for when we're up the mountain. If you do not need flour, then I will have it sent back to the Victoria tomorrow." Cassidy gestured to Jet who made a poor attempt of finding a stable boy to order about. Neither Leroy or Sidney seemed to care that Cassidy and Jet had carried it themselves to find them.

"Ah Miss Smith, if you don't mind me asking how did your father pay for this guide?"

By the time Cassidy and Jet returned to the Victoria Hotel, her spirits has lifted. Leroy would pay Shelton $15 tomorrow and another $15 when they arrived unharmed at Twin Lakes. Beaming with her latest scheme, the rough piano and strings ditty that bled through the double doors worked its way through Cassidy's corset she didn't even think about asking for a second pitcher and basin.

"I like them paying Shelton, but Sidney is someone to watch."

"Nothing Shelton's broad shoulders can't handle."

They wandered past the double doors on the way to the staircase and Cassidy's curiosity got the better of her, her gaze focusing on the men inside and the women that pawed over them. Only one man stole the air from Cassidy's lungs.

In the center of the room, one table engaged in a game of poker, the cigar smoke wafting through the crowd like a serpent of doom. A large puff of smoke escaped from Shelton's lips only to drift through the curls of the woman who sat on his lap. One arm curled around the blonde woman's waist as he the lay his cards down, only to pick up his tumbler and take a sip of dark amber.

"Cass," Jet's word sizzled through her ear.

Unwavering from her gaze, she stepped closer to the threshold of the parlour. Steel grey eyes met hers from across the room; his blond fringe slicked back with two strands dangling over his forehead to rest against his crooked nose. He popped a cheroot into one side of his lips and took another drag.

Jet's words of caution dissolved in the heat that roared through Cassidy's body, making her legs tremble. Shelton titled his chin upright in defiance, smug at his blatant disregard for the fraudulent agreement. With Shelton's position clear Cassidy finally took a breath, only to have it stall in her throat as his hand wound through the Dove's blonde curls to the rear of her neck, tugging the woman's painted face closer to whisper in her ear. The woman laughed, a tinny cackle that rode through Cassidy's spine like iron nails across stone.

The timber boards creaked under foot as Cassidy's heels drummed across the distance. Her boot toe slid out and struck its target. The leg of Shelton's chair shifted backwards. He over balanced. Both hands slapped on the table and Shelton managed to stay upright.

A screech squeaked through the air as the violinist reacted, the pianist stilled his hammering as the room fell silent to watch. Cassidy stood over Shelton, schooling her features to calm. The embarrassment leaching through her bones did nothing to sooth the ache in her ribs. *Did he think she would cower and retreat?* The panic in his wide sugar grey eyes told Cassidy the truth. Satisfaction slowly replaced her anger, bolstering her confidence.

"Ah excuse us Darlin'" Shelton said as he lifted the woman from his lap. "What is it, Precious?"

All of her energy pooled into her gut and she pumped her fists to release it, "I've secured you another guide contract for tomorrow morning."

"You what?" Now Shelton leaned forward on his chair.

"Tomorrow at dawn at the stables," was all Cassidy said before she turned on her heel and left the gambling parlor. Three times she turned her locket before she felt a measure of relief.

The music restarted as Cassidy stepped into the foyer, Jet's face as dark as a thunder cloud.

"Hey!" Shelton shouted as he entered the foyer behind her.

The fury inside Cassidy hadn't abated and she rounded on Shelton faster than he anticipated. With liquor slowing his reactions she collided with his chest. Stumbling back, Shelton snatched at her waist. Scents of stale tobacco washed over Cassidy so fast her nose crinkled and she coughed. Within an instant Shelton had released her, his eyes ablaze, lips thin.

"You did what?"

"Leroy Barnes needs you to take him and his family safely

up to Twin Lakes. Tomorrow morning he'll be here at dawn and he's paying you $30 for the privilege, so maybe you should be a little more professional in your conduct."

"My conduct, Precious? Pot calling the kettle black there ain't ya?"

"You have your guide fee Shelton, since there is no husband of mine to pay you, I found you another." Cassidy took measured steps to the stairs trying to forget the image of the Dove in Shelton's lap. It was no good, the man had wounded her.

"And if I don't agree, what happens to your scheme then?" Shelton pursued her across the foyer stairs, his grip locking onto Cassidy's elbow as she stood two steps above him.

Jet stood by Cassidy's side, his blue eyes flicking between Shelton's arm and Cassidy's elbow, until Shelton let go. "You have no qualms of agreements when quick money is on the line, Shelton. Perhaps if you want to keep this payday, you'll keep your hands off his wife."

Shelton stepped back his brow furrowed, "Fine, no more schemes or set ups or contracts you hear me." Shelton shouted as Cassidy stormed up the stairs.

Shelton ran his fingers through his hair as he watched the woman stomp her way to the next level. He figured Cassidy would try something to force him up the mountain despite her lies. What he hadn't anticipated was her storming right into the bar and kicking the chair out from under him. Nor had he anticipated she'd find him work. His eyes tracked her navy skirts all the way to the top, a lead weight sunk in his chest at his own deplorable actions. The Dove had been a nice distraction, serving her purpose to chase Cassidy away, only now he'd lost all taste for her or any other. The fury he'd witnessed in Cassidy's eyes had set his skin on fire, he wanted those chocolate brown eyes on him, melting in his arms and warming his bed. Only he'd gone and shot himself in the foot right and proper. He didn't have time or the funds for a wife.

Jet reclined against the stair bannister, arms crossed over his chest, one boot resting on the wall.

"In the parlor... just now ...I...."

"I'm sorry for lying to you, Shelton and I know what you're doing, I ain't stupid. But pushing her away, making her see something you want her to see... well you disrespecting my sister is on your head, is all I'm gonna say."

"Your sister...." Shelton started but his anger and the liquor got the better of him, "She ain't even your real sister..."

"Say what you want to say about Cassidy, Shelton but don't say she ain't real." The boy's eyes narrowed. "She's the closest thing I've got to a family and that's pretty real to me."

Jet had said it so quietly and calmly that Shelton wanted to kick his own arse right now, "I didn't mean that I meant..."

"Yeah I know what you meant Shelton, she played you and you're pissed. But don't forget her father played her too with this agreement. She had to fall in line or get out of his life altogether."

The timber creaked under Shelton's weight as he climbed the stairs beside Jet. As if Shelton hadn't felt bad enough, now he wished his words back in his mouth. What kind of father would say that to his daughter? Even worse, how bad could it have been that Cassidy refused her father's offer to take a chance on a stranger and a frozen mining claim?

"Then why she'd go through with it?"

A slap landed on Shelton's shoulder as they reached to top level where their rooms had been allocated, "Haven't you worked Cass out yet?" Jet smiled, "Don't ever call her bluff."

So she had a backbone, and brains, distractingly beautiful, and now Shelton had gone and stomped all over her dreams. It shouldn't matter when it came to the Blue Cow. His Ma and Pa counted on him to bail out the ranch. He couldn't afford the time or the money that a wife and her fraudulent kid-brother would demand, even if it was Cassidy. Jet farewelled him in the corridor.

"I stick to my word Jet, if I can't find you work with us, I'll find you work somewhere."

The boys eyes widened and he shook Shelton's hand, "I knew you would."

After closing the door, Shelton undressed and crawled into his covers, the scratchy blanket adding another layer of irritation to his already whiskey-heated skin.

Hugo had set him up magnificently as well. Hugo had substantial funds and technically he owned the mining lease, earning fifty percent of whatever profits they dredge out of the river. Perhaps Cassidy might find her worthy husband in Hugo. Shelton had to at least offer her the option by taking her to the claim.

Chapter 13

The silvery light of dawn slipped through the slate grey clouds as if to mock Shelton's hangover, the sunlight not strong enough to heat him, yet the light bright enough to add an ache behind his eyes. He'd spent a restless sleep wishing caramel strands curling through his fingers, those velvet doe brown eyes scalding him, daring him to take her lips again. Damn, he owed Cassidy nothing, but would see her safely to the top of the mountain, safely to Hugo and she could decide for herself if she could make a life out of Colorado or its men.

Shelton crossed the road from the Post Master, after sending an update to Cade only to watch the Barnes' arrive with as much calamity as Shelton expected. One mangy horse pulled a laden wagon stacked too high and the weight too far forward from the axle. The small infant carried by the wife, had already begun to wail.

"Shelton Murphy is it? Leroy Barnes, the name." The shorter fatter man sent his hand out and Shelton shook it. "This here is my wife Alice and Oliver and my son Sid."

"Pleasure to meet you."

"Did you really train with the Texas Rangers?"

Shelton shook Sid's hand as well, the boy's knuckles squeezing tight and Shelton met the challenge, letting go only when he heard something crack. Sid hissed and stepped back, his fingers ringed in red and white. "Only one, but he's the best." Shelton replied. What the devil had Cassidy and Jet told them? "You'll need to restack your weight here to ease your horse."

"Ole *Missy* here can handle anything." Leroy patted the worn out horse on her withers.

"Your weight is too far forward of the axle. Restack it." Shelton ordered.

Leroy's piggy brown eyes narrowed but he clicked his fingers at Sidney and together they reorganized the wagon. Jose from the stock yards arrived with six of his best for Shelton, the mules wary of the tired horse. Shelton set about loading each mule in turn with their bundles of goods, still Cassidy was no-where to be seen. Jet had materialized out of thin air and lent a hand. When quizzed about Cassidy, the boy just shrugged his shoulders. Well, without Cassidy to distract him, it gave Shelton time to assess his new charges.

Leroy seemed more than ten years older than Shelton, his dark hair receding as his middle seemed to increase. Lines of wrinkles creased as he furtively watched and then copied how Shelton tied his loads. Every now and then the man would re-tuck a piece of canvas near the right side of the wagon, no doubt where his long arms had been stored.

The wife Alice seemed Shelton's age, the child in her arms not yet a year old. She watched as Shelton instructed her husband, nodding silently, her dusty bonnet tucked over her auburn hair, the hem of her skirts frayed. She tried her best to speak to Sidney who simply ignored her. The boy Sidney had already raised the hair on the back of Shelton's neck, tall, solid, although smaller than Shelton, he seemed about 17 or 18 years of age, his expression only changing from sullen or contempt when a young lady would wander by. Alice seemed too young to be his mother and Shelton filled in the blanks for himself.

By the time, *Tango* was finally saddled Cassidy appeared on the steps of the Victoria, her fancy travelling dress had been replaced by a white shirt and green woolen skirt with jacket to match. The emerald color highlighted her natural warm tones and Shelton was glad he'd finished his work before now. His anger at her deception had disappeared like fog at dawn and he even smiled when he saw her dragonfly boots, before he caught himself.

"Morning Miss Smith." Leroy said.

"Morning Mister Barnes."

Sidney stopped at the edge of the wagon, and lifted the brim of his hat with one finger, "Yeah morning Miss Smith." His voice seemed deeper than before. Jet turned to Shelton and narrowed his eyes. Shelton nodded at Jet's unspoken concern. Sidney Barnes would be an issue. Shelton remembered himself at that age and Cassidy was only two years older than the boy, standing in all her splendor, illuminated by the early morning sunshine, she looked radiant. Downright irresistible, if he didn't say so himself. Shelton regarded Sidney, until the boy met Shelton's gaze. The boy took another languid appraisal of Cassidy making sure he returned his gaze to Shelton.

Shelton smiled. The kind of smile that didn't reach his eyes, a lopsided grin that bared half his teeth.

Cassidy took the steps carefully, ignoring Shelton's heated gaze. She didn't want to think about what happened after she stormed off last night or whether the dancing girl from the parlor made it to Shelton's bed, despite Jet's excited exclamation as he returned to Cassidy's room. "He said *us* Cassidy," he repeated. *Us*, the word Shelton has used to suggest finding work for Jet, the *us* that Jet believed meant Shelton and Cassidy.

Cassidy wasn't a fool, but a tiny part of her still held hope and she hated herself for it. Shelton had simply misspoken; that was all. He had no intention of honoring the lease agreement, and even less of a chance at honoring Cassidy. He could glare all he like, she had managed to find him payment for his services, even if they all had to suffer the company of Leroy and his insolent son Sidney.

"Thank you so much," Alice rushed up to Cassidy, "For the flour and for...." She darted a gaze to her husband, "Everything."

"It's no trouble. My fee to Mister Murphy has already been paid, and the addition of your family is a welcome distraction from his tedious company." She didn't shout, but she didn't whisper either. Shelton's snort of derision raised the hair on the back of Cassidy's neck. Would he ruin it now, if he called her Precious in front Barnes and his family? How far was Twin Lakes?

"Mount up," Shelton ordered and wandered down to Cassidy's side. She put one boot toe in the stirrup and leaned forward. Shelton's warm hands on her waist made her flinch, the sound of his voice at her ear, made her spine melt, "Tedious hey?"

"Your friend certainly looked bored last night." Cassidy sneered.

"She wasn't by the end of it." Shelton added.

The ground disappeared, the horizon lurched and the saddle slipped under Cassidy's grip. She didn't have time for a response and instead threw one leg over the other side of the saddle.

"Aren't ladies supposed to ride side saddle?" Shelton asked.

"Only if they want to fall off Mister Murphy," Cassidy snapped as she straightened her split riding skirts. The dancing girl wasn't bored by the end of it? Jet swore he saw Shelton enter his room alone. Cassidy couldn't concentrate on staying upright and dealing with the asps that circled her ribs to compress her lungs. The mule owner, Jose came down the line of animals and handed Cassidy the reins.

"Her name is Carlota." He said as he rubbed down the mule's dark slate coat, "She is as sure footed as any animal, *lo mejor para transportar la carga más preciosa.*"

Shelton clearly understood what Jose said as his brows furrowed. Instead of replying he stalked off to *Tango* and climbed into the saddle.

As they crossed the Colorado countryside, Cassidy's shoulders began to relax. Shelton hadn't spoken to her and Jet hadn't left her side. A cool breeze lilted through the party as they made their way northwards, every now and then Shelton would pull *Tango* back to check everyone was still managing. The ground seemed to climb straight out of Pueblo, the scenery filled with emerald pillars of fir, pine and spruce. The woody scents called to Cassidy and she inhaled deeply of the sylvan flavors that signaled her fresh start. Shelton's wounding remained so fresh in her mind it felt raw. His beige Stetson bobbed up and down as *Tango* negotiated the rocky road. At the first break, Shelton moved as if to assist Cassidy but she dismounted before he reached her.

Alice rushed around their wagon to retrieve the provisions and Cassidy ate sparingly of the salted meat they purchased in Pueblo. Ten days Shelton had said and she would have to endure nine nights in his company, hoping her tongue didn't slip with another insult, or worse, her willpower didn't dissolve if he ever looked at her, the way he had on the bank of the Little Arkansas River. Cassidy pulled her gloves off to undo her water canister and took a long sip. Despite the cool air, she felt parched. At least, she'd finally get her wish; sleeping underneath the stars, no roof or walls to pen her in with her nightmares.

Shelton rested them in a flat area surrounded by sandy foothills, some sprouting firs, others stout shrubs. The Arkansas River bubbled past and Leroy and his son marched over to the bank. Cassidy brought *Carlota* to the closest shade, a bandy hackberry, while Shelton meandered down the line checking the animals. He moved towards Cassidy, his eyes running head to toe over her condition. Cassidy squared her shoulders, making sure to lift her nose and pucker her lips before she turned her back. Jet strolled over, unbuttoning his checkered shirt and rolling up the sleeves.

"He'll come around."

"This time Jet, I'm almost certain you're wrong."

Jet leaned against the rump of *Carlota* and fidgeted with the saddle blanket, "Did you think to apologise."

"For what exactly Jet? I read the fine print?"

Jet shrugged his shoulders, "I dunno not being honest straight up."

"And if I had, we'd have never made it as far as Waco."

Jet snorted as he picked up a handful of pebbles and tossed them into the bush, "Don't go selling yourself short there Cass, you've brought us this far."

One pebble spun through the foliage, the leaves rustled and a squeak of some animal erupted. Cassidy jumped and then giggled as a brush tailed squirrel dashed up the next higher branch to safer ground.

Jet chuckled as well and offered Cassidy his hand to help her back in the saddle. She waved him away, "I'm fine Jet, I'll manage."

"All right but give us your canister, I'll fill it up again before we head out."

Cassidy relented and handed it over. She patted *Carlota* between the ears, the grey pelt soft under her fingers.

"She's definitely a looker."

Cassidy flinched and turned to see Sidney had returned from the river. Slicking back his dark hair he placed one boot on a rock and leaned his elbow across his thigh. He pulled a strand of grass from between his teeth and smiled, "Don't ya think?"

"She's certainly not ordinary." Cassidy suddenly felt the urge to pull her jacket closer at the intensity from his ice blue eyes. Instead, Cassidy turned back to the mule, whose ears flicked back and forth. For a moment she forgot about Sidney and wondered how *Tango's* size and bulk had Cassidy on edge, and yet with *Carlotta's* daintier build, soft grey fur and wide black eyes, Cassidy felt at ease.

"Yeah there's something about her, for sure." Sidney's words grated Cassidy's nerves and she turned to find him closer.

"Is there something I can help you with?" Lead solidified in Cassidy's bones, her retort ready to send Sidney on his way whatever his response, "Otherwise..."

Sidney stood upright, his eyes narrowed over Cassidy's shoulder, his hands on his hips, chest pronounced.

"You looking for something Sidney?" Shelton stood on the other side of *Carlotta*, his hand splayed wide on the mule's rump, the other on her reins.

"I ain't decided yet."

"I'll decide for you, mount up." Shelton's words inspired action but the man himself didn't move. With both arms outstretched his chest seemed cavernous, his forearms tensed and tanned. Even his blue checkered shirt now appeared two sizes too small around his shoulders.

Sidney shoved the blade of grass between his teeth in a half smile and walked down to his father's wagon. He smacked *Missy* on the rump and the tired mare leaned into her harness. Alice who sat feeding Oliver on the rear had to clutch the canvas to stay seated.

The locket inside Cassidy's corset begged to be twisted as she waited for Shelton to leave. His beige Stetson cast a shadow across his face, turning his sugar grey eyes into a thunderstorm. Color climbed her neck and flushed into her cheeks, before the man even moved a muscle.

"You all right?"

"Always." Cassidy said as she put one boot into the stirrup and heaved herself upright, trying not to wince. "Don't dally on my account. I wouldn't want to waste a single moment of your precious time."

Shelton held Carlotta's reins and brought the animal and Cassidy backwards until her thigh came in line with his chest, "Clever, which textbook taught you those quick retorts?

"You can't learn everything in a textbook, Mister Murphy."

"And that's another thing, when are you gonna drop this Mister Murphy act?"

"When you've been paid."

Shelton rested his hand on the pommel of Cassidy's saddle, the mule's front hoof stomped as both the animals' patience dwindled just like his own. Sidney's presence around Cassidy had added another dimension to Shelton's confusion. The youth needed to be watched, but Cassidy was in need of a husband.

"Since you fixed my guide fee, I have a mind to fix your lease agreement."

Fine brows arched, thick black lashes blinked, and Shelton tore his eyes away from her widening gaze, he needed to say his piece and say it quickly, "I'm not the only one in business on your father's land. My business partner, for want of a better word, Hugo James shares the claim. We agreed on a Fifty-fifty split."

Cassidy's shoulders slumped, her bottom lip thinned. Within an instant, her expression had glazed over, the prim and proper high society façade returned, the glacier in full blizzard.

As the words tumbled, his own gut sunk, "Perhaps you'll find what you're looking for with Hugo. It's at least an option to consider."

Maybe that would keep Sidney from Cassidy's mind. Shelton looked up, the noon sun haloed her caramel strands, except now her eyes were downcast, her teeth bit into her bottom lip and if he had a dime to his name, he'd bet she wanted to twist that damn necklace of hers.

"Good."

"I haven't agreed on anything." She snapped.

"But you'll consider it. You knew nothing but my name before you stepped onto that boat. Now you know Hugo's name."

The sandy gravel trembled under his boots as he tore himself away and clambered onto *Tango*. It would serve them right, two schemers tied together by a shifty contract. Hugo had finances, more than Shelton. Cassidy needed a husband. An image of grizzled jawed Hugo holding Cassidy's hand stuck in Shelton's mind. Damn. He hadn't made it three feet from her, before he wanted to eat his words.

As Shelton led them further north, shadowing the Arkansas River, he filled his mind with thoughts of the Blue Cow. The spinifex, the dusty fields, his Pa's thinning hair and his Ma's blistered hands. He had left Dew Springs, Texas for Colorado gold because his family depended on it. They halted for lunch, only allowing enough time to swap the mules. This time they started out walking beside the animals and Sidney worked himself to the front.

"So you're a trail boss?"

Shelton gave Sidney a side glance and nodded. Cassidy and Jet had spun some tales!

"Who's Frankie Delgardo? "

"Huh?"

"A gunslinger from Wichita, he had a smart mouth but his fists weren't fast enough." Jet said from behind as he gave Shelton a wink, "Now that we're out of Pueblo when are you gonna teach us to shoot?"

Sidney snorted, "Who needs teaching?"

"Only a fool thinks he knows everything." Jet replied.

"Are you calling me a fool?" Sidney snapped.

Laughing, Shelton had to cool the youths temper before it came to blows, "It means, there is no end to learning, we're always learning, all of us, all of the time. And yes, Jet, when I can, I will."

"Good I'll let Cassidy know." Jet smiled.

"That Miss Smith is going to learn how to shoot?" Sidney whistled between his teeth.

"I'd cool it right there Sidney," Shelton didn't like the heat in his voice, but his throat wouldn't relax, "She's on her way to meet her new husband."

"Is she now?" Jet brought his mule closer, his round face expectant, his brows raised.

As quickly and as confidently as he could, Shelton explained Hugo James and the deal he had made before signing the mine lease, without letting too much slip for Sidney's ears.

"Remember what I said Shelton, don't call her bluff." The boy pulled the reins of his mule and let Shelton pull away. Sidney thankfully had taken his place back with his father as the gradient increased.

Once night fell, Shelton would have to manage Cassidy in camp, with Sidney sniffing around like a stray hound. Not only would he have to keep an eye on the Barnes' boy, he'd have to manage his own lingering thoughts. Shelton turned to catch a glimpse of Cassidy on the other side of the Barnes wagon. Sidney reached out with his hand to help Cassidy across a rocky patch of the trail. Shelton groaned.

Thoughts of his father's almost bankrupt ranch seemed to evaporate. Cassidy Smith would be a burr in Shelton's side all the way to Oro City and beyond. If she settled with Hugo James, Shelton would have to work the claim side by side watching James covet his new bride. Shelton's gut twisted and he took a long sip of his water canister.

On the outskirts of Canon City, they made camp for the night, Shelton ordering Sidney to gather firewood, while he assisted Jet and Cassidy setting up their tent. She didn't speak to him. Well not in any civilized terms. She followed instructions with heavy sighs and eye rolls, her pout thin, her spine steel straight.

Only when Shelton started the fire, and set his own tent upright did he get a reaction from Cassidy as she shifted the poles and ropes of her tent to take her further away. Sidney appeared behind her tent and offered to help, assisting her to increase the distance from her canvas to Shelton's.

Shelton didn't need a tape to measure the distance between Cassidy's tent to Sidney's camp. *Did he warn her? No, Jet had said, never to call Cassidy's bluff.* If Jet was right, all Shelton's warning would do, would send her running to the youth to make Shelton jealous. He stirred Alice's beef stew that hung over their fire and laughed. Cassidy hadn't lifted a finger and already Shelton's envy had begun to take hold. Cassidy Smith was trouble all right; the kind of trouble that Shelton ran from at every chance and now, he questioned whether to surrender.

Chapter 14

Cassidy could feel the flames of the fire lick over her skin only slightly less heated than Shelton's narrow eyed gaze, as Sidney assisted with her tent. The sun had only a finger to go before it retired for the night and the soft sandy gradient had fatigued Cassidy's muscles enough that she wasn't far behind. Only night time brought her nightmares she wished she could happily leave behind in Pueblo. The scent of beef stew trickled through the camp, the flavors tempting Cassidy's palate and teasing her empty stomach. She should have offered to help if she hadn't been so caught up with her tent. The minute the first embers floated upwards through the air, Cassidy counted the steps from flames to her sleeping mat, the distance falling hauntingly short.

"I heard you're on your way to meet a husband in Oro City." Sidney smiled as he pulled a rope line and dragged the peg backwards.

Sighing, Cassidy didn't turn. At least she hadn't flinched this time. She had no chance surviving the Colorado wilderness if she kept letting men sneak up and scare her.

"I wouldn't put that there, Sidney, that's shale, not good for support." Cassidy said. Sidney tilted his head down and despite her instructions tried to stake the peg through the loose gravel only to strike the substrate, the dark slate colored soil breaking apart and the peg pulling from the gravel the moment Sidney tightened the guide rope. "Here is better, the soil is more clay and sandy loam."

In her peripherals, a beige Stetson lifted. Cassidy ignored it and hammered her own peg in the correct soil. Jet tried to snatch the peg from Sidney, only to have the older boy hold on tighter and wander over to Cassidy's new location.

"What's he to you anyway?" Sidney asked.

"Mister Murphy?" Cassidy tightened her rope and looped it over the tip of the pole Jet held. She then tightened the next one, "He's nothing to me."

"He doesn't look at you like nothing." Sidney said, his voice deeper than before.

"He's our guide," Jet snapped. "On three ready, one, two, three." The boys raised the center poles and the wedge tent took its final shape. Cassidy tightened the last front ropes until Jet and Sidney could finally let go.

"Just another name for a courier." Sidney wandered around the back of the tent. As Jet rushed to pull the remaining ropes tight; the tent holding steady.

"All done, thanks for your assistance, Sid."

Cassidy thought she heard a snort and even Sidney's head tilted to the fire.

After dinner Cassidy's fatigue caught up with her full stomach and she excused herself for the night. Crawling into her tent, she tied the front flaps closed and then undid her travelling dress in the dark. She redressed in her sleep gown and wrapper, glad to feel the pillow under her head despite the rocky ground under her rump. She fell asleep dreaming about the starlight ebony that watched over her. Why did the stars turn steel grey?

Shelton checked the animal lines one more time, checking Sidney had laid his sleeping mat near his folks' wagon while Leroy and Alice had climbed into the flat bed. Finally satisfied, Shelton lowered himself down to his own mat halfway between the fire and Cassidy's tent.

"Wake me if you need to." Shelton said as he pulled his Stetson over his eyes. He had no intention of sleeping not until he heard Leroy take over. Only then would Shelton get some rest before Leroy woke him for his final shift in the early hours of the morning. He told himself it made sense that he take the last watch at morning then on just after dawn. Besides he liked the morning best, the new light cascading over the nights dew, sparkling like diamonds on emeralds. That's what he told himself, not that early morning seemed to be the worst for Cassidy's night terrors, that had nothing to do with it. Nothing at all.

Sounds of crickets chirping filled the air, including the buzz-saw call of Dog Day Cicadas calling for their mates. Off in the distance the shrill bark of a Northern Saw-whet owl echoed around the pines. A chill crept into Shelton's bones as the earth cooled through the darkness. He turned to warm himself on the fire, his ears prickling to the noise of Leroy chastising a sleepy Sidney for not waking him earlier. Leroy then woke Jet.

Shelton let his mind wander in dreams of warm caramel until sleep overcame him.

"Mister Murphy...." Leroy's voice cut through the darkness, "your turn." He grumbled around a yawn.

"Thanks Leroy, any trouble?"

"A few snapped twigs here and there."

"My money is on a raccoon or elk rather than mountain cat or coyote as the animals didn't baulk." Jet said as he wiped a hand over his tired features.

Shelton agreed, "Smart boy Jet, donkeys are great guard animals that way, thanks. Sleep well."

Leroy wandered off to his wagon, not a peep could be heard from the baby thankfully.

"Night Shelton."

"Night Jet."

Shelton spent the next few hours warming himself by the fire and trying to place the Katydids that chirped around him. Movement in the brush caught his attention and like Jet he checked the animals for any unsettled reactions, none; likely a coon or even pika crawling through the underbrush in hunt of bugs.

Murmurs of the feminine variety stirred just before dawn. Shelton was on his feet, loitering at hi tent when he heard Jet offer the smallest comfort.

"Cass we're in Colorado not Chicago."

Shelton listened as the woman's voice dwindled to a soft agreement. Just as the first rays of the Colorado sun trickled through the Douglas firs and juniper bushes did Cassidy emerge from her tent. Sunlight splashed down on her pale skin turning it a warm alabaster, her messed hair shining like spun gold. She turned her chocolate gaze upon Shelton and he felt his whole body harden. Damn.

"Morning Precious." He growled unhappy as to how thick his voice sounded.

Cassidy's shoulders straightened highlighting her corset-less figure and how her sleeping garments bunched around her breasts. He ran his fingers through his hatless hair, dragging his hand down to his lips, as he watched the realization dawn on her face. True to form she didn't retreat instead she faced him, which only made Shelton groan as the light illuminated her slender form under the sheer garments.

"You wanna cover up when ah the guests are awake, Darling."

"Do I now?" Cassidy said as she walked towards the river.

"Where do you think you're going?"

"To wash, of course."

Now Shelton noticed the bundle under her left arm, clothes and a small bag no doubt containing soaps and oils that brought about her enticing blackcurrant scents.

"Wait." He rose too fast for his liking, his denims too tight in all the wrong spots but he couldn't let her walk off unprotected. "Here," he pulled his pistol from his hip and cocked it. "Point and pull the trigger. At any animal that disturbs you, you hear me."

Cassidy smiled, "What if I shoot..." she didn't finish her

sentence, clearly Shelton wasn't going to disturb her bathing and the disappointment irked her, "Fine." Cassidy gingerly took hold of the pistol, their fingers touching for the briefest moment. "You haven't taught me how to use it."

"Something tells me you can handle it." Shelton grunted and returned to the fire.

Damn, nine more nights of this!

Shelton set the coffee to brew while he waited. Sidney rose next, his eyes immediately shooting over to Cassidy's tent. With perfect timing Jet stretched his arms through the tent flap and Sidney retreated.

"Where's Cass?"

"Bathing."

"Alone!"

"Yep,"

"Shelton!"

"Relax, Jet" Although the time had ticked past and still no sight of her, "I gave her my pistol, anything or anyone disturbs here we'll hear of it."

Jet lumped himself down on a fallen log beside Shelton, "And you think that's wise?"

"You got a better idea."

The boy laughed, "I do Shelton but I don't think you'll agree." The boy set about making breakfast, frying some bacon and beans.

Shelton ignored him and stretched his legs, watching as Alice rose to the noise of Oliver squealing. The sound cut through the chilly mountain dawn. Children. Cassidy would no doubt want children with her new husband. *What man wouldn't want to have children? A man who wasn't done living yet, that's who!* Twenty-four years old was too young to settle down with a wife and kids. His parents depended on him striking it rich in Colorado. Not breeding more mouths to feed. Shelton took a long sip of his coffee. He pushed aside his thoughts and set about packing the animals. By the time Shelton poured himself a second cup of coffee, his nerves had gotten the better of him.

"Jet go check."

"I ain't getting myself shot, Shelton."

"And I should!"

"You gave her the pistol, man!" Jet smiled as he undid the tent ropes and folding the canvas. "Or I can see if Sid's brave enough."

"Don't get me thinking." Shelton cursed to himself, he didn't want Sidney getting shot and he sure as hell didn't want the boy stumbling on a half-naked Cassidy. Then Shelton's mind spun a thousand different images of Cassidy in various state of undress.

"Something wrong?"

Shelton jumped as Cassidy spoke. Then she giggled, a gentle chuckle that sung through Shelton's chest. "Don't mind us Precious."

Cassidy ran her hand down her long damp strands twirling them into a bun and pinning it above her neck. Her dark grey split skirts seemed cleaner than possible, a light blue blouse appeared damp around the collar from her wet hair. "I was washing some clothes too." Cassidy rolled a bundle of fabric tighter and the water leaked onto the ground.

"Don't take so long next time." Shelton snapped.

"Or?" Cassidy added. Her doe brown eyes alight, her cheeks tight.

Shelton froze as if blasted by the freshest blizzard. Did he take the bait? Tease her with Sidney and Shelton might as well declare game over now. "I'll send Leroy to find you."

Cassidy narrowed her gaze, "So you and Alice can get to know one another better?"

Shelton exhaled through his teeth, "Gees Precious, you don't give me much credit."

"Do you deserve it?"

Possibly not, Shelton mused. When Cassidy first met him, he had been courting Mimi back to his cabin, and then he'd spent half his time courting Cassidy with bad intentions. Then the Dove. He had meant to scare Cassidy away by showing her who he really was. He should be happy she thought him despicable, only his gut clenched. Did her deserve her praise?

"Never." Shelton replied as he marched himself to the horse lines. At least *Tango* had improved his manners. He retrieved a fresh shirt and headed to the cool water and hopefully a cooler temper.

Cassidy sighed and packed the rest of her things. Would the rest of the journey to Oro City be like this? Throwing barbs at one another to prove a point? Cassidy wanted a husband, a good, honest, reliable man. She didn't need him to be handsome with strong shoulders, a cheeky smile or worse, a sense of humor and a second sense for trouble. Shelton stalked down to the river.

By the time Shelton returned, Cassidy had her saddle bags packed. He strolled up the hillside, his crisp white linen shirt bare of the normal leather vest, the remnants of his bath plastered the shirt onto his sculptured chest. Slithers of desire trickled through Cassidy's veins, threatening to take hold of her good sense. Turning away she found Jet wandering through the bush after his own bath, pulling his grey cap back on his head before clambering onto the mule.

The morning passed achingly slow, through Canon City and north-eastwards, the trail constantly climbing, on occasion dipping into a shallow valley before climbing again. Shelton called a halt for lunch in shady woodlands littered with tall pine trees.

"If we keep this pace, we'll pass through the Royal Gorge and camp at Sulphur Gulch." Shelton said.

Jet took the hat off his head and wiped his brow, his cheeks pale as he sought the closest shade. Colorado's sun had beat down upon their trek without clouds for reprieve and even Cassidy shifted in her layers as the sweat trickled between her shoulders blades. Glad for the rest, Cassidy climbed down to the ground and helped Alice prepare a quick meal of salted beef and bread with canned peaches for dessert. Cassidy brought a plate to Jet where he lounged in the shade. Surprisingly the boy refused his serve of peaches.

"You all right?"

"Yeah, I think it's just the heat." Jet used his hat to fan his cheeks.

"We should take more breaks, I'll have a word to Shelton."

Jet snatched Cassidy's wrist, his eyes focused on Sidney, "Although I'd love you to talk to Shelton, Cass, please don't."

The man himself rested on his haunches, his eyes dark under his hat as he conversed with Leroy. Sidney snatched his plate from Alice and sauntered over to within Cassidy's eyeline. His blue eyes tracking over Cassidy first and then Jet. He smirked.

"All right."

"Good." Jet drank deep of his canteen and then belched. "I'll be right as rain."

"Always." Cassidy smiled.

"I promise."

As they entered the gorge, Cassidy gulped. She held onto the pommel of her saddle until her knuckles ached. One moment, the walls clawed to the horizon blocking out the heat, the next the mules peaked to sheer drops to the Arkansas River. More than once Cassidy held her breath, praying to whoever that Carlotta's hooves were as surefooted as any mountain goat. Soothingly the animal seemed to plod haplessly over well-worn rocky paths, whereas *Tango* seemed to dance with danger at the slightest bend. Cassidy watched Shelton as if by pure willpower alone she could keep him in his saddle. Every hundred yards, Shelton's Stetson would turn, checking the party of riders.

At one bend, the wagon bed, although narrow, skirted the edge too fine and Shelton called a halt. He marched to the rear of the wagon, ordering Jet and Sidney to help. Cassidy almost opened her mouth, except Jet sent her a curt look. Cassidy watched on in awe as Shelton shouldered the weight around the apex. Slick with sweat the shirt clung even tighter to his back muscles and Cassidy concentrated on the predicament rather than how Shelton's taunt bulk rippled under pressure.

As the afternoon sun slunk past the high peaks, the party finally reached flat ground opposite a wash out that Shelton called Sulphur Gulch.

Although Cassidy had enjoyed marveling in the high cliffs and wild horizon, the basin like appearance of their camp, eased her shoulders. The bubbling Arkansas River carved between the sharp peaks, the hush and gurgle further soothed Cassidy's nerves. A burnt section signaled where previous campers had kept their fire and Cassidy set about distancing her tent position from this epicenter. Sidney came over to help and Cassidy had no option as Jet rested on a boulder, his head in his hands.

Boot steps in gravel came to Cassidy's ears and she didn't turn as she recognized the owner. Shelton marched past his arms filled with firewood, the fabric of his shirt strained under the thickness of his biceps.

"What brings you to Twin Lakes?" Cassidy asked Sidney.

"My father was a glazier, and then a farmer. But Alice doesn't want to be a farmer's wife."

Cassidy nodded as she pulled the canvas upwards, the peaked roof rising as Sidney did the same, "And what about you?"

"I wanna get rich or what's the point to all this." The young man gestured to the steep peaks that rose around them.

The afternoon sun sat crisp over the tallest mountain, half a crescent still pouring golden light onto the opposite hillside turning the juniper bushes a bronzed olive and the blue spruces, silver.

"Oh I don't know." Cassidy mused. The harsh landscape had been muted by the tangerine sunset rays, the wild beauty glorified, even more amplified by the grandeur of their surrounds. Cassidy yearned to hear Shelton describe it in his words, the silver tongued rogue who could paint a picture with only a dozen words. She watched him now as he crouched to start the fire, his denims tight around his thighs.

"See something you like?" Shelton teased.

"Rocks." Cassidy must have rocks in her head, to look at Shelton like she did now, after his incident with the Dove.

"Igneous rock, if I'm not mistaken." Shelton said with a smile.

"Correct."

"See I did read your books."

Cassidy's lips twisted and she turned away to hide her smile. Was he trying to test her? See if she'd tolerate an unfaithful husband. Perhaps Shelton wanted his cake and to eat it too? Cassidy wouldn't settle for second place.

"Reading is one thing, appreciating a deeper understanding is a different thing entirely." Cassidy threw back. Shelton would never come to understand Cassidy or her motivations. He lived for the immediate rush, whether it was gold or women.

Shelton blew into the fire, the sparks igniting the dry tinder, "That's true, I just want to know where the treasure is." She saw Shelton's lips shape another word, she knew all too well. Precious left unsaid in Sidney's company.

Just this once Cassidy let her mind wander to the opposite, seeking the instant fulfilment that Shelton represented. "Some men don't have the patience or courage for either."

"I guess that's true about anything," Jet interrupted, "Even hunting, am I right?" Jet's cheeks still lacked color, but his blue eyes were alight.

Shelton nodded, "Yeah, you could say that."

Cassidy enjoyed the tingling sensation that rushed down her spine when Shelton turned his sugar grey eyes back to her.

"Good!" Jet slowly rose to his feet, and retrieved his notebook and pencil. Opening a fresh page he wandered over to Shelton. "First things first, what do you call each of the parts of a rifle."

"Now Jet?"

"Now is as good a time as any, I'm half a mind to join you and see what you can do." Sidney added, his shoulders broader, his chest a little more pronounced.

"Shouldn't you really rest." Cassidy shot a sharp look to Jet.

"I'm good, was just thirsty that's all." Jet smiled.

Shelton rose from beside the fire and ran his hands down his thighs. Raking her eyes down Sheltons longs legs, Cassidy sighed. She did need to know how to shoot and likely she wouldn't find a library book on the subject. Existing in Colorado wasn't enough, Cassidy had to learn how to survive. By herself. Shelton looked at her as if an eagle might swoop down and take her at any moment. If anything, Cassidy needed to show Shelton, she wasn't timid or useless, she wouldn't be a hindrance in the Colorado wilderness.

Chapter 15

Cassidy closed one eye and she stared across the long barrel. Three empty peach tins mocked her from 50 yards away.

"Line these sights up with these before you pull the trigger." Shelton's breathe caressed Cassidy's cheek. The barrel dipped.

"Pull it tight into your shoulder." Shelton whispered as his fingers wrapped over the top of her collarbone, his palm heating her shoulder. Shelton stood behind her, and Cassidy's finger twitched. The trigger spring tight, she squeezed gently. Nothing.

"It's got a kick so lean in," Shelton's breath caressed her cheek. A boom slammed into her chest, the retort crackled in her ears and the peach can tumbled backwards off its boulder.

"Ah ha!" Jet shouted raising his notebook in one hand and pencil in the other, "That's better than me."

Cassidy would have cheered right along with him if she hadn't stumbled backwards into Shelton's bulk, his arms around hers, hands sliding down her forearms to retrieve the rifle.

"Nice work."

His praise worked its way under her skin sending a rush of color to her cheeks. Cassidy stepped away. Sidney rested on a boulder next to Jet with both elbows on his knees, his hands cupping his chin.

"Do you want another try Jet?" Shelton asked as he reloaded the rifle.

"Ah," he mocked re-reading his notes as he wiped his brow, "Not just yet, maybe tomorrow."

Cassidy tilted her head and regarded the boy's condition.

He had perked up somewhat, but still his cheeks were pale. He needed a full belly and a good night's rest.

"I'll have a go." Sidney stepped off his stone seat and stalked over to Shelton. Taking the rifle in one hand, the older boy wandered over to the peach can and took it further away.

"Wanna wager?" Sidney whispered as he returned next to Shelton. The high slopes of the mountains echoed every tiny sound. Shelton knew Sidney ran headfirst into trouble, and trouble always found Shelton.

"What did you have in mind?" Shelton said.

"A shoot out."

"Oh yeah and what's the prize?"

"I ain't a fool Shelton. I know somethings amiss with you and Cassidy and I want a shot."

Shelton found his lips twist and tried to work it into a smile, "You want a shot at Miss Cassidy Smith?"

Sidney grinned, "I'm 19 next month and I know there ain't much women up the mountain."

"There's a few."

"Yeah and if they aren't already taken, they don't look like her." Sidney said as he brought the rifle up to his eye-line.

The kid was right, they don't look like Cassidy. They wouldn't be as smart or as charming. They might be more honest though? What happens if he won? Shelton thought to ask, but he already knew the answer. "Take your best shot, kid."

Cassidy shivered at the sight of Shelton and Sidney whispering to each other. Shelton stood taller, and broader, his movements languid and confident. "I should get back, Alice will need help with dinner."

"Alice looks like she's enjoying the break, Cass."

Turning, Cassidy saw Alice standing over the pot while Leroy rocked awkwardly back and forth on his heels with Ollie in his arms.

Jet leaned his head on Cassidy's shoulder as they sat together on the rocks, "When you're married you can cook all the dinners you want, right now enjoy the show."

"What show?"

Jet just grinned.

Cassidy wrapped one hand around Jet and the other clutched between her knees, as a chill crept into the air. Sidney's jaw cinched as he raised the rifle. One peach can flew backwards, then the next and then the final can tumbled to the gravel. Shelton reset the cans and took his shot. Faster the retorts sounded, the smoother the action between shots and reloads. All three cans struck.

Sidney picked up the cans and paced further out, when he returned, he handed Shelton the rifle.

Again the three peach cans blasted off their stone perches, as Shelton reset the cans for the younger man. Sidney shot all three without struggle. It wasn't until the fourth round that Shelton took a moment's hesitation between each shot as dusk brought with it a firm breeze that corralled between the valleys, kicking up dust to blind the shooters. The cans tumbled backwards, one, two three.

In the fifth round, Sidney cursed. The second can remained upright. He levelled the rifled and aimed again. The third can wobbled but stayed upright.

Shelton took the rifle from the boy grinning as he did so. His shoulders ached, the recoil of the Winchester echoed through his muscles, but he couldn't let the boy know that. He waited until Sidney turned his back and then squinted at the targets. Shelton took another moment to wipe his brow. Damn the boy could shoot. Then again, Shelton had grown up with Marcus who, together with the red-haired hell-fire Jewel Daniels, had sharpened Shelton's skills. For a moment, Shelton thought of Cassidy meeting Jewel and laughed out loud. Sidney growled. Shelton lifted the barrel and aimed. One. Then he thought of Cassidy meeting Cade's wife, the blonde wildcat, Evie. Two. Finally the image of Cassidy meeting, his mother, the matriarch, Temperance Lovena Murphy popped into Shelton's mind. Three.

The youth's jaw cinched as he shook Shelton's hand, "You can shoot."

"So can you kid, what's next boxing?" Shelton joked.

"Just say so." Sidney replied, not an ounce of mirth about his words.

Shelton snorted. Damn he'd thought the boy would be subdued, "You're still on first watch."

"Fine."

"Next time we'll hunt, see how you go with a moving target."

Sidney murmured something under his breath and Shelton ignored him, as they made their way back to their audience. At each step, Shelton let his mind wander again. The distance decreasing as he approached Cassidy where she sat, perched on a boulder with her knees high, the hem line of her split skirts revealing the dragonfly boots. Cassidy stood and for a moment, Shelton thought about Cassidy waiting to greet him. The boulder became the Blue Cow back porch, the Colorado jagged sky line a perfect Texas sunset. Cassidy's cheeks blushed, she licked her lips and Shelton resisted the urge to encircle her waist with his hands. The ache in his arms would ease immediately if soothed by Cassidy's suppleness.

Before Shelton could say anything, the woman retreated to the fire without so much of a 'congratulations', while Jet stood to shake their hands. Shelton tracked her movements as Cassidy sat next to Alice and engaged her in conversation. Within moments Leroy approached with Ollie in his hands and lowered the sleeping child awkwardly into Cassidy's arms. Shivers of ice slid down Shelton's spine. Cassidy's eyes met his across the flames, her luscious pout now thin, her shoulders slumped.

Marriage came with children and children meant more responsibility. Instinctively Shelton's finger dug under his collar and tugged. The quicker he could get this lease agreement sorted with Hugo, the better he'd sleep.

After Shelton washed up, Cassidy dished out the dinner.

"Do you mind?" Cassidy whimpered and Alice, only too happy to oblige delivered Shelton's dinner instead of Cassidy. Shelton thanked Alice with his best Delano grin, adding a flurry of compliments as an afterthought. Across the fire, Cassidy clicked her tongue. Shelton winked.

Jet slowly shoveled the stew past his lips giving up halfway. "I'm beat, I think I'll turn in. Don't forget to wake me Mister Barnes. Now that I know my way around a rifle, I don't want to miss out."

"Sure thing boy." Leroy raised a mug in Jet's direction as the boy made his way to Cassidy's tent. "I s'pose I better turn in soon too." He grumbled. "But not until I wash the dishes, come on Sid you can help me."

"Washing is women's work."

"When you whine like that? Come on, son." Leroy motioned to clip Sidney over the ear and the boy leaned backwards out of range.

Shelton took his opportunity and handed his empty bowl to Sidney. "I'll check the mule lines." He didn't want to, he wanted to sit opposite Cassidy and make that icy glare of hers melt. The crackling flames consuming the logs until nothing but ash remained seemed to mock Shelton's plight. Without fire, the fallen wood weathered away enjoying a long but boring existence. Yet with fire, the spark of life, it became consumed, changed beyond repair. Shelton wandered down the horse lines pushing thoughts of ice and fire out of his mind.

"Um Shelton."

"Yeah Precious."

With the fire at her back, shadows eclipsed Cassidy's features, "I wanted to apologize for not..." She cleared her throat, "...making my position known earlier, about the claim and the lease agreement." A quaver in her voice tugged in Shelton's chest.

Damn! He closed the distance to meet her. Now her shoulders shuddered, she inhaled a short sharp breath. Like a whirlpool of trouble, Shelton found himself within inches of Cassidy. One finger slid under her chin as he stepped past her, tilting her face to the light. Not a single tear could be seen on her pearlescent cheeks, "What are you playing at?"

"Nothing, I just wanted to apologize." Cassidy retreated, her lips tight, brows furrowed.

"Now, now you're up to something." Shelton's voice came thick and smooth to Cassidy's ears.

She had wanted to make amends, more to the point she had hoped her apology might initiate his. She didn't want to bicker the entire way around the mountain range. Honesty. She had sworn to herself to live an honest life in Colorado!

"I thought since I said I was sorry..."

Shelton's head tilted back as a rich laugh rumbled from his throat, "I've got nothing to apologize for, Precious."

Cassidy's fists pumped, a rush of heat clawed at her veins, "Is that what you told Frankie Delgardo's wife?" She turned on her heel and headed for the fire.

Shelton's hand caught her elbow; he spun her onto his hard chest, his breath now ragged. The pressure at her elbow released. With the half-light of the fire, Shelton's sugar greys eyes turned to pits of mercury. Shelton whispered, "Frankie Delgardo laid into his wife so I laid into him."

Shelton's gaze targeted Cassidy's mouth as his arms slunk around her waist. She clutched his biceps as suddenly Shelton leaned forward and tipped her off balance.

His lips captured hers and met no resistance. Cassidy savored the slow slake of his tongue and the coil of desire it unfurled in her abdomen. Winding her arms around his neck she pulled herself forward, her breasts compressed against his bulk. Shelton's arms tightened, one tracked southwards to cup her buttock, pulling her hips hard against his. Cassidy gasped and Shelton relented, only briefly to kiss along her jaw. She drew breath and finally spoke, "And the Victorian Dove?"

Shelton stepped back, retreating until Cassidy stood safely on both feet, "You saw exactly what happened. Everything. Nothing more." Fingers wound through Cassidy's and pulled them from his neck. Without another word, Shelton disappeared into the darkness beyond the animal lines.

Shelton Murphy wasn't worth it! Straightening her hair and skirts, Cassidy stalked back to the fire. She'd apologized and his slick moves had her climbing into his arms without a word of sorry from the man. He'd purposely plopped a painted lady on his lap and hadn't the nerve to apologize. Even after she'd made amends! Damn the man to Purgatory. At least she had enough composure to bid good night to Alice before she retreated to her tent. Jet didn't make a sound or move from facing the canvas wall as Cassidy undressed and dressed in the dark. Her lumpy pillow caught her head and muffled her tears.

Shelton waited until he saw Cassidy's tent close before he returned to the fire. Sidney and Leroy returned from washing the dishes in the river, Sidney's eyes darted to the empty spot and Cassidy's closed tent before he shrugged his shoulders and sat down. Shelton handed him the rifle and set his own sleeping mat into position. The boy would have to step over Shelton to get anywhere near Cassidy's tent.

He listened as Alice chatted away to Leroy, plans she'd made for their future, in between feeding and soothing the baby Oliver. Shelton droned out her words with thoughts of home. He had tried to use the Dove to push Cassidy away, and yet, with her in front of him, her pout calling him forward while her eyes tried to burn him to dust, he couldn't resist. He'd undone all the distance he'd created with his ruse in Pueblo. Damn! Her lithe frame against his arousal had sent shockwaves through his body. Shelton needed to think about cattle, specifically the Blue Cow cattle starving, the dry grass and the tick fever and his Pa's grey hair. Shelton's sister had gotten herself a husband and solved her problems and now their parents suffered. Perhaps Cassidy was doing the same? He resolved to ask her; only this time, from a distance where his palms wouldn't twitch to hold her.

"Your turn Shelton."

Shelton focused on the rotund shape of Leroy standing over him, the rifle in one hand, both eyes encircled in red.

Shelton sat upright and scrubbed a hand over his face, the whiskers on his cheeks seemed longer overnight. He'd shave in the morning. Wait it was morning. He looked around the camp, an eerie stillness settled through the early hours. The fire had dwindled down to healthy coals, only the surrounding logs were bare.

"Where's Jet?"

Leroy yawned, "I tried to wake him, but he didn't come out. I didn't think it proper to go in."

Shelton slapped him gently on the shoulder, "Good man." Jet shirking work? Not that the boy seemed keen about heavy lifting, but he had been excited to have the rifle by his side. "Any trouble?"

"None. Not a peep, not even an owl."

A shiver stole over Shelton. Silence wasn't good.

Shelton kept his opinions to himself as he rose, stretching he surveyed the darkness beyond the reach of the fire. What kind of predator lurked out there in the shadows, man or beast? Retrieving his rifle, Shelton bid goodnight to Leroy and wandered around his normal position in front of the dwindling flames. He tossed more logs onto the fire until it billowed a healthy amount of light before he set off behind the tents. Slowly Shelton made a full circle of their camp, crouching low and weaving through the animal lines he paused. *Tango* stayed silent, as did the mules. Even *Ole Missy* dozed on her feet.

Shelton completed another full lap, stopping every so often to listen as a chorus of chirps and clicks erupted in the underbrush. Soft murmurs and moans rippled from Cassidy's tent. For a moment his mind imagined those same noises under very different circumstances. Shelton scolded his despicable thoughts as he returned to the fallen log at the front of the fire.

He made himself a cup of coffee enjoying the cool that sunk through his limbs only to have it melt by the warmth of the fire and the bitter brew. These were the easy nights, the calm before the storm. The moment he arrived at the claim, he'd be put to work. Gold needed to be unearthed. The placer boxers had to be built, with Jet's design in mind of course, and then a shaft to find the lode, head frame and so on, if Hugo hadn't started already. Not to mention repairing the second cabin fit for human habitation. The claim had one main cabin already built, with loft bed and stove. The second outbuilding had been built for the previous grubstakers on Smith's claim. The roof had caved in with Colorado snow at some point and never been repaired. Would Cassidy want to take residence at the claim? Shelton couldn't see why not. If she found Hugo James amenable, if he agreed to her lease marriage, then of course she would live with her husband. Shelton squirmed where he sat at the idea of sharing a roof with Cassidy and her new husband.

Soft light of pre-dawn crept across the landscape, the murky browns and muted greys blooming in pinks, peaches and lilacs, sliding down the sharp peaks, to illuminate the valley they camped in. Cassidy's tent shifted, the canvas parting as the woman herself stepped into the light.

"Shelton?" Her cheeks were pinched, lines of sleep still pressed into her skin.

He rose instantly at the sharpness of her voice, "What is it?"

"It's Jet, he's not waking up."

Shelton took long strides that brought him right up to Cassidy. She opened the tent flaps and followed him inside.

Jet lay on his side, his mouth slack, his skin pale. A lump rose in Shelton's throat. He knelt beside the boy and placed a hand on his forehead, almost retracting it instantly as if scolded. "He's burning up, Jet! Jet!" Shelton gently rocked him with no response. Shelton held his breath and rolled him again. This time, a dull moan rumbled from Jet.

"Jet, please....Jet." The crack in Cassidy's voice shattered something inside of Shelton.

He rocked him again, "Jet, man!"

"I'm fine." The boy whispered, his eye lids fluttering, lips parched.

Shelton pulled back the blankets to reveal Jet's arm clutched across his abdomen. The boy winced.

"You don't look fine." Shelton said.

Jet didn't reply, his features twisted again.

Shelton looked to Cassidy. Her eyes wild and filling with liquid, hands covering her mouth. She looked at Shelton. His heart leapt into his throat. Think damn it! Shelton ran his hands over the boy's frame. Jet groaned again.

"He was unwell yesterday, said his head ached." Cassidy's words tumbled over one another, "I told him to rest."

A myriad of illnesses and diseases ran through Shelton's mind. Was it an infection? "Did he hurt himself?" An infection could bring a fever, the fatigue, yet the pain in his stomach was something different.

"Not that I know of..." Cassidy sunk down to her knees and pulled Jet's head into her hands.

Snake? "A cut, a bite, a sting....." Shelton paused. He tore Jet's clothes from his shoulders, lifting his arms one by one. Not a snake but a pest all the same. Parasite to be exact.

"Shelton be careful!" Cassidy hissed as Jet groaned louder, his arm returning to hug his stomach.

"Tick, look for ticks, in any soft flesh..." Shelton lifted Jet's trouser leg and tugged off his socks. Nothing.

"Shelton!"

His eyes met red ringed chocolate. Cassidy's hands trembled as she turned Jet's head to one side. Behind one ear a swollen coffee colored lump could be seen.

Relief flooded Shelton's system as he sighed. He offered Cassidy a thin smile as he wiped his fringe back from his eyes, "Got any tweezers?"

Chapter 16

Cassidy scrambled to her vanity case and pulled out a thin pair of tweezers and handed them to Shelton. He pinched the patch of skin behind Jet's ear and dug under the insects head. The skin stretched with the first tug, the sections wanted to separate. Shelton calmed his tremors and slid the tweezers further under. With one swift movement he pulled it clear. Cassidy exhaled as Shelton crushed it under his boot heel.

Liquid rushed to fill her eyelids, Cassidy turned her back as Shelton moved over Jet, pulling and tugging his clothing, double checking all he could of the boy's weakened frame. She was responsible for Jet and she'd let him become sick. Of course she'd read about ticks and other dangers in Colorado. Why hadn't she thought to warn Jet? She'd been too busy pining for Shelton. He touched her shoulder and she leapt in her skin.

"He needs water and rest."

"I'll get it," Cassidy rose to her feet.

"No I'll get it Cass, you need to check yourself. I won't have both of you going down sick." Shelton strode through the front canvas, leaving Cassidy frayed. His voice had been darker, a snap, irritation that she hadn't done her duty in looking after Jet. Was he worried the boy's condition would slow down his mining dreams? She clawed over her own body, checking all the soft spots she could before Shelton returned. Cassidy worked her way back to Jet's side.

"Jet," She ran her hands through his brown fringe, the hair damp. A drop of blood could be seen where the tick had been. She wiped it with a cloth and then wiped his brow again. "You'll be okay, Jet, wont you?"

Someone coughed outside the tent entrance.

"Come in."

Shelton dipped under the low canvas roof and knelt beside Jet. Cassidy wet a handkerchief and wiped Jet's face. Under the cool water the youth stirred. Shelton tipped the flask to his lips, "Drink a bit and then some more." Shelton ordered.

"Shelton can you take me outside?" Jet moaned.

"I can..."

"No Cass," his voice soft yet determined. Jet focus seemed to waiver.

Shelton looped one of Jet's arms over his neck and he brought the boy to his feet. Wobbling, the two of them gingerly made their way outside. Cassidy threw herself down against her blankets, covering her face with her hands and her sobs with the pillow. As if a hammer rested on her ribs, she sucked down deep breaths. She couldn't bare it. Jet sick and all because of her and now she couldn't even help him.

Twigs snapped, as boot heels dragged across the ground.

"What's wrong with him?" Sidney's harsh tone cut through the morning air.

"Mind your own..." Jet tried only to be cut down by Shelton.

"Tick. Check yourself before we move out."

Cassidy gasped. Move out? Shelton intended on travelling with Jet in this condition? Clearly Shelton didn't want to delay his payment from the Barnes, or his claim couldn't wait. Perhaps Shelton wanted to be rid of Cassidy. The sooner the better, she mused. Wiping away her tears, Cassidy dressed for a battle. Jet would not be moved for Shelton's greed.

By the time Shelton brought Jet back to the tent, the boy's cheeks had flushed with color, his fringe still damp and legs still wobbling.

"Listen."

Shelton froze as Cassidy rounded on him.

"We're not going anywhere until Jet is better."

Shelton snorted as he helped Jet back to his sleeping mat,

"Nice try Precious, but we're packing up and moving out."

"He's not well enough to travel, you said so yourself, he needs water and rest."

Shelton stalked out of the tent with Cassidy hot on his heels.

"With any luck he'll be fine."

"Any luck?" Cassidy's voice sounded higher than she liked. "It wasn't luck that brought this on." Cassidy crossed her arms clutching her own stomach. If only she'd thought to warn Jet. Take precautions. Tears threatened her composure.

Shelton pivoted at the entrance way, trapping her against the canvas. "Yeah that might be so, but we can get the boy some medical attention in Texas Creek or further along in Coaldale. Not here."

"Oh." Cassidy said, and bit her lip.

"So get ready to leave in half an hour. Leroy," Shelton hailed the older man, picking up his own sleeping mat in the process.

Cassidy lingered a moment longer to watch Shelton inform Leroy and Alice, their wagon would become a stretcher. Alice busied herself with the wagon while Leroy just nodded. Sidney stood to one side watching Cassidy and then Shelton before turning away.

She didn't have the energy or the time to decipher Sidney's mood and instead ducked inside the tent to set about her task.

"I'll be all right Cass, just you wait and see." Jet whimpered.

"Always." Cassidy beamed her best smile at him as she rolled her sleeping mat, "Only a few more miles to go and you'll have the best seat in the house."

Jet snorted and closed his eyes, fresh beads of sweat broke out on his forehead.

Shelton hurried to take what he could of Leroy and Alice's belongings, shoving them into the saddle bags attached to Jet's mule. He then redistributed the weight around where he'd placed his sleeping mat and where Jet would eventually rest. Cassidy's harsh blizzard had scolded him to his core; no doubt she was placing the blame squarely at Shelton's feet. He'd never been good with responsibility, always only one step ahead of mortal danger himself, how could he look after others. Not a wife, children, not even a fourteen year old street kid who'd done fine surviving on his own.

Shelton's shoulders eased as soon as he'd seen the tick. Tick fever he could deal with, any other mystery illness and the idea of watching Jet slip away helplessly would cut Shelton in half. As it was, watching the agony on Cassidy's face at the boy's condition had sliced through to his heart. He considered setting *Tango* in the harness, only worried the big animal would balk at carrying the wagon. He'd try after Texas Creek. Shelton ran his hand down the rump of Ole Misty, she whinnied and stomped her hooves. Clearly she didn't think highly of Shelton either. Seeing the disappointment in those doe brown eyes of Cassidy's, and her comment, it wasn't luck. Yeah, Shelton counted on luck too many times.

"Pretty weak." Sidney snorted.

Shelton's fist shot out, twisting around Sidney's collar, "You know nothing about Jet. I'd wager on him to outlast you any day."

Sidney twisted in Shelton's grip, his balled fists came up to smack down on Shelton's wrist. One aimed at his gut but Shelton turned his hip and the blow missed.

"How about from now on you keep your opinions to yourself." The fabric slipped through Shelton's fingers and Sidney stumbled backwards. Blue eyes blazoned a path of fury at Shelton and the boy's shoulder retracted. Shelton stepped to the side, his other arm pushing Sidney's flying fist towards the wagon. The youth struck the timber with a grunt.

"Oi!" Leroy's shout came over the side of the wagon.

Shelton exhaled slowly. He wasn't about to hit a kid even if the boy had a smart mouth.

"You listen to me." Leroy barked.

Here it comes, Shelton sighed. Now he'd have Leroy on his back too.

"Don't you give Shelton any lip you hear me boy. Do as you're told and pack up."

With a tug of his shirt, Sidney jaw cinched. He turned on his heel and stalked away. Shelton stabbed his fingers through his fringe. He was wound tighter than a two dollar watch. Never took himself for a bully, but Sidney had been riding his last nerve. He reached over to lift the last crate of cans when he realized Cassidy's presence; standing next to a cluster of hers and Jet's things, with one hand clasped around her locket and the other on the middle of her narrow waist. Damn! She'd seen him snap. On seconds thoughts, Cassidy should see him as he is, raw, exposed, unfiltered including his language, gambling, drinking and carousing right down to his temper. Tilting his head, Shelton acknowledged her. Cinnamon gemstones glistened in the bright dawn light.

"You ready?" He snapped.

Her brows furrowed, a scowl reset on her face, "Yes."

"Good."

Why did his shoulders suddenly itch? Turning he saw Cassidy watching him, her cinnamon gaze had melted to chocolate, her pinched lips now turned upwards at the corners, the hand at her locket now clutched between her breasts. Wistful? Only for a second before she flinched and her scowl returned. A grin split Shelton's cheeks.

Cassidy tried not to let Shelton's grin affect her. Too late. She rolled her lips inwards to hide her burgeoning smile. Then he winked. Cassidy turned away as she caught the chuckle in her throat. She'd heard him tear down Sidney for Jet. The fierceness of his words threaded a golden ribbon into Cassidy's chest, working its way through the pressure she felt at Jet's condition. She needed to remember Shelton wanted the claim for gold, gold and quick satisfaction with any woman. Not a wife. Likely he saw Jet's sickness as Cassidy's fault, rightly so. She had brought Jet out from the city, to fulfill her selfish dreams of finding a husband.

Try as she might Cassidy's heart sank further and further into a quagmire. The hope of a resolution from Shelton seemed unlikely, yet her yearning intensified. It was high time Cassidy was honest with herself.

As soon as Jet settled in the back of the wagon, Cassidy clambered into her saddle and throughout the trail kept *Carlotta* as close to Jet's sick bed as possible. The sun climbed the high peaks, the scenery changing from gentle peaches to vibrant pinks. The skyline reminded Cassidy of shattered steel, the fragments sharp and uneven, some daunting cliff faces, others rounded crests blanketed in emeralds and saffron.

With each stop Shelton ordered, Cassidy crouched beside Jet and gave him sips from her water canister, protesting that he was fine and should be riding a mule instead. By the time they reached Texas Creek at lunch, he'd fallen asleep again.

Cassidy stomped up the timber stairs to the Druggist, her navy hems dusted with fine grey silt of the gravel trail. The inside of the false-front building, Cassidy's eyes adjusted to the darkness. Lines of shelves ran down each side, the goods sparse, some bottles coated in a thick film of dirt. At the far end a narrow bench ran from wall to wall, the table top littered with bottles and jars, books and powders. The scent of mint and the sickly almond scent of arsenic blended together.

The Pharmacist stood behind the counter and pulled down his rounded glasses, to peer at Cassidy, one hand hovering over his scales with a small pouch of leather.

"Can I help ya, Ma'am?"

"Wait ya turn!" barked a man who leaned against the grim coated window. He wore a black Stetson, and his wiry beard touched his chest, his moustache twisted at both ends.

"Did I hear that right?" Shelton stepped into the apothecary, and pulled his hat off his head. With his broad shoulders, he almost blocked the light from outside.

The man stood upright, both hips heavy with holsters.

Shelton didn't move. With his crooked nose he looked like a seasoned brawler. The pistol on his hip hinted otherwise. They couldn't delay with a fist fight in the streets. Or worse.

Cassidy tried her sweetest voice, "Excuse me, us for intruding sir, my brother is ill, we think, with Tick Fever. We were hoping you had something that might help him."

The chemist lowered the pouch of leather, his eyes glued to the tiny stream of gold flakes that tumbled onto his scales, "Have you removed the tick?"

"Yes."

"Then there's nothing I can do." The chemist reset his glasses as he watched the scale move in tiny increments. He dipped his hand into his waist coat pocket and sniffed.

The miner crossed his arms over his chest and resumed leaning against the window. As Cassidy stepped further inside, she wanted to hold her nose against the onslaught of the men's body odor. Shelton stepped forward and Cassidy gestured for him to stay quiet.

"Surely there is something you can do?" She took stock of the ingredients on the bench, quickly reading the labels, and assessing the chemist's skill. She could see creams, bitters, tinctures and a pill press. His fingers were stained in orange. Although his focus remained on the scales, his other hand hovered over his vest pocket.

"That's only 2 grains worth there."

"Two again!" The customer slammed his palms down on the bench.

Cassidy's patience had worn out. She eyed the scales, a stray piece of metal caught her eye.

"I said there is nothing I can do," He pushed his glasses up his nose and began to mark down his ledger. "The fever will take about ten days from start to finish. All I could offer is pain relief for the aches."

"Well, if you don't mind, Mister...." Cassidy addressed the miner who now chewed a toothpick between his teeth.

The customer clicked his tongue, "Me names Joe."

"Right, Mister Joe, if you would indulge me the time to speak with Mister...."

"Franklin, Herbert Franklin." The chemist twitched. "I said I could offer pain relief, although it's unnecessary."

Cassidy moved between the men and placed her hands on the bench. Joe snorted as Cassidy leaned over the counter. "You could, but you wont?" She didn't even waste the effort trying to bat her eyelids.

"No."

Joe took three steps back as Shelton closed the distance.

"You what...?" Shelton said.

"Shelton please," Cassidy interrupted. She could handle this. She watched the chemist twitch, the sweat beading on his top lip. She could more than handle this.

The chemist ran his finger under his nose and sniffed, "There's really no need to waste supplies."

Cassidy ran her eyes over his disheveled form, certain she knew exactly where the pain relief supplies were going.

"Mister Joe, why don't you ask the good Franklin here, to weigh one of his bottles instead?"

"Excuse me!" The Chemist hissed.

Cassidy's eyes tracked to the sliver of metal that had been jammed into the main fulcrum, "Ask him, if he doesn't mind to weigh one of his bottles. This one perhaps." She pointed to the largest murky glass container she could see that would fit in the gold scales. "Perhaps the bottle will be more than 2 grains worth, perhaps it won't."

"Hey?" Joe grunted, digging in his ear.

She leaned forward, Shelton's hand touched on Cassidy's shoulder and she shrugged it off, she needed to be closer, "Mister Franklin knows full well, that bottle is going to weigh more than 2 grains but his scale ain't gonna move." Cassidy took a step to the side, bringing her closer to the end of the bench.

The Chemist's blew out his cheeks, his piggy eyes wider than before, he dab his nose again, "What are you insinuating?"

"You're scales are faulty and you ain't doing a thing to fix them."

"Herbert Franklin!" The miner boomed as he pulled out his pistol, "Weigh the damn bottle!"

Franklin retreated from the firearm levelled at his nose and stepped into Cassidy's orbit, her hand was as swift as her tongue, "Thank you for your time Mister Franklin."

A pressure on her elbow pulled her towards the door and she shook off Shelton's grip as she landed in the street.

"Happy now?"

Cassidy pulled out the chemist's personal supply of Laudanum, the brown opium laced tincture only half full in its slender bottle. "Jet needs pain relief."

"And you would do anything to get it?"

"I..." Cassidy's gut clenched as Shelton's nostrils flared, "I wasn't leaving without it."

"From you, I expect nothing less."

Bile climbed the back of Cassidy's throat, her fingers numb begging to be pressed into her churning gut. She held her breath until Shelton stalked away.

"Hey!"

Joe, the miner, stood in the street, one hand clutched his leather pouch while crooked fingers on his other hand gestured to Cassidy, "No heavy hands with that stuff, you hear."

Cassidy looked down to see the bottle of Laudanum she held, "Sure."

"Serious." Joe tipped his black brim to Cassidy and then to Shelton who hovered unannounced over Cassidy's right shoulder.

Lifting her navy skirts, Cassidy climbed into the back of the wagon and lifted Jet's head. He stirred and sat upright, squinting at the bright sunlight. "What's this?"

"It'll take the pain away."

"Hell yeah." Jet held a hand over his forehead as Cassidy added a drop under his tongue.

"That's all you get. Are you hungry?"

"Maybe later Cass." Jet laid down on his mat and threw an arm over his eyes.

The wagon jolted and Cassidy vacated the timber structure while Shelton eased *Tango* into the harness. First he ran his hand down the beast's mane, then down to his withers, whispering all the while Shelton advanced. *Tango* retreated, whickering as he moved into position. Patiently Shelton worked his way down the animal, muttering reassurances as he affixed the harness. *Tango's* neck twisted, his muzzle touching Shelton's shoulder. The man ran his hand down the animal's nose and patted his rump.

"You gotta trust me Boy." Shelton's voice drifted to Cassidy where she stood by the wagon's side watching as he calmed the big animal. Such a shame the man was unreliable and kept unsavory company. And he had the nerve to chastise her for her dishonesty. Cassidy's stomach rolled again. She'd promised herself to live an honest life. *Why did it have to be such a difficult path?*

Shelton's palm itched as the coarse hair of *Tango* slid underneath it. He'd thought the horse would baulk at the harness and had been happily surprised. Cade had trained the horse well. Shelton just had to sooth the beast's nerves. He almost laughed. Out of his peripherals he could see Cassidy waiting by the side of the wagon, her eyes judging his every move. She had been fierce inside the Chemist. Fierce, determined and wily. For Jet, for her family. Shelton had no doubt that Cassidy would be a loyal wife. Except he didn't have time for a wife. Not yet anyway.

Chapter 17

Shades of ochre, aqua and saffron blended together like dyes from cheap silk, leaving the Colorado sky awash with tender hues that caressed the dusk. Cassidy exhaled slowly as the cool night air seeped into her bones and refreshed her weary limbs. Shelton had finally called a halt to their journey on the outskirts of a place he called Howard, and Cassidy had rushed to complete all the camp tasks she could, leaving Jet more time to recover. It meant she had to spend more time with Sidney assisting her tent and winking as he did so. She contemplated slipping the teenager a dose of Laudanum to calm his amorous glances.

Cassidy took no time excusing herself to help Alice, knowing full well, Sidney did all in he could to avoid his new mother. With dinner served and Ollie needing feeding, Alice excused herself. Within moments, Sidney had settled next to Cassidy, offering her a sip from his coffee mug.

The scent of whiskey tickled Cassidy's nose, "No thank you. I better check Jet."

"Shelton has him." Sidney added with a wink.

She made a mental note to thank Shelton for shouldering Jet to the woodlands where he could relieve himself. "Well, he will still need to eat." Excusing herself, Cassidy stooped to the pot of bacon and vegetables and filled an extra plate.

"Gee it smells good." Jet grumbled as he limped to the fire, Shelton behind him. Cassidy rushed to his side with plate in hand. Gingerly he sat down and with trembling hands took the plate from her.

"How do you feel?"

"Fine!" Jet grunted, "Fine, thanks Cass, I'm fine." He added, his eyes like slits as he watched Sidney from across the fire.

"I see." Cassidy said, taking her place on the fallen log beside him. He didn't need her fussing all over him, weakening him further in the eyes of the older boy. "Well, you didn't miss much."

"Not the way I hear it." Jet mumbled around a mouthful of dinner, "Fixed a pair of crooked scales in Texas Creek."

Cassidy looked to Shelton on instinct, his blue grey eyes downcast, his lips thin. The man had badmouthed her to Jet? The younger boy grinned, a smear of grease on his chin. What was Shelton playing at, running her down to her family? Did he expect Jet to support him? True, Jet had forced Cassidy to own up to her deception with Shelton and the lease agreement. Who knew the boy would become such a tattle-tale?

"Well I did the right thing." Cassidy said.

"That's open to interpretation." Shelton smirked.

"No it isn't." Cassidy replied. Jet needed medicine, the Chemist was a crooked thief. She ought to know.

"How did you know what he was doing?" Sidney asked, his words slurring together.

Cassidy inhaled and twisted her locket twice for good measure. "My father told me some of the tricks they try up here in the mines." Told or taught? Cassidy mused. Taught. Julius Smith had tried his and Cassidy's hand at multiple fraudulent practices. Weighting the scales had only been one. "Plus, the tine of metal he'd used didn't match the plated gold of his scales. Easy to pick when you know what you're looking for."

"Your father was a smart man." Sidney added.

Shelton paced behind the younger boy and took the cup from his fingers, he took a whiff and tossed the contents onto the dirt, "You're on first watch."

Sidney twisted his neck slowly to look up at Shelton, who held the younger man's gaze. Sidney nodded.

Jet snorted and the cutlery jangled on his plate.

Leroy rose to his feet. "I'm beat, after I wash these dishes, I'm turning in. Don't forget to wake me and don't go giving anymore lip you hear me boy."

Sidney grunted as he handed his plate to his father, only to have Shelton hand him a fresh mug, the steam wafting from the bitter brew.

"One of us will." Shelton said.

Cassidy yawned into her fist. One of them? Was Shelton doing a double watch? "I'll lend a hand."

"Rubbish, you've done enough for today," Leroy said as he snatched her plate, "Get some rest."

Cassidy stole away to the tent and took her time undressing and redressing for bed. Once she'd tugged her tea gown around her, she folded her clothes, ready to wash them tomorrow morning. She set the bottle of Laudanum nearby, ready if Jet needed it during the night. Joes' warning echoed in her mind. Eventually she curled up on her sleeping mat and tucked the chilly blankets around her.

A gust of wind slipped through the canvas as the front flaps flew open, "Sorry." Shelton rushed as he assisted Jet through the tent. "I'm fine Shelton, seriously tomorrow I'll be on guard duty I promise."

"Uh-huh." Shelton said, catching the slightest grin from Cassidy. He didn't dare linger too long, the tent thick with tantalizing blackcurrant scents, the woman herself all soft and luscious curled up in her sleeping blankets like a luxurious feline. "Until then, rest easy, my man." Shelton turned on his heel, glad for the icy blast as he entered the night air.

With one eye on Sidney, Shelton moved his sleeping mat closer to the front of Cassidy's tent. If Jet needed him in the middle of the night, he needed to be close. Right? That's what he told himself anyway. Sidney sipped his coffee, the rifle tight in his grip as Shelton reclined on his mat with one saddle bag behind him for support.

"Up ya get Shelton," Leroy's gruff voice cut through the fog. The crackle and hiss of the fire soothed his irritation at being woken.

"Yeah I'm up." Shelton yawned, "Anything?"

"Nothing. Animals are fine."

"Good. Night Leroy."

"Night." The older man rubbed his shoulders with his hands and crept over the gravel to climb into his wagon; the man's bed already warmed by his wife Alice. Lucky Leroy, Shelton thought until he replayed those words in his head.

Shelton stretched and shivered, walking off the cool by checking the mule lines and building the fire up brighter. He'd trade the cold for the warmth of a Texas sun and a good woman any day. Shelton shook his head. Brewing coffee should keep his mind off Cassidy, so he set about making himself a pot.

No sooner had he finished his first cup that a murmur spoiled his composure. Feminine, quiet, and filled with agony, Cassidy's voice cut through the thin mountain air. Shelton crawled to the outside of her tent, closest to the edge he knew she slept near, "Cass."

Sounds of fabric ruffling competed with her frantic mumblings.

"Cass, I'm here." He tried louder this time.

"Huh?"

Shelton moved back from the canvas, "Cass I'm here, you were ah...." Shelton sighed, "Are you all right?"

Silence.

He waited a moment more before moving back to the fire, settling himself down with his back on his saddle bag and her tent blocked from view, he made himself another cup. Without warning the canvas twitched.

"I can't sleep Shelton." Her words, soft, vulnerable and alluring sparked his imagination.

"Well...." Several ideas sprung to Shelton's mind all of which they would likely regret by morning. "You have plenty of books to read." He slid down on his saddle bags, his hands resting uneasy in his lap as he looked upwards to the night sky.

"I suppose."

He could hear blankets rustling as Cassidy fussed inside her tent. Suddenly he heard a thump and turned around to see Cassidy had moved her pillow to the edge of the tent, only feet away from his saddle bags. She lay down on her back, and rested a book on her ribs.

"What are you doing?"

"In case you haven't noticed, Shelton there is no lantern inside."

Shelton twisted his head to the side. If he wanted to, he could touch her cheek without straightening his elbow. "I can build the fire up."

"This is fine."

The hair on the back of Shelton's arms stood up, the scent of Cassidy so close pumped warmth through his blood, competing with the fire's heat. He could sense the sleep-warmth that radiated from her soft body, his mind conjuring up all sorts of sensations wishing he could explore under her frilly layers. He needed to concentrate, this woman was nothing like she portrayed. "What's bothering you Precious?"

"Jet."

Shelton's ardor cooled, "Yeah about that."

"I didn't intend …." Cassidy started.

Shelton cleared his throat, "I'm sorry I never meant him to get sick."

Cassidy rolled onto her side, the book slipped to the blankets, "You didn't do anything Shelton, Jet is my responsibility."

"Exactly, Precious, I didn't do anything."

"I mean you've done enough Shelton, carrying him, taking regular breaks, you've taken care of him better than I can." The faintest waiver entered her voice.

This time Shelton turned on his side, "He's a tough kid. Still, I should have warned him, warned you all."

"I knew too Shelton," her voice lowered, "If I hadn't brought him out here…."

Shelton rolled onto his back, the tightness in his ribs lessened, "You think Jet would have stayed behind? No way." Judging by how close they were, the minute Cassidy had decided to take up her father's offer, nothing would have made Jet stay behind. "What kind of businessman was your father?"

He heard Cassidy's tone thicken, "A busy one."

"That's not an answer, Precious."

Cassidy rested the book against her chest, "He was into mining, rail bonds, and jewelry, a bit of everything. More to the point, for all his efforts, some less scrupulous than others, he never made more than he could survive on. Forever, chasing the next big city, the next big.... deal."

Shelton nodded. He'd seen a few gamblers behave the same way, winning enough to throw in the next pot and never walking away. "So it was your father who taught you how to pick pocket?"

"No."

"Your mother?" Shelton exclaimed.

"No, she died when ...." Cassidy's voice turned to a whisper, "Before then, from time to time we stayed in an orphanage, waiting."

Her voice caught in her throat and Shelton wished the words back into his mouth. Cassidy had spent time in an orphanage? How much of this was the truth? He ran his eyes over her, the book had been reset, propped against her chest, her eyes scanning the tiny letters, yet he could see the glint of a tear along her lids. If Cassidy had been scheming she'd have made more of a show. He'd seen enough now to know the difference.

The woman seemed to wear a mask, her features schooled to portray a certain emotion. Once to convince him to take her to Colorado, with Jackson and the rail guard, even when she'd attempted to inspire his own apology. With the Barnes' family, Cassidy had pretended to be a high society lady. In the chemist, the woman had shown a different mask altogether. Cassidy Smith was wily like a fox. Was she a fox or a vixen?

"What about your father?" Cassidy asked.

Shelton sighed. Should he discuss his family? They were far from perfect, yet his upbringing didn't share the same hurdles as Cassidy's. "Well, he's tough as old nails and quiet as a church mouse on Sundays. When it rains he can't stop from grinning." Only when it rains, Shelton mused.

The long years on the ranch had worn him down, the once happy go lucky man had turned to fret and worry. His face, suntanned and wrinkled, popped into Shelton's mind. "He's a rancher so his humor needs work, but he's a salt of the earth kind of guy. Works from sun up to sun down and when he's not in the paddocks, he's chasing Ma around the kitchen for a piece of her apple pie."

Shelton thoughts wandered to how his folks would be fairing now, reminding to send a telegram at the next post office; one telegram to his folks and another to Cade. His family would lie to him, tell him the Bank hadn't moved to take back the Ranch, but Cade would tell him the truth. Shelton thought of his sister with her Banker husband, not caring a lick for the trouble at home. It had fallen squarely to his shoulders. But he had broad shoulders, he chuckled. "So where's your father now?"

Cassidy shrugged, "Last I heard he was in Chicago."

"At least he provided an education for you, he did that right I guess." Shelton tried. He didn't know the man from Uncle and he didn't need to defend him, except his father had provided for him and Vivian to get an education; his sister even more so since Shelton would be working the Ranch.

"Libraries make great babysitters." Cassidy said.

"You never went to a proper school or had a tutor?" Shelton asked, turning to watch her directly. The glow from the fire caressed her peach cheeks, her long lashes highlighted by the amber glow. Her lips twisted to one side as she shook her head.

"The nuns taught me to read and I've read everything I could since then."

Shelton pummeled his saddle bags and rested his head back to look at the stars. The blanket of ebony sparkled above him, each pinprick a diamond amongst an ocean of black. The more he pondered Cassidy's predicament, the more his chest ached. His hands fidgeted in his lap, an overwhelming sense of something, yet the nature of it remained elusive. Not pity, or sorrow but something certain. The concerns he held for Cassidy's need to make this journey and secure a husband seemed to solidify. No wonder she shared a special bond with Jet, like him she grabbed at the opportunity to build a life.

"The sky is so bright from here, not like in the big cities." Cassidy broke Shelton musings.

He couldn't provide that life for her. Cassidy needed to make Colorado a success just like him. Only Shelton's troubles waited for him in Texas, not left behind like Cassidy.

"A thousand different possibilities, a thousand different adventures." He rambled. If he'd never left Dew Springs he wouldn't have signed the mining lease or met Cassidy. The woman would marry whoever's signature had landed on that page and he best remember that.

The book rested on her chest, as she looked upwards, "With a thousand different names."

"I know that one is Jefferson the baker." Shelton joked.

Cassidy clicked her tongue, "It's Virgo the virgin."

"Where is Shania the Strumpet?" Shelton laughed.

Without missing a beat, Cassidy replied, "She married the Archer and flew away on Pegasus."

Shelton's gut clenched and he whistled between his teeth. He couldn't be Cassidy's Archer or Pegasus, "Well he'd be happy then." He heard the blankets ruffle.

"Would he?"

"Oh course, if he loved her it wouldn't matter...." Shelton paused. He shifted against his saddle bags, his feet feeling swept away on a conversation he didn't intend. Shelton cleared his throat, "So Chemistry, biology, mining, is there anything you don't know about?"

"Men."

Pulses of heat radiated down Shelton's chest, sending a rush of energy through his limbs and into his loins. Damn! If he didn't know how much she'd lost already, and how much she risked on this journey he'd take her in his arms right now, "Well, all you really need to know is how to wrap them around your little finger."

He tried to build walls around his thoughts, blocking out the sweet blackcurrant scent that called to him only a foot away. Her voice soft, too soft, husky with a hint of apprehension, shimmered the air between them, "I guess we'll see."

Shelton swallowed hard. Somehow her words sounded like a challenge, and worst, curiosity gnawed at Shelton to find out. "Good night Precious."

"Night Shelton." Cassidy said.

Without turning around Shelton rose and took his rifle in hand. The sky remained black against the wooded forests, the fire crackling and hissing like the desire that coursed through Shelton's body. He tried to calm his thoughts, listening to the lull of the animals as they slept, the crickets of the night, an owl hooting to its mate. Well, at least he'd have no trouble staying awake now.

He skirted the edge of the animal lines pausing every now and then to listen. The eerie silence from the other night hadn't returned and that, at least, eased some of the tension. Thoughts of Cassidy, Hugo, even Sidney spiraled out of Shelton's control, and worse, he had to let it. His folks depended on him. The Blue Cows debts had to be paid. And no amount of pouting or battered eyelashes would stop Shelton from saving the Blue Cow.

Chapter 18

It took another two full days of travelling until Jet regathered enough strength to ride in his saddle, and Cassidy took the success to indicate the use of Laudanum could now cease. She stashed the bottle at the bottom of her vanity case if needed again; relieved the boy had no withdrawal symptoms.

Cassidy rolled her shoulders as she sat in her saddle, the long days on the gravel trail and the chilly nights had worn its way through her muscles. Shelton had kept his distance and over the last two nights Cassidy's exhaustion had prevented any more night tremors. Now before her head hit the pillow her mind filled with thoughts of marriage and anatomy and sugar grey eyes, before sleep consumed her.

On the outskirts of Granite, Shelton called a halt for the night. Cassidy rubbed her rump as she stretched, stepping out her legs leaden, pins and needles tingling through her tired limbs. Once the pain had numbed, Cassidy headed to the river, canteens in hand, only to stop as a chill ran down her spine. Out of the corner of her eye, she saw Sidney shadowing her. For a brief moment she considered asking Shelton for his pistol, except the man had already walked out of earshot, staking out the animals.

Cassidy exhaled as she slowed her steps. She knelt down to the river and carefully dipped each canteen refilling them one by one. A weight dropped in her stomach as Sidney's boots paused by her side.

"Thought I might catch you here."

"Oh?" Cassidy rushed the next canteen. She hadn't been ignorant of his heated stares or his uncoordinated winks.

"Do you mind?" Dipping down on his haunches, he held out his canteen. "I'll help with your tent, if you're happy to help."

Cassidy tilted her head to one side, "Sure."

Sidney rose, "Thanks."

"You're welcome."

He wandered up the hill and Cassidy called after him, "Thank you, Sidney, for helping with my tent."

The young man tipped a finger to his brim and smiled, "If you need a hand with anything else, let me know."

As the last rays of the sun disappeared behind the jagged mountain skyline Cassidy finally sat down with an *oomph* to eat dinner. What she wouldn't give for fresh produce instead of tinned food! Grimacing at her plate, she caught Shelton watching her and took a taste, trying not to sigh at the bland mush.

"Tomorrow we'll reach Granite, and when we do," dark notes entered Shelton's voice, "No-one steps more than a foot away from me or the wagon, at any one time."

"What gives you the right?" Sidney snapped.

A breeze, almost glacial now, they had travelled higher up the mountains, sliced through Cassidy's riding jacket.

"Trust me kid, Granite is one of the most lawless places up here, you'd do well to keep a cool head and follow my lead."

Sidney snorted, "Your lead?"

"Two murders a month Sid, and no hangings, what does that tell you?" The sound of Shelton's cutlery slowing scraping across tin remained the only noise disturbing the icy air.

Sidney's cheeks fell flat.

Shivering, Cassidy spooned another mouthful of mush. Surely Granite couldn't be any worse than Chicago or Philly or the slums of New York. Shelton finished his dinner and for the first time during their journey, Cassidy watched Shelton clean his firearms and measure his ammunition.

After completing her evening routine, Cassidy bade goodnight to Shelton, rolling her shoulders before lying down. The flicker of tangerine light across the canvas wall almost rhythmic until Cassidy's tongue turned to lead and the faint trace of ash climbed her throat. She rolled over.

A cool breeze trickled through the flap of the canvas and Cassidy stirred to see the grey light of dawn revealed Jet stepping crouched low over their belongings.

"Everything all right?"

Jet jumped, "Yeah Cass, I'm just sick of these clothes, was looking forward to being clean, you know."

Cassidy nodded and rolled over knowing how she felt after being ill; a good wash to cleanse the sickness away. "Soaps at the bottom," she said.

"Uh-huh." He replied. A *woosh* of the tent flap signalled his exit.

Cassidy resigned herself for another bumpy ride atop her mule, before she'd rest again. She pulled her gold locket from between her breasts and turned it in the early morning light. She heard Shelton greet Leroy beside the fire. Perhaps she should hide it in her belongings? She didn't want to catch anyone's attention. Well, nobody in Granite anyway.

Cassidy dressed for the day, as demure as she could manage, in her dark emerald traveling suit with bonnet, tucking the locket deep within her layers. Shelton rode at the front, chatting easy with Leroy and his wife while Sidney and Jet brought up the rear.

On *Tango* at the front of the convoy, Shelton had his head together with Leroy, while Alice sat on a mule beside her husband. Every now and then she'd check on the bundle in her arms, between laughing at whatever Shelton said. Leroy patted the taller man on the shoulder, a wide grin split his cheeks as well. Sidney and Jet brought up the rear, both boys throwing dark looks at each other like thunderheads brewing on the horizon.

When Shelton called a halt at just outside of Granite, Jet pulled out his writing journal. At least he felt well enough to start drawing again, Cassidy thought.

Shelton issued another warning, as they rested on the edge of the trail.

"We're just buying supplies so I don't know how much trouble you expect us to get into." Alice laughed, jostling the baby at her hip.

"Oh enough." Shelton sent a quick look to Sidney, then Jet and finally Cassidy, the edge of his brim cast a shadow over his eyes.

As an afterthought, Cassidy lifted the gold chain over her head and tucked it into her backpack. The absence of the locket's weight cooled her limbs and instinctively she rubbed her upper arms.

Jet's flicked back a few pages of his journal, "You know," Jet squinted at the sunlight on the pale pages, "I've been thinking about these sluice boxes."

Sidney wandered behind Jet's shoulder, "What do you know about sluice boxes?"

"I know enough."

Sidney eyes targeted Jet's notebook and the younger boy folded the cover backwards and leaned towards Cassidy.

"Well either way I'm glad to see you're on the mend, kid."

Sidney lifted Jet's saddle bags and Cassidy's backpack, "You rest." He said as he wandered back to the mules.

Jet's face contorted, and Cassidy shrugged her shoulders. Despite, Sidney's snap at Shelton last night, he seemed almost pleasant this morning. Perhaps Shelton's influence and the weariness of the journey had softened his bite. Cassidy made a mental note to thank Sidney later.

Shelton pulled the wagon up outside the Granite trading post. Nestled between two hills, Granite consisted of a handful of muddy streets lined by log cabins with false fronts. The sounds of metal on metal competed with men singing, drifted up from the river that snaked below. Across the street, the Saloon doors suddenly swung open, a loud crack silenced the organ music as a waft of smoke parted to reveal one man clutching his chest and another on his heels. His pistol held high, as his foe stumbled another step as the second retort echoed off the false front buildings. Cassidy gasped. Jet whistled between his teeth.

"Don't take too long." Shelton said to Alice, as the assailant, holstered his weapon and returned back inside.

Sidney clambered off his saddle and reset his hat, "I'll go with her."

"Ah all right Son," Leroy stammered, as the boy took Alice's elbow and lead her up the stairs to the boardwalk.

Shelton watched them go, he had supplies of his own to buy, food and oil, shoes and nails for *Tango*. Like it or not, he didn't dare leave Cassidy alone until Sidney returned. The more chaperones the better. Shelton considered giving her his Welby Bulldog, the snub barrelled five shooter would be perfect for Cassidy to hide in her layers. Except, Shelton couldn't be sure she'd wouldn't use it against him! Although he did appreciate her effort of choosing less fancy clothes, especially not the navy dress with the buttons, but even dressed down, in tired emerald, the woman shone brighter than sunshine. Narrowing his eyes, he watched Cassidy fuss with her bags.

"Looking for something?"

"I thought I could trade...." Her arm slid further into her backpack and came up empty. She dug in again, her brows furrowed. "It's gone."

"Huh?" Jet said.

"The laudanum, Jet did you take it?"

The boy's cheeks fell, his nose twisted, "What?"

"Jet don't mess around, did you take the laudanum?" The color rushed out of Cassidy's bottom lip, her hands trembled. "And my locket!"

"You think I'd steal from you?"

No sooner had the woman uttered the words then her cheeks paled, "No I just –"

Jet's heels hit the muddy street.

"Jet!" Shelton shouted in unison with Cassidy, but the boy scurried through the winding streets and like a ghost, he vanished.

"Shelton!"

"Yeah Cass, just...." Shelton pushed Cassidy's shoulders until her back touched the edge of the wagon. Her lids had already begun to fill with liquid, glistening along the bottom of her lashes, her amber iris like pools of burnt honey, "You stay here." Shelton pointed a finger at Leroy's bristling cheeks, "Got it."

"Got it." The older man hefted the rifle to the crook of his elbow.

Shelton stalked through the crowd, slipping his shoulders from side to side, trying to avoid contact with other patrons as best he could. The main thoroughfare bustled as the miners downed tools and filled the saloons. Shelton worked his way up the street, checking behind each log cabin, for a glimpse of the runaway in the grey woollen cap. Only Jet wasn't any ordinary runaway. Shelton took a turn down one of the backstreets with shanty style huts for the miners. Shelton couldn't fathom his luck with the timing of Cassidy's words or Jet's reactions. The woman had been careless, and the boy irrational. He didn't have time for delays and especially not in Granite.

Shelton rushed around the tents, trying his best to not seem out of place. Between a circle of tents, a bunch of miners set up a gambling ring. From somewhere beyond a woman screamed. Splintering timber spilled across Shelton's boots as a man tumbled through the wooden door of a nearby cabin. Shelton worked his way through the cabins and tents. If anything happened to Cassidy while he was off chasing Jet, when Shelton did find the boy, he'd ring his bloody neck.

Jet scrubbed the back of his hand across his eyes. His foot stumbled in a divot as he made his way down to the river. Damn Cassidy! Did she really think he'd steal from her? Was it Sidney making eyes at her or Shelton ignoring her that sent her batty? She had no right to accuse him. Not when he'd done everything for her! Jet sighed as his tired legs carried him further down the hill. If he'd been better he'd run again. The crowd of miners returning from the riverbank got thicker, so Jet rested against the edge of a cabin and sucked in deep breaths. Damn this tick fever. He felt hollow. Sniffling he exhaled slowly, knowing it wasn't just the illness. Slowly he slid down the edge of the cabin and rested on his haunches. He'd done his best to stay honest in Colorado. Cassidy hadn't. Jet leaned around the corner, to see if anyone had pursued him. He shouldn't have run off. Shelton would kick his arse when he returned. Another figure, long and lean crouched around the external of a cabin. Jet didn't think twice. He rose to his feet and set off to shadow his quarry as Sidney Barnes slipped between the tents.

Cassidy rested against the wagon, her toe tapped in the dirt. A trail of miners wandered through the town, at first a trickle and now a steady stream. Several stopped to run their eye up and down Cassidy and even a few whistled. Leroy straightened his shoulders as wide as he could and tapped the butt of the rifle every time a man tried to approach. Cassidy curled her fists into a ball and released them. Worrying about any addictive effect of laudanum had rushed the words from her mouth. Shelton was taking way too long. He should have been dragging Jet back by his collar, so she could apologise straight away.

"Could you give me a hand Leroy, hun?" Alice stood atop the boardwalk with bundles of tins in her hands.

"Where's that boy Sidney?" Leroy stumbled up the steps.

"Dunno, he took off the minute we got inside." Alice handed Leroy the tins of food as she balanced the baby on her hip.

The hairs on the back of Cassidy's neck stood to attention. Sidney! His offer of helping her with her tent now made sense. With Leroy's back turned, Cassidy slipped through the crowd.

She'd find Jet and apologise, after all, she knew where Jet would run.

Shelton returned to the main thoroughfare and cursed. From this distance he could see the wagon, Leroy scratching his balding head and Alice's pinched features. Cassidy gone. Shelton cursed again, this time loud enough a bunch of miners halted.

"Hey, watch it!" one man spat a wad of tobacco into the muck just shy of Shelton's boots.

"Yeah, I'm watching it." Shelton sighed and opened his vest to reveal his six-shooter. He didn't have time for this. The other men moved on, the spitter lingered, harrumphing and casting another wad of tobacco to the street. "I guess, there's no such thing as an easy pay day is there?" Shelton added.

A wide grin split the man's grizzled cheeks, "Ain't that the truth."

Shelton slapped a hand on the man's shoulder.

Leroy waved Shelton down, "Sidney's gone too."

Why the devil would Sidney run off? The pennies dropped one by one in Shelton's mind. Sidney had a one tracked mind. Jet on the other hand, was quick as a whip. But Cassidy had run off after Jet. Shelton had to think. Granite wasn't a big city like Philly or Chicago. Where would Jet go? He was a boy grown on the streets. The darker streets might call to Jet, make him feel at home. Searching for her brother, Cassidy would surely search for Jet in all the haunts Shelton had tried to warn them about.

Shelton followed the stream of miners as they made their way to the drinking halls. Stopping at the double doors, Shelton's fingers danced across his holster. Cassidy. He needed to find her before dusk and he knew she'd be chasing Jet. Except, neither of them would walk through the front doors of a tavern! Either one of them could be picking pockets from the poor souls sent on their way out the back entrance.

Stalking around the side, something struck Shelton's

chest. He clutched his ribs, sucking in a sharp breath as the assailant stepped back. Shelton's hands clawed the dark grey fabric and brought the boy to the mud.

Jet cursed. Shelton grunted.

"Oh God Shelton, quick it's Sidney...." The boy jumped upright and snatched at Shelton's arm. Shelton clutched at his ribs and double checked his pistol.

"Wait," Shelton tugged the back of Jet's shirt, "Sidney can wait, Cass's gone."

"What?" Jet stopped in his tracks and cursed again. The boy rubbed his fingers across his bare chin, "I'll find her, but I swear, Shelton, I don't think Sidney can wait."

Shelton followed Jet to the rear of the tavern where rows of linen had been strung up between the cabins, an area had been roped off like a boxing ring. Sidney slumped to one side of the arena, and spat, a splash of blood mixed with the mud. Across the other side, a shirtless man, cracked his knuckles and grinned. Shelton counted more ribs than teeth as he curled the edge of his moustache and laughed. A group of men leaned on the far side ropes, one man in particular lifted a bowler hat higher on his forehead, sweeping salt and pepper hair as he moved. He wore an emerald green vest that had seen better days and a silver shirt tucked haphazardly around his narrow waist. Flanked by two more thugs, his piggy brown eyes starred directly at Shelton.

"Hey, now, what's this?" Shelton smiled as he entered the section, the crowd of onlookers swivelled their heads his direction.

The man with the emerald vest raised his chin, "This boy one of yours then?"

"Piss off Shelton," Sidney hissed, his front lip swelling.

"He might be," Shelton cocked his head to one side and spread his vest wide, tucking his hands in his pockets. "What's it to you?"

"He touched up lil' Jenny here without paying."

Shelton whistled between his teeth and regarded one of

two women that stood beside Emerald Vest, "A fine lady she is, what's the damage?" Shelton had a few bank notes left, and he'd add it to Leroy's total.

"I paid her!" Sidney shouted.

"Uh-uh, he tried to swindle her with a trinket," Emerald vest wandered around the edge of the ropes.

"And then snatch it back, don't forget that McIntyre!" Jenny hollered.

The man, McIntyre shrugged his shoulders, "So, now he's got to work off his debt."

"Surely we can make an arrangement?" Shelton said, he didn't have time for this, but could he send Jet back to find Leroy and pay his son's debt for a Dove? Would that get back Cassidy's locket, that 'trinket' McIntyre held as 'lil Jenny's payment?

"Yeah, the boy owes me three fights and I don't think I'm going to get a second out of him. You see the lads up here, need a bit of entertainment, fresh blood you know, the same old bets on the same old horses get a bit predictable." McIntyre rubbed together his hands covered in fingerless knitted gloves.

The Dove twirled a blonde ringlet through her fingers, the nails dirty, "Jerry's next." She winked, as one of McIntyre's thugs rolled his bald head on his thick skull. "Then Remmy." The other thug had a scar pulling down the hood of his right eye. He grimaced at Shelton.

Shelton shook his head, "Where's my invitation?"

McIntyre's eyes sparkled, his grizzled cheeks split wide, "I like it."

"I'll give you one to clear his debt, I ain't got time for more than that." Shelton unclicked his gun belt and handed it to Jet before rolling his vest off his shoulders.

"One?" McIntyre laughed, a crackle that hinted at long nights with the pipe.

"I don't need you to fight my battles." Sidney moaned.

"You sure?" Shelton tugged off his shirt and stood bare-chested in front of McIntyre, "Cause it doesn't look like it, from where I'm standing."

Sidney stretched his jaw from side to side and winched, he tried to stand only his knees gave way.

Shelton snorted and he beat either side of his chest with his knuckles, building the heat against the chilly air. Shelton rolled his shoulders as he turned to face the crowd.

Jenny gasped and then winked. McIntyre ran his eye up and down Shelton, hoping that the man would see the long hours worked on the ranch as worthy of the thug Jerry. "You didn't bring them here to watch a boy get punished, you want a fight don't ya?" Shelton shook out his arms as he addressed the crowd, a few cheered, and he cracked his knuckles on his palms. "What's the wager? Three rounds?" Shelton pulled Sidney back from inside the ropes. He helped Jet drag him to an upturned barrel. He dropped his voice, "Where's the locket? McIntyre?" Shelton asked.

Sidney put a finger to the side of his nose and cleared the blood, "Yeah."

Jet cursed again and then patted Shelton on the shoulder, "I got it."

"No you don't Jet, trust me."

"Quick on your feet, Shelly." Jet rushed and slipped through the crowd.

"No Jet," Shelton rose but the boy was gone. He stretched one arm across the other, "What's the rules?"

"Rules?" McIntyre snorted.

Shelton's gut clenched. If the hours working alongside his dad had built his strength, the many days and nights wrestling and fighting alongside Taylor, Marcus and Cade had honed his skill. He threw Sidney a dark look. If he hadn't started all this mess, Shelton could sympathise with him.

"Who decides the winner?"

"Mud or blood."

"Right." Shelton inhaled slowly. Knock Jerry out or draw enough blood the man couldn't continue. He needed to find

Cassidy, and this detour had cost him enough time already. Around the ring, patrons rushed to bid and wager. The noise filtered through to Shelton. Time ticked too slowly.

Shelton ducked under the ropes and stood in one corner, Jerry did the same. Next, Jenny stood on the lowest rope and whistled. Bouncing on his back foot Jerry advanced. Shelton paced to the long side and waited. Jerry's jab flew straight, followed by another and a hook. Shelton ducked and weaved. Bringing his fist upwards, knuckles collided with sternum. A crack silenced the crowd, followed by the slap of Jerry's knees landing in the mud. Shelton ratcheted his shoulder back. Jerry's jaw snapped as Shelton's overhand right pushed the man into unconsciousness.

"No!" Jenny howled.

McIntyre smiled, "Lucky."

"No," Shelton shook his head. "Now the debts paid."

The shadow of Jet slipped between McIntyre and Remmy. If the boy was successful, as soon as McIntyre discovered the theft, he would shoot them dead in the street.

"Debt's paid, sure you don't want to make some more money? Remmy's without an opponent?"

"Now that you mention it," Shelton leaned back against the ropes, "I'll take the trinket the boy offered."

McIntyre flicked the brim of his bowler hat upwards, and leaned his forearms on the ropes, "Sounds interesting."

"Except I don't want Remmy," Shelton needed to end this and end it quickly, "I'll take you."

McIntyre nodded and pulled off his shirt, a dark purple line coursed around his neck, with long wiry limbs, and a chest that looked like it had been carved from marble, Shelton suddenly doubted his decision.

"Next you'll be wanting the girl as well." McIntyre laughed as he stepped through the ropes.

Shelton mumbled, his throat tight, his fists curled, "No I already got a girl."

Chapter 19

Cassidy kept to the edges of the gravel trail, every now and then she stepped to the side to slip past the crush of men. Keeping her bonnet down, she watched their mud-caked boots stop and turn, but she moved too fast. Jet always ran to the river, for some reason the bubbling rush of the water soothed him. Even in Kansas when *Tango* had rebuffed his attention, the boy took off to feed the ducks. Cassidy let gravity take charge of her ankles and she dashed further down the hill. Any moment now she'd reach the plateau and see Jet tossing pebbles into the rippling water.

The cabin's thinned and now tents pock-marked the scarred landscape. As Cassidy descended, the gravel slipped under foot, she fell backwards, something speared the palm of her hand and she winced. Cassidy pulled her feet underneath, hoping her boots didn't slide out again. A weight closed over her upper arm, the skin pinching between rough fingers as Cassidy rose to her feet. Spinning, a grizzled jaw faced her, the teeth black along the gums, the man's blue eyes like pitted sapphires.

"Hey girly."

Cassidy reefed her elbow backwards only to bring the man closer. His stale tobacco breath turned her nose.

"You lost?"

"I'm looking for a boy."

The man ran a stray strand of her hair through his gnarled fingers, "You should be looking for a man."

"Hey!"

At the dark shout, the man released his grip.

"Hands off my wife."

The strength in Cassidy's knees fled, tension leeched from her limbs. Three strides brought Shelton to her side, his shirt half unbuttoned and jacket in hands. With one movement he lifted Cassidy onto higher ground and stood between her and the miner.

"Wife, hey? You sure she's not mine," The man cackled, folding one side of his woollen coat over the other and puffing out his chest, "I ordered one of them meself, but she ain't turned up."

Shelton pushed Cassidy up the hill, his hands warm against her waist, "Posts been delayed these few last weeks, I'm sure she's on her way." Shelton laughed.

They retreated to the riverbank and Cassidy's heels rushed to keep up with the weight at her back. The scree slipped and Cassidy's hands found gravel. Encircling her waist, Shelton brought Cassidy back to her feet. "How did you find me?"

"I asked Jet where would he go, if he hadn't been chasing…"

"Jet! You found him!"

Shelton offered a soft laugh, "Yeah I did, he's back at the wagon waiting for you."

Sure enough as the cabins gave way to the main street, Jet stood up in the wagon bed, his face white, his eyes wide. Cassidy threw him a quick smile, and the boy sat down, settling a scowl on his lips. She had to apologise!

"Come on." Shelton said.

Cassidy's heat flipped inside her chest as she looked down to see Shelton on one knee, one hand forward waiting for hers. Shelton's sugar grey eyes, like liquid silver held hers, sending warmth flourishing through her veins. "Shelton," She looked at either end of the bustling street. *Here and now the man wanted to propose?* She slid her hand into his, "I thought you didn't want to I mean, of course….."

"Ah…" Shelton's cheeks paled, he tugged back his hand, and reached for her ankle, "No Precious, I mean mount up."

Like a bucket of ice doused Cassidy, she sucked in a tight breath. Damn this man! Liquid welled in her eyes and she turned away, snatching Carlotta's saddle and heaving herself upwards without assistance.

Shelton lingered, his voice now a whisper, "What I said at the river, the words...."

"Were just words, Shelton." Cassidy snapped.

The man clicked his tongue and dug into his pockets. Cassidy's heels itched to get Carlotta moving, only Shelton's hand held the mule's reins, his knuckles red and bruised. Gold glinted off the late afternoon sun, stinging Cassidy's eyes, as Shelton plonked the chain with locket into her lap. "You owe Jet an apology."

"I know," Breathless, Cassidy snatched at the jewellery.

"And Sidney owes you one, for this and the laudanum."

Without hesitation Cassidy slung the chain over her neck and tucked it into her bodice, "That means I owe you a thank...."

But Shelton had moved on already his hips swaggering from side to side as he stalked back to *Tango*. Cassidy regarded Sidney, one eye black and blue, a split lip and a swollen cheek. Leroy shook his head and Alice busied herself with Oliver, a fleeting smile to Cassidy, her eyes downcast.

Had Shelton laid into Sidney for her necklace or something more sinister with Jet? Cassidy ran her eye over her brother. Despite him refusing to look at her, Jet looked unharmed.

"Move out." Shelton ordered and Leroy flicked the reins on *Ole Missy*.

As the climb became steeper, the mood of the travelling party became darker. The sun caressed the fir tree bordered peaks, off in the distance, Cassidy could see the snow-capped mountains dwarfed the ridges they now passed. She pulled her jacket tighter, wondering where she packed her gloves. Leroy had only spoken curt words to Sidney after the boy delivered a poorly worded apology to Cassidy. Jet still refused to look at her and Shelton didn't talk to anyone.

Making camp set an eerie tone for dinner. With Alice no longer trying to lighten the mood by talking in high pitched optimistic tones, the sudden gusts of chilly air whispering through the forestry set their nerves on edge.

It wasn't until Alice handed Shelton his plate that the man spoke. A simple 'thank you' before he spooned the beef, awkwardly with his bruised knuckles. Jet sat by himself, the paleness washed away by the glow of the fire. He opened his notebook and rested it on one knee, jotting away as he balanced his plate on the other. Cassidy handed Leroy his dinner and he mumbled his gratitude. When the plates where clean, Leroy finally spoke.

"You gonna tell me what this is all about then?" He pointed to Sidney's busted up face.

"Sometimes you gotta let boy's learn from their mistakes love, otherwise they never grow up to be men." Alice said.

Across the fire, Shelton's gaze met Cassidy's. Jet looked from Shelton to Cassidy and then at Sidney.

Leroy snorted, "Is that right Pet?"

"It is." Alice said with such finality, that Leroy stood up. "Well now, we'll be cracking open the whiskey. It's our last night before we go our separate ways, and I won't have this end on a sour note. You hear me." Leroy winked as he took Cassidy's plate.

"You're still on first watch." Shelton said.

Sidney's cheeks tilted to one side of his mouth and he hung his head and nodded. Suddenly his hand shot out. Shelton slowly shook it.

"Here," Leroy poured a finger of whiskey into Cassidy's cup and then passed the bottle around. After one quick cheer, Cassidy gulped the harsh liquor down, the heat searing her throat and into her lungs. She covered her cough with her elbow. Shelton necked his own and then rose, dragging a measure of canvas from his saddle bags, stepping it out to the far right of Cassidy's tent. She watched as Shelton set up his own tent, his breath fogging as he worked.

"Too cold for you tonight?" Leroy asked as he poured himself another whiskey.

"Glacial." Shelton replied.

As soon as Jet excused himself, Cassidy cut him off at the entrance to the tent.

"Jet, I'm sorry."

"Yeah." The boy stooped in through the entrance and started scooping his belongings into his arms. "I know you are."

"What?" Cassidy watched as he grabbed his blankets, "What are you doing?"

"Shelton said I could sleep in his tent."

"Oh, of course." Boys needed to turn into men, Cassidy thought as she straightened her shoulders, letting her grip drop on his arm. "I mean it Jet, I'm sorry about the laudanum, I didn't even think about the locket."

"The medicine?" Jet rubbed his forehead.

"Yes the laudanum is extremely addictive, I thought I'd given you too much, driven you to seek it out and then...."

Jet snorted, "You should know that nothing can make me do anything I don't want to do."

She smiled and Jet returned it, the weight in her stomach lifted. Cassidy threw her arms around Jet's shoulders. The boy tugged backwards, "I don't care if you think you're almost grown." She pulled him tight and pressed a kiss to his head. "I wouldn't care too hoots from a barn owl, if you never got my locket back, so long as you are safe."

Opening her arms, Jet stood back and Cassidy took a moment to wipe her eyes, "I mean it Jet, I'm sorry. I should never have accused you, I'm sorry."

"I forgive you, Cass."

"Thank you, and thank you for my mother's locket."

"Don't thank me, thank Shelton. I was going to pinch it from McIntyre, but he knocked him out instead."

"McIntyre?"

Jet's brow furrowed, he pulled his lips inwards, "Look, it's all Sidney's fault, he tried to pay for a Dove with that and then steal it back. The girl's handler made Sidney fight to pay his debt. Only Shelton stepped in."

"And knocked McIntyre out?"

"Well first he knocked out Jerry."

"Who's Jerry? Actually, never mind." Images of Shelton's bloodied knuckles sprung to mind. The man had stepped in, or more to the point, stepped up to protect Sidney, of all people. The echo of Shelton's words and her foolishness rang in her ears. Like a gong, it thundered down her neck and into her chest. "I'll thank Shelton later."

"Right." Jet put a hand on her shoulder, "I'm only the next tent over, Cass and you're far enough from the fire."

"Yes of course."

A blast of fresh air gusted through the canvas as Jet left. Cassidy didn't bother bidding any of them goodnight. Shelton didn't see her as a wife, he saw her as a debt, a liability. How could she change his perception? Did she want to? The memory of Shelton's caress, his eyes raking over her, tempting yet temporary. Cassidy undressed and dressed in the dark, sliding into sleep, her locket safely around her neck.

The flames curled under the door, like fingers from the devil, drawing higher up the timber. The air heated and thinned and Cassidy gasped. Her eyes flew open, fingers struggling to find purchase in the dark. She rolled onto her side and sat up. Licking her parched lips she reached for her canteen and drank deep, the cool water soothing her dry throat. Darkness enveloped her as she wrapped the tea gown around her shoulders. She pushed the canvas to one side and stepped into the cold. Embers drifted upwards, dancing across the soft breeze as Shelton sat silent by the fire with a red and black checked blanket about his shoulders. He turned at the sound of the canvas falling back into place. Cassidy slid into her dragonfly boots and carefully tiptoed around the rear of her tent; the pressure in her abdomen forcing her to brave the cold. Shelton had chosen to camp alongside the Arkansas River, at the base of a deep gulch, their backdrop was a thick woodland that rose dauntingly over their camp.

Cassidy thanked the half-moon that hung low on the horizon, lighting her path between the giant trees.

Shelton had only sat down from his nightly checks, when Cassidy appeared, dishevelled, stoic, and cold outside her tent. She'd disappeared into the dark and Shelton had a want to follow her. The last few nights, he'd sat in the dark waiting for the disturbance that brought silence to their camp to show itself. He knew Texas and it's wildlife like the back of his hand, why then, did silence settle over the Colorado ranges so irregularly at night. It made Shelton's skin twitch. He should have given her the Welby Bulldog. He could kick himself for his error at the riverbank. Seeing the miner with his rough hands on Cassidy made him speak without thinking. Calling her his wife! He let that thought drift through his mind, only to have it yanked out when he heard a twig snap.

Cassidy exhaled slowly. She'd only just stood up when she heard the breathing. She fixed her tea gown with minute movements. The sound of heavy footfalls over leaf litter, crisp, determined and yet meandering. Fighting the urge to turn, Cassidy stepped to the next tree for cover. The back rough under her fingers, the low hanging branches scratching against her neck. Her hair tugged backwards, as the leaves snagged her strands. Counting to three, Cassidy moved again. Something snorted. Slivers of amber flickered through the underbrush. Cassidy counted her steps until she would reach the campsite, and Shelton. Another snort and Cassidy broke into a run.

With trembling thighs, Cassidy stumbled into the ring of light around the camp, as if enveloped by a halo of safety she called out.

"Shelly!"

The man already stood, rifle levelled over her shoulder, his blanket discarded across the fallen log that separated him from Cassidy. One arm shot out, and Cassidy's fingers stretched, her legs leaden in the chilly air. Shelton's hand trapped hers and with such speed, Cassidy almost tripped over her own heels, shoved Cassidy behind him. Her hands clutched at his shoulders, her head half buried in his back.

"What was it Cass?"

"I don't know, big, heavy...."

"Bear?"

"I don't know." Cassidy whimpered.

She heard the hammer of the rifle click. Under her hands, Shelton's shoulders tensed, the leather of his vest cold, however the warmth of his body seeped into her limbs. Something tickled her ankle and Cassidy shook her boots. She craned around Shelton's broad back, her eyes staining in the dark, waiting to see what beast crossed the threshold.

Shelton snorted, the muscles under Cassidy's fingertips suddenly released, "Moose." He whispered.

Cassidy's gaze caught the outline of the giant creature, long limbs slowly meandered at the edge of the light, antlers heavy and multi-pronged. With a dip of his head, he tested the air, blowing out puffs of hot air from his nostrils. Black baubles glistened in the amber of the camp fire. Shelton stalked the animal with the rifle barrel .

"You can't kill him." Cassidy whispered. Her calves began to itch.

She felt a small chuckle through Shelton's back, "I'm just watching him."

"Oi," Cassidy kicked her boot. Heat rushed upwards as weight sunk against her legs. Spinning Cassidy's eyes flew wide. A scream stuck in her throat, coated in ash, and searing her lungs.

Shelton heard Cassidy yelp behind him. He shifted to the side, only to see licks of flame curling up the hem of her tea gown. Frozen in place, the reflection of Cassidy's eyes now black consumed by tangerine. Without thinking Shelton, lay down his rifle and tugged the fabric from her shoulders. His boots rained down on the charred fabric to no avail. By the time the flames extinguished more than half of Cassidy's gown had turned to ash. Shelton looked at Cassidy. Bent over, she slapped at her legs, over and over, the sound from her chest, less than a whimper. Shelton snatched his blanket and tossed it around Cassidy, she flinched. Shelton stepped out to catch her, only his sleeping mat stubbed his toe. His knee struck the fallen log and they tumbled, legs entangled blanket askew.

When Shelton pulled back the fabric, Cassidy lay in his arms, her face pressed into his chest, tears streaming down her face. Slowly he dragged his hand over her hair, running the silky strands through his fingers. "It's alright Cass, I'm hear. It's gone. I'm here."

The moose had better be gone! He leaned backwards, hoping Leroy's whiskey kept everyone else asleep. Cassidy's sobs slowed, her ragged breaths evenly paced. Shelton looked down to see Cassidy's eyes open, red rimmed and staring at the flames, her face cradled in the crook of his elbow. "You all right?"

"I am now." Her breath was hot against his throat. She rubbed her cheek against his chest.

Shelton needed to move. The feeling of Cassidy, warm, supple, and all woman, in his arms had stirred the blood through his veins, "Well let's have a look at you." He lifted her upwards and rolled, landing on his back on his sleeping mat. Except Cassidy over balanced. He grunted as Cassidy landed on top of him, her knee in his ribs. Exhaling, he dragged her ankle to one side and regretted it instantly.

Cassidy giggled as Shelton pulled her leg the opposite direction. She tugged the blanket around her, and crouched low across his chest as she now straddled his hips. A groan reverberated in Shelton's throat, his hands captured her thighs. A thousand butterflies took flight in her abdomen as she leaned back. Sugar grey slaked over her form, his lips parted. The fire are her back ignored as Shelton's hands trailed down her thighs, slowly curling behind her knees and down the backs of her ankles, igniting a thick, wicked heat that multiplied.

"Are you hurt?"

A very different kind of ache demanded Cassidy's attention.

"No," the word a whisper, she tilted her face to Shelton's and licked her lips.

Shelton tugged the ribbon free from the braid at the base of her neck. He ran his fingers through her strands, fanning it out to one side, like a cascading shield from the fire, "Good." His palm cupped her cheek and brought her lips to his.

Chapter 20

Cassidy's lips parted and warmth unfurled in her abdomen, circling upwards in rhythm with the slake of Shelton's tongue across hers. On instinct, her knees tightened, clutching at his hips, her hand splayed across his chest. Shivers broke across her skin as Shelton's palms captured her thighs. With the blanket around her shoulders, and her hair shielding them from the fire, perched atop her husband, alone and yet together in the Colorado wilderness. Deepening the kiss, Shelton pulled her downwards, ending her errant thoughts until only carnal energy remained. As if on high alert, Cassidy's body responded, her breasts swelled, the centers demanding attention, her breath shallow in her throat. Shelton worked his hands underneath her night dress and under the thin fabric of her shift, insufficient barriers to Shelton's desire. His long fingers captured her buttocks. Rolling her hips, he brought her down on his arousal, the hardness unyielding as it pressed into her soft flesh.

Shelton captured Cassidy's whimper, the tightness in his throat only slightly more bearable than the tightness in his denims. Cassidy may be naïve, but she learned fast. Where he rocked her hips once, she now took over, gliding herself over his arousal with the deftest of pressure. Shelton skimmed his hand upwards, the soft warmth of her flesh searing his skin. Upwards he pursued until he captured her swollen breast. A moan vibrated against his lips as he scored the tight center with his thumb. Damn she was soft, so soft and supple. Her blackcurrant scent infiltrated his senses, wrapping a chain around his ribs, like the woman who clung to his hips. One button undone, and then another, until Cassidy's trembling fingers trailed across his bare chest. Like a snake made of pure desire, Cassidy slithered atop him and he felt his restraint slipping joyfully away. He wanted Cassidy to melt, to paw at him like he knew she wanted. Shelton broke away from her lips and trailed kisses down her neck. The blanket had fallen about her waist, the golden glow of the fire highlighting her curves, the shift puckering around her taunt centers. He couldn't help himself, and brought one to his lips, fabric and all, licking, supping and sucking as Cassidy's garbled moans spurred him on.

Cassidy thought she'd been trapped in a firestorm, her internal heat competing with the pure wildfire that Shelton wrought as their bodies collided. Surely, he was her man now. An ache filled her chest, she wanted him to see her as his woman, his wife. Tentative fingers worked under the lace of her drawers. Soon, soon he'd ask her, surely. For now, she succumbed to the pleasure his kisses caressed across her breasts.

Shelton dared not say a word as Cassidy writhed on top of him. Her back arched as he cupped her sex. Her slick heat like a whip to his body, he brought Cassidy's lips to his, her thighs trembled, her breaths now ragged. His tongue delved into the soft corners of her mouth as he stroked her silken core. Tendrils of desire clogged his veins and controlled his movements, his buckle unclipped. Cassidy tore her lips away, her words lost in his demand to fulfil his own satisfaction, "Huh?"

Cassidy stared down at Shelton slowly kissing along his jaw line, "Have you got something to say?"

Shelton's hands didn't stop, stroking, gliding, circling. *Did she want an apology?* Well his mouth had gotten him into enough trouble already. He captured her lips, mumbling his answer against them, "I don't want to ruin it."

In a flurry of fabric Cassidy was on her feet, the blanket tossed around her shoulders. Her lids brimming with liquid, "You were never going to…." She turned on her heel and strode to the tent.

Damn! he hadn't said anything and he was right back into trouble. Standing he tugged his shirt closed, shivering against the sudden onslaught of the cold, "Cass." He stalked over to her tent and paused. *What? What could he offer her? Nothing.* He was a scoundrel, he knew it, but she had straddled him! He almost laughed, who was he kidding, he knew exactly what he was doing and a small part of him didn't regret it. He should, but he didn't.

"Can I at least...."

The tent flap opened and his blanket tumbled into the dirt,

"Thanks." He grunted and returned to the fire. He'd think about apologizing tomorrow. He wrapped himself in the blanket and resumed his watch, his senses overwhelmed with the scent of Cassidy. He'd never sleep again.

Morning frost crunched under foot as Cassidy packed her belongings. The Barnes had already packed their wagon and set Ole Misty in the trap. Shelton milled about the camp, his chin high, not even slightly ashamed of his forwardness. Cassidy had to accept he was never going to make her an honest offer. The man had no scruples, no honor and no loyalty. Cassidy couldn't look him in the eye without the memory of his touch on her skin. She exhaled slowly hoping the chilly air would cool her ardor. She needed to be sensible. Once they fare welled the Barnes' at the pass to Twin Lakes, then Oro City lay ahead. If Shelton had been right, Cassidy would find a husband from easy pickings in the high mountain town. From the maps, she remembered the claim lay not far from Oro City. Soon she'd have her feet on her land. Her future awaited and Shelton could stay in the past.

Jet sat high in his saddle, a rifle tucked into his saddle bags. *What the hell was Shelton thinking giving the boy the long arm?* As if he read her thoughts, the man stood over her shoulder, "Once Leroy and Sidney are gone, its just me and Jet."

Cassidy cheeks colored.

"Unless you want to trade the claim for a life at Twin Lakes?"

Cassidy resisted the urge to stomp her foot. What game was Shelton playing now.

"I'm going to take possession of my...." She cleared her throat, "Land and whatever else I find up there."

Shelton smirked. He ran his eyes down her physique in navy blue. "Is that why you chose that dress?"

Questions fizzed and popped in Cassidy's mind. This dress, Shelton liked this dress? Could she use that to her advantage? Cassidy shook her head as Shelton wandered away. She would not trap a husband. Well, no more than her father already had. A thought did cross her mind though, "Since you're not honoring the lease agreement, Shelton, I can choose any husband I deem fit." There, let him chew on that. Cassidy clambered into Carlotta's saddle and struck the reins, bringing her mule alongside Jet at the head of the procession. At least Jet had forgiven her. She knew the day would come when the boy would want to become a man, and increase his distance from her, only she wished it hadn't come at a time where she felt so lonely.

"How'd you sleep?"

Cassidy cleared her throat before she answered, "Well enough."

"I'm glad. I know you don't like the night Cass, but I'm almost a grown man."

"Almost," Cassidy smiled. "I know Jet, and I understand. I'm just glad you're here."

"Always Cass."

"And how do you feel?"

Jet sighed and squinted, "Better, my head still hurts every now and then, and I can't wait till bed but I don't feel dizzy anymore."

"Good." *He'd never told her about being dizzy!* "Then when you're good and rested we can put that big brain of yours to working the claim."

"And these," Jet tapped his shoulders and winked. Cassidy rolled her eyes. "I can't say I'm sorry to see the back of him though." Jet jutted his chin out towards Sidney. The teenager stalked over to the wagon, hat low over his brow.

"Neither can I," Cassidy mumbled.

"Did you really see a moose last night?" Jet asked.

Cassidy's fingers reached for her locket and she snatched her saddle instead, "Yes, giant antlers, long muzzle," She kept describing the animal while Jet pulled out his notebook and began scratching.

They reached the divergence right on lunch time, Alice insisting they eat before they farewell each other. Rubbing her rump Cassidy stumbled to the wagon, meeting Alice at the supplies.

"He's quite the charmer your man," Alice grinned.

Cassidy cleared her throat, "My relationship with Mister Murphy is purely professional."

"For now." Alice grinned as she single-handedly broke apart biscuits. Oliver squeaked in his swaddling, wide brown eyes taking in the new scenery. "I see how you too look at each other. I reckon we don't think you'll need a tinderbox to start the fire up the mountain."

Oliver warbled again as Alice moved around the food supplies.

"Do you want me to take him?" Cassidy offered.

"Uh-uh, you don't want that man thinking of children when he looks at you, I wished you-da said something earlier and I wouldn't have had you hold him so much."

A sigh escaped Cassidy's parched lips, she wanted Shelton thinking of marriage and Cassidy was certain she wasn't going to put the cart before the horse. Only Shelton didn't want marriage or children or a wife!

"You go take him this," She handed over a biscuit with jam.

Cassidy shook her head, and scooped up Oliver, "It'll be my

last chance for a cuddle, Shelton does like your biscuits."

She watched as Alice waddled over, a smile upon her cheeks. Shelton took one look at Cassidy and turned away. Good, she needed him to see what lay on the line. Cassidy wanted a future, not a fleet of fancy by the fire. Looking at Shelton's broad shoulders, the narrow taper at his waist and the way his denims clung to his thighs, the flight of fancy drifted through her mind. No. Cassidy would not settle.

Shelton put the sight of Cassidy with child out of his sight, but the memories of her melting in his arms, would not shift. She wanted what he couldn't offer. Not yet anyway.

"Thank you Shelton," Leroy shook his hand, "For bringing us up here and taking care of Sidney. He's a thorn in my buttocks most the time, but Granite seems to have straightened him out."

"I told you hun, boys make mistakes, that's how they become men." Alice appeared beside Shelton and handed him two jam biscuits. "I'll leave the recipe with Miss Smith for you Shelton."

"That's mighty kind of you Alice, but..."

"Nonsense." The woman handed her husband another two biscuits and his canteen before she excused herself and wandered over to Sidney.

"You know Shelton, she's my second wife."

"I gathered Leroy."

The older man went on without pause, "She's easy on the eye, she can cook, she looks after me and Sid and of course gave me Ollie, but do you know why I married her?"

Shelton bit into his biscuit, thinking of all the wrong answers, The conversation had travelled into territory that made Shelton want to tug his collar, and straighten his fringe. "Do I want to know Leroy?"

"It's the long nights and early mornings I cherish. Sometimes I just let her talk, God knows what she's on about but I do love the sound of her voice. When Sidney goes, even when

Ollie is grown, who will I spend my days with? She's always making plans for us, a future. That's why I married her, the girl can't sit still even if her life depended on it. Plus she thinks the world of me! I'd be just as happy if she never lifted a finger so long as she kept talking to me the way she does."

"Company?"

Leroy snorted, "Oh sure there's plenty of women that can provide all sorts of company, temporary as it may be, even for an old soul like me." He patted his belly, "But there's only one woman that's right for me. Just like there's one woman that's right for you."

Shelton almost groaned, he knew where Leroy was headed next, "Save your breath old man, we don't share the same ah, common goals." Shelton wanted Cassidy in his bed, Cassidy wanted his name after hers.

"You don't fool me Shelton, you both court close to danger and don't back down when it shows up. I know what you did for Sidney in Granite, and a lesser man would have walked away."

"He still got flogged Leroy, I couldn't prevent that."

"Aye and he no doubt deserved it. I know, I was a young man once too, twice, and take it from me; you don't even know what you're running away from let alone why. I seen you with her brother Jet, I wouldn't be surprised, given another week on the trail together that I would have had you holding Ollie."

Shelton almost spat out his biscuit, "Responsibility doesn't suit me."

Leroy laughed, "I ain't seen anything but from you this whole time! But that's my opinion, that you didn't ask for, do what you like with it." Leroy put out his hand again, "Thanks again Shelton, and I hope to see you and Miss Smith up at Twin Lakes sometime."

When Shelton finally swallowed the cookie crumbs he shook Leroy's hand, "Safe travels old man."

Leroy handed Shelton the remainder of his guide fee and

Shelton tucked it into his vest pocket. He'd send it straight home to his folks. No, he'd do one better and send it directly to the bank. "You're wrong about me running Leroy," Shelton said, "It's about timing."

"Ah," Leroy shook his head, "There's no such thing as good timing with women."

Cassidy watched Shelton shake hands with Leroy and then Sidney before both went over to shake Jet's hand. Sidney even tapped Jet on the shoulder. Cassidy said her farewells, hugging Alice and giving little Ollie a kiss on his dark curls. Butterflies stirring within her stomach as they climbed back on their mounts and continued towards Oro City.

The trail narrowed as it ascended, the fir tree line thinned as the gravel screes and sharp escarpments replaced thick woodlands. The Arkansas River snaked through the barren landscape only this time it seemed to carve through the earth. Gaping valleys yawed on either side as they climbed.

They broke for a rest briefly as the sun levelled with the snow-capped mountains along the horizon. The sounds of hooves approaching their party warned of the impending township. The miner lead his mule with wagon attached up from the river and northward, tipping his head in greeting. He meandered along the trail, thick beard and mud stained clothes, looking back every few feet to look at Cassidy. She tried to ignore Shelton's heated gaze and decided to pick a text book to read instead.

After resuming their pace, the land flattened out, smoke from chimney's visible through the sparse trees. The sun slipped beneath the horizon and for a moment Cassidy stared at the sunset, the sky filled with vibrant pinks and tangerines, lilacs and blues, so colourful in stark contrast to the slate and stone they trekked through.

"Well camp here for the night, and then head up to the claim tomorrow morning."

Cassidy eyed the expanding settlement, clumps of tents

loitered on the slopes, the sound of cooking and men singing, flitted through the chilly air. The soft glow of several campfires flickering amber light over the canvas could be seen. How many men camped here?

As Shelton greeted the onlookers, Cassidy scanned the features of the citizen's in the fading light. She couldn't hear his words, but one man pointed to the furthest edge of the tent city. Shelton tipped his hat in acknowledgement and lead *Tango* around the mass of tents. Cassidy caught sight of a few women, scarves over their head, babes in arms, or food in their hands. Overwhelmingly the crowd were men, and almost all of them came to the edge of their procession to stare and whisper at Cassidy.

Shelton looked over his shoulder several times as they walked, his head swiveling from crowd to Cassidy and back again. *Well she couldn't very well pick a husband in the dark!*

They reached the final tents, before the ground rose to a sharp escarpment. Three tents had been set in a circle and a fire crackled in the space between Cassidy could smell beef and beans and whiskey as she approached. Five men at the fireside stood up, two smiled, one winked. Cassidy offered a weak smile and ducked her head.

Shelton ordered Jet and Cassidy into action, and two miners stumbled over, "Need a hand me lady?" One said.

"Of course she does Benny."

"Ah thank you but I'm sure..."

"Ah rubbish, me and Gareth ain't busy."

Benny scooped up the side of Cassidy's tent and began hammering nails, and tying ropes.

"Thank you." Shelton said as soon as they were done, "Mind if we share your fire?"

"Be our guest," Gareth hiccupped. Both miners stepped back, looking Shelton up and down twice before returning to their stools by the campfire.

Cassidy watched the flames dance across Shelton's cheeks, the thinnest whiskers graced his square jaw, in this light it added a golden glow to his cheeks. She felt pressure on her waist, Shelton's palm curled around her hip and pulled her towards him. She wanted to push him away, only her hand rested on his chest, her fingers soothed by the pulse of his heart.

"Here."

Another type of pressure entered her abdomen, she looked down to see Shelton holding something. Fumbling with her grip, she closed her fingers over cool wood and steel.

"What's this?"

"Protection. I should have given it to you earlier."

When Shelton took a small step back, her eyes focused on the weapon she held in her hands. "What for?"

"In case some uncouth miner decides to crawl into your tent tonight."

Cassidy wanted to laugh, that's exactly what she wanted. No, she wanted an honest offer first! Instead she simply nodded and tucked the stub nosed weapon into her pocket. She looked at Jet who had finished setting up his own tent. Perhaps she should ask Jet to stay with her? No, the boy was almost grown. Here, in Oro City, their new life had begun, and she couldn't reduce him in the eyes of the men he might have to work with. Shelton had kept her safe so far, surely, he wouldn't fail her now. Although, her mother had thought that of Julius Smith and it had been her undoing.

Chapter 21

Cassidy stretched her legs, the warmth of the fire heating the soles of her dragonfly embroidered boots as the lump of timber carved into a stool, turned her rump numb.

"From Chicago, yes." Cassidy answered.

The miner who sat to her left, whistled through his teeth, "Big city girl, hey." He grinned. Perhaps if he combed his knotted curly brown hair, he wouldn't look so rough. His deep set brown eyes sparkled in the firelight, his nose straight and narrow. Was he closer to twenty or thirty, Cassidy couldn't tell.

"Me names Harold," He shot out his hand, "Everyone round here just calls me Harry."

Cassidy took his hand and shook it. She looked down to see his nails edged in something black and seemed too long for Cassidy. Plus, could she really marry a man who said 'me' instead of 'my'?

"Pleased to meet you Harry, and your name is?" She turned to her right to greet the thickset man beside her. His ginger beard reached halfway down his chest, his flaming hair slicked back into a tail, with glasses on his nose.

"Eddie," The man said softly, his blue eyes holding Cassidy's gaze, unblinking. His lips turned gently up at the corner. He didn't say another world but continued to stare at Cassidy.

"Well it's a pleasure to meet you both." She said. Across the fire, another miner stood, one knee bent, his heel on his stool and blew steam off the top of his coffee. With broad shoulders, he stood half a head shorter than Shelton. His eyes looked like black pits from this distance. He tucked a curl of brown hair behind his ear and ran the palm of his hand down his whiskered cheeks. He hadn't said a word to her so far, and Cassidy couldn't help but shiver when he looked at her.

She tried her best to make beef and bean stew without Alice to guide her, a young man named Sandy came to stand over Cassidy's shoulder with a lantern. Jet started talking and soon, his conversation drifted to the people and rumors.

"So who's the dark horse?" Jet whispered.

"That's Johnny Twobit Jones, he keeps to himself, but some reckon they seen him on a wanted bill from Kansas."

Cassidy watched Johnny wander out of the reach of the campfire and disappear into the darkness. She pressed her hand to her pocket and felt the cool steel still concealed. One night, she only had to make it one night, before they would be safely up at the claim.

When she served dinner to Shelton, he held onto her wrist, his eyes tracking down her dress and then over to the far side of the fire where Johnny had disappeared.

"I know, I saw him." Cassidy whispered and pulled her hand back.

Jet sat next to Cassidy eating slowly, staring at the fire. Although he remained still, seemingly disconnected to the world, Cassidy knew his ears pricked to any slip of information.

Cassidy looked to Shelton, a sudden worry entering her mind that they sat amongst criminals and hoodlums, Jet and Cassidy felt at home. Shelton was just a rancher. Her eyes fell to his broken nose and busted knuckles. Nope, the man wasn't 'just' anything. She sighed.

After dinner, she excused herself and Jet walked her to her tent. "I'm going to keep watch with Shelton for a bit."

"Sure." Cassidy said. Inside the canvas she hastily dressed in her nightgown, and then her riding jacket and finally tugged on her boots. Tucking Shelton's tiny revolver under her pillow, she turned on her side and pulled the blankets tight around her. The low sound of men's voices discussing gold filtered through the canvas. Slowly, as the weariness of the journey bleached into her muscles and sleep claimed her.

Shelton watched as Jet's lids grew heavier, the boy was beat and he needed his rest. "Off you go, but stay alert hey." He whispered.

Jet stifled a yawn and shook his head.

"You're no good to me tired, boy." Shelton added. "If I need you, don't worry I'll holler."

Jet rose to his feet slowly, and wandered into his tent. Shelton's elbow touched his holster. Six. He took a sip of his coffee and nodded to the men around the fire. Four.

"Yeah, he's a dancer, not a cutter so I got him for a steal." Shelton said.

"He's a looker," Harry said.

"They both are." Johnny had returned not long after Cassidy had taken to her tent. Something about the man unnerved Shelton. He'd seen his type before, silent, watching, anticipating. As if the man waited for a trap to spring, and then like a carrion eater he'd swoop to eat the carcass.

Shelton nodded his head, "Yep she is, and her husband is paying me to bring her to him, unharmed." He emphasised the last word.

Johnny didn't move when he spoke next, "How much?"

Shelton met his dark gaze, "Enough."

"I'll counter offer." Johnny said. The other miners froze. At least Eddie had the decency to look down into his mug.

"Trust me, it wouldn't be enough." Shelton said. It would never be enough, he thought. Shelton stood upright and stretched, cracking his neck from side to side and rolling his shoulders forward one at a time. He could sense Johnny sizing him up. Shelton couldn't help himself and let his vest gap, the holster of his six-shooter dipped forward, as Shelton adjusted the one around his waist. For a moment, he considered cracking his knuckles.

Johnny smirked.

How else could Shelton ensure Cassidy's safety? Shelton regarded their two isolated tents behind him. Cassidy as always had set hers further from the rest. If he could have it his way Shelton would knock Johnny's grin from his narrow cheeks right now. Except the man hadn't done anything. Yet. Shelton cleared his throat and tossed his coffee onto the stones surrounding the fire.

"Well I'm turning in for the night, thanks for your hospitality."

Murmurs and grumbles fare-welled Shelton, one voice louder than the others.

"Sweet dreams." Johnny said with a click of his tongue for emphasis.

Ice ran down Shelton's spine. He couldn't shoot a man on his first night in Oro City, could he? He stalked to the tents, each step bringing him closer to his decision. He knelt at the edge of the threshold, hands tentatively opening the canvas. The scent of blackcurrant, violet and amber searing bewitching Shelton's good sense. As he crawled his way into the tent, his eyes adjusted to Cassidy slumbering on her side. Suddenly she leaned up and Shelton froze.

"Shelton?"

How could she see him in the dark? "Yeah it's me Precious," He crawled to the side of her sleeping mat. The long hours of sentry duty at the fire for the past week had taken it's toll and now, this close to Cassidy, weariness and contentment brought him down to the sleeping mat.

"What's wrong, is it Jet?"

"No, Precious I'm just tired." He brought an arm under his head and rested on his back, staring upwards into the darkness.

"I could have shot you."

He didn't want to argue, he wanted to find comfort in her soft warm curves, "I'm too tired to keep watch and this is how I'm going to keep despicable miners from crawling into your bed at night."

The blankets shifted, and a giggle reached his ears, "Are you sure, there's not one here already."

Shelton snorted, sleep finding him more rapidly then he'd like, "I know," he mumbled.

"I will be choosing my own husband Shelton."

Restraint fled like his strength to stay awake, "Fine. Tomorrow. In daylight." He turned on his side, finding her pillow with his cheek, he wrapped his arm around her waist, the softness of her hair tickling his nose, "For now, just this."

Cassidy waited, except Shelton didn't finish his sentence. She squeezed her eyes tight and slowly dragged her thumb back and forth across his forearm that cuddled her waist. In response his body curled around hers, knees behind hers, groin against her buttocks. This, Cassidy told herself, was how it was meant to be. Tomorrow they would reach the claim, and the terms of the contract could either be enacted or void. She hadn't bothered to ask him about Hugo and truth be told she wasn't interested. She needed to try though, this was hers and Jet's future. She needed to be realistic. This. This meant nothing to Shelton and although it sliced through her insides to admit it, this would have to be the last indulgence she allowed.

The light grey dawn slithered in through the canvas. Cassidy's cheek rested against Shelton's chest and she listened to the deep breaths as his warmth kept her glued to his side. Any minute now, and he'd wake, the spell would be broken and Cassidy would have to face her future and see through her convictions. Underneath her palm, the man twitched. She closed her eyes and tried to remain still.

The blankets shifted as he lifted his head. A short groan made her heart sink. She felt her pillow dimple as he rested his head again. If she opened her eyes, would she want to see his expression? Disappointed, angry, annoyed?

Long fingers danced along her forearm, down to her elbow and back again, as Shelton's other arm tightened around her waist. He thumbed her back, his movements steady and then slowing until Cassidy felt sure he'd fallen asleep again.

"Cass," Shelton whispered.

She sighed, "Mmm."

"Time to get up."

"Is it?" She mumbled. Once so eager to reach the claim, now her limbs filled with lead.

Shelton pressed a kiss to her hair as he gently pried her off his chest. She tucked the blankets under her chin and rolled over, the illusion broken.

"I should check on Jet at least." A blast of chilly air gusted through the tent.

Cassidy sat up to see the canvas settle in place, Shelton gone and with him, her hope.

It took her a full twenty minutes before she felt ready to exit the tent. The scent of bacon and eggs had become too much. Eddie and Harry sat around the fire, their heads together whispering as they watched Shelton ready the mules. As soon as they saw Cassidy they stood, Eddie rushed to put two eggs on a plate, and Harry handed her a fresh mug of coffee.

"Thank you," She said.

At the sound of her voice, Johnny appeared on the other side of the camp, two holsters on his hips and a well-worn grey Stetson pulled low over his eyes.

"Morning Darling," He said with a wink.

Shelton's shoulders tensed.

"Ah morning," Cassidy said and took her plate to the closest stool. Jet slumped down beside her, his plate filled with bacon and bread.

"Heading out this morning, or going to stay around Oro City for a while?" Johnny asked taking the only other stool next to her.

"We'll be heading out, I believe." Cassidy said.

"Not straight away mind you." Shelton took three steps that brought him over Cassidy's shoulder. "Going to stop by the Post Office and send a telegram or two."

"Oh yeah," Johnny ran his fingers down his beard. "I can show you the sights, the view from the peak is quite alluring at dusk."

Shelton brought himself right between Johnny and Cassidy, "Not that long Johnny, was it two-bit Jones or Jones two-bit?"

Johnny's smile turned down, his cheeks flat.

"First I'm going to send a few telegrams, one home, one to Kearby, you remember Kearby don't you Jet."

"Kearby, Kearby...." Jet tilted his head to one side and then smirked, "Oh yeah, the Texas Ranger Kearby."

"Yeah, gonna send him a telegram that we arrived safe and made some new friends." Shelton patted Johnny on the shoulder. At each tap, the man's cheeks changed another shade of white.

"Is that so?"

"Yeah." Shelton smiled an empty expression that deepened the coldness in his eyes.

Cassidy rolled her lips inwards. *Clever, very clever,* she thought. "Oh he'll be up in no time to visit then."

"How very decent of him." Johnny managed before he stood up. His dark eyes narrowed over Shelton's only for a moment before he turned on his heel, "Pleasure to meet y'all, Miss Smith."

"Pleasure is all mine," Shelton answered.

Johnny stalked to the tree line, as soon as the fir trees engulfed him, he broke into a run.

Shelton winked at Jet, who leaned forward to Cassidy, "See there is a benefit in living an honest life in Colorado Cass."

"Otherwise Shelton will call Marcus Kearby on us?" She replied.

Jet laughed and bit into a strap of bacon, "Uh-huh."

As they clambered into their saddles, Shelton finally spoke to Cassidy, "You lost another suitor."

She couldn't help but laugh, "I don't mind so much about that one."

When Shelton's laugh echoed off the tree-lined slopes, she continued, "I don't fancy my name as Cassidy Two-bit anything."

His laughter lightened the ache in her chest if only for a moment. She still had to face Hugo James, and still Shelton hadn't made any offer, not even an apology.

The trek up to the claim wound around the mountain side, the Arkansas river always to one side, the rush of water became a torrent at places, others it split wide over irregular plateaus. A loneliness crept into her bones, wishing she could float her way back down the river to the grassy plains of Texas and Kansas, where the sun shone on fields of wildflowers. The landscape filled with pinks, and purples, tangerines and cherries, rather than the emerald and slate filled scenery that now surrounded them.

Just before lunch, Shelton lead *Tango* off the trail, a narrow path snaked between tall pines and firs, marked only by a steel peg driven into the earth and topped with a hessian bag. Cassidy pressed her hands to her stomach as they wandered deeper into the woodland.

The trees gave way to a sandy flat, the Arkansas River curled wide along the bank as a large hill boarded the rear boundary. The hillside peaked in a large escarpment that loomed over the property, disappearing out of sight to another thick forest of fir, pine trees and aspens. For a moment, Cassidy imagined how many moose and bear would be roaming wild in the dark woodlands. Two huts had been erected up from the plateau but spaced several feet away from the hillside. A long and wide log cabin had a pitched roof, with smoke curling from the chimney, the other smaller and more rustic with a flat roof that had been overwhelmed by leaves.

A figure rose from beside the river, his brown trousers and coat dusty around the hem. He placed down the panning tray and lifted his hat higher on his forehead. Hugo James stood for a moment, his head titled to the side watching Shelton lead Cassidy and Jet to the largest cabin.

Cassidy dismounted and straightened her skirts, while Shelton met Hugo halfway across the field. Hiding her profile behind her mules rump she watched as Shelton stalked over, arms on his hips shaking his head. Hugo threw his head back and laughed. From this distance she could see the long strands of salt and pepper hair curled behind his ears, his short beard more grey than brown, and eyes that crinkled at the corners. He made his way to them.

"So this is Julius Smith's daughter." Hugo pushed his hand forward and Cassidy shook it.

His beard was short and neat, with a moustache that curled across his cheeks, the wrinkles around his eyes showed he was near ten years older than Shelton, but his deepest, brown eyes seemed to radiate warmth in the bleak landscape.

He stood shorter than Shelton but taller than Cassidy, his hand solid, but gentle. Cassidy smiled. "It's a pleasure to meet you Mister James."

"Please call me Hugo," He smiled, straight white teeth beamed at Cassidy. "And you're her brother Jet, is that right?"

"Ah yes." Jet straightened his shoulders.

"Well we could always use more hands around here, how are you with a shovel?"

"Fair enough."

"Good, well I'm hungry, Shelton did you get the supplies?"

Shelton nodded, his gaze lingered on Cassidy as she smiled at Hugo. He struggled to find words as if a weight had been dangling inside his chest, and Hugo just cut a support rope. He directed Hugo to the line of mules and together they unpacked the items.

"What you playing at, you knew you set me up to sign that document."

"Did I?" Hugo mused, his eyes returning to watch Cassidy saunter into the main cabin, "I thought she'd be one of those, farmer's daughters, you know, all plain faced scowls and checked aprons." Hugo lifted one bag and it tumbled to the gravel. Shelton picked it up and shoved it at the man's chest.

"And now?"

"Well, I'm surprised you haven't made an attempt, or have you and she told you to take a hike?"

"I'm not here for a wife, I've got the Blue Cow to think of."

"Yeah, mores the pity." Hugo slapped Shelton on the shoulder and lumbered up to the main cabin.

The urge to throw something at Hugo's back trembled Shelton's hands. He had hoped that Cassidy would find another husband so he could be free of the contract, only now it didn't sit right. He reached the tiny patio of the cabin just before Hugo did and he pulled back on the man's shoulder, "You going to marry her then?"

Hugo's face screwed up, and he readjusted his burden, "Marry? Unless her Daddy up and dies before we find a shit tonne of gold what's the point in marrying her?"

Because Cassidy wanted marriage, that's why, Shelton thought. Well, Cassidy had swindled her way up the mountain and now she could contend with another wily businessman. Perhaps they suited each other? The heaviness in his ribs hadn't shifted. What could he do about it? Nothing. Yet. If he started in earnest, paying off the Blue Cow debt, perhaps he could make Cassidy an honest offer before Hugo won her over?

Shelton entered the cabin and the warmth forced him to blink. Cassidy stood in the centre of the room looking at the rustic contents. A pot belly stove creaked in one corner, the door ajar and glowing with coals. A tiny sink had been bolted underneath a narrow window. A wonky table with two chairs filled out the space between the fire and the double bed that had been built against the far wall. Beside the bed a rough hewn ladder climbed to a narrow loft bed above.

"It's not much but it'll do us."

"First things first, I suppose," Hugo took hold of Cassidy's backpack and tossed it onto the double bed. Next he pointed to the upper bunk to Jet, "If you wouldn't find fixing a spot of lunch, Shelton and I will see about the hut's roof. Come on Shelton."

Shelton nodded. So, Hugo would play the chivalrous host despite his intentions? Shelton gave one last look to Cassidy and followed Hugo out the door.

"We'll see which one of us she invites first to supper." Hugo said to Shelton as they crossed the distance to the ramshackle outbuilding.

"Fine." Shelton said and tossed an offcut of timber at Hugo. The older man snatched it from the air and winked. Shelton thought he knew, except with Hugo's slick ways, now he wasn't so sure.

Chapter 22

"Now that the hut's got a proper roof on it, I'll head into town tomorrow morning and buy those supplies you missed at Granite, Shelton." Hugo said around a mouthful of pork and peas.

Cassidy sliced a thin sliver of her meat as she watched the exchange between the men. Hugo's hair still damp and slicked back, Cassidy had been surprised the man had scrubbed up for dinner. Even his nails looked clean. The scent of sandalwood and musk reached her from where she sat on the bunk. Jet sat beside her, while Shelton took the other stool at the table.

"While you start cutting for the head frame."

Shelton nodded and pushed his plate to the centre of the table, "Sure."

"Is there anything you need from town Pet?"

Cassidy couldn't be sure if Shelton burped or growled. His long fingers splayed across the table, he lounged in his chair, only he didn't look comfortable.

"No I'm fine thank you," She answered politely. Hugo's jaw looked solid under his short beard and his shoulders were thick. She eyed his forearms, tanned and tensed as he manoeuvred his knife and fork. He had manners and he wasn't unattractive, she mused.

Shelton took his plate to the sink, "Do you feel up to lending a hand tomorrow Jet?"

"Sure, Shelton." Jet answered.

A squeak erupted as timber dragged across timber and Shelton pulled his chair closer to the bunk, "Give us a look at those drawings again."

Jet complied and handed Shelton his notebook. Hugo

scraped his plate and craned his neck to take in the sketches that Shelton and Jet now discussed.

"Nice," Hugo said. Jet offered the man a weak smile.

Cassidy dug into her backpack and brought out her geology text book, "It might be worth having a look around to see where the best place to...."

Hugo's head raised over the top of Jet's and he looked at Cassidy, "I wouldn't mind a spot of coffee would you?"

"Um," Cassidy paused at the interruption, "Coffee? Sure,"

"No worries, I take it two sugars if you don't mind."

Cassidy's breath froze in her lungs, Jet's brow furrowed, his hand moved as if to close the notebook. "Of course."

"Only when you finish your grub, Pet." Hugo added.

Cassidy looked at her pork and peas, the flavour of ash suddenly coated her tongue, "I'm done." Rising she stalked past the table and Hugo's plate shot out. Cassidy's cheeks coloured. She was a fool. A wife should want to wait on her husband; dote on him and indulge his every whim. Hugo hadn't worried about the formalities; he clearly knew how this arrangement worked. She reached for his plate, only to have Shelton snatch it away.

"You make the coffee." He said as he manoeuvred around the tiny space to reach the sink.

Cassidy listened as Hugo and Jet nattered away, discussing measurements and supplies on how to build the sluice boxes. "Well you and Shelton can get a good start on them tomorrow then before I get back. Then again, you might want to build Cass, a linen line too from the scraps, can't have her stringing up the washing between the trees."

The spoon in Cassidy's fingers trilled against the coffee cup. She heard a sigh from Shelton.

"Is this how you imagined it?" Shelton's question barely a whisper.

"I don't mind doing laundry Shelton, but I wont be taken advantage of. Not by anybody."

She held his gaze just long enough for the man to look

down into his sink, the suds slipping over his hands, as his long fingers circled the plates. "You want an apology from me?"

She gritted her teeth to hide her heated whisper, "It wouldn't hurt." She ached inside at his dismissal, the disregard for her feelings and the selfish satisfaction he sought for himself. Her pain echoed by the hearty breeze that rattled the tiny pane of glass.

Cassidy tossed her spoon into the sink with a clatter. Shelton's soapy hand closed over her wrist, "I'm not going to apologize for wanting you, Cass."

Against her desire, she slid her arm from his grip, his fingers trailing down hers, "You want me for now, Shelton but I need forever."

His shoulders slumped, a strand of his blonde hair rested across his crooked nose, "I can't give you forever."

"Then that's how it is." Cassidy took Hugo's cup to the table, he didn't even raise his head in thanks. She let him and Jet discuss the logistics of their build as she curled up on the bunk bed. A lantern clung over the dinner table, allowing enough light for her to read the text on geology. Damn that man! She'd show him that Cassidy Smith was worth the trouble.

Shelton tossed two more logs into the pot belly and closed the grill. Hesitating at the cabin door, he saw Cassidy slumped to one side, her eyes closed. Jet had already crawled up to the bunk before they'd finished going over his sketches. Three steps took him to her bedside and he tugged the geology book from under her fingers. The sight of her braid askew and long lashes fanning her cheeks increased the urge to crawl under the blankets until it almost overwhelmed Shelton. How long would it take him to pay the Blue Cow debt? Instead of lowering himself to the mattress, Shelton turned on his heel, extinguishing the lantern before he closed the cabin door. Ten steps from Cassidy, the hut waited for Shelton. An orange glow seeped from around the crooked door sill, as smoke rose from the stone chimney. He'd have to share the tiny hut with Hugo, thankfully Shelton hadn't had to settle the matter with his fists. Although, knowing Hugo there'd be an angle to his benefit somewhere. Shelton crept into the heated interior and took his place on his sleep mat. He'd build himself a bed, while he cut for the headframes and sluice boxes. Both him and *Tango* would be busy tomorrow pulling last years felled logs and any others that had fallen in the meantime.

Hugo had sprawled across the single bunk, his snores already tearing through the chilly air. At least the man had set a fire. Shelton had sent his telegrams before they left Oro City and would wait at least a week before checking any replies. In the meantime, he'd ask Cass to look around the claim. Clearly with her geology knowledge she'd have a least an even chance as Hugo's mining experience.

He rolled onto his side, he didn't want to think of Cassidy Smith. Not until he struck gold. Everything up until that point was speculation. He pulled his blanket up to his shoulder, groaning as he sensed her blackcurrant and violet scent lingering in the fabric.

Cassidy cooked straps of bacons and a sad helping of beans for breakfast. A lopside grin disturbed Shelton's clean shaven cheeks and she couldn't wait until Hugo left for town before she could find a quiet spot to bath.

"As a matter of fact, I think I might want something after all." She said. If Hugo wanted her to play 'house' then she could play along. "Some chickens for eggs would go nice, don't you think."

Hugo leaned back in the slender chair smiled, "Sounds tasty."

"Oh and maybe some lye and vinegar."

Hugo dug a finger into his ear. Shelton's fork paused halfway to his mouth.

"Well the lye is for the laundry and that window could do

with a lick of vinegar, white vinegar if you don't mind, a jar of baking soda wouldn't go astray either, I like to bake."

Hugo threw Shelton a smirk and the other man raised his eyebrows. Shelton finished his breakfast, his eyes narrowed at Cassidy. Maybe Shelton did know the common household ingredients could also find gold. If he did, he didn't say anything.

"Sure thing Pet," Hugo put his hat on his head. For a moment she thought he'd lean in to peck her on the cheek. At the last minute, he must have thought better of it and simply strolled out the front door.

Shelton picked up Hugo's plate and his own. Cassidy stopped him at the sink, "It's fine Shelton, please leave it."

"Baking?"

"I thought it was a bit too much to ask for ammonia."

A thick laugh trickled out of Shelton's broad chest and she wanted to throw herself against it and feel his arms around her.

"Besides, Alice gave me her jam biscuit recipe."

"Good, Precious." Shelton cleared the table of the coffee mugs before he grabbed his Stetson and placed it on his head, "I do like those biscuits."

It wasn't until the cabin door shut, that Cassidy replied, "I know."

Shelton hitched the rope to the back of *Tango* and then handed the care of driving the horse into the field with the dead trees behind him to Jet. The morning had passed fast, with each log they split. He'd been careful to rest Jet more than needed. The boy still wobbled sometimes, squinting in the sun, and Shelton caught him more than once clutching his abdomen. Sometime around noon, he'd given up on his shirt, the damp fabric hampering each swing of his axe. He scooped up the tool now and rolled one arm then the other.

After breakfast, he'd caught sight of Cassidy slipping down the river, with a bundle in her hands. It seemed to Shelton that he counted every breath until she resurfaced, her braid wet, her navy dress gone, replaced with her blue split riding skirt and light brown shirt.

As she wandered around the other side of the cabin, Shelton found himself transfixed as she draped each piece of clothing over the branches of a scrawny tree, including a selection of lace.

"Shelton?"

"Huh?"

"Ready now," Jet clicked his fingers at Shelton's face.

"Yeah ready."

An hour later, he'd watched Cassidy slip from the cabin to walking slowly along the base of the hillside, following it south to the woodlands opposite where Shelton and Jet worked.

Now as he picked up the axe again, he found himself counting moments until she would wander out of the thicket.

"Should we check on her?"

"Didn't you see that book in her hands? She's probably found a quiet spot to sit."

"Bears, Jet. Bears."

"I'll stay here with Tango." Jet said.

Shelton reached for his rifle just as a slim figure appeared from the tree line, head down book open across her arms. She walked laboured and Shelton hazarded a guess she'd filled her pockets with rocks.

"She's fine Shelton." Jet said as she ran his hand down *Tango's* nose.

"Just you worry about that horse."

"He's no trouble."

Shelton snorted, "He has taken to you now, you've done well."

The boy grinned, "Yeah I think we understand each other now." Jet slipped another slice of apple under the animal's nose.

Shelton just hummed as he turned back to his pile of timber.

An ache seared through Shelton's shoulders as Cassidy re-appeared with a tray full of sandwiches and fresh mug of steaming coffee. Sighing Shelton reclined against the felled timber, waiting until she reached him. As she neared he caught her gaze drifted over his frame, right down to his belt buckle and he fought the urge to tense. Blood thundered through his veins, her intoxicating scent catching on the wind, and his tired arms sung, thirsting to reach for her.

"Thanks," He said with the bitter brew tart on his tongue as he stood bare-chested in the brisk breeze.

Cassidy's plump lips rolled inwards as her cheeks filled with colour.

"How did your survey go?" Satisfied the redness on her cheeks deepened, Shelton smiled.

"The landscape is pretty ah, um, rugged, so the results are unresolved."

Shelton took an excessively large bit of his sandwich, not trusting his next words.

"How are the boxes coming along?" Thankfully Cassidy moved to Jet, and Shelton could relax.

"Shelton thinks we'll have enough timber to build my design. We're starting after lunch. Hugo's already got all the mesh and wire. He pointed to crates stacked beside the tiny shack.

"The double layer is genius." Shelton added. Cassidy loved it when he praised Jet. He could see the edges of her lips curl upwards. "Hopefully we can halve our time and wastage." Anything that would pay the Blue Cow debt, and then perhaps Cassidy would be warming his bed sooner. He almost scoffed, suddenly he'd become too cautious. Cassidy was a grown woman, she knew the risks and could make her own decisions. The memory of her hips rolling across his, strummed a chord in his chest that speared through his loins. "Come on, back to work then."

Cassidy collected their plates and headed back to the house.

"Let me know when your survey results are in." Shelton hollered after her and picked up the axe.

Cassidy washed the plates in the tiny sink first and then with soapy fingers she washed the rock specimens she'd collected including a nice sample of quartz to soak in vinegar when Hugo returned. She'd followed the natural lay of the land, looking for intrusive rock formations, even remnants of gas pockets or metamorphic structures that might lead to precious gems. Cassidy trekked an aspen gully down to the edge of the main Arkansas River before she'd circled back. Hopefully, once soaked in vinegar or tested with acid, her samples would reveal gold.

She spent the next hours tidying up the cabin to what she imagined a wife would do, wiping down the table, tucking chairs in and dusting every other surface. Despite the cold, she left the cabin door open; the sound of axe striking wood oddly satisfying. Every now and then she paused to watch Shelton and Jet working together. The first sluice box had been erected, resting on its timber frame at the sandy bank of the river. Fuelling Cassidy's curiosity, Shelton still worked shirtless, her fingers twitching to caress his sculptured chest. Would it be so bad to satiate her curiosity? How quickly could that turn into craving? Something told Cassidy if she tested her desires with Shelton that it would be total surrender. Shelton twisted, his eyes shaded by his Stetson, as he faced the cabin. Cassidy felt the air drawn out of her lungs and heat blossom in her abdomen. How much trouble was Shelton Murphy?

A gust of wind tore up the Arkansas crossing the field as it buffeted Cassidy's skirts against her legs. She decided to cede defeat over her washing, and collected it from the chilly air before it froze solid. The last piece of lace tugged free from the tree when Hugo returned with his mule tired and his rickety cart full, including two very frazzled looking chickens.

Shelton and Jet wandered over to assist and Cassidy tossed

her damp clothing on the bed before stepping out to help.

Hugo greeted Cassidy with a broad smile across his cheeks and one hand behind his back. With a wink of his eye he revealed a bunch of white wild flowers, "For you my Pet."

Cassidy didn't dare look at Shelton when she heard his groan, "Thank you although the chickens were enough." She lowered her head hoping Hugo wouldn't see the falseness in her reply.

As they brought the goods inside Hugo sighed loudly, "You've almost let the fire go out you daft –"

"Hey," Shelton's snap brought Hugo's head around, "I spent all day with the sluice boxes and didn't get enough timber up."

Hugo nodded, "Well, did you get the linen line done?"

Shelton sat down and stretched one leg across the edge of the table, "Nope been building boxes all day, I reckon they're ready."

"Yeah well, I'll be the judge of that." Hugo slammed down a tub, then a jar and finally a tin on the table, "I got them all just like you asked."

Cassidy simply nodded.

"You're welcome. Now what's for dinner?" Hugo turned his attention to the pot belly. Opening the grill, he tapped Jet on the shoulder, "Get some wood Boy."

Jet's eyes met hers, "I will, and then I'll sort out those chickens."

Cassidy retreated to the sink. Her head had been so full of Shelton she hadn't thought about dinner.

"Oh and Delilah wasn't happy she heard you're back in town and didn't dropped by to say hello Shelton." Hugo added.

Fast as lightening, Cassidy faced the window, wishing she could snap every stem of the dainty flowers. Who the devil was Delilah? Hugo kept talking except Cassidy couldn't hear a word he said as the heat climbed her neck and clogged her ears. "I'll take this to the icebox." Cassidy scooped up the remaining supplies including a parcel of lamb wrapped in paper. The cabin door creaked as she stormed to the narrow box dug into the ground at the edge of the cabin.

"Hey?"

Not trusting her emotions, Cassidy stayed crouched over the tin-lined ice chest. Shelton leaned against the exterior of the cabin, one boot flat against the logs, both hands in his pockets. "You want me to chase off another suitor?"

Cassidy stood slowly, trying not to shiver, "And have him chase us both off the lease?"

Shelton crossed his arms, his gaze wandering out to the river, "What do you want Cassidy?"

"A husband."

"And what's inside is what you want?"

"It's the best on offer at the moment, isn't it?"

Shelton's jaw cinched, his brows furrowed, "I think you should consider altering the terms of this agreement, work in a few new clauses and conditions of your own." He pivoted against the edge of the timber, bringing her waist within his orbit. Raising one hand, he gently ran the back of his fingers along her frozen cheek, "Maybe consider adding terms that are mutual beneficial to all parties."

"Is that so?" Cassidy's locket seemed so cold, it could burn her skin and she longed to turn it, to heat the metal and feel the warmth that Shelton had awoken. His hand trailed down her neck, behind her shoulder and dragged her by the waist against his body.

"Surely we could negotiate a merger of sorts," His lips brushed against hers and Cassidy relented, melting against him, "At least for the short-term."

Lengthening her arms, Cassidy's palms pushed against his solid chest until she'd retreated out of his reach, "Short term...."

"I meant..."

Cassidy re-entered the cabin to see Hugo standing at the pot belly warming his hands, "I made you a pot of coffee, Pet."

With a deep inhale Cassidy smiled, "Thank you." She knew

the 'short-term merger' Shelton referred to and, tempting as it was, she knew she could never act. She wasn't against hard work and would rather build her marriage from scratch than like a flash of gold in the pan, she'd be chasing forever. Hugo's unusual attempts at courting had gained Shelton's attention. Cassidy didn't want to trap a husband, but she knew the effect of demand and supply, distraction, and sleight of hand.

Chapter 23

After Cassidy's reasonable attempts at dinner, Shelton and Hugo returned to their cabin leaving Jet and Cassidy alone.

"I don't like him, I don't trust him and I don't understand why Shelton hasn't made you a proper offer yet. I'm going to speak to him."

Cassidy almost blanched, "No Jet, I'm working on it, but I share your sentiments. He's Shelton's business partner and we - well I've already cost Shelton time and money. If we stay here, I know I can find something of value."

"And if you don't?"

"I'll do laundry in Oro City."

Jet snorted looking at the pile of wet washing still on her bunk, "You better hope that geology book sets you straight."

"I know." Cassidy sighed.

They retired that night, Jet scrawling designs for an extravagant chick coop in his notebook while Cassidy checked the pot belly's grill three times to make sure it was shut before she eventually fell asleep.

Cassidy woke to the smell of bacon filling the dark corners of the cabin. Shelton stood at the pot belly, his back to her, while she listened to the crackle of the bacon.

"What are you doing?"

Cassidy crawled out of bed, and she heard Jet groan above her. Shelton looked over his shoulder and slowly ran his eyes over her sleep-laden form as she stood there, the sheer fabric clung to all her curves as she pulled her hair to one side of her neck.

"I'm hungry." Shelton picked a piece of bacon from the pan

and slipped it past his lips. "Aren't you?"

Wishing her cheeks would cool, Cassidy relented and tugged her jacket on, tiptoeing to the table, "Please let me do it."

Jet crawled down from his bunk rubbing his head over his unruly hair, "Smell's good, I'll check the chickens for eggs."

"Its fine Cass," Shelton snatched the coffee pot from her hands and reset it on the top, "I wanted an early start this morning that's all. We only have two days to build the boxes before tools down for Church on Sunday."

"Church?"

"It's not much, but it gives the town a lift and an excuse to rest. Afterwards, if there's time, I'll take you up the escarpment and show you why your father named it Pips Pit."

She couldn't help the smile that worked across her frozen cheeks, "Thank you, that would be nice." Cassidy would make time to take a few samples from way up there up on the ridge. Surely when her father had acquired this place, he'd known its value. Somewhere, somehow Cassidy would find the vein of gold. Cassidy sat down at the table and watched Shelton move about the kitchen, his tall frame moving gracefully in the tiny space. Cassidy had already found something, only Shelton Murphy was more like Fools gold than anything else.

The next two days passed in a blur, all three men spent long hours in the open air. Jet constructed the most elaborate chicken coop this side of the Rocky's and when he'd finished, Jet helped Shelton build the head frame for the shaft. Hugo had spent his time, at the river sending shovel load after shovel load into the sluice boxes.

Each night they trudged in for dinner, Cassidy eventually got one egg from her frazzled chickens to make a batch of biscuits. She'd hope to make another round to the woodlands however Hugo had added a pile of mud soaked clothes to her task list. She still checked her samples every day, nothing but dirt and debris. Nothing sparkling at all.

Cassidy had dressed in her navy outfit that morning and a thin film of dust coated the fabric as she rode in the back of the cart, led by Hugo's mule. Shelton sat atop *Tango* as they made their way down the mountain to Oro City. The journey didn't take nearly as long as it had when they arrived and this time in daylight, Cassidy could survey the town. The tent city cascaded on the low side of the town all the way down to the Arkansas, however Oro City's main street ran parallel on higher ground. A trading post, which doubled as the stage coach stop rested beside a saloon with rooms on the second story likely for rent by the day or the hour, then a barber shop and the post office. Cassidy spied the canvas rears behind the false fronts of the newer buildings, and further out, the long sloping roof of the stamp mill could be seen.

Indeed, as Shelton described, the community had erected a narrow building at the high end of town overlooking the river and the main street. Inside the church Cassidy sat at the far right hand side and tried to listen patiently as the pastor delivered his sermon. When had she last been at Church? Certainly her father hadn't made an effort, despite Cassidy's upbringing at the orphanage, she couldn't recall the finer details of worship. Something she could remedy. Shuffling in her seat she tried to pay attention, only Shelton's long leg rested only inches away. She clutched at her abdomen as she heard him softly clear his throat. His usual plum scent suddenly overwhelming irresistible. Jet's head lolled on Cassidy's shoulder and she twisted to adjust, her hip colliding with Shelton's. Against her best intentions, Cassidy's body didn't want to respond. The sermon ending before Cassidy moved away.

As Church spilled out into the chilly Colorado air, Cassidy found Hugo at her elbow, hooking his arm under hers, "I'll introduce you to the Pastor."

The air froze in Cassidy's lungs, the Pastor? Was he going to try and marry her here and now? On trembling knees Cassidy allowed Hugo to direct her to the Pastor where he stood near the main door.

Shelton watched as Hugo and Cassidy approached the Pastor. As if his heart had been sliced in two, Shelton stumbled backwards. Jet nudged him in the ribs. "I see, Jet."

"And you're just going to let him marry her?"

"I'm working on it, Jet."

Jet snorted, "Cass said the same thing."

"Your sister needs a future, and I can't give her one Jet. Not now."

"Not ever?" Jet's voice dropped to a whisper.

"I don't know."

With so much poison fueling his veins, Shelton needed to move. He stalked down the muddy street and wandered to the cart, where Hugo had left it, outside the trading post.

"Shelly?"

Nasal tones cut through the back of his skull, and he almost winced, "Hey Delilah."

"I heard you'd come back around."

"Yeah." Shelton turned to see the buxom brunette saloon Dove wandering over, a shawl around her best assets, the hem of her tangerine silk skirt coated in dust.

"Yeah that's not all I heard."

Shelton reclined against the cart, arms crossed over his abdomen, he tried to look relaxed, except every nerve ending seemed dipped in vinegar. Cassidy would march down the aisle with Hugo despite her lack of attraction to the man. She couldn't hide it from Shelton, he knew, just the same as he felt when he looked at Delilah.

"I heard you've got yourself a wife, well half a wife."

"Half a wife, that's new."

"Oh look here she comes now."

Shelton ground his teeth as he tried to exhale, only one look at Cassidy's ice cold stare made him twitch.

"Cass, ah Miss Cassidy Smith, this is Delilah um..."

"Musgrave." Delilah put out her lace gloved hand and Cassidy courteously shook the other women's hand.

"Pleasure to meet you Delilah Musgrave."

"Pleasures all mine, is it still Miss is it? Tell me 'ow do you manage 'aving two 'usbands?"

As if an arctic blast gusted across Cassidy, she trembled, "I don't have any husbands Miss Delilah, but you're welcome to either." Cassidy stalked past, chin high, brown eyes likes river stones in the snow.

"Nice talking to you Delilah," Shelton said as he followed Cassidy up the boardwalk and into the trading post.

"You wanna talk to me some more Shelly, you know where I am."

Shelton crossed the threshold of the trading post, as Cassidy strolled down one set of shelves. He decided to wait at the door while Cassidy spoke to the storekeeper. She handed over a bank note and collected a small vial in return.

"More laudanum?"

Cassidy didn't look him in the eye as she marched back down the boardwalk and to the side of the cart, "Mercury."

"Considering poisoning my dinner?" Shelton said, glad the cool air diluted the sweet blackcurrant scent of Cassidy.

"Not today."

Shelton chuckled, "Perhaps I better swap plates with Jet at dinner."

When Cassidy didn't reply he tried a different tact, "About Delilah...."

"I know Shelton," Cassidy took his hand as he lifted her into the rear of the trap, snatching back her fingers faster than double struck lightening, "She's one of your short term contracts."

Shelton whistled through his teeth, Cassidy had him there, "How was the Pastor?"

"He's a right gentleman," Hugo shouted from the other side of the cart, "He's not busy next Sunday, hey Pet?"

Shelton pumped his fists, the only thing that stopped Shelton from throwing his knuckles into Hugo's face, was how much Cassidy bristled at the back of the cart. Jet dragged his hands down his cheeks and then shook his head.

"Next Sunday, nice." Shelton climbed into *Tango's* saddle and led the horse into the street. He didn't wait for Hugo or his cart and let the animal stretch his legs. The countryside fled under hoof, as *Tango* raced up the trail, passing carts of other citizens. Shelton took a turn into the fir forest, letting *Tango* pick the route. Together they leapt over fallen logs and Shelton clutched the pommel leaning low when the horse careened too close to the trees. It wasn't until both horse and Shelton had blown out their steam that he turned them back towards the claim. Cassidy had set her sights on marriage and it didn't matter who. If he had a lucky strike would he ask for her hand? Of course, he told himself. With every step of *Tango* wandering slowly up the mountain Shelton's certainty solidified. One average win-fall and he could pay off the Blue Cow's debt. Then he'd have more than enough to ask Cassidy for her hand. Shelton patted *Tango* along his neck, "Well that's that." He told the horse, "I have until Sunday to find gold."

Cassidy chopped the lamb into chunks and pushed it into the stock until the meat was totally submerged. She hadn't seen Shelton since he tore off on his tantrum after Church. If the man ran off at the slightest hint of pressure then perhaps he wasn't the right type of husband for Cassidy. She chopped the silver beets into slices and then the onion.

"That lamb will cook nicely and I even got us a lick of whiskey to celebrate." Hugo rubbed his hand down his chest just as Cassidy heard the step of dancing hooves across field. She clicked her tongue. She didn't want to be cooking when Shelton arrived back; not cooking, cleaning, washing or any other wifely duty. Brushing her hands down her skirts, she put the dish on top of the pot belly.

"I'm going to take a walk up the ridge, while I wait."

Hugo harrumphed, the back of his fingers tapped Cassidy's

rump as she scuttled out the door. Throwing her riding jacket around her shoulders she took her canteen of water and set off to the northern end of the hill.

Without looking back, she trudged up the slate and gravel ridge, ever so often the stones would slide out under her heel and her arms shot out in front to balance. She picked up a branch to help. So far she managed to stay on her feet. Only when she reached the last few yards before the summit did Cassidy have to snatch at tree roots and boulders to pull herself up. Finally she straightened her back and stood atop the ridge.

Looking down she could see both huts, with chimneys puffing trails of white smoke into the air, Cassidy took a breath. From up here the uneven ground looked like a plush carpet, the sluice boxes like thorns along the vine of the Arkansas River. She allowed herself a few sips from the canteen before she used her walking stick to poke around the shale. Crouching down she found a regular line of rock, so regular it looked out of place. Square edges collided with rectangle stones. *Yes!* On her hands and knees she crawled around the rock, picking, chipping and crushing. Surely there would be something here! The time whittled away, she heard a shout from down on the field and saw Hugo waving hat over head up to Cassidy. Without reply, she bent her neck and focused on the stones. Let him cook his own dinner. It wasn't that she wouldn't enjoy looking after her man, fawning over him, feeding him after a long day of work, only it wasn't the right husband. She brought her hammer down on the next section of rock, enjoying the resulting smash.

"Find anything, Precious?" The hammer skittled across the stones.

"Nothing worthy." She snapped back.

A long whistle slipped between Shelton's lips, as he strolled past her and retrieved her hammer. Crouching beside, he handed it over handle first, "You might be digging in the wrong spot."

"It's not the location, it's the strata."

Shelton's brow furrowed and Cassidy let her anger wind out. "Too many layers, they keep changing." Cassidy wanted to berate him, only when she looked up, he was watching her intently. His Stetson balanced high on his head, blonde strands pushed back, crooked nose and all, she couldn't stay angry at the man.

"I thought I said I'd take you up here, what happened?"

"I didn't want to wait."

Shelton turned and sat down, pulling his long legs up in front of him and resting his arms on his knees. "Patience isn't your strength?"

Cassidy relented, putting down her hammer she shuffled her skirts so she sat next to Shelton as they overlooked the field. "Why did my father name it Pips Pit?"

Shelton smiled, one arm shot out and he traced the horizon, "The far edges of the range over there, envelope the land as if carved by the hand of God himself while these two," Shelton pointed to two large collections of round rocks, "...spaced evenly apart, seemed to have tumbled from Lucifer himself." He leaned his head closer to hers, "See how it looks like a dice. The two black pips, only sunken in."

Cassidy let her eyes adjust to what Shelton described; their heads together, sharing the same perspective. If only he shared hers about marriage! The lay of the land inverted in her eyesight and she could see it how Shelton described. As if a square dice had been pushed into the dirt, the two black pips of the 'two' had been made by the boulders. A weight sunk into her stomach. The field was a pit; perhaps an old marsh or an ancient seabed. She pushed away the dark thoughts of her father's business dealings. She'd read that gold could be found in sedimentary rocks and alluvial deposits quite often in dry creek beds. Hope blossomed. Cassidy's eyes were drawn back to the shape of the land.

Pip's Pit.

Julius Smith had chosen a name synonymous with gambling. Cassidy stared at the boulders, Shelton saw them as a 'two' on a single dice, but she knew her father better than that. What Cassidy saw when she looked down at the land, resembled snakes eyes, the worst possible throw in the game.

She shivered as the afternoon breeze lifted, icing her cheeks and cutting under the riding jacket. Freezing as it may be, the lead in her legs wouldn't shift. Snake eyes. Forcing her gaze from below she focused on the horizon. The sky streaked with soft clouds, the late afternoon sun painting them cream, gold and silver. The blue Colorado sky seemed to soak up every shade of blue, from deep violet to cornflower blue.

"Do they have sunsets like that in Texas?" Her teeth chatted like milk bottles in a crate.

Shelton tugged his jacket free and wrapped it around her shoulders, "We do, only bigger." His lips thinned.

Plum and cedar wood and smoke and leather enveloped Cassidy and on instinct she rubbed her cheek along the collar.

"Cass," He cleared his throat, "Hugo's not going to marry you."

Heat surged through her chest and into her jaw, "He said he would."

Shelton ran his hand along his mouth, "Cass um,"

Did his cheeks just redden?

"Trust me Cass, he's not."

"You don't know that." She stood up and handed back his jacket. In one swoop she picked up her collection of rock samples and pocketed them. Grabbing her walking stick she turned on her heel.

"I can, Cass wait."

She didn't wait. Her ribs ached just as bad as her feet. Cassidy needed a husband who would stand tall when needed, be reliable, responsible, stand by his word. Shelton hadn't made her any offer, in fact he'd asked her to compromise her morals. If Shelton wanted Cassidy as his wife, all he had to do was say the words. The fact he hadn't, spoke volumes. By the time she reached the pit floor, Shelton caught up to her.

"I said Cass wait." Something dark about his tone made her pause. Up on the ridge, the light had been bright, warm, majestic. Here on the pit floor, in the slate grey shade of the escarpment, the scenery had an unhealthy blue tinge.

"Why?"

He reached her in three long strides, "I'm serious Cassidy, I want you to wait for me."

The air rushed out her lungs in one long gush, her knees suddenly without strength. *Shelton wanted her to wait for him?*

Her words tumbled over her lips, "Wait for you, for what?"

"Until I find gold."

Julius's Smith had named this awful place Pip's Pit for a reason; her past unworthy of her father's attention and her future unworthy of his legacy. Tears welled behind Cassidy's lids and she threw a hand to her face.

"Hugo has no gold and has made an honest offer."

"It's not honest."

"An offer is an offer Shelton."

Cassidy could feel her throat tightening the words strangled,

"I have responsibilities I have to take care of."

"To who, to *Tango*? Shelton you've swept your way from Texas to Colorado without an ounce of worry."

He took a step back, "I have people relying on me."

What about me? Cassidy thought as the tears begun to fall.

"Gambling debts you need to pay?" Cassidy turned on her heel only to have Shelton's fingers clamp on her elbow, "In a marriage, Shelton responsibilities are meant to be shared."

She couldn't dare spend any longer in his company without wanting to strike him or sob uncontrollably or both and so stalked off. At the door to the cabin, she took a moment to gather her breath, wiping her hands down her cheeks until she felt strong enough to enter the cabin. Damn Shelton and his wishy-washy comments. Hugo had made an honest offer, despite Shelton's misgivings. *If she had never met Shelton would she still have married Hugo? Very likely.* Her stomach twisted.

Would she have? She used two cloths to take the casserole from the pot belly and rest it on the sink and she pushed away the doubts that niggled at the back of her mind.

Chapter 24

Shelton ate dinner in silence that night, watching the interactions between Hugo and Cassidy. The man grinned like a fox in a hen house, while Cassidy's jaw twitched intermittently. She could say what she wanted to Shelton, he knew different. Every time Hugo neared Cassidy her body stiffened as if bracing for a glacial blast. If only the woman could see sense. He pummelled his pillow and turned over. What good was having a husband if he made her skin crawl? His frustration would delay his usual dreams of Cassidy melting in his arms, although that thought made Shelton smile, remembering the way Cassidy's body responded to him. Well he'd made an offer. Almost. He rolled onto his back. Sunday, he had until Sunday. He couldn't expect Cassidy to marry a man with not a lick of money to his name, worse, his parents almost bankrupt. Cassidy needed a future and right now Shelton couldn't provide for himself, let alone a wife. He heard gravel crunch under foot and soon enough the tiny hut door nudged inwards. Hugo hummed a ditty, unfamiliar to Shelton as he sat on the edge of his bed and tugged off his boots.

"She kept nagging about the rocks, did my head in. I reckon she's ...."

"Careful," Shelton said. He stuffed the pillow with his fist, "She is going to be your wife, remember."

Hugo snorted, "Yeah, she said the western edge of the ridge, but I reckon we just stick to the plan, the original shaft her Pa dug."

Shelton hummed his agreement. Gold. He had left Dew Springs on the hunt for gold. He needed to stay focused.

"Good." Hugo said as he tossed another log onto the open

fire and then laid down to sleep. "She sure is pretty."

A spike of heat slammed into his chest. Pretty? To Shelton, Cassidy was a delicate dew drop on the first morning of spring and he the parched ground desperate to consume her.

"Night." Shelton grunted.

"Night." Hugo replied.

An hour past dawn and the sun finally broke over the looming cliffs, the golden rays touching the ground and heating Shelton's tired shoulders. He'd erected half the head frame and now he needed a rest. Smoke trailed from both chimneys and the scent of bacon drifted across the distance. He'd love breakfast to satiate his hunger and the sight of Cassidy right now would add motivation. As if she read his thoughts the cabin door opened, and the woman stepped down the gravel slope to reach him. He spied Jet behind her, the boy tugging on a jacket and wiping sleep from his eyes.

"Thanks." He said as he took the plate of breakfast and a mug of steaming coffee.

Cassidy just nodded and Shelton spied dark circles under her eyes, "Bad night?" Cassidy's cheeks paled despite the rosiness from the chill. Behind her Jet's expression said it all.

"Well it's promising to be a beautiful day, I can feel it prosperity in the air." Shelton tried.

A bellowing yawn broke from the hut's doorway as Hugo greeted the morning. Cassidy picked up her emerald skirts and headed back to the log cabin, her head down, long caramel braid bristling in the breeze.

"Don't ask." Jet said as he put hands on hips, "It's a fair start, except I think you need some wedges here for support."

Shelton scoffed his breakfast as the boy walked him around the frame. The horse *Tango*, nibbling on grass a short distance away lifted his head and snorted as if to agree.

Cassidy had only crossed the cabin threshold when Hugo waltzed in after her. His salt and pepper hair disheveled, a frown crinkling his forehead, "You know when we're married I expect I'll be the only man you'd be bringing breakfast too."

"Shelton's been up since dawn, I thought it only fair."

"Mmm"

"Besides he did bring Jet and I all the way up here."

"He did."

Cassidy plated up the last of the bacon and placed it down on the table. Hugo stayed standing, while she shoved the pan into the tiny sink and poured hot water straight from the kettle over the top. Without hesitating she started to scrub, hoping distraction might shift the ash taste from her tongue. Last night's horrors seemed to haunt her, the flames multiplying until she woke. When she eventually did fall asleep again, the dream picked up right where it left off, as if Cassidy was stuck in a quagmire of infernos.

"I've been meaning to ask you, if Shelton voided any of the terms."

"Huh?" Cassidy scrubbed the steel around the pan, the suds colliding with the grease.

Hugo sounded closer now, "If Shelton got a bit hands on when he brought you up here?"

Cassidy swallowed hard, "No of course not he was a gentleman." She couldn't face him without her lack of sleep affecting her concentration. Cassidy knew she needed a fraudulent mask, one demure, naïve, smiling and innocent. Only she didn't want to. She wanted to shout in Hugo's face that her heart and her body belonged to Shelton, only the man wouldn't take delivery!

"Good." Hugo grunted.

Cassidy felt a pressure against her neckline and she turned to see Hugo only inches away. His eyes ran over her form, stopping at her breasts and then again at her hips, as his fingers slithered down her spine, circling her buttocks and then back to her buttons. "I think, since we're getting hitched and all…"

"Hugo!" Cassidy said, careful not to put too much heat into her words.

She felt a button unclip as Hugo's lips suckled at her neck. She shied away from his wet lips as another hand fussed with her layers. Her hem pulled upwards and Cassidy recoiled. Hugo's body pressed against hers, trapping her against the sink. "Come on Pet."

"No, Hugo I don't think it's wise."

His scent of musk and sandalwood turned to bile in the back of her throat as his hands worked under her clothing. "Don't think Pet."

Cassidy pushed against the sink, regretting it instantly as Hugo's groin collided with her. "Don't you think we should get acquainted properly, I mean....." She would try anything to get Hugo away.

"It's not necessary," As Hugo's fingers closed around her jaw, the pressure biting into her cheeks, he twisted her face towards him. Without a second thought, Cassidy's hand curled around steel. Her elbow sprung like a trap, the frypan landing true. Hugo howled as he stepped back.

Clutching his ear, Hugo cursed.

"Church was only yesterday Mr Hugo James..... of all the ...." Cassidy didn't know enough to keep talking. Dropping the pan, she threw her hands to her mouth. The tremors in her legs as real as her outrage including the tears that tumbled down her cheeks. "Get out!"

Hugo winced as he rubbed his ear, his right eye closed as a red lump began to swell on the edge of his eyebrow. "The nerve....."

Hugo slammed the door behind him and Cassidy pushed a chair against the door before she threw herself onto her bed and let the sobs overtake her.

Shelton watched as Hugo stalked from the cabin, both hands to his head, muttering under his breath as he reached the hut.

"Maybe you should check on her?" Shelton said to Jet.

Jet shrugged his shoulders, as he yawned, "Maybe you

should, Shelton."

Shelton lifted his cup of coffee and sipped the last remnants. Maybe he should give her time. Judging by Hugo's trudging through the gravel, he'd been his usual distasteful self. Maybe Cassidy would come to her senses. When Hugo made it down to the construction of the frame, Shelton stood up. Instantly he could see a red welt brewing on the side of Hugo's skull, just above his eyebrow.

"You right?" Shelton didn't care one lick about Hugo, he wanted to know about Cassidy.

"She's a frigid little thing. Nothing warm hands won't fix."

Jet dropped his hammer, throwing Hugo his darkest look, as he made his way up the slope to the cabin.

Shelton's fists pumped, his fingers wrapped in Hugo's shirt collar and he dragged the smaller man up to meet his nose, "What happened?"

"Nothing, she hit me with a frypan, can you believe it, after I made her an honest offer and all...well honest enough." Hugo's hands came down on Shelton's just as he let go of the fabric and Hugo stumbled backwards, "Believe me, she's not worth the trouble. I'm done and when I'm done here, I'm going to take my warm hands to Delilah."

Shelton knuckles cracked, "You do that, but not before you lend a hand here."

Hugo nodded and picked up Jet's discarded hammer.

Not before too long, Jet returned, his eyes narrow at Hugo where they worked in the sun. Shelton hitched *Tango* and together they dragged the structure to the base of the slope. Only after *Tango* had helped winch the structure up the slope and into position above the shallow shaft, did Shelton find time to talk to Jet without Hugo hearing.

"She said she's fine, said it was a miscommunication and told me to help you."

Shelton ran his fingers through his fringe, "Fine? Miscommunication?"

Jet shrugged, "I'll go back after lunch."

Shelton patted Jet twice on the shoulder, he'd been avoiding this long enough. How he really felt, telling her the truth about his parents, asking for her hand, "I will."

The boy tilted his head to one side and smiled.

At noon, Shelton wandered down the slope to the cabin, disappointed to find the door still shut and three plates of food on a stool at the door. He knocked twice. Silence.

"Cass it's me."

Silence. Shelton looked at the lamb rolls with gravy. He knocked again, "Cass."

Her voice trickled through the logs, "I'm fine Shelton."

Resting his head against the timber, he lowered his voice, "Are you sure?"

"Yes Shelton. I'm working on my cross-stitch and don't want to be disturbed."

Shelton snorted and picked up the plates, "Fine, Precious."

When he made it back up the slope, Hugo had sat down on part of the frame, as Jet drew a diagram in the dirt, "It's not going to work."

"It's a good idea to set a weight on the drum and let gravity do half the work." Jet replied with a touch more heat in his voice then Shelton was used to. Well the boy had found his spine, plus hardly got any sleep by the looks of him. "Tell him Shelton."

"If we set the sheer at the base of the ridge, with the sheave wheel at the top we can work the drum from the ground. As the boy... as Jet said, with the angle from the slope we can add some weight to the cable and cut our effort in half."

Hugo stood up, "You're siding with the boy now? Well, it's my equipment, my drum, my wheel, my cable."

Shelton pointed at the lines in the dirt, "Except this makes perfect sense for three of us, we don't have teams of men to be lifting the ore."

Hugo crossed his arms, "Maybe I'll get teams of men to work the shaft."

Standing his ground, Shelton put his hands on his hips, "You going to pay teams of men?"

"There's four of us, if she's not putting out, she's going to be pulling her weight."

The dirt kicked up at Shelton's heels as he closed the distance, only Hugo tumbled backwards on the gravel, and Jet's palms smacked Shelton in the chest. "There's no gold for anyone if we can't work this out."

Hugo stood up, "You two figure it out, I'm heading into town."

"You do that."

Without a look back, Hugo wandered down the slope brushing the dust from his clothes. He clambered on top of his mule, his heels kicking it's flanks until the animal sped up.

"Is he going to kick us off the claim?"

Shelton sighed, "He can't, technically it's my name on the lease agreement. What he can do is take all his gear and leave us with shovels." He'd never pay the Blue Cow debt with a single shovel. "But Hugo wont." The man cared about his money. He knew Shelton would work from sunup to sundown to save his family's ranch. Only when Shelton should be gaining traction, the man had run out on them. He couldn't afford any more delays. "Come on let's see if we can get this up."

"My way."

"Of course."

By the time the frame had been set into the ground and the sheer secured, Jet scaled the timber to secure the sheave wheel. They ran the cables to the drum, and let it dangle as the night closed in on them. Crossing the field, Shelton looked at the log cabin, the narrow window dark. A thin trail of smoke curled from the chimney. He set *Tango* in his horse line for the night, although he didn't' think he needed to anymore. The horse was trained by Cade Hamerton, it would stay where it was told. Shelton continued onwards until he reached the river, wondering if he should build a pen for the gelding.

Splashing cool water over his sore limbs refreshed him, as well as cooled his temper. Jet followed him in for a dip and before too long the iciness wore them down and they redressed and retreated to the cabin. Jet reached the door first, leaning against it with his shoulder only it wouldn't budge.

"Cass?"

The boy yawned as Shelton pointed to the stool, two plates of lamb casserole had been left out. Jet picked up one, talking around the spoon in his mouth, "It's cold but I'm beat. Mind if I sleep in the hut."

"Go ahead, I doubt Hugo's coming back tonight."

Jet grumbled his reply, balancing his dinner with one hand, he scooped up two logs of timber with the other, "Night."

"I won't be far behind, Jet." Shelton tapped his knuckles on the door, without waiting for Jet's reply. "Cass."

Silence. Shelton knocked again and pressed his ear to the cool timber. Silence. He looked at the plates. Two. She'd seen Hugo ride away, taking her future with him. Well Shelton had had enough. He needed to set her straight. He leaned back and rammed his shoulder into the door, the timber creaked, something squeaked and he crossed the threshold.

"Cass?" Shivering, he closed the door, the pot belly cold. Not a single lamp had been lit, not even a candle. Shelton shivered. How long had it been since breakfast? Cassidy had let the fire dwindle, and now the darkened interior felt glacial. Shelton retrieved two logs and crouched down in front of the pot belly. Sparks fluttered into the coals, as Shelton gentle blew into the barrel. He stripped bark and twigs, only throwing a log in once the flames had built. Closing the door but opening the grill, Shelton turned to watch the tangerine light flickering over the inside of the cabin. A lump, unmoving, huddle on the bed, caught his eye. The blankets had been pulled up to her chin, her braid messy with caramel strands spread across the pillow. She lay on her side, her eyes closed, the long lashes gently resting on her cheek.

"Cass, I'm here." Shelton said as he lowered himself onto the bed. He put a hand to her forehead. Even with his body fresh from the river, she felt icy. Her eyes opened. "Cass you're freezing!"

Cassidy sighed and brought the blanket higher up her nose. The mattress dipped where Shelton sat, a cherry glow from the fire painting one side of his face gold and the other in shadow. How did the man look so irresistible?

"Are you sick?"

"Yes." She said. *Lovesick over a man who didn't feel the same,* she thought.

"Is it a fever?"

Cassidy tried a weak laugh. Where his fingers touched her skin, a spark ignited spreading warmth as he dragged his caress down her cheek. "I'm not sure." She managed.

"We need to get you warm."

The blankets lifted and Shelton crawled underneath.

"Boots off," Cassidy said.

He clicked his tongue and then she heard the *clunk-clunk* onto the timber slats. Curling her arms around his neck, he pulled her against him. One hand wrapped around her back the other rested on her waist.

"You should have called one of us down for the fire." He murmured, his breath ghosting across her hair as he reset the blanket around them.

"It's fine. You were busy working."

"Yeah..., what happened with Hugo?"

Cassidy sighed. She could feel the color flushing her cheeks. Did she dare admit that although she agreed to marry him, her husband-to-be repulsed her? Cassidy chose her words carefully, "He wanted to enact some of the terms before the final settlement date." Underneath her hands, Shelton tensed, "So, I hit him with the frying pan."

Shelton sat bolt upright and took one leg out from under the blankets, "I'll have a word to him."

Cassidy brought herself upright and pushed a palm onto his chest, "Please don't. I have no intention of seeing through the agreement."

Now that her decision had been spoken, tension eased through her limbs. She'd spent half the day worrying about how to repair the damage she caused, then the other half deciding whether she really wanted to. The answer had been a resounding 'no'.

Shelton leaned his back against the wall of the cabin and Cassidy leaned against his, her cheek pressed against his chest with his heartbeat pulsing beneath. With wrapped her arms around his waist as his arms curled around hers. One hand continued to stroke her spine. The warmth from the fire chasing away her shivers, and Shelton replacing them with a very different kind.

"I've had enough of letting men direct my future, Shelton. First my father, then Jackson,...."

Shelton could be included in that list, with his refusals to marry her, only this time she didn't care. To secure her future, Cassidy would grab what she could with both hands and make do. Cassidy had checked her vinegar samples, with no result, so tomorrow she take more samples from all along the ridge, until she found gold. For good luck, Cassidy twisted the locket around her neck and let it fall. Besides, it was something she owed the memory of her mother, taking control of her own destiny, without waiting for any man to see her true worth.

Shelton tugged the blankets around her shoulders, skimming his hands across her skin and down to her throat. He picked up the locket and ran it through his fingers, "You talk about your father, but not your mother. Tell me about her."

Cassidy took a deep inhale and shivered. The nightmares still seemed so fresh, so vibrant, the flames scouring the room, the ash returned to coat her tongue. She cleared her throat and exhaled. Where did she start?

Chapter 25

"She died in Chicago when I was fourteen."

"Tell me Cass," The softness in his words strummed an ache in her chest. He wrapped his arm back around her waist and pulled her closer against his chest.

Cassidy let her eyes drift to the orange glow through the grill of the pot belly.

"For a long time, we lived on and off in the city and taking shelter in Homes for the Friendless or other orphanages. My father would return for a few months, move us out to a new place with my mother full of hope. He would stay for a while, then one morning he'd be gone. Usually she would find something missing the next day, food, cash and sometimes jewellery. She told me that it was a borrowing game they used to play, and when I was younger I believed her. When he was gone we had to rely on the shelters, always waiting for his return. When he did eventually come back, he would always bring presents, only sooner or later they'd disappear too." Cassidy thought of the long nights her mother pined for Julius. Regaling Cassidy with stories of her father's exploits, only looking back, it seemed none of it was likely true. "She loved him, more than he deserved. More than once he took me with him to the streets, rubbed muck down my face, gave me a pan and taught me to beg."

Shelton's chest heaved underneath her hands and she slowly worked circles across the fabric. Perhaps she should stop?

"Go on, Cass, please."

A tear leaked down her cheek and landed on Shelton's shirt, she wiped the rest away. "One day in a boarding house

254

on the south side, a few heavies came, she gave me this and told me to hide. When they were gone, she swore she'd never let him come back. I believed her, I think I was about ten then. We begged for food, sharing what we could but eventually we had to return to the orphanages." Cassidy took a breath as the memories flooded back to her, the darkened interiors, cots lined wall to wall, women wailing as their child succumbed to fever, the constant need to protect yourself and your food supplies. She learnt how to steal back her treasures quickly. Everyone tried their best to make the food stretch as far as it could. Cassidy scratched her nose at the memory of the itchy blankets.

Shelton's arms curled tighter around her waist. Wishing being in his arms didn't feel this good, Cassidy let her cheek fall against his chest, listening to his heart beat; strong, steady and constant.

"He came back in September 1871 and rented a room close to the city. My mother assured me it was the last time. That this time it would work. Julius Smith was older and wiser and loved us, she said."

Cassidy's words clogged her throat, the ash taste almost unbearable, "She kept to that, when the fire spread across the river. Told me for certain he was coming back." Cassidy turned her face inwards to Shelton's chest. The ache in her chest speared through her ribs, driving a slice of pain into her heart, she swallowed hard, the words harsh in her throat. "I think she didn't want to leave, hoping if she stayed there would be something for Julius to come back to." Cassidy sucked in a shallow breath, "Even when the flames curled under the door." She let the tears fall as Shelton tugged her closer, running one hand down her spine.

He whispered soft reassurances, as she felt him press a kiss to her hair. She couldn't continue. The sound of her mother's cries echoed in her ears as she pushed Cassidy through the window frame. Strong hands that yanked her downwards and onto the street, holding her back as she wailed for her mother, the flames licking across the timber, the roar of consumption as the wooden structure until nothing but ash remained.

As the sobs abated, Cassidy snuggled into Shelton, his bulk warm and reassuring. She'd promised herself no more dictating her fate with consideration or consultation from a man. Looking upwards she rested her chin on his chest and focused on his sugar grey eyes, now like molten mercury. Her conviction waivered, shimmered under the sizzling heat of his gaze, like the Plains in the middle of summer, "I'm sorry Shelton."

"Don't be sorry, Precious." He cupped her cheek, "I understand your night terrors now." His thumb and forefinger gently trapped her chin infusing a flush of fever across her cheeks.

"I wasn't sure how much you heard."

"Don't worry Cass, I tried to bring you some comfort."

"You did." She rolled her lips inwards as his hooded gaze lingered, his lips parted. Sweet plum ghosted across her tastebuds, he was so close and yet so far, closed off, hesitant. "More than I anticipated." Cassidy sat more upright, bringing their noses only inches apart. His heart beat quickened under her palms, matching the cadence of her own, "I miss that." Senses numbed from the cold, now returned at full volume and Cassidy let the blanket fall from her shoulders.

Callused hands held her tight, "So do I Cass."

How could this man feel so solid under her hands, yet so fleeting? With a quaver in her voice, Cassidy couldn't leave the words unsaid, "You could give me something sweet to dream about."

Shelton chest heaved as a rumble reverberated in his throat, "I want to Cass." His bicep tensed, dragging Cassidy upwards and onto his taunt body. Sugar-grey targeted her lips, and Cassidy shuddered. The anticipation and curiosity spiking thorns of desire that unfurled in her abdomen and slicked between her thighs. Nothing about Shelton felt fleeting as his lips seized hers. The slow slake of his tongue into the soft corners of her mouth sent another wave of desire through her body. Cassidy savoured the wild plum scent, wishing she had the courage and the knowledge to make Shelton her man. With trembling fingers she unclipped one shirt button and then the next as Shelton's palms ran circles down her back, across the top of her buttocks and around her thighs.

"I want to Cass," He repeated.

Cassidy's whisper almost stalled in her throat. "Then show me."

The thin fabric lifted towards her waist as Shelton scored a trail of tender caresses upwards. The pressure constant, the height increasing at each pass across her goose-bumped skin.

Shelton kneaded Cassidy's lithe flesh and pulled her thigh up to his lap, his arousal ached, trapped behind denim while this woman writhed in the linen. Cassidy's naivety and eagerness spurred him on, tearing through his paper-thin restraint. Shelton wanted to hear caution, hear some hesitation in her words to bring him to order. Waiting for the moment when good sense prevailed and she pushed him away. Melting Cassidy had come easily, his desire winning out against restraint, except now, he sensed the weightiness, the responsibility that came with his actions. Responsibility didn't suit Shelton and it certainly didn't slow his words.

"I have a few ideas." Shelton smiled against her lips as his palm trailed up the soft velvet of her outer thigh. When the linen shift bunched around her waist, Shelton trailed his fingers along the outside edge of her undergarments. Her suppleness thawing in his hands, the woman coming alive by his touch fuelled his addiction. "You're all sweetness and light, Cass."

The heat from Cassidy radiated through the denim multiplying his arousal. "And you make me hotter than Hades." He needed to go slow despite Cassidy's gasps that drove lightening into his chest. "I want all of you Cass, all to myself, until I can't breathe without tasting you."

Another gasp shredded his control. Cassidy expected

much more from him than pretty words. Scoundrel, leech, rogue, Shelton admonished himself. He could at least be honest with her, "I have nothing to offer you Cass," Curling a caramel strand through his fingers he looked down at her, as she caressed his chest. Nipping along his jaw line, melted chocolate, now rich cognac. "Except me, Cass, that's all I have to offer you, no gold, not titles, just what you see."

Cassidy sat upright her hand undoing another button from his shirt and pulled it wide exposing his bare chest down to his belt line. "That's all I want Shelton."

Dipping to savour her kiss Shelton succumbed. Cassidy rolled his shirt from his shoulders and unrelenting, like a firestorm, her caress seared across his chest. As if Cassidy had severed an invisible ribbon around Shelton's ribs, he brought her hard against him. When her fingers trembled at his belt line, he grabbed her wrist in warning, "Cass."

"I want to touch you Shelton, like you touched me."

How could he argue with that? Methodically Cass worked each button free until nothing but will-power kept him still. He seized her lips again as she curled her grip around his arousal. He didn't think he could become any tenser until her delicate manipulations echoed in his blood.

Slow at first, tentatively, Cassidy stroked the full length of his hardened flesh, flooding his system with desire. Kissing her wasn't enough, he needed more, to slake the appetite threatening to overcome him. With each motion Shelton worked higher under Cassidy's linen shift until his thumb pad scored with her taunt nipple.

Cassidy moaned against his lips, her tongue frozen in rapture. Working the shift over her head, he broke her grip. Cassidy sat still her creamy skin bathed in golden light from the fire and all the more irresistible. As if seeing Cassidy for the first time, all woman, waiting, wanting, and eager, drew all the air from his lungs. He reached for her, savouring her velvet soft skin as he kissed his way down her neck, her quickened breaths surging him downwards, until he pulled one tight bud into his mouth.

Cassidy arched backwards as he sucked, licked and kissed his way across her chest, one arm curled tight around her waist, the other massaging her other breast; his pressure gentle yet direct sent wave after wave of pleasure rocketing through her body. She stroked him, the man himself groaning as she worked her way down his long hard flesh. Time seemed to slow against the rapid beating of her own heart, the ache she felt that tore through good sense, only Shelton's touch to anchor her in the present. Surely he could see her as his woman, what his caress did to her, the melody they made together?

The edges of her undergarments pealed back as Cassidy's thoughts drifted from the future to the present. When there had been tears before, now Cassidy only wanted his caress; to feel the carnal energy ignite as Shelton slid across her silken folds. The rhythm of his movements surging, leaving tremors in their wake. She withdrew from his kiss, teasing his tongue with the tip of hers, as he wrought waves of pleasure between her thighs. "Besides, you said you wanted to negotiate conditions."

In no way could she think straight, not with his deft strokes, and she hoped Shelton couldn't either.

Shelton smiled as he sucked and nipped the tender flesh of her throat. She swallowed hard, her breath ragged as her breasts swelled, demanding his attention again. Suddenly he leaned backwards, "I did, didn't I. Well there are some finer details to consider."

"Fine?"

"The finest." Shelton brought her knee over his hip to settle Cassidy on his exposed arousal, the damp material of her underwear the only barrier between them. "You're beautiful Cass, more than beautiful," His pressed a delicate kiss to her lips, she followed his retreat and he added another, then another, drawing her closer, "Like the dawn after a storm, when the lightening still lingers in the air, I'm on the edge of danger, breathless." The tight centre of her breast scored his thumb, his tongue met it's mate only to break away, his words tumbling over one another, "You may think you don't know about men, Cass, but you've had me transfixed from the first time I met you."

Shelton faulted, trembling with Cassidy's shivers, drawing the tight centre of her breast past his lips. Cassidy's touch became frantic, echoing his own building desire. As she speared her fingers through his hair, he savoured the sweetness of Cassidy, his craving running unchecked and Cassidy melting under his touch. The molten centre of Cassidy shredding his nerves, his desire pulsating as her frustration and hesitation seeped into her movements. He brought her onto him; a thin lace barrier preventing Shelton's advancement.

Unsure of what to do next, Cassidy remembered the night at the campfire, and rolled her hips backward, the resulting groan from Shelton ricocheting through her body. She'd gotten lost, somehow, the terms of her negotiation dissolving into sweet talk and moans. "The things you say Shelly."

"No, Cass, Shelly is the fast talker."

"The silver tongued rogue, I know," she laughed.

His voice hit a dark chord, not angry, but tender, "Shelton is who I am, all of me, raw, true and honest."

Cassidy's ribs tightened, as she moved the strand of blond hair that fell across his nose, tucking it behind his ear. Without closing her eyes, she touched her nose to his. "That's who I want Shelton."

His kiss thawed her remaining doubts and the mattress caught her shoulders as Shelton kept one knee on the bed and placed one foot on the floor. His bulk shaded her from the fire as his lips worked down her belly, her skin trembling under his delicate kisses, long fingers entwined in lace and dragged it down and off her ankles. She lay there frozen unable to turn away as Shelton stood. His shirt already gone, now he discarded his denims. Cassidy's eyes trailed over his hard body, like oak where the sun had touched him, marble everywhere else. She felt ashamed that she didn't turn away, enjoying the glory of his naked form.

"It's your trust Cass, the way you look at me with such certainty, it's frightening and alluring all at the same time."

"I do trust you Shelton."

"I know." Shelton paused, "It buries deep with a man, that kind of trust." He tapped his chest as he spoke.

Cassidy didn't think her heart could swell any further. The glow from the fire bathed them in gold and Cassidy couldn't have imagined a more perfect vision. She opened her arms.

His weight settled over her, safe, comforting, all man. She wrapped her arms around his broad shoulders as his knee parted hers. Sinking her teeth into her bottom lip, Cassidy braced for the pain she'd been told to expect, only to have Shelton settle between her thighs.

"Shelton?"

"I don't want to hurt you, Cass." Curling both arms under her shoulders, he cupped her face, his thumb dragging along her bottom lips as the tip of his arousal came to rest against hers.

"I trust you, Shelton." Cassidy whispered.

Their eyes locked together, the moment suspended as Shelton's sugar grey eyes, shimmered like copper in the firelight. Cassidy pressed a kiss to his lips, once, twice, three times until his tongue met hers and he slowly thrust his hips forward, grinding his rigid flesh against her satin.

The soft velvet of Cassidy taxed him, testing his metal, to temper his desire and bring her to her edge. He wanted nothing more than to bury himself in her, make her his woman forever. He needed to be patient, only Cassidy's trust bolstered him, lifting him until he felt rock hard, potent and invincible. How could one woman's confidence charge him with such strength?

"I want no other man Shelton."

Lost, adrift in the pleasure of his woman, Shelton thrust forward again. The silken folds of Cassidy parted as he slid further, Cassidy's knee hooked behind his. He'd thought he could resist, that her frostiness would keep him at bay, how wrong had he been.

"Cass...."

"I trust you, Shelton."

"I know," He rolled his hips backwards, slaking his arousal across her dewiness; he seized her lips, thrusting his tongue deeper as he advanced, sensing the precipice of surrender only moments away.

"I am safe with you Shelton."

He'd been open and honest and still she beckoned him onwards. The shield of his slick words discarded, his heart exposed. "I will keep you safe, Cass." An ache echoed in his chest, his mind racing to forestall his next word, lest he spoil it and fail to deliver.

Forever, Cassidy told herself. As their limbs entwined, Cassidy steadied her hips. The pressure increased until Cassidy winced, the slightest sting as their bodies became one. Cassidy wound herself tighter, his strength the shelter she chose, tethering her heart to him.

"Cass?"

"I'm fine," her breath tangled with Shelton's, inhaling deeply as the pain dissolved to tiny ripples of pleasure. Withdrawing, Shelton's steel gaze locked onto hers, he moved slowly, Cassidy's body responding to his rhythm, thawing beneath the blaze that Shelton ignited. "I'm more than fine."

His lips kinked to one side in a cheeky smile and Cassidy couldn't help but smile with him. The strength of Shelton soothed and reassured, while he built waves of torrid heat that threatened to overtake her. Only Cassidy didn't shy away from this inferno, instead she raced towards it, the wildfire roaring through her veins; a symphony of embers engulfing Cassidy as they rocked together.

As if an avalanche of white heat trembled out of reach, Cassidy writhed to meet Shelton, the muscles of his back bunching under her grip, her ankles locked behind his thighs. The fire thick, she gasped for breath, only to have Shelton's kiss steal it from her lips, his tongue curling around hers. Encircling her body with his solid arms, Shelton thrust forward, again and again, driving deeper with his rigid flesh into her slickness. Wave after wave of pleasure crashed over Cassidy as his fingers gently stroked the nape of her neck, at odds with the potent carnality he wrought from their union.

Cassidy's eyes closed of their own accord as she arched backwards and succumbed to the firestorm. Captured by Shelton's tenderness and enthralled in his sensuality, Cassidy surrendered, letting the winds of carnality tear her away to drift amidst the tornado of pleasure. The sensation built, a barrage of energy demanding to be released and Cassidy rocked against Shelton with a rhythm of her own, knowing at the end, rapture awaited. Like lightening erupting through her veins, tremors spreading out from her abdomen and Cassidy shuddered against Shelton's bulk, curling her arms tighter around his neck.

Shelton unable to control the growl that rumbled in his throat. The blood thundering in his ears until all he could hear was the crackle of the fire and Cassidy's strangled breaths. As he sensed Cassidy's peak, Shelton checked himself. The tenderness of this woman, writhing underneath him, loving him, had melted his defences. The Cassidy he thought he'd known was gone, and in her place, replaced by this Cassidy, her thirst meeting him in kind, open and without pretence. He felt soothed by her trust and humbled in her love. He swallowed hard and thrust forward again, trying to ignore the word that slid under his ribs and attached itself inside.

"Cass?"

Tilting back, she raised her lips, already parted, tongue seeking his. Shelton captured her kiss as he drove forward, his resolve shredded. Like bolts of silk, Cassidy curled around him, her silkiness unending, his desire demanding release. As her fingers speared through his hair, he thrust deeper, fast and longer, the edge of his cliff rapidly approached. He wanted to linger in her love, basking in the light she brought to his chest, only, her own slick tremors brought him undone. He withdrew sparing her his seed, collapsing in her arms, he rolled onto his back. Gently pulling her with him, Cassidy sprawled across his chest. Words failed him, the weight in his chest unsettling.

"You all right Cass?"

"Of course," Cassidy's breathless laugh ghosted across his skin.

Shelton sighed. Cassidy Smith was trouble. More trouble than Shelton could handle. Worse, he wanted to handle her, for now and forever and that unsettled him even more. A problem for another day, Shelton told himself as he drifted off into sleep, where his dreams were filled with Texan sunshine and chasing Cassidy through the Blue Cow fields.

Chapter 26

A twang of metal on metal woke Shelton and he dragged his hand down his face to see a blanketed form standing near the pot belly. The grey light of dawn pealed through the narrow cabin window and memories of last night speared through his veins and hardened his flesh. Damn. He looked down unashamed that the sheet barely concealed him and watched as Cassidy, wrapped in their blanket, put the kettle on the stove. *Their blanket?* Shelton shook his head and the weight returned to haunt his chest. Thoughts of Cassidy in Texas made him shiver. He'd been honest with her. Then why did his ribs feel so tight. He could sense his surrender, the truth he refused to voice, and sat bolt upright. Pulling on his denims he wandered into the kitchen. He would set her straight. Last night had meant something to him, only not what Cassidy wanted. As he neared he could hear her humming, and couldn't help but smile. This close to Cassidy, her intoxicating blackcurrant scent trickled past his defences. She'd pulled her caramel locks to one side, and his fingers itched to trail the silken strands.

Wrapping his arms around her waist, Shelton sunk his lips to the exposed skin at her neck. Cassidy jumped and Shelton chortled.

"Morning Precious." His voice, too thick for his liking. He cleared his throat, ready to set her straight.

"Morning Shelton." She leaned back and one hand stroked his neck as she lengthened her own. The edge of the blanket dipped.

The briefest glimpse of pearl coloured skin caught Shelton's eye "Cass, you're not dressed." He mumbled against her neck.

"I wanted to make you coffee, first."

"Forget that." Shelton spun Cassidy. His lips seized hers as he lifted her into his arms. Cassidy wrapped her legs around his hips, her warmth seeping into his bare chest as he worked his hands under the blanket. The softness of her skin sent shudders down his thighs into his already hard arousal. Parting the blanket with his teeth, Shelton found her taut bud with his lips. Cassidy arched backwards and he could feel his resolve waiver. He had meant to set her straight, instead he set her down on the table, gripping her thighs he pulled her hard against him.

The sound of her own heart pumped in her ears, drowning out the sound of her doubt, the taste of plum on her tongue drove away her worries. Cassidy wrapped her arms around Shelton's neck, her body taking over, answering to Shelton's caress. Dragging her nails down his back, she hesitated at his waistline. She could feel her body's reaction, the slickness eager for Shelton's attention. Cassidy pushed his denims down, and within seconds, his hard fleshed entered her. A cry strangled in her throat as he filled her, the pressure building immediately. *Coffee, she had intended on making him coffee!* He kissed her, his lips hard, tongue demanding, urgent, seeking the release they shared last night. Cassidy answered his call, tightening the grip with her thighs. She felt the table shift and she ran her hands down his sculptured chest, then over his ribbed abdomen as Shelton leaned her backwards. He thrust forward again and again and Cassidy whimpered, the pleasure too much, the precipice of her climb, too close.

Shelton sucked her bottom lip until she gasped, "You all right, Precious."

"Don't Shelton."

"Don't what?" his teeth nipped the tender flesh at her throat.

"Don't stop."

He chuckled and circled one bicep around her waist, pulling her forward in time with his rhythm, "Not yet, Precious."

The blanket forgotten, Cassidy surrendered, the rhythmic pulses Shelton wrought overcome her and Cassidy tumbled. Deeper, harder and faster until nothing but Shelton remained. His name branded across her heart.

Shelton cried out as Cassidy shuddered around him, he withdrew with only seconds to spare. He watched her expression change from rapture to confusion, and he himself unwilling to admit that he too felt disappointment at their discarded union. He stood upright unable to turn away from the exquisite cream and gold beauty that lay beneath him. Unashamedly Cassidy ran her trembling fingers down his bare skin, his chest heaved under her fingertips. Breathless, lost and sinking, Shelton captured her wrist, pulling her to sit upright. She dove into his embrace and slowly he wrapped the blanket around her shoulders. He pressed a kiss to her silken threads, his chest too tight to speak.

He wanted Cassidy beyond reason. Not just this, he wanted her to look at him with that trust and certainty until the end of his days. The finality of that truth struck his heart like a gong. Shelton scooped her up in his arms and over to the pot belly removing the kettle from the shelf.

"Don't you want your coffee?"

"I'll make breakfast later." Shelton wandered over to the bed, and gently lay Cassidy down amongst the ruffled sheets before he stretched out beside her. She curled into his chest. "For now I just want this." Was all he managed to say.

Cassidy squeezed her lids together to no avail as a tear leaked from one eye and trickled onto the sheets. The man felt solid under her hands, yet his heart seemed so fleeting. Cassidy pressed her cheek to his chest and relished the strong beat there. No, maybe not fleeting, just stubborn. She let herself drift off to sleep in his arms only to wake to sunlight streaming through the open cabin door. Shelton stepped inside with an armful of timber, closing it behind him.

"Jet's awake."

"Oh."

Cassidy pulled the blanket upwards.

"I told him if he wants me to cook him bacon and eggs he better wash up first."

Cassidy smiled. Knowing full well how much Jet hated soap. She dressed as fast as she could pulling her shift over her head and eventually her riding skirt and jacket. Turning she saw Shelton leaning against the tiny sink, one hand on the pan and his gaze locked on her. "I would have thought a gentleman would give a lady some courtesy."

"I tried Cassidy but I couldn't turn away." He smirked. "Besides I ain't a gentleman."

Cassidy inhaled slowly, his plum and cedar scent still lingered on her palate as the memory of his caresses ghosted across her skin. Cassidy began braiding her hair as she wandered past the tiny kitchen table, placing herself just out of his reach, "I suppose I don't want a gentleman."

She smiled as he clutched her waist, his solid bulk enveloping her as his mouth clamped down on hers, slow, haunting and possessive. Cassidy wound her fingers into his collar, his leather vest smooth and familiar. "That's just fine by me Cass." He said as he withdrew.

The cabin door creaked and Cassidy pushed herself backwards, her hands rapidly finishing her hair.

"Morning Jet." She pretended to look for a pin as she carelessly made the bed.

"Morning." Jet sighed.

"You look clean."

"Mmm" He harrumphed, tossing his grey cap down on the table and taking his seat. "Sleep well last night?"

"Uh-huh." She managed, resisting the urge to press her hands to her blushing cheeks.

"Good, cause we want to start on the shaft and I'm starving."

Cassidy gave up and returned to pull out three chipped plates, placing them carefully on the table. "Well I'll try to do my best keeping up with your appetite." She heard a noise from Shelton but couldn't face him. "I'm going to check for eggs."

"No need." Jet pulled out two speckled ovals and handed them to Shelton.

"Thanks, but I'll have you on the sluice boxes." Shelton ordered.

"Hey that's not fair, if there's gold down there...."

Shelton cracked the eggs one handed and Cassidy found herself admiring the simplest of tasks.

"It's not about being fair, I'm not having you down the shaft until I have the lining complete. No sense rushing in and risking a cave in."

Cassidy tried to control her cheeks, except her smile wouldn't budge. She found the coffee pot and poured out two cups. Jet seemed to watch her and Cassidy shrugged her shoulders.

Jet looked to Shelton and back again to Cassidy, a slow smile wrinkled his youthful cheeks. "Sure."

Seizing the opportunity to keep Jet talking instead of thinking, she asked, "How are your sluice boxes going?"

Jet leaned back in his chair, "Yeah good, except the damn black sand."

"They had trouble with that in Oro City too, that's why I think the shaft is our best bet for gold." Shelton took his coffee cup from Cassidy, their fingers colliding briefly. That was enough for a rush of color to enter her cheeks and Cassidy retreated to the table.

"Black sand?"

"Clogs it up. Alright, fine, but you'll need help with digging."

Shelton brought the fry pan to the table and portioned out the straps of bacon, on egg for Cassidy and one for Jet. "I will have help, whenever Hugo returns."

As if a spear of ice slid down Cassidy's spine, she froze. She eyed the frypan, her previous weapon. What would happen when Hugo returned to the claim? Would Shelton have words with him? Had Cassidy broken apart a crucial business relationship? Looking up she saw Shelton's half smile and then he winked. The chill passed and Cassidy exhaled. Shelton took his plate and sat on the edge of the mattress.

Cassidy rose and pushed her egg from her plate to his, "You'll need your energy." She relished Shelton's surprised expression as she returned to her seat. Well, she had no intentions of becoming Hugo's wife and every intention of being her own woman. If that meant enjoying every inch of Shelton and his company, well she'd suffer. She threw him a wink of her own and Shelton almost choked on his bacon.

The hours passed slowly in the trench as Shelton dug through the hard rock and assembled the timber structure support around it, that would prevent the shaft from collapsing on his head. The long hours drew out how similarities of the narrow tunnel to Shelton's current predicament. He discarded his shirt before midday. Distracted and frustrated, Shelton took a breather and rested on his shovel. The heat had melted his mind. Instead of gold and ore, he daydreamed of cream and caramel, of delicate porcelain skin and fine silken wrapping around his sore limbs.

He needed to find gold. The sooner the better. Then he'd make Cassidy a real offer, not some flimsy paper contract with a false name. His offer would come from his heart and it would be for life.

He watched the cabin, as the smoke trailed steadily from the chimney. *Did he have enough to sustain Cassidy for her life? Wealth, status or even appeal?* The woman herself emerged carrying plate and drink.

"You look beat."

"I'm fine." Shelton took the sandwiches and a canteen of

cool water, before reclining on his dwindling stack of short timber set for the shaft lining. "How's Jet managing?"

"He says his fine. He said he is cured of tick fever, but I'm going to make him help me after lunch and that should make him rest."

Shelton snorted, "What are you doing?"

"I want to take more samples from the woods, there's a line of aspens that I want to dig around. I'll make him sit down with my sample bag, so he doesn't overwork himself."

"It's not Jet I'm worried about." Shelton took another bite, and watched as her gaze drifted across his bare chest. Her chocolate brown eyes seemed to blaze across the divide. He swallowed hard, thanking the canteen and cup for keeping his hands from her waist. "Take the pistol and the rifle."

Shelton washed down the rest of his sandwich and let Cassidy take his plate. "I will." Her wide chestnut eyes held his for a moment longer. "When Hugo returns..."

"Don't worry about Hugo. I'll let him know exactly where he stands."

"Good" *What about me, where do I stand?* The way Shelton reclined his sculptured bare-chest basking in the sun and long limbs resting but tense, he reminded Cassidy of mountain cat, elegant, powerful and waiting to pounce. A tremble infiltrated her knees and she turned on her heels.

"If I need your fry pan I'll holler." Shelton called after her.

Halfway down the slope she looked over her shoulder. Shelton sat as she'd left him, his gaze unwavering from her as she returned to the cabin. Once inside she took a breath, pressing her hands to her abdomen. This time the unrest in her stomach resulting from butterflies in anticipation of dusk. The table caught her eye. Not that daylight seemed to worry Shelton. She needed to concentrate and pushed her thoughts aside.

In the woods, the afternoon slide by fast with every slick of the shovel and Jet's protesting that he could help. She made him sit to dig the ridge line that descended to the riverbed, while the late afternoon sun sunk behind the aspens.

"What if we find nothing but more black sand?" Jet said.

"Maybe I should take a sample of this sand hey?"

"It's sludge Cass, it's not worth it."

"Surely there is something worthwhile here." Cassidy cracked open the rocks with a back of her short pick. She picked up the mottled colored lumps of brown and grey turning them over in her hand, "Sphalerite?"

"Gold?"

"No I think it's Black-jack."

"That doesn't sound like gold." Jet crawled over to where she sat and started sifting through the pile of rubble at her knees.

"No, it's a zinc ore, I think." She dusted the crumb between her fingers and brought up to her nose. Wincing, Cassidy pulled back as she detected a faint trace of sulfur.

"You don't sound sure Cass."

"I'm not sure, they call it Black-jack, Steel-jack or even Ruby-jack but it's real name is Sphalerite, named after the Greek word *Sphaleros*, meaning treacherous or deceiving, because it's has a variety of appearances."

"Sounds just about right for you, Cass."

Cassidy elbowed him gently in the ribs. He clutched his stomach pretending to be mortally wounded then laughed as Cassidy narrowed her eyes. He picked up a handful of the stones and rubbed it between his fingers. "What's that smell?"

"Black-jack is a sulfide, that's sulfur."

"Is it valuable?"

"For zinc yes, but it's also commonly found with other ores, including those that contain copper, silver and gold."

"Now you're talking."

A breeze skipped through the emerald and gold leaves of the Aspens and Cassidy shrugged into her riding jacket. She stood up and scanned the darkening horizon, "Time for dinner anyway,"

"And wash up I suppose."

"Now that you smell like that, yes, don't forget the samples." Cassidy scooped up the rifle, listening to the gusts rustle through the trees, hoping that she didn't hear any twigs snap or bears grunt.

They made it to the clearing and she sighed as she saw a steady stream of smoke still rising from the cabin's chimney. She eyed Shelton still shoulder deep in the shaft. Well if Hugo had returned at least she didn't have to make a fire. As the hour was late, she'd have to rush to make dinner. She hurried down to the river to wash up. When she returned to the cabin she peeked inside. Empty. Perhaps Shelton had come down and added more timber? Just in case she sent Jet next door to the shack, while she busied herself with the beef and vegetable casserole. It did nothing to calm her nerves, waiting for a confrontation with Hugo irked her, only half as much as waiting for Shelton to walk through the cabin door.

Jet's return made her jump.

"It's empty too Cass, but the fire was on, it must have been Shelton."

"Must have been."

"So who are you marrying on Sunday?"

Cassidy stirred the casserole, deciding it needed more flour to thicken, "With my luck Jet, no one."

"I'll talk to Shelton."

Cassidy almost dropped the flour, "No Jet. This is between Shelton and I. Don't worry about Hugo, he knows where he stands."

"And you Cass?"

Turning, she looked at Jet's furrowed features, his words echoing her own. "I guess I'll know by Sunday."

Jet nodded, "And if not by then, I'll have a word to him." His voice deeper than before.

"If not by Sunday, I'll be having words myself."

The door swung inwards as Shelton stepped into the cabin. River water from his wet strands dripped onto his collar dampening his fresh shirt. Navy this time, and the dark blue color highlighted his tanned features.

"Any luck?"

"Cass thinks she found something called Black-jack."

"Zinc ore?" Shelton smiled, "See, I read your books." He met her at the pot belly. Leaning, he hovered over her shoulder, his lips dangerously close to her cheek, "Smells delicious Precious."

"Better than Black-jack." Jet laughed at his own joke.

Shelton straightened up and his hand rested for a moment in the small of her back before he moved past. Cassidy spine melted and she yearned for his presence to linger longer.

As they ate dinner, Cassidy's stomach settled, sure that now darkness had fallen, Hugo would remain in Oro City for another night. With each forkful her mind drifted to thoughts of last night and Shelton, punctuated every now and then, when Jet asked Shelton another question about Dew Springs. The tales grew taller as the cold night closed in and this time it was Jet who washed up.

"What are you going to do with the Black-jack?" Shelton dragged his fingers slowly across the table top and it took another prompt before Cassidy answered.

"Um look for more, it's a good sign that I'm looking in the right spot. I'm not sure whoever dug that shaft knew where to start, I didn't see anything of note..."

Shelton raised his eyebrows.

"Geologically speaking." Cassidy offered him a half a smile. He winked.

"With the damn sand in the boxes, I reckon we set our sights on Cass's river bed."

Shelton's cheeks fell flat and he turned to the watch the pot belly. His steel eyes unfocused at the orange glow through the iron grill, "No need to rush in Jet, I want to be sure first."

"I thought you liked taking risks Shelton?" Jet teased.

Shelton did like taking risks and usually trusting his gut

had lead him down some dark alleys and gotten him out of some wild places. He knew trouble like the back of his hand. Except Cassidy was a different type of trouble. If he married her, living up to her idea of a husband might be too much. He looked at her now, as her cheeks colored with Jet's comments. As she carried the rest of the plates to the sink, it seemed Jet sensed her mood and shifted just out of her reach. What if Shelton failed her? He already had his parents counting on him and judging by his progress, the Blue Cow would be under by the time winter came. Shelton needed to be responsible, for both his and Cassidy's sake.

Chapter 27

After coffee Cassidy handed out biscuits, Jet scoffed two and snatched another two as he made for the door, "I'm beat. Wake me in the morning this time Shelton."

Shelton took his coffee cup up to the sink to rinse it out, "Sure thing. Not too early though I need my beauty sleep."

"With a nose like that you certainly do." Jet shut the door just as the cloth hit the timber.

Cassidy scooped it up and brought it to the sink. Now they were alone, Shelton couldn't resist any longer. He wrapped his arm around her waist and pulled Cassidy until she was hard up against him.

"What do you think, Precious?"

Cassidy ran a single finger down his crooked nose, "It's growing on me."

Following her fingers, Shelton leaned forward, dipping Cassidy until she had to clutch his neck to hold on. "Growing on you?"

For a moment Cassidy tried to object except Shelton clamped his mouth down on hers. Her spine seemed to meld to his arms as her breasts swelled against his chest. Carrying Cassidy toward the bed, Shelton forgot all about risk and focused on the reward.

When Cassidy's feet returned to the floor, she unwound her grip, dragging her hands down the front of his shirt, undoing buttons as she went. "Although you're too tall." She stood on tips toes to pull the shirt from his shoulders. The joke lightened her heart, and distracted from the words she wanted to hear from Shelton. His silence on their arrangement frustrated her only half as much as his touch comforted her.

"And too handsome."

"Too handsome? I like that." This time it was her buttons that fell aside as Shelton worked his way down her blouse. Tugging it free, his callused palms skimmed her skin and raised goose bumps in their wake.

She turned his hands over in hers and kissed them one after another, "And too rough."

Shelton pulled the ribbon from around her skirt, unclipped the buttons on the hip and slid it over her thighs until it bunched on the floor next to her blouse. Cassidy stood in her shift and nothing else, the shear fabric dimpled as the brisk air cooled her skin. Shelton kicked his boots off, "Too rough? I tried to be gentle, Precious." His lips claimed hers, the slow sweep of his tongue, flooding her body with thirst.

Without a second thought, Cassidy reached for his belt buckle, she pulled back enough to whisper, "And too slick with words."

Shelton withdrew, his thumb captured her chin and he tilted her backwards. His brows furrowed. The reflection of the flames in his steel grey eyes appeared like smoke across a mirror, "I care about you Cass."

The sincerity in his voice as he called her name, struck a chord in her chest. "I know."

Shelton watched the emotions pinch Cassidy's features. He understood that Cassidy had taken a leap of faith in his arms, and he hadn't made an offer in return. "To me Cass, you are like the first stars after dusk, lightening the way to guide me home."

"Oh." A rush of color blossomed in her cheeks. He wanted her to see past his words, to see what she meant in his heart.

Bringing his hand from her cheek to behind her neck, he brought her closer, "And with the dawn, I mourn my loss," He pressed a delicate kiss to her parted lips, "Only for a moment," He brushed his lips across her mouth, "As I know you're there."

Teasing his tongue along her bottom lip, he tasted her hot breath, "... waiting for me when I'm lost." This time his kiss lingered and his chest tensed as Cassidy ran her hands across his bare skin, downwards until she pushed his denims from his hips.

"You're intoxicating Cass, when I revel in your light, I want more," Slowly he lifted her shift, "To cherish it," He kissed her breasts one by one, advancing until Cassidy's knees bumped the edge of the bed, "To bask in your splendor." In a single movement, he brought Cassidy gently down to the mattress. Kneeling, Shelton nipped and sucked his way down between her breasts to her navel, "Until there are no more dawns or dusks," He parted her thighs as he sunk to his knees, "Only us until the end of our days."

Shelton savored the delicate heat of Cassidy's velvet core as her mews of pleasure intensified his own arousal. Flickering his tongue across her most intimate flesh, proved too much as Cassidy's hands suddenly speared through his hair and Shelton's control almost slipped. Stroking her silken folds, Shelton rose, kissing the creamy flesh at her abdomen and then drawing a taunt nipple into his mouth. Cassidy's thighs clenched around his hips and Shelton drove forward, growling as he entered his woman, slick with rapture.

Cassidy surrendered, the maelstrom Shelton wrought had overwhelmed her. Now as he filled her, Cassidy tumbled over the precipice and succumbed to the deluge of ecstasy. The sweetness in Shelton's words echoed through her mind, dusk and dawn, until their end of days. If this was dusk, then how would she ever survive the dawn?

Just when she thought her euphoria began to ebb, Shelton's rhythm built another vortex within, intensifying until sheets of bliss cascaded through her body. Trembling, she held on as Shelton's muscular back tensed and his own peak paralleled hers, erupting once again in the sheets.

He rolled to his side and pulled Cassidy tight against him.

Leisurely he stroked downwards, circling her breasts and curling around her bare thigh. With sweet whispers he kissed her hair and she let her cheek loll against his chest, "And then there's the eclipse, Cass, where neither of us can tell where the other one ends."

"I don't want to be apart."

"Neither do I Cass."

Cassidy let sleep claim her, lying satiated, safe and secure in Shelton's arms.

Cassidy heard a horse whinny. Furrowing her brows she kept her eyes closed, the strong heartbeat of Shelton pumped under her palms. The warmth from his skin heated her, and like a lizard on a rock, she didn't want to move. A man's voice whispered through the walls of the cabin and Cassidy sat upright.

"Shelton," Gently she rocked his chest. "There's someone here."

Shelton moaned beside her and scrubbed a hand down his face, "Huh?"

Cassidy didn't have to answer as the man spoke again, "This too, Hugo?"

"All of it." Hugo whispered back.

Shelton shot out of bed and tugged on his denims, he had half his shirt on by the time he stormed out the door. Cassidy dressed in a rush, finding yesterday's clothes and her dragonfly boots on. She twirled her hair in a bun and rushed out to the cold to witness Hugo standing by his cart while half a dozen men walked around the claim, picking up cables, ropes and pulleys.

"What the devil do you think you're doing?" Shelton shouted at Hugo, his fists curled by his side as he stormed over to the shorter man.

"I'm making a smart business decision. We are through, Silver-tongue Murphy, I should never have agreed to your deal in the first place."

"You can't."

Cassidy spun her mother's golden locket at her throat. Hugo would really end a business deal on a shonky mail order marriage?

"I can and I will. Met an interesting friend of Miss Smith in town yesterday, he seems to know her and her father quite well."

"Who?" Cassidy snapped.

Shelton intercepted one of the miner men and reefed a coil of rope from his hands, "This is mine." Shelton palmed him in the chest with ease and the man stumbled onto his buttocks.

"Mr Wilfred Gerald Jackson Esquire."

"Jackson's a liar and a thief." Jet hissed from beside Shelton. He had thrown on a shirt but no jacket and stood with his fist clenched.

"Yes he said the same thing." Hugo smirked, "He also said her old man is a crook, a counterfeiter who was arrested over that railway bond fraud not long ago. Jackson says the land's worthless, her old man died in prison last month. The damn mine is probably salted. Either way, I'm taking me gear to Sully's gulch, you can keep this pit."

Cassidy's knees buckled the ground rush to meet her and she slumped on the side of the cabin. Her father was dead? Jackson was here?

"I don't understand."

"Said he came for what's owed and her old man owed him big. Had plans of her shacking up with some miner so they could scam everything out from under him."

As if the air filled with ash, Cassidy's lungs wouldn't work. Liquid rushed over her lids and streaked down her cheeks. Jet suddenly filled her vision, his mouth moving but the sound not reaching her ears.

Shelton's gut churned, and his limbs began to shake. The sun breached the grey dawn clouds and suddenly everything about Cassidy seemed to make sense. The masks she wore,

Jackson, and all the stories she'd shared about her father. He caught sight of Cassidy with Jet by the cabin except the white heat in his veins clouded his judgement.

"Jackson's in town?"

"Over at the royal. Had his pockets emptied yesterday and his hands full last night? Don't blame yourself Shelly, grifters come in all shapes and sizes even pretty ones such as her."

Shelton stepped forward, his shoulder ratchet back, ready to land knuckles on Hugo's jaw.

"Whoa! Nancy!" One man called as his horse backed up to the head frame.

"Hey!" Shelton shouted.

"I want my wheel Shelly." Hugo snapped.

"Jet!" Shelton pointed to the top of the head frame and the boy scrambled to obey. His blue eyes were like sapphire daggers at Hugo. Within moments, the boy had reached the top and levered out the wheel while another miner wound up the lengths of cable. "Take it, but you lay a hand on all but one of those sluices boxes and it'll be the last thing you do."

"The sluice boxes are...."

"No, you built one, the rest are Jet's." Shelton's throat tight. He'd love to pummel Hugo into the gravel right now, only his six other miners might have something to say about it. Sizing them up, he could take at least three of them. But Cassidy and Jet would be at risk. He didn't want a shot fired. "Jet's boxes stay. You ain't gonna need them over at Sully's gulch anyway, despite what he's promising you it dried up years ago."

"We'll see ole Silver-tongue." Hugo sneered. He pointed to the first box that Hugo had erected and two men shifted it to the cart. Jet scrambled down to the ground with Hugo's wheel and handed it over.

"If you need any work, you head on over to Sully's gulch you hear." Hugo tapped Jet on the shoulder.

"Not if my life depended on it, Hugo. As you said, grafter's come in all shapes and sizes." Jet dipped his hat and half bowed in mockery, "From one crook to another."

Hugo raised his shoulder as if to backhand the boy, Jet squared up to the older man and Shelton stepped between them, "Get your gear and get out."

Hugo looked upwards as Shelton stood over him, the ground had not yet heated from the sun, and their breaths ghosted before them in the chilly morning air.

"Right." Hugo murmured and stepped back. "Get the burros too."

"You leave two. One for Cassidy and one for the.. one for Jet. It's the least you can do to pay him for his work so far."

Hugo nodded to his worker, "Two."

Shelton stood in the shade line of the fir trees and watched Hugo's men collect the remainder of the property and load it onto the wagon. When the final mule meandered out of sight, Shelton turned on his heel down to the sluice boxes.

The bubbling river water almost soothed his rage. Cassidy had lied. The mine had been salted and now the Blue Cow Ranch was out of his grasp once and for all. He'd pegged all his hopes on this mining claim paying out. He picked up the black sand that clogged Jet's timber design. Worthless. He turned back to the cabins. The tiny shack with its repaired roof seemed a symbol of one failure decades ago. Then the cabin, with its trail of smoke wafting into the air, had been the latest attempt to turn this pit into something worthwhile. Cassidy. His gut clenched, the rush of fury seizing his lungs until his hands began to tremble. He couldn't bring himself to think about her deceit. Back in Dew Springs, his Ma and Pa counted on him to make something work up here. He could have stayed in Texas and worked every minute of every day of his life to pay some of the debt. Now he'd wasted time and money to get up here and for what? For nothing! An image of the Blue Cow's front lawn dusty and the homestead empty, popped into his mind. The ranch was as good as gone thanks to pointless effort. Bending down to the river, Shelton washed his trembling hands in the cool water. Damn Cassidy. Damn Jackson.

Shelton stalked up the cabin, wishing the sunlight could dim to match his dark mood. Entering the Cabin he saw Cassidy at the table, her red rimmed eyes searching his face for something.

"A counterfeiter?"

A sound choked from Cassidy's throat, "That's why I don't paint Shelton, I learnt with inks and stamps."

"And the mine? Did you know?"

Cassidy moved to rise and Shelton extended his palm, wishing he could settle the rage that made his hands quake. Cassidy halted but remained on her feet, her narrow chin raised just an inch and she met his gaze with eyes the color of desert jasper. "I thought.... " She inhaled, a shaky breath with a hiccup, "I knew my father and what he was capable of but I had hoped..." Her shoulders hunched, "Then when you showed me Pips Pit I knew. It's not a two on the dice," Cassidy's lip thinned as the color drained from her cheeks, "It's snake eyes, I guess there's always a chance with the Black-jack, if I can just -"

"Damn it Cass!" Dragging his fingers through his hair, Shelton paced to the sink and back. He'd reached his limit, reckless and infuriated, his words tumbled end over end, "I found your sense of loyalty admirable, but now I see its folly. There is nothing here. Worthless. You said so yourself, your father took everything he could and then some. You're a fool if you think he'd leave you anything of value."

"Is that what you think too Shelton, that all this is worthless?"

Shelton closed his eyes against the onslaught of her stricken face, and the image of the Blue Cow ranch, derelict and barren, appeared in his mind, "I need gold, Cassidy and I'm not grubstaking on a worthless piece of land." Shelton pulled the door tight, hoping the slam would sooth his temper. Only the hinges squeaked.

"The lease agreement is terminated."

Shelton's boots froze, "What?"

"With my father's death this claim reverts to me. I,..." Cassidy gulped, "I'm terminating the agreement you had with my father."

Cassidy sucked in a quick breath, "The lease agreement is void."

Shelton didn't reply. By the time he reached the shack, Shelton's mind had been set. He stepped over the threshold to see Jet's unmade bed and Shelton's gun belt over the bedhead. Wrapping it around his waist, he pulled on his vest and Stetson. If Jackson stirred up a hornets nest, then he'd get stung.

Shelton mounted *Tango* with Cassidy still standing on the threshold of the cabin. He couldn't look at her lest she'd see the betrayal in his heart and the depth of the wound she'd caused. He booted *Tango* in the flanks and tore off towards Oro City.

Gold dug into the flesh at the rear of her neck as she tugged and twisted on her mother's locket. Julius Smith had died in prison. She hadn't known he'd been caught. A raft of thoughts rocked through her mind and she clutched her knees. Had he suffered? Fraudulent railway bonds? Perhaps Julius Smith was awaiting the hangman's noose? Would anyone come for her? She had nothing to offer anybody anyway. Perhaps dying in prison could have been the best Julius Smith could hope for. A fitting end for a fraudster, a thief and a counterfeiter, only he was her father.

"What did you say to him Cass?" Jet asked.

"I terminated the lease agreement. I set him free." She said.

She watched as Shelton, atop *Tango*, tore down the trail. She'd hoped she made the right decision. With his silver tongue, Shelton had shown his true colors. His words had rung crystal clear. Worthless.

"Free from what?"

"Obligation."

With shoulders hunched and his Stetson pulled low over his brow, Shelton and *Tango* covered the ground in leaps and bounds taking her heart with him. The cool timber leached through her thin blouse as she sunk to the ground. Hiding her face into her elbow, Cassidy let the fabric catch her tears.

"I'm sorry to hear about your father, Cass." Jet sunk to the porch and threw his arm around her neck.

"I think I am." Cassidy winced. Shelton's anger had sliced harder and faster than her father's death. It should be the opposite and the realization of where her heart lay sunk in her boots. "I'm not sure."

"I guess you're more crooked than I gave you credit for, Cass." Jet offered a tiny laugh and Cassidy tried to match it.

"He certainly was a crook."

Jet's voice softened, "And your father."

Leaning her head against Jet's shoulders, she let the tears fall again. "I didn't love him, but I didn't wish him ill."

"Nobody does I suppose."

Cassidy looked at Jet and the boys blue eyes reflected her own sorrow.

Julius Smith hadn't loved Cassidy, she had become a tool in his schemes and when she refused, Cassidy had become a commodity. He hadn't cared for her at all, and now, he likely had swindled her like he did so many others. Had Julius Smith really left his daughter a worthless piece of dirt?

"Some day, when you're ready, you can tell me about him. I'll just listen Cass, no judgement."

Cassidy settled her breaths as she nodded and scrubbed the back of her hand across her cheeks. Well Shelton could be angry, and tear off in a temper. Cassidy would prove him wrong. Prove Jackson and her father wrong as well. Perhaps Julius Smith had salted the mine, it sounded like something he would do, even downright practical. Only he couldn't have buried a false lode of zinc ore. Cassidy rose to her feet. She would turn her father's snake eyes into a win with Black-jack.

Chapter 28

Jackson reached the bottom step of the tavern wearing a three piece brown suit that had seen better days and a pair of boots coated in trail dust. His belly looked slightly leaner and his hair slightly thinner. Shelton nodded to the dove Delilah who strode down the stairs, winking over Jackson's shoulder to Shelton. The light of midmorning trickled across the worn timber slats, highlighting every stain from the nights before, including cigar, whiskey and blood. All the time spent atop *Tango* cooling his temper had dissolved at the sight of Jackson here in Oro City.

"So you finally figured out I'm right and she's not worth the trouble."

"Tell me why you're here Jackson." Shelton could feel the itch at the back of his neck.

"Her father owes me so I came to receive payment."

"What?"

"You heard me, now he's dead, the land reverts to her and he only ever paid me ten percent of what he owed me, always promising more than he could deliver."

Those words echoed in Shelton's chest and doused his temper with ice cold realism. Over an hour ago, Shelton had done the same. Rushing off to shake the truth from Jackson, when he should be consoling Cassidy about her father's death. She'd lied. The woman had more masks than manners. The sight of her red-rimmed eyes tore through his anger. The least Shelton could do was run the man from town.

"If you say the mine is salted then what's the point?"

"It's what you call a honey trap Mister Murphy," Jackson took the final step to the tavern floor and pulled out a chair from the closest table. He pointed to the empty seat opposite. Shelton remained still and crossed his arms, if only to stop from striking Jackson now. "Suit yourself, but a sweet gal like Cassidy all alone in the wilderness and looking for a husband and with all that land and not knowing what to do with it. I could sell it for a fortune to the next unlucky bastard that came along."

"You'd re-salt the mine?"

Jackson clicked his fingers to the tired barkeep who just snorted. "I had half a mind to bring some prospectors up here when I followed you from Waco."

"And what of Cassidy?" *What of Cassidy?* Shelton challenged himself. She'd terminated the agreement and booted him from the land. The betrayal still stung, and his harsh words seemed like vinegar to his wound.

"She'd get a husband one way or another." Jackson pulled at his own three day old vest before sliding his hand through his thinning hair. "You could help me guide the prospective prospectors up here, you could earn some good coin. What do you say?"

Thunderclouds pulled around Shelton's mind, his limbs singing with lightening as he glared at Jackson's rounded cheeks.

"It's not going to work."

"Why not, you've seen how well it worked." Jackson snorted.

As the words tumbled off Shelton's tongue, the clouds parted in Shelton's mind and the tightness in his chest replaced with rays of golden warmth. "It's not going to work Jackson," Shelton's fingers speared through Jackson's collar and he dragged the portly man into the street. "Because she's already got a husband."

"Ha!" Jackson rose to his feet.

"You heard me, now get on your mount." White heat poured through Shelton's veins as the dawn broke over his thoughts. Cassidy was his woman in everything but name. The thought of this man trying to bargain her off to others crystalized in his mind to the point where he couldn't focus on anything else except Jackson's pudgy face. Shelton pumped his fists.

"Now listen here I didn't come all this way to be stopped by some hotheaded rancher, I want what's owed to me."

Jackson's hand went to his waist coat but Shelton had already launched. Squeezing the man's forearm he twisted and Jackson's knees buckled. He pulled the older man's arm free and with it came his colt. Shelton squeezed tighter and the pistol tumbled to the dirt. Jackson leaned to one side. His fist ripped upwards into Shelton's ribs.

Grunting Shelton stepped back, connecting fist to nose, then jaw and then eye. Jackson yowled and bit the dust just as the crowd spilled onto the street.

"You have until I count to ten, Jackson to get on your mount and leave Colorado."

Jackson scrambled to his feet.

"Colorado you hear, not just this mountain."

Jackson tried a hearty laugh, only to crouch over, hands on his knees and spat in the dirt, "To the count of ten and then what?"

Shelton cracked his knuckles, "And then I'm hitching you to Tango and dragging you all the way to Texas."

"Texas?"

"One..."

"You're not serious!"

Shelton rolled his shoulders, "Two."

Jackson dashed to a spotted pony hitched to the front post and rushed to climb into the saddle. Only his foot missed the stirrup and he clutched the pommel to stop himself falling on his buttocks.

Shelton wandered slowly to *Tango*, "Three."

"I'm going Murphy! I'm going!"

Shelton reset his Stetson over his brow and glared at Jackson "Four."

"What are you doing? Why are you still counting?" The man's jowls wobbled as he lifted himself into the saddle on his next attempt.

"It was just a head start Jackson. I'm going to make sure you leave this mountain."

Jackson booted his animal into action and Shelton continued to count. He'd dog Jackson down the mountain until he felt certain the man was gone. It felt like the right thing to do, only he wasn't sure for who? Cassidy's father had just died and the jackals had come circling, starting with Jackson. Shelton didn't know what Cassidy would do with the claim now that she'd rescinded the lease. He only knew it was her decision. Dust streamed behind Jackson's spotted pony and Shelton steered *Tango* to follow. Only when he felt sure Jackson was done and wouldn't return, would Shelton head back to the claim and ask for Cassidy's hand. Hopefully then the cool mountain air had soothed her pain like he had failed to do.

Cassidy rechecked all the ingredients she had laid out on the table, lye, vinegar, mercury and ammonia. She had nested three pots inside of each other and pulled out her geology textbook. Next, she went to the shack to riffle through what was left of their equipment for something she could use as a mortar and pestle. When she returned inside the main Cabin, she could smell bacon cooking in the pan.

"What are doing Jet?"

"Cooking you breakfast. It's still early and I figured you could eat before whatever this is."

"Thank you, you should eat too." Cassidy said just as Jet popped a strap of the salted pork into his mouth. Cassidy reminded herself she did the right thing, freeing Shelton from any obligation he had to her so he could find the gold he chased. She would prove him wrong and her father wrong. Trash could also be treasure.

"Right, well, I'm taking a few things out to the Aspen gulch, if you don't mind helping me."

"Sure but then ..."

"Yes?"

"I want to work the sluice boxes."

Jet suddenly found interest in his shoes, whatever he was hiding Cassidy had to trust him.

"Sure, I'll have the pistol, besides I just want you to start a fire for me."

"Huh?"

"A little one so I can test my samples, you know like a camp fire with rocks around it to keep it safe."

"Sure Cass, but..."

"Don't worry I'm going to bring a bucket or two with me full from the river, like always."

"Always. Ok."

Jet waited until the logs had ignited and turned to glowing coals before he retreated, the leaves crunching under his feet. "I'll be back soon, Cass."

Cassidy waved over the edge of her book. She'd be safe, she always was around fire. He had lugged her two buckets full from the river and she had the pistol. Besides, he needed to get to town before it was too late. He sneaked across the field to the group of mules milling about. Thankfully, Hugo had agreed to leave them two. Jet's first honest wage! He saddled his mule and climbed aboard. Cassidy would be fine. She was quick and clever and never messed around when it came to fire. Jet had told Cassidy he would talk to Shelton and now the time had come. With one last look to the aspens, Jet headed into town.

Shelton stretched in his saddle, glad that Jackson hadn't dallied as he scampered down the trail. At each hoof step of *Tango*, Shelton's decision solidified. Now he only had to reach Cassidy and apologize, hoping she'd forgive him for his insensitivity. The lines of tents of Oro City came into view and Shelton's stomach growled. He rested at the trading post, although the scents of a beef roll were tempting he couldn't eat. Instead he decided to see to the post master. He needed to be honest with his family. The mine had been a bust. Secondly, he'd send his sister a telegram demanding she think of someone other than herself. Her husband, the banker surely could do something.

Entering the post office, Shelton pulled his Stetson off and let his eyes adjust.

"I wondered when I'd see you here."

"Oh yeah." Shelton grabbed a pad and pencil off the counter and started writing down his messages.

"Yeah, you've got a few messages here."

Shelton held out his hand as the post master handed over the telegrams. Shelton read the first one, from Cade. He'd reached Dew Springs safely and surprisingly he'd met Marcus Kearby and Jewel Daniels on the trail. The telegram ended with his news of Evie's safe delivery. Twin girls. Shelton smiled, who would have thought Cade Hamerton, the family man. Shelton laughed. He'd never thought he'd see himself married either and hopefully he wasn't too late.

He read the next telegram, this time from his Ma. Her message was short and sweet but he could read between the lines. She told him they were fine, that they couldn't wait to hear of his adventures and to come home and not to worry.

The third telegram gave him pause. He read it and re-read it until he remembered when he demanded Cassidy send a telegram to her husband.

Shelton, I have known your name for weeks. Now I have glimpsed your heart. I hope by the time we reach Colorado that I will have earned both.

Shelton's hand came down on the counter as if he'd been kicked in the stomach. Wichita, Kansas. Cassidy had so much loyalty and faith in him. Wichita, Kansas. Shelton had still been messing around, enjoying thawing the glacier that had been Miss Precious, without a care for either of their futures. A vision of Cassidy standing amongst the fields of the Blue Cow ranch came to mind and Shelton tucked the telegram into his pocket. As he sent his two telegrams, Jet stormed into the Post Office.

"Shelton Murphy, we need to talk."

"Jet? Where's Cassidy?" He touched his vest pocket gently. "Is she alright?"

"She will be eventually. But you and me need to talk."

Shelton replaced his Stetson and patted Jet on the shoulder. The boy shrugged it off but followed Shelton out to the street all the same.

"I thought you were worthy of her Shelton but you ran away like a coward."

Shelton's jaw cinched and he exhaled slowly, "Hey, I came to confront Jackson and see him out of town." Shelton threw his hands up in mock surrender, "I'm heading back to the claim now."

Jet's frown eased and his mouth opened and then closed. He pointed at Shelton's nose and then crossed his arms, "What are you going to do when you get there?"

"Ask Cassidy to marry me. Proper. None of this lease agreement nonsense."

Jet smirked, "Well she kicked you off the claim anyway."

"I know." Shelton clambered onto *Tango* and looked at the worn out mule that Jet mounted. "Come on. I'd race you except he looks beat." Just when Shelton wanted to hurry back, he'd have to pace their rides up to the claim.

"Don't wait for me Shelton. I have no intention of being around when you two make up."

Cassidy wiped her hand over her brow as she read and reread the instructions. Chemistry seemed so similar to baking that she felt confident all she had to do was follow the recipe. She stepped cautiously around the flames, watching the pot hanging over the tripod as she rechecked the amount of lye she needed.

It had taken her over an hour to ground down three separate measures of rock in the mortar and pestle, watering it down into an ore soup. One for gold that now required a dash of mercury, one for silver currently being heated in the coals, next to a third she kept an eye on in case it revealed copper. Cassidy decided to hedge her bets and instead of concentrating on gold, she'd test for all three.

Shelton would eat his words when she found something. *Worthless.* The word echoed through her heart and tightened her throat. She inhaled quickly and reset her shoulders. Nothing was ever worthless, it's true purposed hadn't been revealed yet. Cassidy knew she'd find something. Not because her father had bequeathed it to her, but because Cassidy had studied the geology and if there was anything, she'd be the one to find it.

Picking the wide shallow pan filled with the sample for gold, Cassidy carefully balanced it on a fallen stump and undid the stopper on the mercury. With a steady hand, she added the silvery element to the mix. After replacing the stopper, Cassidy swirled the pan around to blend it before moving to place it on the ground. The heat of the day plus being this close to the fire made her sweat and she wiped her forehead on her elbow as she crouched down.

The fire sparked and hissed. A section of glowing coals collapsed inwards. As the silver pot tilted, Cassidy reached out. Wincing she pulled back her singed fingers. The gold pan slipped and Cassidy gasped. As one pot splashed onto the other, the contents fizzed and hissed. The tripod tumbled next and Cassidy's face heated so fast she dropped the pan and shielded her eyes.

A wild vapor rose from the flames and Cassidy stepped back. Her throat tightened and she dry retched. Coughing, she covered her mouth and frantically waved the smoke away. Cassidy's heart echoed in her ears as panic set in. Her lungs didn't seem to work. The air she desperately sucked down turned sour and she tasted metal.

Heaving and coughing, Cassidy wiped at her eyes. The scene of the woodlands looked unfamiliar as the toxic fumes obscured the trees.

She tried to call out, only her tongue felt thick. Bent double, she coughed into the leaf litter. *What had she done?* Crawling, she reached one bucket and splashed the water on her face. She drank deep of the cool liquid, thankful it eased her throat. Trembling, Cassidy squatted and splashed more water on her face and over her jacket and down her dress. Only when she felt strength return to her legs did she finally stand.

Smoke curled through the aspens and the leaf litter seemed a carpet of flames. Cassidy picked up the bucket only her shaky arms couldn't lift it. The water splashed into the dirt at her boots.

Calm, she just needed to stay calm! Her gaze darted from bucket to flames and back again. She stumbled over to the second bucket. Crouching down she heaved it towards the flames. The liquid splashed onto the fire and pushed the potion further into the leaves. The bubbling and hissing continued only this time everywhere she looked.

Time ticked slower as her legs numbed and the flames sped through the underbrush. It seemed to Cassidy that the tangerine curls climbed higher and faster, nipping the low branches and consuming fallen logs. Cassidy wiped her stinging eyes and backed away until a tree trunk stopped her. Turning, she squinted through the smoke to the escapement. *Damn!* She followed the line of rocks until it came to an end. In front the rocks climbed to the horizon, behind her the flames heated her back. Cassidy eyed the flames, like fingers of a demon as they clawed towards her, leaping from leaf to leaf, the embers floating upwards and sparking anything it touched.

As the walls pressed in Cassidy's knees failed. The dirt bit into her skin as the darkness clouded her mind. The scene shifted in her eyes, suddenly everything doubled and the ground slanted under her body. She would die here, on her father's land, surrounded by fire, just like her mother.

No. Your land, your fire, she thought. Her fingers speared through the gravel and dirt as her mind cleared if only for a moment. Down lower the air seemed sweeter and Cassidy pressed her face down to the dirt and drew deeply of lighter air. She would not succumb like her mother did. She would move and keep moving until she was free. Cassidy tilted her head to one side placing the escarpment to her left meant the river was down to her right. As if to double check her estimate she speared her arm across the sloping ground. *Yes. Down, towards the river.*

Cassidy brought her wet jacket up to her head crawled on hands and knees. The heat hugged her right hand side, but she moved one hand over the other and scrambled down towards the bank.

Swirls of smoke wafted through a row of aspens and Cassidy covered her mouth. She caught the narrowest glimpse of river and hastened her crawl. As she neared the smoke, Cassidy's head began to throb. Dizziness struck and Cassidy pressed her cheek into the gravel. *The river, just get to the river.* She knelt only to suck down another mouthful of the noxious vapor. Cassidy bent over and coughed. Suddenly a voice boomed nearby.

Shelton's name stuck on her thick tongue, the air all but gone from her sizzling lungs.

"Cass!"

The last thing she saw was a giant liver colored horse charging through the flames before darkness claimed her.

Chapter 29

Shelton leaned low over the saddle as he saw the line of smoke spiraling through trees. As he neared, he could make out just how high the flames had reached up the trunks. A weight sunk in his gut.

"Cassidy!" He shouted, "Cass!"

Something moaned and Shelton didn't wait for another sign.

"Dance boy, dance." He pleaded as he booted *Tango* in the flanks. Shelton shifted his weight with the animal as Tango leapt. He smelt singed hair and didn't look down as the flames licked the belly and hooves of his horse.

They came down hard on the other side of the fire and Shelton had to shield his eyes from the heat. The air tasted sour and stung his nostrils. A lump of fabric caught his eye and in one movement Shelton left his saddle and tumbled on the ground. Scooping Cassidy up, he tossed her over his saddle and remounted. *Tango* baulked as the flames encircled them. Shelton took the moment to resettle Cassidy in his lap.

"Yar!" Shelton shouted and *Tango* moved. The ground tilted and Shelton held onto his precious cargo with all his strength.

As they cleared the fire, Shelton steered them to the river. *Tango* dashed into the bubbling current without delay. Shelton cursed as he slid into the water dragging Cassidy with him. She lolled in his arms, her head against his chest. She had to be alright. She just had to be. As he splashed the water over her hair and face, the dirt and ash came away. Carefully he shook her in his arms as he ran his other hand over her body. Was she injured? Bleeding? He pressed his ear to her chest except his own panic made it impossible to hear.

"Cass, come on Cass. I'm here. Come on." Shelton pleaded.

"Is she all right?" Jet hollered from the shore.

Shelton waded through the water and laid Cassidy down on the river bank. He pealed back her jacket and pressed his ear to her chest again.

One cough. One cough was all it took for Shelton's heart to start beating again.

"Cass?"

Rolling over, Cassidy coughed again. Shelton whistled and *Tango* returned to him. Within seconds he found his canteen from his saddle bags and filled it. Cassidy sat upright and Shelton gently pressed the canteen to her lips.

"Cass?" Jet's cheeks paled, his blue eyes filled with liquid.

"I'm fine." She croaked.

"Jet take *Tango* and get the Doctor."

"I'm fine." Cassidy coughed again and this time she took the canteen herself and drank deeply.

"I'm on it." Jet raced to *Tango* and pulled himself into the saddle. The horse whinnied but obeyed as the young man pushed the big horse into a gallop.

Shelton dashed to the sluice boxes redirecting the narrowing channel of Jet's design so that the water splashed onto the river bank. From there Shelton removed the top section, turning it upside down he used it as a pail. Setting himself between the fire and the edge of the woodlands, he pushed the water onto the embers that breached the border. With every wave of the river, with every scoop of the sluice box lid, he looked back to Cassidy still sitting on the edge of the bank. Shelton rolled his shoulders as the afternoon wind gusted through the trees and pushed back against the fire.

When Shelton was satisfied the cabins were safe and the fire had turned tail to burn its way out beneath the escarpment, he returned to Cassidy.

"How are you?"

"I'm fine." Cassidy croaked. "How's the fire?"

"It's done its dash."

Shelton couldn't help it and he pawed her arms and legs checking for any break or burn. Another knot released from his stomach in relief. He pushed her wet strands back from her head and regarded her red rimmed eyes and pale cheeks, "You scared me Cass."

"I scared myself." She tried a laugh only it rasped her throat. "I'm fine Shelton."

He pushed his damp fringe out of his own eyes and scooped one arm under her knees and the other under her arms.

"I can walk."

"I don't care." He mumbled into her neck.

When they reached the cabin, Shelton sat her down on the side of the bed while he built up the fire. He left the door open worrying just how much heat would be bad. Cassidy looked shaken but relatively unharmed, except Shelton could still feel the tickle in his own throat at the noxious fumes she'd made. He chewed his bottom lip as he approached.

Cassidy rested one hand on the table as she stood, the ground tried to slip away from her but she held on. She didn't want Shelton to see her folly. Almost beaten by her own experiment. Cassidy shivered and suddenly Shelton stood in front of her, wet and dripping, his sugar grey eyes like the softest mink.

"Thank you." She mumbled as her bottom lip trembled. She needed to be strong.

"Cass I'm sorry."

Shelton's fingers began to pluck her buttons and she tried to turn away.

"Relax Cass, I'm trying to get you warm."

"I know how that ends." She threw back, her throat less scratchy.

He laughed. A deep rumble that sent tingles down her

spine and ending in her chest. "I'm serious you're shivering and I'd rather have you dry and warm before the Doctor comes."

Cassidy surrendered and let Shelton remove her wet clothes. When it came to her shift she turned away until she'd pulled the fresh one down to her ankles. Shelton helped her with her navy dress, only doing up half the buttons.

"I'm sorry I took off Cass, when I should have been here for you. For your father."

"It's okay Shelton. I understand your disappointment. You came here for gold." She swallowed hard and took another swig of the canteen.

Shelton gently pushed her shoulders until she sat back on the bed.

"I realize, I never told you why I came to Colorado."

"You did, gold."

Shelton fluffed up the two pillows behind her back and Cassidy reclined. He pulled the chair to her side and sat down. Gently he pulled her hand into his. "Yeah gold, but why I need it."

Cassidy felt her resolve waiver. She should tug it back, only she wanted to pull him into bed with her and curl up with his arms around her.

"The bank is going to foreclose on the Blue Cow if I can't pay the debt by winter. My Pa is working from sun up to sun down, but there's not enough feed and he hasn't got the money to buy more. What we've got is not enough to sell and pay the debt."

Shelton replaced Cassidy's hand on the bed, "I shouldn't have left when Hugo gave you the news about your father. I'm sorry. But I found Jackson and chased him out of town."

Shelton dipped his head and rubbed his palms slowly together, "This land it yours by right now Cassidy, no lease agreement with your father, no extra conditions."

His lips kinked to one side.

Cassidy held her breath.

"I figured, I'd like to renegotiate terms."

As if the toxic fumes had returned, Cassidy clutched at her chest, her throat dry and her stomach lurched. He wanted to talk business. Now? She remembered the way he described the Blue Cow, the colors of the sunset and the live oaks by the river. He clearly loved his family. They counted on him and her father had cheated him. Julius Smith had cheated them both.

Cassidy slowly pulled her mother's locket from around her neck. She opened his palms and placed the locket between them.

"What's this for?" Shelton sat upright.

"You said you need gold." Cassidy shuddered. She slunk down into the linen of the bed and rolled over.

"Cass, I can't take this."

Liquid pooled in her dry eyes and leaked onto her pillow. She tried to wick it away without Shelton seeing. "Take it."

The silence stretched out. Only the crackling of the pot belly echoed around the tiny cabin.

When Shelton did speak, his whisper was dark, "You have so much faith in me."

Her emotions boiled over and Cassidy tried to choke back her sob, "In us, Shelton."

Shelton turned the gold locket over in his hands. What was it worth? Judging by the weight it could pay some of the Blue Cow debt. But what was it worth to Cassidy? Slowly Shelton pinched the hinges and gasped. Ice slid down his spine as he stared at the empty frames.

"It's empty Cass."

The girl had worn an empty locket? Of course. Shelton cringed at his own foolishness. No picture, not even a lock of hair to remember her mother by and here Cassidy offered it to him for his family.

"Don't pity me, Shelton."

If his heart didn't ache, he would have laughed, "I don't Cass. I'm in awe of you."

That made her roll over! The woman's chocolate eyes ablaze as she regarded him.

"I can't take away your past Cassidy. I wish I could but I can't. The only good that I can find is that it led you to me." He gently placed the locket in her hand. "I'm in awe of you, because despite all of this you can still trust and love. You're brave and adventurous and clever and kind." He ran his finger down her cheeks, "You have so much trust in me it's daunting to live up to, I'm afraid to let you down. I'm no good with responsibility." He laughed.

Cassidy sat upright, her caramel strands fell about her face, "You're wrong. What you are doing for your parents, everything you've done for me, and how you are with Jet. Even Sidney Barnes!" Her bottom lip trembled. "I came to Colorado for a husband Shelton, but I don't want just a husband, I want you."

Her wide brown eyes only drew him in further. Shelton pressed his forehead to hers thankful she'd seen through his foolishness. "I want to be everything you need Cass."

Her hands circled his neck and he watched her close her eyes, her long lashes gracing her cheek, "I only need you to love me."

Shelton laughed and pressed a kiss to her delicate lips, "I already do Cass. My heart is yours and if you're not busy Sunday I'd like you to take my name."

Cassidy rose the next morning slowly crawling out over Shelton's sprawled frame. The doctor had checked her out late yesterday afternoon advising rest and plenty of liquids. He insisted she visit him today in Oro city for another check-up which Shelton commented suited him just fine since he needed to speak to the Pastor as well.

After a small dinner last night exhaustion overcame Cassidy and Shelton carried her back to bed. The flames had returned to haunt her only this time the dream ended when Shelton arrived. She heard him muttering reassurances to her again and curled into his flank drifting safely back to sleep. Now she wandered out to the chickens and collected the eggs as if she floated on clouds. Returning inside the cabin, Shelton had woken and greeted her with a kiss. Leaning into him she kissed him back disappointed as Jet wandered into the cabin for breakfast.

"When you're ready, we'll slowly head into town."

"I'm fine Shelton. I feel much better today." She straightened her shoulders as Jet delivered her breakfast.

"Well I'll see the Pastor and then I'll see about finding some work."

"We could sell the land?" Cassidy offered.

"For what and to who? Thanks to Jackson nobody would buy it." Jet scoffed down his bacon and pushed his eggs onto a slab of bread.

Shelton sipped his coffee slowly, "I'll take work on one of the others claims, maybe running supplies up from Pueblo or Howard, I'll think of something."

Cassidy sighed. When Shelton took her into town she would sell her locket. There was no other option to consider. They were lucky Hugo couldn't transport his food. They had supplies for a while, but eventually they would need more. She could sell her locket and maybe her geology text book. *Oh damn!* Had the fire consumed it? Cassidy suddenly ate her breakfast with purpose and then stood up.

"Where do you think you're going?"

"To see if my text book survived. I figured we could sell it in town."

"Cass!" Jet snorted.

"There's a chance someone might buy it." Cassidy put her plate in the sink

Shelton sighed and took his plate to the sink, "Wait for

me."

Shelton and Jet both accompanied her into the woodlands where a wide circle of her devastation could be seen as soon as they entered the trees. Picking her footing carefully Cassidy stepped over the debris until she stood in the ash. Her pots lay overturned and their contents spilled. She wandered over to her failed experiments.

"Is this it Cass?" Jet picked up a half singed lump, the blackened pages tumbled into the ash.

"Oh." She picked up one pot and looked inside. Charred sludge slid out to greet her. She tossed it aside and moved to the next.

"I don't think it's salvageable." Shelton kicked the dirt over the ash coals. He pointed to the path of the fire as it steered towards the escarpment. "Lucky."

"I have others to sell." Cassidy turned the second pot over and a sliver of something sparkled amongst the black.

"Cass you don't have to sell anything. I've sent a telegram to my sister."

"That's what husbands and wives do, Shelton, they share the burden. Give it some time and I can sell this land." She mumbled into the blackness, her breath lifting ash from the pot's inside.

"Until then we've still got to eat." Jet added

Cassidy scrapped the char with her fingernail, "Silver?"

"We can't eat that." Shelton added.

"No, silver!" She held the pot up as Jet raced to her side.

"Are you sure?"

Cassidy handed over the treasure and paced down the gulch as if seeing the land for the first time. She continued until she reached the river bank and the sluice boxes. Crouching she scooped up the heavy black silt. "It's Cerussite."

"Cass, speak English not Latin!" Jet rushed.

"It's a lead mineral. This," She took back the pot from Jet, "Is likely Galena. Silver, Shelton. Both Galena and Cerussite are high in silver!"

Shelton's long strides brought him to Cassidy and his arms wrapped around her waist. Spirals of joy flooded Cassidy's system as her feet left the ground. Shelton's lips clamped down on hers, she kissed him back until he withdrew to pepper her lips with kisses, down her jaw and to her throat. "Are you still going to marry me, Miss Cassidy Smith?"

"I will and then I want to renegotiate terms?"

Shelton wrapped her legs around his hips, "Of course, Precious, whatever your heart desires."

"I want to see your home."

"You are my home, Cass."

"I mean Texas."

Shelton laughed against her lips, "I'd be more than happy to spend winter in Dew Springs."

Jet hollered from across scorched ground, "This means pie!"

Shelton kissed Cassidy slowly, and she lingered in the bliss. He pulled back again, "Besides you want to meet the rest of your new family, am I right?"

Cassidy smiled, her heart couldn't swell any further, "Before we start ours."

Shelton groaned against her lips, kissing her deeper holding her just that little bit tighter, "I agree to your terms."

The end

Epilogue

Cassidy opened the cabin door as the sound of metal on rock pealed across the brisk Colorado air. She handed Jet her latest platter of roast beef with a smile while she retrieved half a dozen coffee mugs. She wanted to tussle Jet's hair only he'd shot up so much in the last six months she couldn't reach it.

"What's for dessert?"

"It's only been a week since Texas and every day you've been asking for dessert. I'm sorry to say that this is Colorado and I believe Temperance Murphy spoiled you rotten."

"I know Cass. Has it only been a week, it feels like a month. I do miss her pies." Jet said wistfully.

"Well lucky for you she gave me the recipe." Cassidy's heart had warmed so much in the time she'd spent with her husband's family that by the end of the winter, she hadn't wanted to leave. She knew that silver waited underneath her boots for her and Shelton to seize.

Within the two weeks after finding the silver, they had paid off the Blue Cow ranch debt and had enough to hire men to dig the excavations. Shelton agreed to give up on the mine shaft and concentrate on what Cassidy called the 'Aspen Gulch'. For the first few months Shelton, Jet and Cassidy had spent every waking hour amongst the rubble, side by side with the workers, digging and crushing the ore until they could take it to the newly built mill to extract the silver. Then Congress had approved the Government to buy more silver and the Murphy's had obliged. Shelton could rest his shoulders and let the workers do their bit, only he didn't. She watched him now, as he dismounted from *Tango*, telegrams in his hand, as he wandered over to the cabin. His navy blue shirt stretched tight across his broad frame and he lifted his Stetson up to push back his fringe.

Cassidy couldn't help but smile at how lucky she was. Seeing Shelton with his family reaffirmed all that she knew about her husband. His heart was good, even if his nose was crooked. He wasn't perfect, but he was perfect for her.

"Give me some time to settle in Jet, and I'll try one of those pies for when the surveyors come." Cassidy set the mugs down on the top of one of the ice boxes.

"That's too long a time Cass."

"It's tomorrow Jet!"

Cassidy bent down to the second ice box and pulled out a pitcher of milk from the cooler.

"What's this shouting about?"

Shelton must have crossed the distance, as now he wrapped one arm around her waist and pulled her up against him. Planting a kiss on her cheek and then her neck and then at the tender join between her throat and shoulder. His grip tightened and Cassidy leaned into his strength, her hands clutching at his thighs. Judging by his lingering kisses, she knew dessert wasn't far away.

Cassidy opened her eyes as she tilted her neck, savoring the delicate kisses he laid along her flesh, "Just speculating about these surveyors. Did the Post Master have any telegrams?"

Shelton released her and scooped up the milk and three of the cups while Cassidy carried the rest. "Oh yeah?"

"I reckon I can sell them some of my designs." Jet said.

"Probably Jet but you got to build them first." Shelton followed Jet towards the workers that rested at the timber table setting that Jet and Shelton had built. A fire glowed nearby and a tripod strung over the flames with a pot of coffee on the boil. Cassidy handed out the mugs and took the milk from Shelton topping them up as requested. Then the three of them sat down on a fallen log a little away off from the resting crew.

"Do you think they're crooks?" Jet whispered.

"News is, they've been traveling all over these mountains buying up places but they're still looking for the main lode." Shelton said.

"And if it's here?"

"I hope it is Jet." Cassidy said. Shelton smile back. Having the warm Texas sun heat her through to her bones, the wide green fields and the long slow sunsets had made up Cassidy's mind. She hadn't wanted to leave Dew Springs as much as Temperance Murphy hadn't wanted her to leave, and the thought of raising a family up here didn't sit right either.

"What are you going to negotiate with them?"

"Why you asking me?" Shelton winked at Cassidy.

Jet smirked, "I guess it takes a crook to know one."

Cassidy threw a pebble at him, "I'd still like to see where their maps are."

"Ask them." Shelton sipped his coffee.

"I intend to dear Husband." Cassidy laughed

After satiating their thirst and collapsing in each other's arms that night, Cassidy dozed gently as stroked Shelton's chest. "Would you mind if I wanted to sell the claim?"

Shelton hummed as his long fingers stroked her bare spine, "My home is where you are Cass and wherever you choose to build our family."

"I've been thinking about that."

"Mmm?"

"I want to live where the land stretches to the horizon, and the fields are green and full. Somewhere I can feel the afternoon sun creep across our porch warming me as much as the timber, while the cicadas sing."

Shelton's chest rumbled with laughter, "I think I know a place, Precious."

"Good."

"I wasn't sure my Ma was going to let us leave when we did."

Cassidy snuggled into the chest of her husband, "You wouldn't mind leaving behind being a Silver Baron to become a rancher again?"

This time Shelton's rumble broke into a hearty laugh, "Silver Baron? Just what kind of offer do you think they're going to make tomorrow?"

"I've been all over this land Shelton and if the geology is correct, then Pip's Pit sits right on top of the lode."

Shelton sighed and pulled Cassidy closer into his chest, "People have been finding silver all over this mountain after we did Cass."

"Little bits, Cerussite but nothing like the amount of Galena we have here."

Shelton pressed a kiss to her hair, "I trust you'll negotiate well tomorrow then." His voice became heavy with sleep and Cassidy let the topic drop. She would ring every last dime out of this deal to secure their future in Texas.

Shelton reclined with his arms crossed over his chest pretending to be the Silver Baron that Cassidy had envisioned. Jet did his part in the background loudly discussing designs for a much larger excavation and an onsite mill. Shelton squinted as he listened to the plans, struggling to imagine how it could feasibly be built.

The two surveyors paced out the land picking up rocks and scribbling in their books. They spent most of their time with their heads together while Cassidy sat at their table and benches and warmed her hands on the fire. Shelton leaned against the table and concentrated on looking disinterested.

When the two men had finally packed up their instruments, they sat in front of Cassidy and Shelton finally took his seat. He added a yawn for emphasis. "What ya got boys?"

The younger one with longer hair and a moustache spoke first, "This is an interesting parcel of land with that escarpment on the outer edge, ah, it would inhibit the work, and the foundations...."

Cassidy straightened her shoulders, her lips thin, "I think that escarpment will be exactly what you need it to be. Besides, I'm sure the amount of trouble you think it will cause you will pay dividends when you finally dig."

As if Jet could read Cassidy's mind he whistled to a worker and gestured wider with his arms. The worker scratched his head but followed Jet right to the base of the slope where Jet repeated the gestures.

The older man, who wore a faded tan jacket with mixmatched grey slacks scratched his grizzled cheeks, "We're prepared to offer you forty."

Shelton almost pulled his ear in disbelief. *Forty dollars!*

"No." Shelton rose from his seat.

"Okay forty-five!" The younger man stood up. Shelton focused on his top lip that suddenly trembled. "That's our best offer."

"I don't believe adding another five is your best offer." Cassidy stood up next to Shelton and swished her skirts out of the way of the timber bench.

The older man stood and "Maybe an extra five thousand is no issue for you, but I assure you it's a substantial feat for us Missus Murphy."

Shelton's splayed his hands on the table, his knuckles white, "Forty-five thousand?"

"Yes Mister Murphy, forty-five thousand dollars for Pip's Pit."

Shelton looked to Cassidy, for a moment her cheeks paled, her eyes widened until she resettled her Silver Baroness mask. "Well I guess we can make a deal at forty-five thousand."

As the ink dried on the documents, Cassidy finally exhaled. Her worthless land had just secured her future. She waited until Jet decided to accompany the surveyors back to Oro City, before she threw her arms around Shelton's neck. He lifted her off the ground and spun her, clamping his lips on hers.

"Where too Precious?"

"Texas."

"Are you sure, what about California, or Nevada, I'd like to see New York?"

Cassidy smacked Shelton's shoulders, "No, Dew Springs."

"Well," Shelton gently placed Cassidy down on the table and rolled her skirt up to her knees, his lips seized hers for a moment before he pulled back, "We did get this yesterday." Shelton picked up the telegram from the table and handed it to Cassidy and she briefly skimmed it.

"Cade's sister Pearl is marrying Jessie Kline?"

Shelton kissed her again, "Yep, I told Cade he was fighting a losing a battle. It'll be the biggest event in Dew Springs in a decade." Button by button of her blouse tumbled under Shelton's fingers, "So the Colorado Silver Barons better make an appearance."

Cassidy looked down as Shelton's thumb caressed the golden locket that hung her neck, "And then we can add to this."

Shelton smiled, "Nothing would make me happier, Precious."

Cassidy's laugh was lost in Shelton's kisses.

Extract from Ash & Stone – Chapter 1

Helena Ash shifted as the hard cushions of the stage coach compounded the heat that stuck her shirt to her back. Unfolding her satchel, she retrieved her notebook. The pages fell by habit to the dog-eared section and her fingers ran down newspaper clipping fastened there. Under the banner Colorado Daily Chieftain a column read:

"Shelton Murphy and wife Cassidy sell silver mine to buy ranch in Dew Springs, Texas."

On the opposite page, Helena had tacked the results of the Pinkerton agents search

"Lena, Shelton Murphy, Blue Cow Ranch, Dew Springs, Texas. Happy hunting, F.J"

Lena studied the small photograph of Cassidy Smith her half-sister. Well Cassidy Murphy now, thanks to their crooked father bargaining the younger woman off with a mining lease.

Lena compared how different they were to each other and her lips thinned. No-one would believe they were related. Lena's hair almost black and curly compared to Cassidy's mousy straight strands. The description read brown eyes and not even the shape resembled Lena's dark blue eyes, nor did Cassidy's pale cheeks match Lena's olive skin. Sighing, she tapped her fingers on the paper hoping a great many things would resolve when she finally met Cassidy. She wanted her half-sister to be safe, and Lena would find a way to free her from her awful marriage. Secondly, she prayed for Cassidy's forgiveness.

As the coach hit a rut, her pistol dug into her hip and Lena winched. Rather than concentrating on the pain, she turned the page to re-read another telegram:

"Helena, if you or any other Pinkerton agent could assist a friend of ours who needs help with cattle rustlers, we'd be much appreciated. Windy Hill Ranch, Dew Springs. Kind regards, Marcus and Jewel Kearby."

It had been over six months since she'd received the message from the ex-Texas Ranger Kearby and his spitfire of a wife. Only when Lena's Colorado contact confirmed Cassidy's direction of travel, then she arranged for herself to be assigned in Texas.

Lena opened the dusty window as the township appeared on the horizon. She ducked her head out, the wind raced through her strands obscuring her view of her horse, *Chester*, who trailed behind the stage. The gelding would need a clean when they finally arrived as his champagne colored coated turned rust by the trail dust. Sitting back down, Lena repacked her journal and readjusted her colt. She didn't know much about cattle rustling and she'd had enough of strikes and unions, so she felt the stars had aligned to bring her and Cassidy together in Dew Springs. Only first, Lena had some explaining to do.

Under the guise of searching for rustlers, Lena would finally find Cassidy and help her in any way she could, to escape her sham marriage. No arranged marriage ended happily. Helena knew. She scooped up her wide brim hat and brought it down snuggly on her head.

As the horses slowed, Lena hung onto the tattered cushions and her knees buckled needing to be stretched. Travelling alone on Chester the entire way would have slowed her down and now that Cassidy had been found, Lena couldn't cope with any further delays.

The stage came to a halt, and Lena didn't wait for the driver to open the door, stepping down into the mid-morning sun she sized up the wide main street. From the timber board-walk to the busy bodies gawking at the front of the café and across the street the double story Bluebell hotel, Lean decided Dew Springs looked like a cow town that never boomed.

As Lena worked her way around the rear of the stage, the sensation of someone watching her climbed her spine. By shielding her face with her bags, Lena scanned the porch of the saloon, surprised to see large glass windows still intact and a sign above that read "Nine Lives".

In the shadows, a figure reclined against the doorway with only his leather boots and denims visible. Lena's elbow touched the position of her pistol, concealed under her navy riding jacket. Tipping the coach master she led *Chester* down the street, keeping on the other side of the horses flank and watching the saloon over the saddle. As she passed, the man stepped into the sunlight, placing a black Stetson over his fair hair and stalking down the boardwalk. Lena immediately sized up his broad shoulders covered in fabric the color of burnt cherry and the colt on his hip. As he drew level, his eyes tracked to Lena. She met his gaze for the briefest moment be-fore she brought her brim lower over her eyes. The man con-tinued straight to the stage coach that still lingered outside the mercantile. Lena made her way down to the Sheriff's office before she checked over her shoulder. The man conversed with the stage driver, who shook his head vehemently at the stranger's words. Hitching Chester to the front, she took off her hat and entered the tiny office.

"Morning."

A Sheriff who was as round as he looked tired sat upright, his eyes blinking independently of each other as he dragged a hand down his face, "Is it still Morning? Oh sorry Miss, what can I do for ya?"

Lena offered him a curt smile, "Hiya Sherriff..."

The Sherriff took his boots off the table and extended his hand, "Sherriff Green, but you can call me Bill."

Lena shook it, surprised at the strength in his grip despite the silver in his hair. She remembered the glass windows at the saloon. Bill Green must be doing all right. "Nice to meet you Bill, I'm Lena. It seems you keep a tidy town."

"Ah thanks, it's mainly due to the trouble makers passing on."

Lena nodded and took off her hat, "Finding other towns to carouse in?" Dew Springs may be tidy but tidy quickly became tedious.

Bill let out a hearty laugh, "On the contrary, Miss they just grew up. Ah so how can I help you today, Lena?"

"I was hoping you could point me in the direction of Windy Hill Ranch."

"Windy Hill hey?" Bill Green jostled his leather belt around his swollen waist, "Ah you can follow the south road until you see the big live oak and then turn off, keep head East until you cross the river, then you'll see it. Or you could take up with Taylor. I thought I saw him over at the Bluebell this morning."

Lena chewed the inside of her cheek. As a Pinkerton agent, Lena was undercover. If Taylor was a hand at Windy Hill then naturally he fell under suspicion. She'd take her chances on the open road.

"Thank you, but I'd rather not delay anyone."

"What business you got with Windy Hill?"

Without a second thought, Lena answered, "Visiting relatives, Bill."

"Oh," Bill's plump cheeks suddenly fell, "I'm sorry to hear about Old George, Miss. My condolences."

Lena pulled her hat upwards to cover her reaction. Clearing her throat she offered him a weak smile, "Thank you that's very kind of you Bill. I'll be around town for a while, I think, if I need any assistance can I count on you?"

The Sherriff extended his hand, "Of course, would you like me to escort you."

"No thank you, I'll find my way."

Stepping out in the light, Lena's head swiveled to the stage coach, now without the stranger affronting the driver. Lena walked *Chester* behind the buildings, attempting to gain another view of the tiny town. She almost whistled between her teeth, even the back streets were tidy. By the time she reached the far end of the town, the stage driver had taken a seat outside the café. Lena spied her opportunity and tied Chester up out the front. First she purchased herself a beef roll and a bottle of lemonade as she scanned up and down the street. The man in the burnt cherry was no-where to be seen.

"I hope you didn't have too much trouble earlier?" Lena asked the stage driver.

He swallowed his last bite, "Nothing I ain't used to, just a misunderstanding over my passenger list."

Lena nodded. So the man was inquiring about her arrival?

"It's not the first time someone's been stood up when I've arrived." He laughed and crumbs tumbled down his shirt front.

Lena took her lunch to go and climbed into *Chester's* saddle. She touched her elbow to her pistol one more time before flicking the reins.

The fields opened wide under the big blue Texas sky, tufts of white drifted across the horizon as the sun beat down on Lena's dark fabric shoulders. Before too long she drank deep of her canteen. How far was this wretched ranch from town? How far was Windy Hill from the Blue Cow? She thought about asking Bill, except that would raise too many suspicions in one day. Instead she'd find Windy Hill and then start asking questions.

Lena found the live oak easy enough, the giant tree and its thick branches wound out at wild directions signaling the trail to the Windy Hill. It wasn't until she'd topped the first rise that she felt the need to circle around and check her back track.

Just as she could see the live oak again she picked up the second tracks. Lena searched the horizon without success. She could take *Chester* across the harder ground; however she was headed in only one direction. Instead she followed the trail and hopefully come up behind the rider.

At the next ridge, Lena checked her tracks again. A shard of panic speared through her stomach as she realized the other rider had also circled back.

Keeping her eyes peeled she found the perfect spot to take a detour and seized her opportunity. Where a crossing sloped gently towards a stream, the bank continued to rise as it wound around the river. Lena took Chester up stream and hitched him to a root poking out of the sandy bank. Then slinking low over the ground Lena crawled back to the crossing and waited.

No sooner had Lena pulled her pistol from her coat than the sound of hooves tumbled through the earth and set Lena's nerves alight. Lena's breath stalled in her throat as she recognized the burnt cherry shirt and black Stetson rider from town, now astride a large black stallion. This close, she could see the man's blonde curls gracing the back of his tanned neck. He stood high in his saddle and Lena couldn't help but admire his physique. His shoulders were broad and the shirt tapered down to his waist where Lena's gaze stuck on his thighs filling out dark denim. Lena bit down a curse when *Chester* whinnied. The man stepped down and Lena could see a trimmed goatee. Something about its neatness almost made Lena forget her mission.

She waited until the man wandered towards her traitorous horse before she rose and tiptoed until she stood above him on the river bank. As the single click of her hammer echoed off the rock, the man froze.

"Wise decision, Bud."

At the sound of her voice, the man turned slowly and the midday sun shifted from his back to his face. Lena found herself staring at his whiskered jaw line and the top button undone of his shirt that hinted at further tanned skin. Lena met his gaze. Dark lashes framed walnut and pinched at the corners so that it seemed, despite the man's stern expression, his eyes smiled.

"All right, what now?" He scoffed.

"State your business."

The man's brow's furrowed, "How does that work?" He shook his head, "You're on private property Miss, so how about you state your business."

Lena exhaled slowly, "I have business with the landowners."

"Do you now?" The man crossed his arms and started to walk back to the main track. Lena's muzzle remained trained on his wide chest. "And what business is that?"

Lena followed his movements failing to notice the narrowing divergence until he stood on level ground. "I'm visiting relatives."

"I see. Considering Old George never had any children, and neither did his sister, then what family are you here to see?"

"Um," Shoot. In her race to reach Cassidy in Dew Springs, Lena hadn't bothered to inquire about her client. Her muzzle dipped, "I'm a second cousin of his wife's first nephew."

"First nephew?" Now the man genuinely smiled as he advanced with his palms open and his slow steps brought him within arms distance, "What's his wife's name?"

Lena lowered her muzzle, "I saw you asking about me at the stage."

"I wasn't asking about you," He smiled, "I was asking about a Pinkerton Agent. You, I don't know what your game is if it's to fool Clementine into some inheritance scheme I won't have it. I'll take you back to town and you can stay at the Bluebell till the next stage."

Lena took a moment to process how this man thought he could drag her back to town when she held the firearm. She looked down at her pistol and then back to him. Well he did stand a good head taller than her. "Wait? Why were you looking for a Pinkerton Agent?"

He didn't answer straight away, instead he lifted the brim of his hat an inch and ran his gaze up and down Lena. "Damn!"

He took a step back and sighed. Placing his hands on his hips he stalked back towards the track. "You're the Pinkerton aren't you?"

"Helena Ash, Pinkerton Detective."

The man's head threw backwards and he stared up at the sky. He sighed again, "How's a woman going to infiltrate the cow Hands?"

A rush of color heated Lena's cheeks so fast she almost clicked her tongue, "Not all Agents need to infiltrate gang's Mister...."

He didn't even look at her when he replied, "Stone, Taylor Stone." Wandering a short distance away, scratching his jaw and resetting his hat on his head.

The sun added another layer of sweat to Lena's skin and she wiped her forehead. She didn't know why she cared about Stone's comments. Pinkerton had lots of female agents and they all did remarkably well. "Jewel Daniels is a Pinkerton Agent."

Taylor Stone laughed; a desperate thin thing that slithered under her chemise. "She is but she's not here, and Mack, Gerry and Lee all know Jewel."

Lena shrugged her shoulders. Cattle rustlers were not trying to assassinate anyone, they weren't the Turner's Gang or train robbers or railway unions. She'd only used Windy Hill as her connection to free Cassidy from her awful arranged marriage.

Taylor stalked over to her, "I need answers and fast, so what other story, other than Clementine's nieces' whatever, have you got?"

In the brief second it took for her mind to take over her mouth, Lena wished her words back in, "Mail-order bride?"

Taylor's smiling eyes mocked her, "No-one would believe that."

Her finger itched on the trigger and she re-holstered her pistol, "No, of course not." Lena's mind echoed other harsh words spoken to her in haste and she blinked in the bright sunlight. Taylor's sneer slowly disintegrated as Lena made her way back to *Chester*. She led him out to the trail and climbed into the saddle, "Tell me about these rustlers then Mister Stone and I'll see what I can do about Clementine's uncles best friends' cousin."

Taylor relented. He'd seen her the moment the stage door opened. Expecting a stiff business like agent only to be disappointed and intrigued when the dark haired beauty had stepped down to the street. Her navy riding skirts said function, and the mess of dark curls that hung around her neck looked delicate if not entirely neat. Yet it was her eyes, deep pools of sapphire, almost indigo peering over the saddle of her champagne gelding that captivated Taylor's curiosity. The way she slunk through town and then disappeared without a trace should have given him warning that she was no ordinary woman. Picking up the unusual tracks on his way home, Taylor had stalked the beast until the river. Now as she sat high in the saddle, Taylor's jaw cinched with uncertainty. He spied the narrow bulge of her saddle bags. Helena Ash looked ridiculously under prepared for her assignment, although her pistol said otherwise.

"Well Mister Stone?"

Realizing he hadn't stopped staring, Taylor cleared his throat and clambered back onto his black stallion, *Saturno*. "I was the leading Hand here at Windy Hill. After Old George passed, Clementine put me in charge of everything, not just the cattle."

"You stood on some toes?"

"A few." Taylor brought *Saturno* alongside Helena's horse, "Last month I've caught more than one weaner with a fresh rustlers brand suckling from Windy Hill stock."

The woman's plump lips thinned and Taylor couldn't help but sigh. She knew nothing about rustling.

"They're long horns. They will travel miles to return to their mama. Someone's cutting the cattle before their properly weaned. It's easy, but costly. I keep losing stock and soon Windy Hill will have to sell."

"Who wants to buy?"

"Who doesn't is a shorter list." Taylor answered. He found his hands tightening on *Saturno's* reins to bring Helena back into his line of sight. She sat straight in the saddle, her hips rocking with the rhythm of her horse and a slight breeze brought her sweet lily of the valley scent to Taylor's nose. He sighed again. He needed someone tough and rough to get amongst the men and find out who was responsible. Not this graceful woman who would be no end of distraction.

"Sounds interesting…" Her words trailed off as the homestead came into sight. Windy Hill ranch had been blessed with two sides of the river and wide level grassy plains. The limestone homestead and surrounding buildings sprawled across the greenery as two large shady oaks decorated the front yard. Taylor smiled as he saw Helena's lips curl. "Impressive isn't it."

She nodded.

"I'll introduce you to Clementine and someone will get you settled." He didn't have time or the patience to see this woman to her room. If she wanted to play Detective she'd better start the clock now.

As they reached the house yard, Taylor dismounted. Instinct made him offer his hand, not the curiosity that itched through his veins. Helena took it, retracting her hand as she reached the ground.

"Lena Ash, long lost second cousin is here to assess whether to buy Windy Hill." She said to Taylor.

He furrowed his brow.

"It will expose any internal saboteurs and force the hand of any external ones."

Impressive, Taylor thought although out loud, he said, "Sounds solid."

Helena strolled ahead for three steps and then pointed to her saddle bags, "My bags?"

Taylor's jaw cinched and he put his hands on his hips, "Did

you forget to pack something?"

"Huh?" Her eyes like sapphires chips narrowed.

He couldn't help but grin as he took her saddle bags in one hand. She'd packed light. "Your manners. You know you catch more flies with sugar than you do with vinegar."

To the woman's credit her pouted lips softened, her blue eyes downcast, "Force of habit, I suppose."

Taylor's gut clenched at Helena's pinched cheeks, the delicate freckles across her olive cheeks suddenly vibrant and alluring. His boots brought him closer and he softened his voice, "I mean to say, if you want something, just ask."

For a moment her thick lashes fluttered and Taylor contemplated returning a wink, "Come on, I'll show you around."

About the Author

Louise Crouch loves all genres of fiction mixed with a healthy splash of romance. When she is not writing, Louise spends her time frustrating her wonderful husband and raising their two marvelous children.

Book 4 of the Belles & Boots series *Ash & Stone* will conclude the series and follow Pinkerton Agent, Helena Ash and rancher Taylor Stone as they search for rustlers in Dew Springs, Texas in 1877.

When Helena discovers her half-sister Cassidy married a rancher in Dew Springs, Texas she ensures she is the Pinkerton agent assigned to the only investigation in the dust bowl town; cattle rustlers at Windy Hill Ranch. Helena knows nothing about cattle rustlers and she doesn't care, she will do whatever it takes to rescue her sister from her arranged marriage.

Taylor Stone needs answers and he needs them fast. After Old George passed away, his widow Clementine, puts Taylor in charge of the Windy Hill ranch. Only not everyone's happy with his promotion. Someone is rustling his calves before cutting season to sabotage Taylor and force Clementine to sell.

Book 1 of the Belles and Boots series, *Hammer & Lock; a Texas Romance* begins when Evelyn Lockwood returns to her hometown Dew Springs to claim her inheritance, the Double E Ranch. Evie's plans to resume her high society life in New Orleans are suddenly derailed when she discovers her fathers' strange bequeath to the rugged and boorish cowboy Cade Hamerton. With Evie staying on at the Double E, Cade is forced to defend not only his entitlement, but his heart, from invasion.

Book 2 of the Belles and Boots series, *Ruby's Texas Ranger* follows Jewel Daniels and Texas Ranger Marcus Kearby across Kansas in 1876. Two years ago, Jewel left Dew Springs, with a broken heart, hoping to have her name plastered across every poster as the fastest gunslinger in the West. After joining the Texas Rangers, Marcus Kearby stopped in at every sharp shooter carnival along the Trails hoping to catch a glimpse of the redheaded girl who still haunted his dreams. When Marcus and Jewel collide in Kansas and discover Jewel's 'Ruby Drawers' has been wrongly accused of murder, Marcus must choose between Jewel and doing what's right. Jewel must decide whether she'll take one last shot for Marcus's heart.

Louise's debut novel was *Even Spinsters Need Company* which is set in Pennsylvania in the 1870's. Hannah Evans arrives in Franklins Shallows to take up the Headmistress position. She soon finds out not all is as it seems in this quaint town especially the Sherriff, Nicholas Hoffman and his devious family tree.

Louise has also delved into the genre of Space Opera with part one of the Sandes Chronicles, *Under the Light*, with part two, *In the Shadow* and the finale *Until the Dawn* to be released later next year.

If you wish to read more of Louise Crouch's books find them here: http://loucrouch.wordpress.com/books

If you want to follow Louise Crouch on Facebook find her here: http://www.facebook.com/LouiseCCrouch/

If you want to follow Louise Crouch on Twitter find her here http://twitter.com/LouiseCCrouch

You can favorite Louise at Amazon: Louise Crouch Amazon

If you've enjoyed Louise's books please leave a review at your favorite retailer.

Special Thanks

A special thanks to my husband and kids who have put up with me at various stages of the writing journey. Thanks for the support, the encouragement and the late night dinners.

Thanks to my extended family and friends who have provided me with feedback, the good, the bad and the ugly.

A big thanks to my Mum; her avid reading habits led me to develop my own passion for this ever evolving genre.

And finally thanks to the readers for their support! I hope you have enjoyed reading these as much as I have enjoyed writing them.

www.ingramcontent.com/pod-product-compliance
Lightning Source LLC
Chambersburg PA
CBHW030020180626
46810CB00001B/134